FOUL LADY FORTUNE

ALSO BY CHLOE GONG

THESE VIOLENT DELIGHTS
OUR VIOLENT ENDS

FOUL LADY FORTUNE

CHLOE GONG

MARGARET K. McELDERRY BOOKS
NEW YORK LONDON TORONTO SYDNEY NEW DELHI

FOR MY GRANDMOTHERS AND GREAT-AUNTS

谨此献给我的阿娘、外婆，
和我的小阿奶、二姨婆、小姨婆

MARGARET K. McELDERRY BOOKS • An imprint of Simon & Schuster Children's Publishing Division • 1230 Avenue of the Americas, New York, New York 10020 • This book is a work of fiction. Any references to historical events, real people, or real places are used fictitiously. Other names, characters, places, and events are products of the author's imagination, and any resemblance to actual events or places or persons, living or dead, is entirely coincidental. • Text © 2022 by Chloe Gong • Jacket illustration © 2022 by Skeeva • Jacket design © 2022 by Simon & Schuster, Inc. • All rights reserved, including the right of reproduction in whole or in part in any form. • MARGARET K. McELDERRY BOOKS is a trademark of Simon & Schuster, Inc. • The text for this book was set in Dante. • Manufactured in the United States of America

Time travels in diverse paces with diverse persons.
I'll tell you who Time ambles withal,
who Time trots withal, who Time gallops withal,
and who he stands still withal.

—Shakespeare, *As You Like It*

PROLOGUE
1928

O
ut in the countryside, it doesn't matter how loud you scream.

The sound travels through the warehouse, echoing once over in the tall ceiling slats, booming through the space and into the dark night. When it escapes, it merges into the howling wind until it is only another part of the storm that rages outside. The soldiers shuffle nervously toward the warehouse entrance, pulling at the heavy door until it slides closed, though the rain falls heavily enough that it has already soaked onto the flooring and stained the concrete in a dark semicircle. The faintest whistle of a train comes from the distance. Despite the infinitesimal chance they will be caught by any soul passing by, their instructions were clear: Guard the perimeter. No one can know what is happening here.

"What is the final verdict?"

"Successful. I think it is successful."

The soldiers are spread out across the warehouse, but two scientists stand around a table at the center. They stare impassively at the scene before them, at the test subject strapped down by thick buckles, forehead beaded with sweat. Another convulsion tears through the subject from head to toe, but their voice has grown hoarse from shrieking, and so their mouth merely pulls wide and soundless this time.

"Then it works."

"It works. We have the first part complete now."

One of the scientists, putting a pen behind their ear, signals to a soldier, who approaches the table to release the buckles in turn: all those on the left, then all those on the right.

The buckles drop, metal clanking to the floor. The subject tries to roll over, but they panic, jerking too hard and tipping off the table instead. It is a terrible sight. The subject lands in a sprawl at the scientists' feet and heaves for breath—heaves and heaves like they cannot fill their lungs properly, and perhaps they never will again.

A hand comes down upon the subject's head. The touch is gentle, almost tender. When the scientist peruses their work, smoothing at the subject's hair, their expression is set with a smile.

"It's all right. You mustn't struggle."

A syringe appears. Under the tall lights, the needle glints once as the plunger goes down and again as the red substance inside disappears right into soft skin.

The pain is immediate: a liquid blaze, overwhelming every nerve nestled in its path. Soon it will reach where it needs, and then it will feel like being unmade.

Outside, the rain pours on. It drips through cracks into the warehouse, puddles growing larger and larger.

The first scientist gives the subject one more affectionate pat. "You are my greatest achievement, and greater still is yet to come. But until then . . ."

The subject cannot keep their eyes open anymore. Weakness turns every limb heavy, each thought in their mind fleeting like ships sighted in fog. The subject wants to say something, scream something, but nothing will form. Then the scientist leans in to whisper into their ear, landing the final strike and piercing the fog as cleanly as a blade:

"*Oubliez.*"

1

The train corridor was quiet except for the rumbling underfoot. Dusk had already fallen, but the windows flashed
every three seconds—a pulse of illumination from the lights
installed along the tracks and then gone, swallowed by the speed
of the train. Elsewhere, the narrow compartments were crowded
with light and noise: the soft golden chandeliers and the rattling of
silverware against the food trolleys, the clink of a spoon tapping
against a teacup and the glowing crystal lamps.

But here in the passageway into first class, there was only the
sudden whoosh of the door as Rosalind Lang pushed it open, stepping into the semi-darkness with her heels clicking.

The paintings on the walls stared as she walked by, their beady
eyes aglow in the dark. Rosalind clutched the box in her arms, careful to keep her leather gloves delicate around its edges, her elbows
held out to either side of her. When she came to a stop outside the
third door, she knocked with her shoe, tapping delicately at its base.

A beat passed. For a moment, only the chugging of the train
could be heard. Then the softest shuffling came from the other
side, and the door swung back, flooding the hallway with new light.

"Good evening," Rosalind said politely. "Is this a good time?"

Mr. Kuznetsov stared at her, his brow furrowing as he made
sense of the scene before him. Rosalind had been trying to secure
an audience with the Russian merchant for days. She had bunkered

down in Harbin and suffered the frigid temperatures without success, then followed him to Changchun, a city farther south. There, his people had failed to respond to her requests too, and it had almost seemed like a lost cause—that she would have to go about everything the rough way—until she caught wind of his plans to travel by train with a booking in first class, where the compartment rooms were large and the ceilings were low, where hardly anyone was around and sound was muffled by the thick, thick walls.

"I will call my guard—"

"Oh, don't be foolish."

Rosalind entered without invitation. The private first-class rooms were wide enough that she could have easily forgotten she was aboard a train . . . if it weren't for the quivering walls, its papered floral pattern trembling each time the tracks grew rough. She looked around a while longer, eyeing the hatch that went up to the top of the train and the window to the far side of the room, its blinds drawn to block out the rapidly moving night. To the left of the four-poster bed, there was another set of doors that either gave way to a closet or a toilet.

A firm thud summoned Rosalind's attention back to the merchant as he closed the main compartment door. When he turned around, his eyes darted along her person and then to the box in her hands, but he was not examining her qipao, nor the red flowers clipped onto the fur throw around her shoulders. Though Mr. Kuznetsov tried to be subtle about it, he was concerned about the box in her hands and whether she had brought in a weapon.

Rosalind was already gingerly lifting the lid from the box, presenting the contents inside with a flourish.

"A gift, Mr. Kuznetsov," she said pleasantly. "From the Scarlet Gang, who have sent me here to make your acquaintance. Might we chat?"

She pushed the box forward with a flourish. It was a small

Chinese vase, blue and white porcelain lying upon a bed of red silk. Adequately expensive. Not expensive enough to verge onto the point of outrage.

Rosalind held her breath until Mr. Kuznetsov reached in and picked it up. He examined the vase by the lights dangling from the ceiling, turning its neck this way and that, admiring the characters carved along the side. After a long while, he grunted what sounded like approval, walked over to a coffee table between two large seats, and set the vase down. There were already two teacups upon the table. An ashtray lay nearby, dusted with a smattering of black.

"The Scarlet Gang," Mr. Kuznetsov muttered beneath his breath. He folded into one of the chairs, his back stiff against the upholstery. "I have not heard that name for some time now. Please, take a seat."

Rosalind walked to the other chair, fixing the lid back onto her box and setting the box beside the chair. When she dropped into the seat, she only perched upon its edge, casting a glance once more at the closet doors to her left. The floor jolted.

"I assume you are the same girl who has been harassing my staff." Mr. Kuznetsov switched from Russian to English. "Janie Mead, yes?"

It had been four years, but Rosalind was still unaccustomed to her alias. Sooner or later she was going to get in trouble for that split-second delay, that blank look in her eyes before she remembered her name was supposed to be Janie Mead, that pause before she lengthened out her French accent when she was speaking English, pretending to be American-raised and one among the many new returnees in the city registered in the Kuomintang's ranks.

"That's correct," Rosalind said evenly. Perhaps she should have made a joke, kicked her feet back and declared that it would be wise to remember her name. The train rumbled over a bump in the tracks and the whole room rocked, but Rosalind said nothing more. She only folded her hands over each other, crinkling the cold press of leather.

Mr. Kuznetsov frowned. The wrinkles in his forehead deepened, as did the crow's feet marking his eyes.

"And you are here for . . . my properties?"

"Correct," Rosalind said again. That was always the easiest way to buy time. Letting them assume what she was there for and going with it rather than spitballing some strange lie and getting caught in it too soon. "I'm sure you have heard that the Scarlets don't deal much in land anymore since we merged with the Nationalists, but this is a special occasion. Manchuria holds vast opportunity."

"It seems rather far from Shanghai for the Scarlets to care." Mr. Kuznetsov leaned forward, peering into the teacups on the table. He noted that one was still half-filled, and so he brought it to his lips, clearing his throat for dryness. "And you seem a little young to be running Scarlet errands."

Rosalind watched him drink. His throat bobbed. Open for attack. Vulnerable. But she did not reach for a weapon. She was not carrying any.

"I am nineteen," Rosalind replied, peeling off her gloves.

"Tell the truth, Miss Mead. That's not your real name, is it?"

Rosalind smiled, setting the gloves down on the table. He was suspicious, of course. Mr. Kuznetsov was no simple Russian mogul with business in Manchuria, but one of the last White Flowers in the country. That fact alone was enough to land on Kuomintang lists, but he was also siphoning money to Communist cells, supporting their war effort in the south. And because the Nationalists needed to snuff out the Communists, needed to break their every source of funding as smoothly as possible, Rosalind had been sent here with orders to . . . put a stop to it.

"Of course it's not my real name," she said lightly. "My real name is Chinese."

"That's not what I mean." Mr. Kuznetsov had his hands resting at his sides now. She wondered if he would try to retrieve a concealed weapon. "I looked into you after your previous requests to meet. And you look an awful lot like Rosalind Lang."

Rosalind did not flinch. "I shall take that as a compliment. I know you must be tuned out of Shanghai's happenings, but Rosalind Lang has not been seen in years."

If anyone claimed they sighted her, they were surely sighting phantoms—catching remnants of a faded dream, a memory of the vision that Shanghai used to be. Rosalind Lang: raised in Paris before returning to the city and rising in infamy among the best of the nightlife cabaret dancers. Rosalind Lang: a girl whose where-abouts were presently unknown, presumed dead.

"I did hear about that," Mr. Kuznetsov said, leaning in to examine his teacup again. She wondered why he didn't drink out of the second one if he was so thirsty. She wondered why there was a second cup poured to begin with.

Well, she knew.

Mr. Kuznetsov looked up suddenly. "Though"—he continued—"there were rumors from the White Flowers that Rosalind Lang disappeared because of Dimitri Voronin's death."

Rosalind froze. Surprise dropped a pit into her stomach, and a small whoosh of breath escaped her lungs. It was already too late to pretend like she had not been caught unaware, so she let the silence draw out, let the anger roil to life in her bones.

Smug, Mr. Kuznetsov picked up a miniature spoon and tapped it to the edge of the teacup. It sounded far too loud for the room, like a gunshot, like an explosion. Like the explosion that had rocked the city four years ago, which her own cousin Juliette had set, giving her life just to stop Dimitri's reign of terror.

If it weren't for Rosalind, Juliette Cai and Roma Montagov would still be alive. If it weren't for Rosalind's treachery against the Scarlet Gang, Dimitri never would have gained the power he did, and perhaps the White Flowers never would have fallen apart. Perhaps the Scarlet Gang wouldn't have merged with the Kuomintang and become one with the Nationalists' political party. *Perhaps, perhaps, perhaps*—this was a game that haunted Rosalind late into her eternal nights, a useless exercise of cataloging everything she'd done wrong to end up where she was today.

"You would know all about the White Flowers, wouldn't you?"

The curtain had come down. When Rosalind spoke, her real voice came out, French-accented and sharp.

Mr. Kuznetsov set his spoon down with a grimace. "The funny thing is, the surviving White Flowers also have enduring connections that feed us warnings. And I was long prepared, Miss Lang."

The door to her left swung open. Another man emerged, dressed in a Western suit, a simple dagger in his right hand. Before Rosalind could move, he was in position behind her, a firm grip on her shoulder keeping her in the chair and the dagger positioned against her throat.

"Do you think I would travel without bodyguards?" Mr. Kuznetsov demanded. "Who sent you?"

"I told you already," Rosalind answered. She tested whether she could crane her neck away. There was no chance. The blade was already piercing into her skin. "The Scarlet Gang."

"The blood feud between the Scarlet Gang and the White Flowers ended, Miss Lang. Why would they be sending you?"

"To make nice. Didn't you like my gift?"

Mr. Kuznetsov stood up. He put his hands behind his back, lips thinning in annoyance. "I will give you one last chance. Which party sent you?"

He was trying to feel out the two sides of the civil war currently moving through the country. Gauging whether he had landed on the Nationalist lists or if the Communists were betraying him.

"You're going to kill me anyway," Rosalind said. She felt a bead of blood trickle down her throat. It ran along her collar, then stained the fabric of her qipao. "Why should I waste time on your questions?"

"Fine." Mr. Kuznetsov nodded to his bodyguard. There was no hesitation before he switched to Russian and said: "Kill her, then. Bystreye, pozhaluysta."

Rosalind braced. She took a breath in, felt the blade whisper a benediction to her skin.

And the bodyguard slashed her throat.

The initial shock was always the worst—that first split second when she could hardly think through the pain. Her hands flew unbidden to her neck to clamp down on the wound. Hot, gushing red spilled through the lines of her fingers and ran down her arms, dripping onto the floor of the train compartment. When she lurched off the chair and fell to her knees, there was a moment of uncertainty, a whisper in her mind telling her that she had cheated death enough and there would be no recovery this time.

Then Rosalind bowed her head and felt the bleeding slow. She felt her skin knitting itself back together, inch by inch by inch. Mr. Kuznetsov was waiting for her to keel over and collapse, eyes staring blankly at the ceiling.

Instead, she lifted her head and moved her hands away.

Her throat had healed over, still stained with red but looking as if it had never been cut.

Mr. Kuznetsov emitted a strangled noise. His bodyguard, meanwhile, whispered something indecipherable and advanced toward her, but when Rosalind held a hand out, he complied, too stunned to do anything else.

"I suppose I'll tell you now," Rosalind said, slightly breathless. She wiped the blood from her chin and rose onto one foot, then the other. "Haven't you heard of me? The Nationalists need to do a better job of their propaganda."

Now it was dawning on the merchant. She could see it in his eyes, in that expression of disbelief to be witnessing something so unnatural before him, connecting it with the stories that had started spreading some few years ago.

"Lady Fortune," he whispered.

"Ah." Rosalind finally straightened upright, her lungs recovering. "That's a misnomer. It's just Fortune. *Catch*." In a smooth motion, she retrieved one of her gloves to clasp the lip of the vase and swipe it off the table. The bodyguard caught the vase quickly when she tossed it at him, likely preparing for some attack, but the vase only landed in his palms softly, nestled like a wild animal made of porcelain.

Fortune, the rumors whispered, was the code name for a Nationalist agent. Not just any agent: an immortal assassin who could not be killed despite multiple attempts, who didn't sleep or age, who stalked the night for her targets and appeared in the guise of a mere girl. Depending on how much flourish was added to the stories, she was specifically a menace for the surviving White Flowers, going after them with a coin in hand. If it landed on heads, they were killed immediately. If it landed on tails, they were given the chance to run, but no target had yet managed to escape her.

"Abominable creature," Mr. Kuznetsov hissed. He lunged back to give her a wide berth between them—or at least he tried. The merchant had yet to take three steps before he crashed abruptly to the floor. His bodyguard stood stock-still in shock, freezing with his hands around the vase.

"Poison, Mr. Kuznetsov," Rosalind explained. "That's not such an abominable way to die, is it?"

His limbs started to twitch. His nervous system was shutting down—arms going soft, legs turning to paper. She took no pleasure in this. She did not treat it like vengeance. But she would be lying if she said she didn't feel righteous with each hit, as if this was her way of sloughing away her sins layer by layer until she had answered entirely for her actions four years ago.

"You . . ." Mr. Kuznetsov heaved in. "You didn't . . . touch the . . . tea. I was . . . I was watching."

"I didn't poison the tea, Mr. Kuznetsov," Rosalind replied. She turned to his bodyguard. "I poisoned the vase that you touched with your bare fingers."

The bodyguard tossed the vase away with a sudden viciousness, smashing it to pieces by the four-poster bed. It was too late; he had been holding on to it for longer than Mr. Kuznetsov. He lunged for the door, perhaps to seek aid, perhaps to wash his hands of the poison, but he, too, crumpled swiftly to the floor before he could make it out.

Rosalind watched it all with a blank stoniness. She had done this many times. The rumors were true: she did sometimes carry around a coin to give the Nationalists fuel for their propaganda. But poison was her weapon of choice, so it didn't matter how far they ran. By the time her targets thought they were being let free, they had already been hit.

"You . . ."

Rosalind walked closer to the merchant, placing her gloves into her pocket.

"Do me a favor," she said dully. "Send Dimitri Voronin my regards when you see him in hell."

Mr. Kuznetsov stopped wheezing, stopped moving. He was dead. Another assignment had been fulfilled, and the Nationalists were one step closer to losing their country to imperialists instead of Communists. Moments later, his bodyguard succumbed too, and the room fell into a hollow silence.

Rosalind pivoted for the sink by the bar, spinning the faucet as far as it would go and rinsing her hands. She splashed the water down her neck next, scrubbing with her fingers. All this blood was her own, yet disgust was bitter on her tongue when she saw the sides of the sink staining while she cleaned, as if specks of a different poison were dropping off her skin, the kind that contaminated her soul instead of her organs.

"It's easier not to think about it," her cousin used to say, back when Shanghai had a blood feud between two rival gangs, back when Rosalind was the right hand of the Scarlet Gang's heir and watched Juliette kill people day after day in the name of her family. *"Remember their faces. Remember the lives taken. But what's the point in mulling on it? If it happened, it happened."*

Rosalind breathed out slowly, turning the faucet off and letting the rust-colored water swirl down the drain. Little had changed in the city's attitude toward bloodshed since her cousin's death. Little except swapping gangsters for politicians who pretended there would be some semblance of law and order now. An artificial exchange, nothing different at its core.

A rumble of voices echoed from the hallway outside. Rosalind stiffened, making a scan of her surroundings. While she didn't think she could get prosecuted for the crimes committed here, she did need to make her escape before she could test out that theory. The Kuomintang had put itself in charge of the country, positioning its governance as an upholder of justice. For the sake of its image, its Nationalist members would throw her to the wolves and disown her as an agent if she were caught leaving dead bodies outside the city, even when their secret covert branch gave every instruction.

Rosalind tilted her chin up, flexing the new smooth skin at her throat while she searched the compartment ceiling. She had studied the blueprints of the train before she boarded, and when she spotted a thin, barely visible string dangling near the light fixture, she pulled a panel of the ceiling free to reveal a metal hatch leading directly to the top of the train for maintenance.

As soon as she had the hatch down, the wind rushed into the room at a roar. She gave herself a foot up using the nearby drawers, removing herself from the crime scene with nimble speed.

"Don't slip," she told herself, climbing through the hatch and emerging into the night, teeth chattering against the frigid temperature. "Do *not* slip."

Rosalind closed the hatch. She paused for the slightest moment, gathering her bearings on top of a speeding train. For a dizzying moment, she was struck with a sense of vertigo, convinced that she would tip over and fall. Then, just as quickly, her balance adjusted, her feet planted steadily.

"A dancer, an agent," Rosalind whispered to herself as she started to move across the train, her eyes on the end of the carriage. Her handler had drilled the mantra into her head during her earliest training days, when she had complained about being unable to move fast, unable to fight as traditional agents might—excuse after excuse for why she wasn't good enough to learn. She used to spend every night on a brightly lit stage. The city had built her up as its dazzling star, the dancer that everyone had to see, and talk moved faster than reality ever could. It didn't matter who Rosalind was, or that, really, she was only a child dressed up in glitter. She swindled men and beamed at them like they were the world until they passed over the tips she wanted to see, and then she switched tables before the song could even change.

"Let me slink around in the dark and poison people," she had insisted at that first meeting with Dao Feng. They stood in the courtyard of the university where Dao Feng was working undercover, rather begrudgingly on Rosalind's part because it was hot and the grass was itching her ankles and there was sweat gathering at her armpits. "They can't kill me anyway. Why do I need anything else?"

In response, Dao Feng punched her in the nose.

"Jesus!" She felt the bone crunch. She felt blood rush down her face and burst in the other direction too, running hot and metallic liquid into her throat and onto her tongue. If anyone had seen them at that moment, it would have looked a scene. Fortunately, the hour was early and the courtyard was empty—a time and place that became her designated training ground for months afterward.

"That's why," he answered. "How are you going to set your poison if you're trying to heal a broken bone? This country didn't invent wǔshù for you not to learn any. You were a dancer. Now you are an agent. Your body already knows how to turn and bend; all you need to do is give it direction and intention."

When he threw his next punch at her face, Rosalind ducked indignantly. The broken nose had already healed with her usual rapid speed, but her ego stayed bruised. Dao Feng's fist landed in air.

And her handler smiled. "Good. That's more like it."

In the present, Rosalind moved faster against the roaring wind, mumbling her mantra beneath her breath. Each step was an assurance to herself. She knew not to slip; she knew what she was doing. No one had asked her to become an assassin. No one had asked her to leave the burlesque club and stop dancing, but then she had died and woken as an abominable creature—as Mr. Kuznetsov had so kindly put it—and she needed purpose in her life, a way to upset each day and night so they did not blur together monotonously.

Or maybe she was lying to herself. Maybe she had chosen to kill because she didn't know how else to prove her worth. More than anything in the world, Rosalind Lang wanted redemption, and if this was how she got it, then so be it.

Coughing, Rosalind waved at the smoke gathering around her. The steam engine chugged loudly, dispersing an unending stream of dust and grit. Up ahead, the tracks ran long, disappearing into the horizon farther than her eye could see.

Only then—movement in the distance interrupted the still picture.

Rosalind paused, leaning forward curiously. She wasn't sure what she was seeing. The night itself was dark, the moon only a thin crescent hanging daintily from the clouds. But the electric

lights installed alongside the tracks did their job perfectly to illu-
minate two figures running away from the tracks and disappearing
into the tall fields.

The train was perhaps twenty, thirty seconds from approaching the tracks where the figures had been lurking. When Rosalind
moved to the end of the train carriage, she tried to squint and focus
her vision, certain that she had to have been mistaken.

Which was why she didn't notice that dynamite had blown an
explosion on the tracks until the sound roared through the night
and the heat of the blast hit her face.

2

Rosalind gasped, lunging down to grip the top of the train for balance. She thought to shout out a warning, but no one inside the train would hear her; nor could they do anything when the carriages were hurtling forward at such speed, heading right for the site of the explosion.

The flames on the tracks, however, faded quickly. As the train careened nearer and nearer to the explosion site, Rosalind braced for a sudden derailing, but then the front approached the dwindling flames and drove right onward. She glanced over her shoulder, grimacing against the wind. The train rumbled over the blast site. In seconds, it had left the site behind entirely, the blast too weak to affect the tracks with any significance.

"What *was* that?" she asked the night.

Who were those people running into the fields? Had they been intending to cause damage?

The night gave her no answer in return. Biting back another cough from the train's relentless smoke, Rosalind shook herself from her stupor and slid down the side of the exterior, landing in the walk space between two carriages. Once she brushed her stray hair out of her face, she opened the door and stepped inside the train, returning to the warmth of an economy-class hallway.

It was busy. Though she had entered the carriage into the company of three people wearing waitstaff uniforms, they didn't pay her any attention. One boy pushed a tray into the hands of another, snapped a few words, then hurried into a compartment. With his departure, the door behind her opened again, and five more servers came through.

One of them gave Rosalind a sidelong glance as he hurried by. Though the eye contact was exceedingly brief, it prickled her skin with a warning nonetheless, ill ease making an instant home in her stiff shoulders. As soon as the server retrieved a tablecloth off the shelf, he pivoted in his step and broke away from the other train staff to proceed forward in the carriages.

Rosalind made to follow. She was heading for the front of the train anyway, though she hadn't decided yet if she was getting off at the next stop—Shenyang—or riding closer to Shanghai. She supposed it depended on how quickly they found the bodies. Or if they found them at all. If she was lucky, they would sit pretty until the train hit the very end of its line and someone thought to clean the rooms.

With a grimace, Rosalind reached into the inside of her sleeve, where she had tucked her train ticket. JANIE MEAD, they had printed on it. Her alias, publicly known for being Scarlet-associated. The best way to hold up a false identity was to keep it as close to the truth as possible. It was harder to mess up the details, harder to forget a past that ran almost parallel to your own. According to their invented story, Janie Mead was the daughter of a former Scarlet Gang member who had turned hesitant Nationalist business partner. Dig any closer into who her parents were—into what her legal Chinese name was underneath this English one she had adopted for her alleged years spent studying in America—and everything would dissolve into dust.

A conductor passed her. Again, there came a glance askew, this one lasting a second too long. Had Rosalind left a bloodstain somewhere? She thought she'd cleaned her neck well. She thought she was doing a perfectly fine job of acting normal.

Rosalind scrunched her ticket tightly in her palm, then stepped into another carriage, where the windows showed their surroundings slowing. The train was nearing the station, green fields turning to small township buildings and electric lights. All around her, the mumble of conversation got louder, individual snippets floating from seat to seat.

Every little hair at the back of her neck was standing upright. Though there seemed nothing amiss, only other passengers hurrying to pull their luggage down and flock closer to the exits before the train stopped, Rosalind had spent years now working as an assassin. She had learned to trust her senses first and let her brain catch up second. She needed to be on the lookout.

Two attendants hurried by, bundling blankets in their arms as they collected them from departing passengers. Rosalind leaned away cautiously to let the women pass, her shoulder pressed to the walls. She almost pushed a loose-leaf calendar right off its hook, but before it could jostle too hard and hit the carpeted floor, Rosalind righted it, brushing against the page it was opened to: 18 September.

The attendants bustled past again, their arms freed of the previous blankets and ready to collect more. There was a *tut*, both of them ignoring Rosalind in their path—thankfully.

"We're stopping in Fengtian?" one asked the other.

"Why are you using the Japanese name? They haven't invaded yet—we don't need to change it back."

Rosalind proceeded forward, trailing her hand along the intricate wooden beams running lengthwise on the walls. *Fengtian*. It had been changed to Shenyang almost two decades ago, after the Chinese took back control of the land, but when she'd studied the region with her tutors, they had used the English she was more familiar with: Mukden.

This new carriage was far more crowded. Rosalind ducked closer to the middle aisle, weaving her way through the passengers. Right in the thick of the clusters, it was easy to tune in and out of the conversations she was passing, conveniently absorbing what her ears caught.

"Have we arrived already?"

"—qīn'ài de, come here before Māma can't find you."

"You'd think there's a fire somewhere with all this jostling—"

"—seen my shoe?"

"—member of the Scarlet Gang aboard. Maybe it is safer to give her to the Japanese until someone higher up can appease them."

Rosalind slowed. She didn't make a visible show of her surprise, but she couldn't stop herself from pausing just a beat to make sure she hadn't misheard. *Ah.* There it was. She'd known something was off, and the instincts pounded into her during her training hadn't led her wrong yet. Sometimes in her work she identified her target before consciously realizing it; other times she sensed that she herself had been made into a target before proper comprehension caught up.

Give me to the Japanese? she thought wildly. *For what?* Surely not the Russian merchant's assassination. There weren't police on board, to begin with, and even if there were, they wouldn't have worked fast enough to have external departments to answer to already, never mind why the Japanese would be involved.

Her eyes made a sweep around the seats. She couldn't pick out where the voice had come from. Most faces in the vicinity looked ordinary. Regular civilians wearing cloth buttons-ups and soft fabric shoes, which told her they were on their way home to their village instead of any big city.

Something larger than her was happening. She didn't like this one bit.

When the train stopped in Shenyang, Rosalind joined the throngs of passengers for disembarking. She dropped her ticket as she stepped off the train carriage, littering the small scrunched ball onto the platform as easily as a coin tossed into a well. Noise surrounded her at every angle. The train's whistle sang into the night, blowing hot steam around the tracks that drew sweat at Rosalind's back. Even as she pushed through the crowds on the train platform and entered the station, the sweat remained.

Rosalind scanned the station. The platform display for arrivals and departures made a rapid *click-click-click* as it changed to show the most forthcoming trains. Shanghai was a popular destination, but the next departing train wasn't for another hour. She would be a sitting duck lingering around the waiting area seats.

Meanwhile, the main exit was being guarded by a line of police constables, stopping every civilian who passed through the doors to make a quick check of their ticket.

Slowly, Rosalind pulled her necklace out from under her qipao, her steps steady while she made up her mind and walked toward the exit. If she made it past, she could situate herself in Shenyang first, then extricate herself in the morning, returning to Shanghai while drawing as little notice as possible. If she didn't . . .

She put the bead of her necklace into her mouth, then undid the thin clasp and slid the string out. There hadn't been time for a change of clothes. Maybe she could have blended in better if she had brought along something else, but now she was the most well dressed in this station, and clearly of some city stature. It didn't take a ticket to mark her.

As soon as one of the constables sighted her coming, he nudged the man next to him, who wore a different pin on his lapel.

"Ticket?" the lapel pin man demanded.

Rosalind shrugged breezily. "I lost it. I don't suppose you're demanding a ticket for me to *leave*, are you?"

Another man leaned in to whisper into his ear. His voice was too soft for her to pick out anything other than "passenger list," but that itself told her enough.

"Janie Mead, is it?" he confirmed when his attention turned back to her. "We need you to come with us. You're under suspicion for collaboration with the Scarlet Gang in conspiracy to cause large-scale damage."

Rosalind blinked. She moved the bead around in her mouth, tucking it from one side to the other under her tongue. So this had nothing to do with her work as Fortune. This was the Scarlet Gang being used as a scapegoat. This was another instance in a long series of happenings across the country, its city gangsters being blamed for incidents left and right because foreign imperialists kept trying to cast blame for failing infrastructure and rioting crowds. City gangsters had been taking the hit when the warlords in control needed a place to point the finger before the imperialists could say the Chinese couldn't control their own people and installed intruder governments in the country instead.

It is safer to give her to the Japanese until someone higher up can appease them.

She should have figured. It was routine at this point: something goes wrong in a city, and the foreigners with interest stationed in that area use that as a reason for why the Chinese needed the land taken off their hands.

The only solution was scrambling to fix the problem before the imperialists could insert themselves, march in with their guns and tanks. For the Chinese authorities here, "Janie Mead" just happened to be in the right place at the right time.

She brought her hands forward, wrists together ready to be cuffed. "Okay."

The men blinked. Perhaps they hadn't expected it to be that easy. "You understand the accusation?"

"The weak explosion, yes?" Rosalind supplied. "Never mind how I did it from inside the train, but I see how it must be easier to search the passenger list than hunt through the fields near the tracks."

Either they didn't pick up on her ridicule or they pretended not to hear it. Her very knowledge of the explosion was evidence enough. One of the constables locked a cold set of handcuffs over her wrists and gave her a push, leading her out of the station. He took one arm; another constable took the other. The rest of the group followed closely, circled around her in precaution.

Rosalind shifted the bead once more under her tongue. Gave it a swirl around her mouth. *Come on,* she thought.

Though activity was filtering down at this hour, there were still plenty of civilians with business at the train station, some being subtle with their curiosity, others outright craning over their shoulder to see who the constables were arresting. She wondered if they might find her familiar, if any of them picked up newspapers from Shanghai and remembered when they used to print sketched renderings of her a year after the revolution, speculating that Rosalind Lang was dead.

"This way."

In the courtyard outside the station, there was only one street-lamp, burning near a water fountain. Beyond, there was a car parked across the street, almost hidden near an alley.

The constables hurried her in that direction. Rosalind complied. Patiently, she walked with them—walked until they neared the police car, its sheen of black paint and the bars across its windows almost within reach.

Then—*finally*—the outer layer on the bead in her mouth melted away. Liquid burst inside her mouth so suddenly that Rosalind almost coughed from the sensation, struggling to control herself as the peppery taste swept across her tongue. A noise slipped from her throat. The constable on her left turned to her.

"No funny business," he commanded, audibly annoyed. "Xiǎo gūniáng, you're lucky if—"

Rosalind spat the liquid into his face. He reared back with a shout, letting go of her so that his hands could tend to his burning eyes. Before the one on her right could register what was happening, she had looped her arms over his head and pressed the chain of the handcuffs around his neck. The constable shouted out in alarm, but then Rosalind pulled hard enough to hear a *crack*, and he fell silent. Her knee shoved into his back. She untangled her hands from his neck.

The other constables lunged forward to close the openings on either side of her, but it was too late. Rosalind was darting away, making a fast scramble down the road.

A dancer, an agent. She would use every inch of the stage, every item in her arsenal. The bead was one of her own little trickster inventions, coated with the same substance that pharmacies used for its pills. The liquid inside was harmless if accidentally swallowed, but capable of blinding someone for a whole day if it got into the eyes.

She cast a glance behind her, sighting the constables falling behind. There were residential buildings lined up to her side, half-collapsed stoops and broken glass windows passing by in a blur. Just as Rosalind approached the turn of the corner, she jumped and hooked the chain between the handcuffs over a protruding light fixture off one of the houses. There would have been no firm grip for her bare hands, but the chain was almost perfect, giving her the prime opportunity to kick against one of the window ledges, then pull herself onto the balcony, the metal handcuffs clattering against the railing. With a stifled yelp, Rosalind rolled over the railing and slammed flat onto the tiled floor. The abrupt landing crushed the breath from her lungs. Below, the constables were already fanning out to find a way up.

"I'm not in good enough shape for this," Rosalind wheezed to herself, rolling onto her side before stumbling upright and throwing open the balcony doors. She entered a dark and empty restaurant, her breath heavy as she navigated through the maze of tables. It didn't sound like the constables had caught up yet when she emerged from the restaurant and ran along the building's second-floor walkway, but they would be coming to search the restaurant because they had watched her climb in, and they would be guarding the ground level around the building because that was her only escape. She had very few viable routes out, and very few places to hide.

"Block the second floor! Hurry up!"

Their voices were entering the building's inner courtyard. Rosalind searched her surroundings, then latched her gaze on a door thinner than the other shop entrances and residential corridors. A water closet.

Just as footsteps started thudding up to the stairs, Rosalind slipped through the door, unmoving on the other side. Someone had done their duty thoroughly in cleaning the squat toilets, so it only smelled like bleach in the small space. Rosalind gauged the width. Looked again at the hinges of the door, seeing that it opened inward.

She pressed up against the corner of the water closet and held her breath, counting one, two, three—

The door slammed inward, blowing back on its hinges before stopping a hairsbreadth away from her nose. Finding the water closet to be empty, the constable kept moving, calling out to the others.

"All clear!"

Slowly Rosalind released her breath. The door to the water closet creaked closed on its own, its knob giving a soft click while the constables dispersed and searched through the residences. She didn't move. She didn't even tend to an itch on her nose so long as she could hear movement.

"Where could the girl have gone?"

"These operatives are tricky. Keep looking."

"Operative? Isn't she Shanghai's Scarlet Gang?"

"Probably Communist too. You know how it is in that city."

Rosalind almost snorted. She was the furthest thing from being a Communist. Her sister, Celia, actually was. Unlike Rosalind, it had been easy for Celia to leave the Scarlet mansion one day and fall off the grid. She had been known as Kathleen Lang while they were in the household, having taken on their third sister's name after the real Kathleen passed away in Paris, adopting an identity upon return to Shanghai that would keep her safe while living authentically. She had been assigned male at birth, and while their father hadn't allowed her to openly be Celia, he *had* allowed her to take Kathleen's place as a protection mechanism, sliding in as someone the city already thought they knew. When revolution swept through Shanghai, when power shifted and allegiances changed and their once-mighty family started to fracture apart, Celia had entered Communist circles with the name that she had chosen for herself rather than return to being Kathleen. If she wanted, she could pretend she was never a part of the Scarlet Gang; after all, the Scarlet Gang had only ever known their precocious heir, Juliette, and her two dear cousins, Rosalind and Kathleen.

While Celia told only a select few people in the organization about her past with the Scarlet Gang, Rosalind was being watched by the Nationalists at every moment as a Scarlet bomb ready to go off. There was a reason they sent her after White Flowers, after all. She and the Nationalists had an understanding about why she was working for them.

Rosalind pressed her ear to the door, listening to the constables as they searched. Their irritated commands to one another grew fainter and fainter, grumbling that she must have escaped unnoticed. Only once their voices had disappeared entirely onto another street did Rosalind dare ease herself out from the corner of the water closet, lifting her handcuffed wrists and nudging at the door with one finger to open it a crack.

The building's surroundings fell quiet. She heaved out a breath, finally releasing the tension in her shoulders. When she opened the door properly, the scene was entirely still before her.

She could almost hear Dao Feng's praise, his voice booming loud and his hand giving her shoulder a hearty thump. Rosalind had more poison tucked in the line of her qipao, emergency powders hidden at her waist, toxin-coated blades in the heels of her shoes. But there was no need for any of it.

"I did as you always say," she muttered to herself. "Run if you don't have to combat. Never strike the front if you have the back."

Rosalind had failed her very first assignment. The knife had faltered in her hand; the blade had been tossed out of her grasp. Her target had loomed over her—seconds away from stamping a boot into her face and testing the limits of her healing.

Except Dao Feng had known to oversee her. He had been following close behind and stepped in to blow a dart of poison before the target had even turned around, letting the target drop like a bag of rocks. Rosalind hadn't thought to say thank you in the aftermath. While she heaved for breath and shook with adrenaline, her only words when Dao Feng came to give her a hand up were a demand: "Teach me."

Rosalind tested the sturdiness of the handcuffs around her wrists now. Without giving herself time to flinch, she pulled her knee up and slammed into the chain. The handcuffs came off, albeit alongside her scraped flesh. Her raw skin screamed, whole ribbons dropping onto the floor with the metallic cuffs, but it would pass. So long as *she* did not scream. So long as she bit the inside of her cheeks as hard as she needed to control herself and remain quiet.

Small droplets of her blood fell to the wooden floor, seeping through the gaps and staining whatever was downstairs. In less than a minute, however, her skin turned from red to pink, then from pink back to lightly tanned brown.

From that first mission onward, she only ever wanted poison. Poison was irrefutable. If there were others like her out there, they could take a blade to the throat, they could take a bullet to the gut, but poison would rot them from the inside out all the same. Her cells had been altered to knit together against any wound; they had not been altered to withstand a whole system collapse. Working with the only weapon that could kill her was a way of reminding herself that she was not immortal, no matter what the Nationalists said.

It was comforting, in its own strange way.

Rosalind stepped out from the water closet and started down the stairs, making her way back onto the street at the pace of a leisurely stroll. She did not want to raise any suspicion if she was sighted, and she managed to trace her steps back to the train station, passing the same alley from before. The black car was gone. So too was the body of the constable whose neck she had broken when she made her escape.

"It is your fault," Rosalind muttered aloud. "It is your fault for combating me. You could have left me alone."

She pivoted, crossing the road. The water fountain had been turned off to conserve energy through the night. Rosalind's fingers trailed along the edge of the basin when she passed, picking up a layer of dust, then rubbing it away when she reentered the train station, her heeled shoes clicking on the tiled flooring. If anyone in here recognized her as the same girl who had been hauled out no less than half an hour ago, they did not show it. The woman inside the ticket booth barely looked up until Rosalind leaned in, one hand braced on the counter and the other smoothing down her hair.

"Hello." Rosalind's voice was honey-sweet. Soft. Entirely innocent. "A ticket for the next train to Shanghai, please."

3

When the grandfather clock struck midnight, its echo rang cavernously through the mansion house. It wasn't that there was a lack of belongings to absorb the sound—plush couches lined every common area, circled by large flower vases and antique paintings hanging on the walls. It was only that the Hong family had been downsizing their staff these recent few years, and now they merely had two servants left, which gave the house a ghostly sort of emptiness that was impossible to counter.

Ah Dou was nearby, adjusting his spectacles as he organized the calling cards that had been stacking up on the foyer cabinet. And on the living room couch, sprawled sideways with his legs over the armrest, was Orion Hong, looking the very epitome of frivolous and relaxed.

"It's getting late, èr shàoyé," Ah Dou said, casting a glance at him. "Are you preparing to retire soon?"

"A bit later," Orion replied. He rose onto his elbow, propping himself up on the couch pillows. His dress shirt wasn't made for such a casual posture, and the white fabric strained at the seams. If he ripped it, maybe it would make him look tough. Disregarding the fact that Orion was the least tough-looking person in the city. Maybe he could scare someone off with his pretentious dishevelment. "Do you think my father will be home tonight?"

Ah Dou peered at the clock, making an exaggerated sound

while he straightened his back. It had rung minutes ago, so they both knew exactly what time it was. Still, the elderly housekeeper made a show of checking. "I would guess he's staying at the office."

Orion tipped his head into one of the pillows. "With his work hours, you would think he's on the front lines of the civil war instead of running upper-tier administration."

It wasn't that Orion was home often, either. If he wasn't assigned on a mission, he was luxuriating somewhere in the city, preferably in a loud dance hall surrounded by beautiful people. But on the nights he did return, it was strange to see the house in its state. He should have been accustomed to it by now, or at least grown familiar with how it emptied bit by bit every year. Yet each time he came in through the foyer, he was tilted off-kilter, lifting his chin to look at the chandeliers dangling off the main atrium and wondering when the last time was that they had been lit at full brightness.

"You have your father's spirit," Ah Dou answered evenly. "I'm sure you understand his dedication to his work."

Orion flashed his best grin. "Don't make me laugh. I'm only dedicated to a good time."

The housekeeper shook his head, but it wasn't true disapproval. Ah Dou was too fond of him for that—before Orion had been sent off to England, he had grown up with Ah Dou hovering over his shoulder, whether to report to his nanny that he was wearing his jacket or to make sure that he had eaten enough for the day.

"Would you like some tea?" Ah Dou asked now, setting the calling cards down neatly. "I shall make you some tea."

Without waiting for a response, Ah Dou shuffled off, his slippers clapping against the marble flooring. He parted the beaded curtain into the dining room, then disappeared into the kitchen, making a clatter of the water kettle. Orion sat up straight, running a hand through his gelled hair.

A single strand fell into his eyes. He didn't bother brushing it out of the way. He only rested his arms on his knees and eyed the front door, though he knew it wouldn't be opening anytime soon. If Orion had wanted his father home during the nights he returned, he could have made a phone call ahead of time and confirmed first . . . but they weren't that sort of family anymore. General Hong would ask if there was anything pressing to be addressed at the household, then hang up if Orion said no.

It didn't used to be like this. That seemed to be his daily refrain. Once, his father would come home at five o'clock on the dot. Orion would run at him, and even though at nine years old he was getting too big to be picked up and swung around, his father did it anyway. How terrible was it that his happiest memories came from such a distant past? England in the years following had been a blur of gray skies, and then nothing was the same after he returned to Shanghai.

A sudden rustle sounded from upstairs. Orion's gaze whipped toward the staircase, his attention sharpening to a point. To the left of the second floor, his father's home office was situated in an open-plan room: a large dome of stained glass shining patterns down onto his desk when the sun was in the right position. In the night, the entire house echoed the loudest from the office; the shelves and shelves of books looped above the desk did nothing to insulate the space. His father had been particularly fond of pacing alongside those books during Orion's youth, always tapping on the railing of the walkway that curled up to the shelves. The bedrooms were to the right of the main staircase. Sometimes Orion would hear the metallic clanging when he was sleeping, taking the sound as a lullaby.

"Phoebe?" he called. He thought his younger sister had gone to sleep hours ago. At his voice, the rustling stopped short. Orion bolted to his feet. The sound wasn't coming from the right, where Phoebe's bedroom was. It was coming from his father's office.

"Èr shàoyé, your tea—"

Orion's arm shot out. Ah Dou halted fast.

"Don't move. I'll be right back." Gone was the easy grin; in slid the operative. Orion Hong was a national spy. No matter how lightly he wanted to take the world, the world came barreling toward him at breakneck speed every second day.

He hurried up the stairs, keeping his footfalls as quiet as possible. Because the moonlight streamed in through the side windows, only certain parts of the office space were visible. When Orion entered, he made no noise, creeping closer and closer to what he thought was movement at his father's desk. If luck would have it, he would find nothing more than a wild rodent that had nibbled its way in through the drywall.

But luck wouldn't have it.

A figure stood up from behind the desk.

Orion sprang forward, fists clenched in attack. With any other intruder, he would have backed away and called the police—the most efficient solution. But this particular intruder had not even concealed his identity, so his grimace was stark on his expression when Orion hauled him by the collar, slamming him against the lower bookshelves.

"What the hell are you doing here, Oliver?" Orion spat in English.

"What?" Oliver retorted, sounding entirely casual despite the wheeze at his throat. "Can I not enter my own home?"

Orion pressed harder. His older brother still didn't look threatened, though his face did turn red with effort.

"This is not your home anymore."

Not since Oliver defected to the Communists. Not since the April 12 Purge four years ago, when the Nationalists turned on the Communists and kicked them out of the Kuomintang party through mass slaughter, throwing the country into civil war.

"Ease up," Oliver managed. "When did you start using your fists instead of your words?"

"When did you start getting so foolish?" Orion returned. "Walking back here *knowing* what would happen if you were caught."

"Oh, please." Even while he was being held down, Oliver sounded so confident and assured. He had always been like this. There was little that the eldest son of a Nationalist general could not demand, and he had grown up with his requests granted at the click of his fingers. "Let's not bring politics into our family—"

Orion reached into his jacket, then jammed his pistol into his brother's temple.

"*You* brought politics into our family. *You* drew division lines in our family."

"You could have joined me. I asked you to come too. I never wanted to leave you or Phoebe behind."

Orion's finger twitched on the trigger. It would be so easy to pull it. Shanghai had become entirely hostile to Communist activity: no known member could walk the streets without being hauled in, either to be immediately executed or tortured for information and *then* executed. He would only be hurrying along Oliver's ultimate fate.

Oliver eyed the pistol. There was no fear in his eyes, only mild exasperation.

"Put the gun down, dìdì. I know you're not going to shoot."

"Qù nǐ de," Orion spat. He was the aggressor, and yet his heart was pounding with terror. As if he had been the one to get caught sneaking somewhere he wasn't allowed to be. "Did they send you to gather information? Kill me?"

Oliver sighed, trying to crane his neck back from the forceful grip that Orion had on his collar, putting wrinkles into the fabric. He was in a Western suit, which meant he was undercover, dressed in pretense of the elite he used to be instead of the politics he believed in now.

"I've quite literally run into you in the field before," Oliver replied plainly. "Wouldn't we have come after you sooner if we wanted you dead?"

Unwittingly, Orion's eyes flickered up to the library walkway, where he had said goodbye to his brother just before Oliver's defection. Civil war had yet to entirely break out back then. It was coming, and everyone in the city knew it, but they were resolute to pretend until it could not be ignored any further. That night, Oliver had made a mess of the books in his search for a journal, claiming that the reason their mother had left was because their father was a national traitor—that General Hong was hanjian, that he did not have the right loyalties.

"He has been cleared," Orion had insisted, holding his hands out, frantic to catch the books his brother was tossing. "Oliver, *please*—"

"Do you believe it? I do not." Oliver hadn't been able to find what he was looking for. He had made up his mind already anyway, and when Oliver made up his mind, there was no changing it. "I'm leaving. You have the same choice."

"I would never," Orion replied, barely able to get the words out.

Oliver whirled around. "You can't keep doing this. You can't keep trying to fix our father's mistakes."

"That's not what I'm doing—"

"It *is*. Of course it is! Joining the Kuomintang? Training as their operative? You don't have any interest in any of that. You're only trying to prove a point to them—"

"Stop it," Orion tried to interrupt. He had been the one to volunteer his services. When the covert branch came to discuss business with his father, he had been the one to follow after the higher-ups and slap his academic transcript on their desks, showing his years abroad and his early graduation from Shanghai's secondary education academy, demanding a job that suited his background. "You don't know what you're talking about—"

"They're *corrupt*. You're going to fall into his same path—"

"I'm not." Orion snatched the last book right out of Oliver's hands. "Treason is not inherited. They'll see. They'll have to see."

It was a long moment before Orion realized what he had said. What he had let slip, and what Oliver would have caught on to immediately.

"So you admit it," Oliver said quietly. "You *do* think he committed treason."

Orion stilled. "I didn't say that."

There was no point fighting that fight. Oliver was intent on walking out; Orion was stubbornly adamant on staying. When the front door to the house slammed shut that night, it had echoed so loudly that one of the glass droplets on the chandelier detached and pitched to the floor at rapid speed, shattering right in the center of the living room.

Orion tore his attention away from the books, from the shelves that he had spent hours afterward tidying. His father had been accused of taking Japanese money against national interests. His mother had abandoned them without any explanation. His brother had defected to the enemy. Orion had grown up as a careless middle child with nothing on his shoulders, and suddenly within the span of weeks that fateful summer, he was the only tool left to prove to the Nationalists that the Hong family name was worth something.

"You shouldn't be here," Orion said. His words were vehement, but he drew his pistol back and released his hold on Oliver's collar. "If you weren't my brother, I wouldn't take my hand off your throat until I had pulled out your tongue with the other."

"Good thing I'm your brother." Oliver straightened his collar, huffing at the creases. "I'm not here to make trouble."

"Then what are you here for?"

"It would be boring if I told you, wouldn't it?"

Orion clenched his jaw. He much preferred to go through life unbothered than angry, but with every run-in—every brief public encounter on missions that collided with each other, every time Oliver was undercover and Orion was forced to pretend he had no clue who this man was even while they were rehashing the same old arguments under their breaths—there was no one who got him angrier than his estranged brother.

"Go, Oliver," Orion seethed. "Before I report you."

Oliver considered the matter. He folded his arms, then seemed to look at Orion more carefully. "Do you know about the chemical killings yet?"

Orion furrowed his brow. Had any of his words even gotten through? "The what?"

"I suspect you will soon," Oliver continued. "My sources say they're putting you on the task. Typical of the Nationalists to start formulating their plan of action without your agreement first."

"Don't—" Before Oliver could lean in and take something from their father's desk, Orion grasped him by the wrist. When Orion turned to examine the desk, he couldn't see what it was that Oliver had been reaching for. Maybe his brother was playing mind games. "Either tell me what you're here for or go."

"You're too trusting, Orion. You ought to be more careful. You ought to look more closely at the people you're working for." Oliver tugged his wrist away and, for the first time that night, winced to show visible discomfort.

"I am not the one working for an ousted party," Orion said dully. "Go. Please."

Don't go, please, he had pleaded years ago. When there was still hope that their family wasn't crumbling into pieces. When Oliver was the prodigy and Phoebe was the baby, and all Orion needed to do was ensure he didn't get caught making frivolous trouble.

But none of that remained in the present. Now Orion worked for the country's legitimate government, and Oliver worked to overthrow it, other interests be damned. Oliver smoothed his sleeves down. That slip of emotion before when he had pulled his wrist back could have been entirely imagined. Nothing more to say, Oliver brushed by and walked away without a second glance, just like the first time he'd left this house. Moments later, Orion heard the front door close, albeit a lot softer this time around.

Orion loosed his tight exhale. Though his breath came more evenly, he was far from relaxed. What had Oliver been looking for?

Orion took a step away from the desk. He tried to put himself into his brother's shoes, see the world from his brother's eyes. Every small thing became a thousand times more pressing, every sudden decision made so much faster. Though he performed a careful sweep of his father's desk, eventually pulling at the drawers too to check what Oliver might have been digging through, he found nothing save for invoices and boring correspondences with assistants.

"Shàoyé?" A knock at the doorjamb. Ah Dou was poking his head into the office, his expression held with careful neutrality. "Is everything quite all right?"

"You didn't hear anything, did you?" Orion asked. His tone indicated what answer Ah Dou needed to give: *No, sir, I heard nothing at all.* In households that played politics, the staff either blocked everything out or risked being removed. Ah Dou was familiar with the procedure.

"Nothing at all," he returned evenly. "Are you looking for something of your father's?"

Orion gave the desk one last scan. He had to admit: yes, he was expecting to find something suspicious. He had to admit: he lived every day afraid that his father would mess up again and that, this time, the case would not fall apart before conviction; this time, he would not be cleared when the evidence proved too insubstantial. He would be hauled in, and Orion would watch the last of his hope fall apart. He didn't know what to believe. Traitor or not, hanjian or not. It was his father. Perhaps it made Orion a bad operative, but if he were ever to encounter incriminating evidence within the walls of his house, his first instinct would be to hide it away.

Orion allowed himself one shaky sigh. Then he transformed his expression into a bright grin, and had he glanced into a mirror, he might even have fooled himself.

"Only some extra paper. You have the tea ready?"

4

There, by the bar: a target, standing.

Under the lights of the dance hall, one might think the women of this city resembled sea serpents: bright colors and formfitting qipao, the curve of a hip and the slope of a shoulder, slinking from wall to wall. A flash of a scale glinting when the lights flare bright, fading into the shadows when the spotlight drops low. Dancing legs and imported shoes gliding along the sticky floors.

Saxophone music reverberates through every corner of this establishment. No one cares much to remember where they are, to hold the venue's name on their tongue and report it in the morning when the previous night's events are rehashed over a game of cards. This dance hall is not one of the big ones, not Bailemen nor Peach Lily Palace nor the Canidrome's ballroom, so it merely blends into one of the hundreds, another blinking light in a ceiling of electric fixtures. Some few years ago, it might never have survived. It would have been competing against a monopoly held by two gangs, but now those gangs have crumbled while the war outside still demands distraction. New dance halls and cabarets pop up every week like infestations on the city—a fast-spreading tumor that no one cares to cull.

There, out the doors: a target, walking.

Much as they are the focus in every establishment, the women of this city are not being watched tonight, here, now, by the eyes in the corner. Any other time, they are tracked everywhere they go; they are bombarded at every corner with posters that promise eternal youth and unwavering health. Chesterfield cigarettes, Nestlé chocolates, Tangee cosmetics. Hollywood starlets with their skirts billowing in the pencil-sketched wind. This is an age of consumption, time speeding by on American flavors and jazz, French literature and a sea of lost cosmopolitan love. If you are not careful, you will be swallowed.

There, by the tables: a predator, rising.

The killer follows their target out the doors. The killer is like every other occupant of this city because this city holds every soul under the sun. In that manner, perhaps no one is alike to anyone, but that only means that they are another one of the masses, another face that does not draw attention, another late-night wanderer trailing along the streets to the *dun, dun!* of the tram chugging on its tracks. They are your neighbor leaning off the balcony; they are a hawker selling peaches; they are that banker hailing the last rickshaw in the area to pursue the night in a different district. They are, quite simply, Shanghai.

Until they grab the man who walked out from the dance hall, throwing him against an alley wall as easily as one would toss a wad of gum.

The man gasps, scrambles. He had been buzzing pleasantly in his drunkenness, barely able to see two feet in front of him; he cannot summon his wits back fast enough to comprehend this attack, nor the blur of an assailant standing above him when he stumbles to the ground.

"Please," he heaves, trying to scoot away. "You want money? I have money."

There, in the alley: another victim, to be taken.

The glint of a needle flashes under the streetlight. Then its wicked sharpness, forced into the soft of the man's elbow. He tries to escape, but the grip on his shoulder is iron, holding him down.

It burns. Like fire rushing through his veins in place of blood, pulsing through his heart and ravaging everything it passes. Though he fights it, though he screams and screams and screams, the noise is only one more added ruckus to Shanghai as the city beats on.

When the needle is tugged out, a single drop of its contents splatters onto the man's clothes.

But the man won't care.

He is already dead.

5

M orning came heavily, dawn rising over the horizon with strain and effort. By the time Rosalind had made it to Shanghai's French Concession and was walking herself home, the roads were murmuring with the chatter of early risers, a light breeze blowing through the willowy green trees decorating the street sides.

She never thought she would end up back here, living in the French Concession, where her memories were slathered like glaze over the marble pillar houses and mosaic pathways. Everywhere she looked, voices followed, hopping along the wrought-iron fences and trailing atop the short brick walls.

Rosalind turned onto a narrower street, angling her head away from two students walking arm in arm to school. Their eyes followed her, neck ribbons fluttering with the autumn chill, but by then Rosalind was already stepping into her driveway. Her apartment was on the second floor of this block, a small one-bedroom space that creaked in the winters. It always felt empty despite her best decorating efforts, but what choice was there? It was expected of someone like her. She had never had a mother. She had never been close with her father—he'd either handed her off to the tutors or left her to the Cais, her cousin's family. And though she had made a home at the Cai mansion, it was now even emptier than an apartment of her own.

Once, the Cai mansion had been the bustling hub of the Scarlet Gang. Once, the Scarlet Gang had been a formidable underground network that ruled half the city. Now it was merely another political arm of the Nationalists, and Rosalind's bedroom in that house had become a storage unit for random objects that the household staff didn't know where else to put. If Rosalind hadn't left, she would have become another one of the odd items, forgotten amid the mess and clutter in that room.

"I was about to contact Dao Feng and tell him that you had gotten killed on the job."

Lao Lao's voice boomed from the doors of Rosalind's apartment. Then the old lady leaned over the second-floor railing to peer down into the courtyard, watching Rosalind make her way in.

"Dao Feng knows it takes a lot more than one job to kill me," Rosalind retorted.

"Oh, goodness. My frail heart can't take shock, you know."

With an amused snort, Rosalind took her pins out of her hair, shaking her mussed locks while she crossed the grassy courtyard. She reached for her shoulder as she climbed up the external steps, rubbing at a small ache of tension that had blossomed to life. Even through the fabric of her qipao, she could feel the raised edges of her scars, stopping just at her shoulder blade. The brunt of them decorated her back like the center of a lightning strike. She had gotten them before her body was capable of knitting itself back together in an instant, and so they remained, throbbing each time she thought about the Scarlet Gang.

Rosalind came upon the second-floor landing, blowing a lock of hair away from her face. When she met Lao Lao's filmy eyes, the old lady merely tut-tutted, turning on her heel and disappearing back into Rosalind's apartment.

"Come eat. The rice is getting cold."

Lao Lao was the landlady of the building. Rosalind didn't know her name, and Lao Lao refused to give it, so a grandmother-adjacent honorific it was. She lived in the apartment below, where there was a rotary dial phone hooked up in her living room to take messages for Rosalind. Initially, Lao Lao had let herself into Rosalind's apartment with her keys and taped notes to the kitchen table whenever there was a message, but sometime two years ago, she had realized how sparse Rosalind's food shelves were and how her clothes were always folded poorly like a seven-year-old's attempt at housekeeping. Since then, despite Rosalind's protests, Lao Lao always had perfect timing with Rosalind's return to the apartment, already in her kitchen and setting dishes on the table.

"I'm concerned about how early you wake up in the mornings," Rosalind said, sitting herself down and eyeing the bowls of food: the yóutiáo and the scrambled eggs with tomato, the century-egg congee and the jiānbǐng. This would have taken an hour at least to prepare.

"I do not require rest like the youth do," Lao Lao replied.

Rosalind picked up a yóutiáo stick, split it in half along its length, and bit down.

"*I do not require rest.*"

Lao Lao shuffled to the kitchen counter, looking very closely before picking up a newspaper. The old woman certainly needed glasses of some sort, but for whatever reason, she insisted on not wearing any. When she brought the newspaper to the table and set it down in front of Rosalind, there was a note taped to the front page, the handwriting bleeding off the edge.

*Meeting with Dao Feng, 5 PM. Golden Phoenix
restaurant.*

"Yes, I know, dear. I hear you pacing at odd hours of the night." Lao Lao shook her head, exasperated. "I suppose it is better than stalking the streets."

"Stalking the streets is a critical part of my job description," Rosalind said, leaning back into her chair and taking another hearty bite of the yóutiáo. She lifted the scrap paper off the newspaper page, meaning to dispose of the note. Before she could stand, however, her attention snagged on the headline that had been hidden underneath the paper. "Lao Lao . . . did you give me this newspaper on purpose?"

Lao Lao had wandered into the kitchen again, organizing Rosalind's soy sauce collection as she glanced over. Really, it was Lao Lao's soy sauce collection, since she was the one who had bought them and she was the only one who used them.

"Ought I have done it on purpose?"

Rosalind shoved the last of the yóutiáo into her mouth and turned the newspaper around. "'Murder in Chenghuangmiao,'" she read, the sound muffled from the dough. She swallowed, then cleared her throat. "I thought we were close enough that you would accuse me of murder outright."

"Oh, *that*." Lao Lao shuddered. The soy sauce bottles clinked. "It is the second one this week. Drug-related deaths, they're saying. Pitiful way to go out. I am sure you would have a lot more flourish."

"That's me, a master of flourish," Rosalind muttered. She turned the newspaper over, reading more closely. "Why are they calling it murder if it is drug-related?"

There were plenty of opium addicts in the city. Plenty of general addicts lumbering through the poorer parts of these streets too, dropping dead without a word.

"I heard the first victim showed signs of a struggle. They did a . . . What are those new age body-cutting procedures called?"

Rosalind wrinkled her nose. "An autopsy? Lao Lao, that's not new age. The Westerners have been doing it for centuries."

Lao Lao waved her off, the jade bangles on her wrist flashing under the morning light. "Either way, whatever science they used said it was murder."

"Who kills someone with drugs?"

"Is that not what you do?"

Rosalind feigned a glare, taking a spoon and scooping up a chunk of the scrambled eggs. The tomato purée hit her tongue with such flavor that she lost her expression immediately, closing her eyes and pinching her fingers together.

"First, you have outdone yourself with these tomatoes. Second, I use poison to *avoid* any signs of a struggle. If there's someone running around the city inciting these headlines"—she stabbed a finger to the newspaper—"they're not doing a very good poisoning job, are they?"

"You frighten me, Lang Shalin." Lao Lao hurried out from the kitchen, coming to push the chairs around the table until they were aligned straight along every edge. "I have to return downstairs because my daughter is bringing her whole parade of children soon, but report to your handler in the afternoon, hǎo ma?"

Rosalind nodded. "Understood."

With a satisfied sound, Lao Lao patted her shoulder as she passed, then left the apartment, pushing the door closed. The apartment fell silent in an instant, its walls thick enough to keep out the rumble and bedlam of the city outside. The French Concession was quieter to begin with, its streets too full of the rich and wealthy and foreign to tolerate the usual screaming that populated the Chinese parts.

Rosalind took another spoonful of food, thumbing through the newspaper absently. The city's affairs flitted by: trade reports, traffic complaints, new store openings. Four years ago it might have been populated with reports of the blood feud between the Scarlet Gang and the White Flowers. Today there was nothing. Nary a mention of the White Flowers, because the few that had survived were actively being culled by her hand. The Montagovs were all dead or gone. Anyone who'd lived in that household had fled, the headquarters turned into a Nationalist base.

Rosalind flipped to the last page, then froze, her hand stilled over the print. So the universe had decided to play a cruel joke. It had peered into her thoughts and chosen to show her cousin's smiling inked face, her portrait side by side with Roma Montagov's, rendered in delicate line art.

Commemorating the Star-Crossed Lovers of Shanghai

Juliette Cai & Roma Montagov

1907–1927

Rosalind closed the newspaper gently. She breathed in. Breathed out.

If they had lived, they would be twenty-four years old now. But the city's rival darlings were dead. All that was left were the city's street rats and failures, the city's sins and awfulness—personified in a girl named Rosalind. Out of all the people who had been allowed to remain, why had it been *her*?

First she had survived the revolution and the turnover. Then, again, when death came knocking at her door a second time. It had been a summer night with sweltering temperatures, months after the explosion that took Juliette's life in April.

"Rosalind, I need you to get on your feet," Celia had demanded.

She remembered her sister's concerned face, hovering over her while the ceiling of her bedroom swirled into a bright white, indistinguishable from the glare of an imaginary sun.

"Leave me," Rosalind begged. "You'll get infected."

Her teeth were chattering, but her skin was red-hot. *Scarlet fever*, the doctors at the Scarlet house said, and Rosalind would have laughed if she had the energy. Of course it was. She had betrayed the Scarlet Gang, and now scarlet fever came ravaging a course of destruction through her body. It was only right. It was only just.

"We're going." Celia's voice left no room for argument. "The doctors here are doing nothing to help. You're dying."

"So let me die," Rosalind returned. She broke into a cough, lungs seizing in agony. "If no doctor hired with . . . Scarlet money can make me better, then the hospitals . . . cannot either."

"No," Celia hissed. "You need medicine. They're not paying enough attention here."

Rosalind had put her hands over her stomach. Clasped them together as one might do to a corpse laid out for their final viewing. "I'm so tired," she said.

"You won't be once we go."

"Celia," Rosalind said quietly. This was how it should have been in April. Rosalind should have paid with her life for betraying her people. The universe was only a little slow in balancing its scales. "Let me die. Let me—"

"Pull yourself together," Celia snarled, and when her sister yanked Rosalind by the arm and tore her sick body right out of bed, it was the most violence she had ever seen soft-spoken Celia show. "Do you think I would let you die? Do you think I would let you waste away in this bed of silk pretending that we have done enough? Then you think so little of me that you should renounce me as a sister this very moment. Get on your feet, and help me *save you*."

Celia didn't take her to a hospital. She took her to a scientist. To Lourens Van Dijk, a former White Flower, holding down the fort in a laboratory that had mostly gone defunct, but still he waved them in at the door, muttering with Celia about what was wrong with Rosalind. They put her in the back, and Lourens looked through his work, trying to determine whether he had anything that would help cure the infection running to its height.

Not long after, Rosalind's heart had stopped.

She'd felt it growing slower and slower, as if the muscles could not go on anymore, before that first stutter when early morning crept in. She felt the darkness come close, felt her thoughts scatter and her consciousness fracture into mere clouds of memories, and the last gasp of relief that crossed her mind was: *This is it.* Balance restored once more.

Then, like being torn through the very fabric of the world, she was dragged out of the darkness and shoved back into her body. She felt the terrifying pinch of pain at the crook of her arm as her eyes flew open, and though her jaw unhinged to scream, she couldn't make a sound, couldn't say a word until Lourens pulled the syringe out of her arm, the long needle catching the light.

"What did you do?" Rosalind gasped. "What happened?"

"Her rash has disappeared completely," Celia added, sounding equally flabbergasted. "What sort of medicine is that fast-acting?"

"You may have some trouble sleeping," was all Lourens said when he put the syringe away. He patted her arm in a grandfatherly gesture of care, then helped her off the table that she had been lying on. The recovery was dizzying. Not because she remained sick, but because she had switched from dying to healthy again in a matter of minutes, and it was impossible for her brain to comprehend.

"Come on," Celia had whispered. "Let's get you home. We'll tell Lord Cai you had a miracle recovery."

You may have some trouble sleeping. Lourens didn't say that she would never need to sleep again. He didn't say that a week later, when she accidentally sliced her thumb open trying to cut an apple, only a single drop of blood would splash onto the countertop before her skin smoothed over as if the injury had never been there.

Rosalind went back to the lab in search of answers. The windows were boarded up, the doors taped down with a large VACANT sign, but none of that was unusual at first. White Flowers hoping to survive in the city needed to be ready to flee at any moment, or at least give the appearance of departure. Even before Rosalind started chasing after them, she knew their tricks, so she broke into the building and crept into the back assuredly, thinking she would find Lourens lying low.

But Lourens's apartment had truly been cleared out. Even the carpeting had been torn away, leaving rectangular patches on the floor. Lourens had disappeared.

Three weeks after Rosalind was cured, she was supposed to turn twenty years old. The eighth of September drifted around, and she blew out her birthday candles side by side with Celia. A month later, Celia was visibly half an inch taller. It would have been nothing strange—even if they had always been the same height, one sibling gaining an inch on the other was normal enough. But Rosalind was already suspicious. In those three weeks, she would close her eyes every night and she would not sleep. She would get up in the mornings and not feel any fatigue, as if she had not spent seven hours tossing and turning.

She was out of options. She went to the Scarlet research labs, asked them to run tests on her and figure out what was going on. They swabbed her skin. Drew her blood. Put everything under a microscope.

When the scientists came back, they had looked to be in shock. Eyes wide, exchanging frantic glances with each other before they were willing to look in Rosalind's direction.

"Your cells are . . . entirely different from what is normal," one eventually reported when he sat down in the seat beside her. "As if they revert back to a starter state the moment they are injured. As if they don't decay at all unless they have been damaged, and then they rebirth instead of dying."

Rosalind hadn't been following. All the words had gone over her head, landing as useless chunks around her feet. "What does that mean?"

The men in the room had exchanged more glances. An eerie sort of silence had befallen like a heavy blanket.

"It means . . . I think it means you are effectively immortal."

So her twin sister had turned twenty. Rosalind Lang was still nineteen. Rosalind Lang would always be nineteen.

The Scarlet Gang passed their findings on to the Nationalists. The Nationalists ran their studies for weeks, months. No matter how hard they tried, their labs could not re-create exactly *what* Lourens had done to Rosalind, and where their researchers failed to comprehend why she no longer slept nor aged, their agents made use of the results instead. They'd come knocking on her door, telling her that she would be critical to their war effort, and Rosalind had almost turned them away with a roll of her eyes, caring little about the sides of the civil war, especially with Celia secretly aligned on the side of the Communists. But Dao Feng, even from that first day, had known how to read her, and he had jammed his shoe through the archway to stop her from closing the door on them. He said that she could be the mightiest weapon the country has ever seen, the savior of Shanghai and the reason for its redemption. There was no telling how long this immortality would last—didn't she want to take advantage of it while she could?

Rosalind *had* wanted to be useful, and the Nationalists were holding power to be used. Rosalind had broken the city; she wouldn't be happy until she fixed it. And it seemed like the only way to do that was to align herself with the people who were offering themselves to her. When Rosalind packed her bags to leave, Celia did the same and whispered that she would go first, knowing that the two could not stay in contact—or at the very least, could not *appear* to be staying in contact—else the two warring parties would take advantage of the situation. Celia believed in what the Communists were doing; Rosalind found convenience with the Nationalists.

So here she was.

Despite her best efforts, she had never found Lourens again, even after she became Fortune and started searching with an assassin's eye. He had disappeared like every other White Flower threatened by the politics in this city. In truth, she didn't know what she would have done if she had successfully tracked him down— whether she was grateful that he had saved her life, or if she would slip into that familiar resentment for all White Flowers and make him answer for his interference. Perhaps it was better to let him get away, even if it meant she would never know what had been done to her.

Rosalind picked up the newspaper before her, her eyes blurring on the portraits. *The Star-crossed Lovers.* Juliette had chosen her departure from this city: an outrageous, explosive one that Shanghai would never forget. When Rosalind's time came, when her unnatural youth collapsed in on itself, she might fizzle out with a whimper, ashes blown into the wind. The scars on her back would never smooth over as her new injuries did. She was stuck in this state, forever locked into the worst part of her life on a cellular level. It wasn't only her body that didn't age; her whole *soul* felt halted too. The damn city itself was telling her to move on, to find the next thing that would occupy her time, but all she wanted to do was burrow back into the past, into the anger she was familiar with, into the comfort of resolving the wrongdoings that had stacked up there.

It is better this way, she always told herself. Better to fix the past, because she would always be trapped in it.

Rosalind stood up with the papers, taking one last look at the familiar portraits. Then, squeezing her stinging eyes shut, she tossed the newspaper into the wastebasket.

6

When Rosalind walked into Golden Phoenix, a server spotted her immediately, nodding a greeting and pointing down the hall to let her through. Though she had never exchanged more than a few words with the people behind the counters, she was a regular at this restaurant, because Dao Feng called almost half their meetings here, and always in the same private room.

It seemed like bad covert work, in all honesty. With just one leak, there could be someone waiting to kill them.

Which was precisely what Rosalind assumed when she entered the private room and a dagger flew at her head.

Rosalind ducked just in time to avoid the blade. It sank into the wall with a heavy *thud*, metal trembling after it made its landing. She whipped back up, a snarl on her lips.

Only it hadn't been an attack.

"See?" her handler said. He grinned, but he was not speaking to her. "She's good."

Rosalind yanked the dagger out of the wall, testing it in her grip. She had half a mind to throw it back at Dao Feng, but there was no telling if her aim would go wide, and she didn't want to look like a fool, so she simply placed the blade upon the nearby table.

"What is the meaning of this?"

Though there was no danger, there was indeed someone else in the room—another agent. The young man looked incredibly familiar, though Rosalind couldn't fathom why. One corner of his mouth tipped up when he met her gaze. He looked nonchalant, lounging on the chaise with his legs stretched out and his ankles crossed, one arm along the back of the seat and the other swishing a wineglass. The tickling in her memory wanted to indicate that perhaps they had met before, but Rosalind had seen too many faces coming and going during her time as a dancer at the Scarlet burlesque club, and this agent looked exactly the type to frequent them.

"Merely making introductions in the most efficient way possible," Dao Feng replied. "This is Hong Liwen, but—"

"But I go by Orion," the boy interrupted in English. "Enchanté."

Orion Hong. Now that she had a name, she suddenly knew why his face was familiar. His brother, Oliver Hong, was her sister's mission partner. She had spent days doing a background check on him, digging into everything she could find the moment Celia gave her his name.

Rosalind's eyes flickered to Dao Feng curiously, but Dao Feng didn't look like he was preparing a trap for her. As far as her Nationalist identity went, Rosalind was Janie Mead. She might already know of this Orion Hong, but he knew nothing about her.

"Charmed," Rosalind said. She strolled toward him, speaking as flatly as her natural cadence would allow. Orion's accent had come out British, but his French was also flawless. Rosalind had been taught English by a Parisian. One slipup while she spoke and he would hear her as Rosalind, not her alias.

She came to a stop before him and extended her hand to shake. "Janie Mead. Nothing else."

He clasped his hand into hers, shaking pleasantly. His fingers were cool to the touch.

"You get my Chinese name, but I don't get yours? Doesn't seem fair."

The very first matter she had stumbled upon during her research was how the Hong family lay in shambles. General Hong, his father, had been accused of treason some years back, and though Rosalind wasn't one to talk when it came to treachery, at least she had only strayed against family allegiance; General Hong had been investigated for taking bribes from Japanese interests, though he had eventually been cleared by the Kuomintang's upper echelons. Still, it had done its damage. Lady Hong left him, packing up for the countryside, allegedly with another lover. His eldest son defected to the Communists when civil war broke out, disavowing the whole Nationalist party for being corrupt.

Amid all the scandal, however, it was still the middle son who got the most press attention. Gossip columns loved talking about the children of prominent Nationalists, and when Rosalind ran a search for Hongs, all she could find was *Orion, Orion, Orion*—a known playboy in the foreign parts of the city who had slept his way through half the student population at Shanghai's top academy before graduating to become a full-time philanderer.

It was a good cover for being a covert operative for the Nationalists, she supposed.

Though that didn't stop him from being only a part-time philanderer.

"You don't need my Chinese name," Rosalind replied. "It's reserved for my enemies before I eradicate them from mortal existence. And the elderly."

Orion lifted a dark eyebrow. The move was practiced, accompanied by his humoring expression and a single lock of hair that had come loose from his combed style with an assumed casualness.

"Are you trying to be funny?"

"Are you laughing?"

He tilted his head back, letting the lock of hair shift away from his eyes. "I could be."

Rosalind didn't bother with any further retort. It had been no less than a minute since she'd met Orion Hong, and he already watched her like he was planning a conquest ten steps in advance. She had half a mind to tell him to give up before he wasted his time. Rosalind didn't feel physical attraction the way everybody else liked to talk about it, didn't understand the idea of looking at a stranger and feeling ensnared by their gaze. A temporary fascination, fair enough, but true desire to engage in pursuit? With her, that had always taken something more: an understanding, a friendship. It was highly unlikely that Orion Hong had that kind of patience when she knew exactly the type of person he was: Beautiful. Arrogant. Conniving. In this decade, who wasn't?

Orion was still holding on to her hand from their exchange of pleasantries. Rosalind tugged away, making a switch to Shanghainese so she didn't have to keep straining her accent.

"As I asked so kindly before, what is the meaning of this?"

While Rosalind and Orion were engaging in their back-and-forth, Dao Feng was standing by the window, gazing out onto the street pensively. For a moment, he did not say anything to Rosalind's question. He simply held his hands behind his back, scrunching up his Western suit. When the soon-setting sun streamed in, his graying hair ran white, aging him past his years.

"Have you heard of the murders happening in the city?"

The newspaper from this morning flashed in Rosalind's head. There were murders every day in Shanghai, and many more that went unlogged in official records. French Concession, International Settlement, native Chinese land—when they were all governed by different hands and no one bothered communicating past their jurisdiction, a body disappeared was a body forever lost. For these murders to be captivating everyone's attention so thoroughly . . .

"The drug-induced ones?" Rosalind asked. "What are we thinking, new gang running products? The streets have gotten a little hungry for leadership since the Scarlet Gang merged into the Kuomintang."

Dao Feng narrowed his eyes.

"No," he said. "The media decided these were recreational drugs used with murderous intent, but they are not drugs at all. They are lab chemicals."

On the chaise, Orion had shifted to sit upright. He did not interrupt. He merely swung his legs down and rested his chin in his hand.

"Lab chemicals?" Rosalind echoed. Her skin prickled. The very lab chemicals that ran in her bloodstream seemed to perk to attention, rushing to the surface to listen in. "What sort?"

"We don't know," Dao Feng answered. "Information doesn't move that quickly, and we have agents in different parts of the country still working. What we do know is where it's coming from. Preliminary intelligence shows the killings are linked to a Japanese business sponsored by their government: Seagreen Press."

"Wait, *this* is why you kept me here after I reported in?" Orion finally interjected. He threw his leg back onto the chaise. "Are you issuing a new mission? Old man, we *just* finished investigating another Japanese business. Couldn't you have waited a single day?"

Dao Feng shot him a scathing look. "Do you think the Japanese are waiting patiently before swallowing our country into their empire?"

Orion set his wineglass down. He harrumphed. "You're keeping me away from the Green Lotus during peak business hours."

Rosalind lifted a brow. Dao Feng shook his head in exasperation.

"Seagreen Press," her handler tried again. "At home, they do media imports. In Shanghai, they run a newspaper for fellow Japanese residents. Their objectives?"

Dao Feng reached for something lying on one of the chairs, then tossed it in Rosalind's direction. This time she didn't duck; she reached out and caught the newspaper smoothly.

"Imperial propaganda," Dao Feng finished.

Rosalind turned one of the pages. Then she turned another, flipping through quickly. "I can't read any of this." It was all in Japanese.

"Exactly."

Dao Feng came and snatched the newspaper away, despite Rosalind's cry of protest. He dropped the papers in front of Orion.

Orion sighed, smoothing out the front page. *"Socialite Inherits Forgotten Fortune, Pledges Funds to—"*

"Here is what we're going to do," Dao Feng interrupted, not letting Orion finish. "The agency is hiring. Domestic help, because it's better for taxes, and new blood too, preferably youths right out of school so they can pay them less. Two positions have opened up—one interpreter assistant and one reception assistant—so we're pulling some strings and sending you both in. There is a whole cell within the agency responsible for planning these poisonings, following instructions from their government to destabilize the city. Root out the cell, we make arrests, Shanghai lives happily ever after and doesn't get invaded like Manchuria."

Rosalind's head jerked up. The explosion on the tracks last night. The frantic scramble among the constables to use the Scarlet Gang as a scapegoat before their national Chinese troops were blamed. Rosalind had looked into it this morning after breakfast—the part of the railway that had taken the blow was indeed owned by the Japanese. She wouldn't be surprised if their own officers had planted the explosion to manufacture Chinese incompetence and provide a reason for marching in.

"Manchuria was invaded *already*? I—"

Dao Feng shot her a sharp look, his eyes swiveling to Orion once. Rosalind swallowed the rest of her words, taking the warning in stride. They would discuss this later: Orion Hong didn't need a briefing into her last task.

But it did raise the question about why he was here in this room at all, being assigned a joint mission with her. Not to mention why *Rosalind* was being roped into a long-term intelligence operation. She was an assassin, the one sent in for quick kills and targeted hunts. Infiltrating a company and finding foreign threats—she could do it, sure. She had been trained to catch information and take on new covers.

Nevertheless . . . why?

"I think that about covers everything," Dao Feng concluded. "Questions? Comments? Concerns?"

"Yes," Rosalind said. She jerked her chin at Orion. "Why can't you send him in alone?"

Dao Feng shook his head. "These are tense times. The country is still in a civil war, even if Shanghai does not feel the effects as heavily as the countryside. Look at how many Communist spies were caught these last few years because they were one young man living alone and it incited suspicion."

Rosalind blinked. "Wait one moment—living alone as opposed to—"

"What does it matter how Communists were caught?" Orion, meanwhile, was asking. "We're not Communists, and the Kuomintang are the ones doing the catching. Just put me into an apartment under an alias and let me be."

"The whole Kuomintang doesn't *know* about you, Hong Liwen. Unless you want our covert arm exposed to the greater party."

Orion pursed his lips thoughtfully but did not argue. It was a loose excuse, and Rosalind folded her arms, her eyes going to the newspaper in front of him again. They had brought *her* into a mission where her skill set did not entirely align. Which meant maybe she was not there wholly for the mission but to watch over the one who was capable of fulfilling it. In this city, if you knew a language, you had associated with its culture in some way or another.

If Orion spoke Japanese and his father had been suspected of being hanjian some years back . . .

"What did you mean," Rosalind tried again, "when you said Communists were caught by living alone?"

Dao Feng waved his hand at her like she was slow for not understanding. "Your cover stories must make sense, after all. If Hong Liwen is entering the workforce under a different name, he cannot remain living in his father's house."

Now Orion was catching on to Rosalind's confusion. "So . . . I shall be living alone?"

"No, no. As I just said, that is too suspicious."

"Then . . ." Rosalind exchanged a glance with Orion. He was equally puzzled. "Where is he living?"

"With you."

The room fell silent. Rosalind thought she had misheard. "I beg your pardon?"

"Sorry, did I skip that part? You're getting married. For this mission, the two of you will be abandoning your present code names and becoming one combined operative. Welcome to the covert branch, High Tide."

Rosalind choked on her spit. Orion's expression brightened, practically manic as he hopped to his feet. "Oh? You should have opened with that."

"That is surely unnecessary," Rosalind wheezed.

"Your new workplace is three streets away from your current place of residence," Dao Feng said to Rosalind. "Taking on a married couple cover gives you the excuse to be a little odd and closed off while you are still getting comfortable. It gives you the excuse to debrief with each other during your lunch breaks and not appear suspicious. It gives you a built-in partner while you discuss with your colleagues their allegiances to their government and discover whether they formulated the plan to kill your people across the city. We might be a little scattered in our war effort, but we are nevertheless professionals who have considered our plan of action very thoroughly."

Rosalind needed to sit down. This was too much. It would be impossible to hide Fortune's strange eccentricities with someone in her space twenty-four seven. No sleeping, no injuries—all of that was a part of *Rosalind*'s identity, not Janie Mead's. If Dao Feng did not fully trust Orion, then why should Rosalind?

Before she could speak another word in protest, however, the door to the private room opened, and a waitress stuck her head in, gesturing to Dao Feng that he was needed. Dao Feng excused himself, but Rosalind was fast to follow, slipping through the door just before it could close.

"Dao Feng," Rosalind hissed in the hallway. "Have you lost the plot? Why would you give *me* this assignment?"

"You are needed," Dao Feng answered patiently, waving for the waitress to go on ahead. "You're a very skilled operative—"

"Stop. I don't want your practiced spiel," Rosalind cut in. She cast a look back at the private room. Usually she couldn't hear anything from the hallway when she was sitting at the table inside, so she could only hope Orion wasn't pressed right to the door eavesdropping. "I work for you to rid the city of White Flowers. I work for you to purge out the enemies who are actively harming Shanghai. I don't work for any other reason."

Dao Feng tipped his chin in agreement. "Correct. And on this mission, I am sending you in to find the city's enemies. I don't see the problem."

"The problem is that you trained me to *kill* them. Not make *lists*. Not to root out a *terror cell* or whatever else is going on—"

At this, Dao Feng finally looked to the private room door in concern, then took Rosalind's elbow and walked them a few steps away from it. When he frowned, the crow's feet at his eyes deepened; sometimes he reminded Rosalind of Lord Cai, who also used to look perpetually in concentration when her cousin was bringing him information he didn't want to hear.

"Listen to me, Lang Shalin," Dao Feng said, lowering his voice. "Hong Liwen is a very good spy. He's effective. He has one of the highest success rates among the covert branch. But this isn't an easy assignment. There's too much about it that doesn't make sense, and the reason for that might involve hanjian. We might have a cover-up. We might have defectors in the Kuomintang. You know how the Japanese are: they bury themselves in the shadows long before they act in the light. And . . ."

He trailed off. Rosalind's jaw tightened.

"And you don't trust Hong Liwen," she guessed.

"I trust him, to an extent," Dao Feng corrected. "But I trust you most. Everyone in this city can be swayed for a price. You, however—I don't think anything under this city's sky could buy you over once you've set your mind on something. I need you to have a hand in this. Give this operation a few months of your time. I promise there will be White Flowers to cull after it."

Rosalind pulled a strand of her hair around her finger. The fight left her shoulders, her posture sagging.

"Well," she said quietly. She shrunk a little more. "What if I'm not a very good spy?"

Dao Feng flicked her on the temple. Rosalind reared back, snapping "Ouch!" but his quick glare stopped her from saying more.

"I didn't raise you with so little confidence."

"*What?* You didn't *raise* me at all."

"Of course I did. I birthed you as Fortune. Now get back in there and speak to Hong Liwen. I will only be a moment."

Dao Feng hurried into the main restaurant, and Rosalind huffed, pivoting back toward the private room. She opened the door and stepped inside, mouth thinned into a line. Immediately, Orion hopped to his feet again, ready to speak.

"Don't," Rosalind interrupted.

His mouth snapped closed with an audible sound. "I didn't say anything yet."

"It was a pre-warning. I'm trying to think."

Orion crossed his arms. "You're very grumpy. I expected my wife to be less grumpy."

"I"—Rosalind barely managed through her gritted teeth—"am not your wife."

"Not yet. Do you think they'll make us a fake certificate, too? I'll get you a ring. What do you like? Silver? Gold?"

"Will you stop speaking—"

"It's okay that you're grumpy. I think it's very cute—"

Rosalind suddenly picked up the dagger that Dao Feng had thrown at her, taking aim. She had thought it would make a mighty fine threat, that Orion might flinch when she raised her arm, but he only grinned, straightening his posture. Their eyes met. His had a wild sort of glee in them, as if he were saying, *Please, go on. I dare you.*

The door to the room opened again. The dagger clattered back onto the table.

"All right. Come with me, you two."

Dao Feng was already gone before he could get a response. Rosalind was first out the door, Orion close on her heels. Despite how quickly she walked, she did not catch up with Dao Feng until they were outside Golden Phoenix, and that was only because he was taking another message from a soldier in uniform.

A car was parked by the sidewalk.

"Get in," Dao Feng instructed.

"Where are we going?"

Orion was already opening the back seat door, gesturing for Rosalind to go ahead.

"It is a short trip," Dao Feng replied in a non-answer. He slid into the passenger seat. "They made it convenient for us, it would seem."

Quickly, Rosalind pulled at the fabric of her qipao, ducking through the open door and sliding along the back seat, biting down on the inside of her cheeks. As soon as Orion slammed his door closed, the chauffeur was driving, rumbling through the French Concession and down Rue Ningbo, passing municipal offices and police stations.

They had entered the Chinese parts of the city. And Rosalind had an inkling of what they were being taken to see.

The car stopped. To the left side, there was a small crowd gathered around an alley, flocked with their shopping baskets still clutched to their chests. She guessed there had to be an open market somewhere nearby, but Rosalind hadn't been to these areas much lately, and the stalls and vendors had moved around too much for her to be sure.

Dao Feng got out of the car. Rosalind and Orion followed suit, both of them quiet now, feeling the tension on their skin that spoke of trouble, the heaviness in the air that spoke of danger. When Dao Feng walked toward the crowd, it parted to show soldiers standing guard by the alley, keeping onlookers back by the threat of their rifles.

The soldiers stepped aside for Dao Feng. He was not in uniform, nor identifiable in any other way, and yet there was barely a nod exchanged before his path was cleared, letting him disappear into the alley.

"Are we supposed to follow?" Orion asked.

"Evidently," Rosalind muttered, hurrying forward.

The alley walls were tall enough to block out the sun. A chill swept her neck as she approached Dao Feng and the dead body he was crouching beside.

Its limbs were splayed in all directions. Its head was lolled to the side at an awkward angle to its neck. This was a rush job—whoever made the kill had been working fast, no time to catch the victim and set them down.

"You see this?" Dao Feng asked. He reached for the body and lifted an arm. The skin had already turned a sickening shade of white, so that the circle of red at the crook of the corpse's elbow practically glowed. "An injection site. Too thick to be from the needle of addicts. Far too bloody and weeping to be a reaction to any normal drug, not when most in this city have been safely circulating since the foreigners brought them in."

"We already believe you," Rosalind said. She felt vaguely nauseated. It was ironic, she knew—a squeamish assassin. "What is the purpose of this?"

"Merely a reminder alongside the frightful bickering I was hearing earlier."

"It was not bickering," Orion countered quietly. When Rosalind tried to observe him out of her periphery, she found his hands to be wringing at his sleeves. He couldn't take his gaze off the body, a greenish tint of disgust marring his expression.

Dao Feng let go of the corpse's arm. It flopped onto the concrete ground with a pitiful *clunk*. It didn't even sound real.

"The papers have reported two. By our count, it is more than ten, stemming back months—perhaps years—prior. I am sure there are others waiting to be found too, knowing how many alleys and nooks curve in and out of Shanghai. Don't think you have a simple task because we have already found the source killing these people. Play your hand before all of them are caught, and they simply re-form to start again. Play your hand before pulling out every foul imperialist root grown into the soil, and they will merely sprout anew when the conditions are right and the sympathetic gardeners return."

Rosalind shifted uncomfortably. As did Orion, going as far as to take a step back when Dao Feng stood suddenly, seeming far taller than his usual height.

"So," he said. The sun disappeared over the horizon. "Are you ready to get to work?"

7

Outside Shanghai's city limits, there was a small photography shop that specialized in engagement and wedding portraits. Business was always slow, given there were not many who could afford such portraits around these parts, which suited the four people who worked at the shop perfectly fine. Day in and day out, they opened the creaky front doors and prepared the light screens for two or three patrons who would wander in and mosey around before walking right out. The townspeople here had only sparse change to spend, better suited for the array of dumpling shops and fish markets along the row.

The lack of business didn't matter much; the shop never checked their weekly profits or calculated their losses. Though they had beautiful cameras and knew how to put together a portrait on the rare occasion that a patron did use their service, the shop was a front for the Communist agents installed outside the city to track their enemy's movement.

"Why are we still open? Don't you people have family to get back to?"

The sarcastic voice bellowed loudly through the doors, and Celia Lang looked up from where she had been sweeping, startled out of her reverie. She had been thinking about their latest maps, the works in progress that the team had been sketching to send to their underground military forces. Their task was being conducted on the outskirts of Shanghai, in what was technically Jiangsu Province, because there were Nationalist forces from the city gathering at the bases here, readying to be sent into the countryside for further waves of war. The four of them had been stationed at this shop for a few months now, and it would likely be only a month more before they finished their reports and were assigned somewhere new.

"Thankfully, all my family is dead," Audrey replied from behind the front desk. "What's your excuse?"

Oliver stepped through the shop entrance, kicking out the stopper so that the door could close behind him. He cast Audrey a wry look. They hadn't expected him back until the next morning, so he had either finished up in Shanghai early or had been chased out. Knowing how Oliver completed his tasks—knives first, kicking down doors, boots scuffed—both were equally likely options.

Oliver rolled up his sleeves. A black bag dangled from his hand, casual in his grip as he leaned one elbow on the front desk and wrinkled his nose down at Audrey.

"If you worked as hard at being a receptionist as you did at being a comedian, business would be booming."

"Don't blame *me* for our lack of business," Audrey countered happily. There was one potential patron in the corner looking at their film prices, but they knew he would wander back out into the cool evening after a few minutes, treating this excursion into the shop as merely another piece of scenery on his nightly walk. "Everyone probably sees your scary face and runs out screaming."

Oliver only frowned deeper, and Celia turned away, hiding her smile against her shoulder.

"Now, what are you giggling about over there?"

Celia smoothed down her lips. Oliver had seen her. Of course he had—there was very little he missed, starting from that first time they'd met, in an alley filled with workers fighting for revolution, and he had guessed immediately that she was a Scarlet elite wandering off from where she was meant to be. He had looked important; she had thought he was one of their leaders. Once Celia joined the Communists properly and was assigned beside Oliver, she found out that the Communists regarded him highly only because he was a Nationalist general's son, and his defection to the other side had been a mighty gesture of commitment.

Though Celia was on equal standing with Oliver now *technically*, Oliver was in communication with their superiors more often. She didn't know why he kept going into Shanghai, and she didn't ask. Not because she didn't want to know, but because their entire line of work dealt in secrets. Leaks could spring in every which direction, and it was better to know nothing if one was ever caught and tortured than have to bite your tongue clean off to protect your fellow agents.

"I'm thinking about the French Concession's coffee," Celia replied, stepping aside to let the wandering patron look at the wall frames. "Did you bring any back for me?"

Though Oliver kept his face blank, there was a glint in his eye as he lifted the bag in his hand and pulled out a thermos. Celia set the broomstick against the cabinet and walked toward him, arms outstretched like she was being handed a child.

"It may be cold by now," Oliver said. "Though I tried my best to keep it bundled close."

Celia pressed the thermos to her face, reveling in her happiness. Nothing mattered at that moment: not their civil war, not her concern for her sister in the city, not the progress of her own mission. Only this coffee, reminding her of simpler days in Paris where she and Rosalind had grown up, making a world of their own.

Audrey muttered something from the desk. Celia startled, glancing over.

"What was that?"

"Oh, nothing." Audrey cast them a wink, scooping up her belongings and readying to retire to the back of the shop, where they all had rooms. None of them returned to real homes anymore. Only makeshift ones, depending on what the Party wanted from them. "I think I hear Millie calling for me, so I'll leave you to close up. Wǎn'ān."

She hurried off, her cloth-soled shoes silent on the linoleum floor. Millie was certainly not calling from the back because Millie went to sleep at outrageously early hours. Though Audrey hadn't repeated what she'd said, Celia thought it had sounded a lot like *Picking favorites, I see.*

Oliver had clearly heard it too. He glared after Audrey for a long moment before loosening his expression. Only—there was a flash of something dark under his collar when he moved, and Celia's hand snaked out quickly, taking ahold of his jaw to get a better look before he could protest.

"What happened?" she demanded. A patch of angry scratches started at his collar and continued down into his shirt.

"A small scuffle," Oliver replied. He was always vague out of habit, even when there was no information at risk, and it infuriated Celia to no end. She pulled her hand away, narrowing her eyes; Oliver stared back evenly. Eventually, though Oliver would never admit it outright, Celia's intimidation won out, and he turned his palms over wordlessly to show her his knuckles too, also bearing scratches.

"Are you trying to end up in the hospital?" Her voice had risen an octave.

Oliver's mouth twitched. "I only need you to tend to my wounds, sweetheart."

"Oh, I'll *give* you some wounds to tend to."

"Ouch, harsh." He scrunched his palms away. "Please don't worry about it. I had a small encounter on the streets—that is all."

"Enemies?" Celia asked. *Nationalists*, she meant, without saying the words aloud, as if the mere mention would invoke their presence.

Oliver didn't answer. He reached out to squeeze her elbow before sidling past. "I'm off to write a missive. Do you need anything?"

"No," Celia huffed. She forced herself to shake off some of her annoyance. "Thank you for the coffee."

Oliver shot her a controlled smile, then disappeared into the back of the shop. Left alone, Celia retrieved a cloth and started to clean up, wiping at the windows and dusting away what would collect after a long day of nothing. She had started to settle into these daytime routines. As much as Nationalist propaganda made them out to seem like competent spies who had stepped out of a Hollywood film, being a Communist agent was nothing more than drawing maps, counting the tanks that would roll in every week, and on the rare occasion, sneaking out in the middle of the night when Kuomintang army divisions were moving down the town's main path to determine their army's next place of settlement. The Communists had gone underground. It would do no good to draw attention to themselves. They were not expected to do anything except maintain the covers of being ordinary people, or else they would get caught, and their numbers were dwindling as it was. Celia was sure that her sister was doing a lot more running around and slashing throats as a covert agent for the actual government in charge.

"Hey."

Celia glanced over her shoulder, her fingers halting on one of the door latches. As soon as she saw it was just Audrey again, leaning against a glass case, Celia turned back to locking up. She would get the left side in place first and then secure the right side once the last patron exited.

"I thought you had retired into your room already."

"It's still early," Audrey returned. She made a show out of listening for movement from the back, as if Oliver would march out to tell her off. "Do you know what the angry man went into the city for?"

"By 'angry man,' I have to assume you mean Oliver," Celia said wryly. "I don't know. Do you?"

Audrey clicked her tongue. "That's why I'm asking *you*, Celia."

The left door clicked in place. The latch was especially rusty when the temperatures were hotter.

"Why do you assume I have information about him?"

"What else are the two of you always whispering about? Don't tell me it's sweet nothings."

Celia threw the dirty rag in her hand at Audrey. The girl shrieked, slapping it away from her face before it could land.

"I mind my business," Celia replied.

With a sigh, Audrey picked up the rag, then spun it in circles as she toddled around after Celia, not doing anything to help with closing up. Their team knew nothing about each other's pasts; Celia could not begin to imagine how someone as lazy and loudmouthed as Audrey got looped in as a Communist agent. She and Millie were both newbies, assigned to this task as training more than anything else. Soon they would be moving elsewhere; it was safer to say less about how they had ended up here, lest someone turn traitor and root out the whole cell. Only Oliver knew everything about Celia—including the fact that she hadn't been born with the name Celia, nor with the name Kathleen—and that was because they had met so much earlier, had had years between them since the first outbreak of civil war. To everyone else, Celia just introduced her-self as Celia—or Xīlìyà among the entirely Chinese crowds—and gave no other backstory.

Well . . . she supposed most of her superiors knew that Celia had once been Scarlet-associated, which had been a matter of necessity more than choice. Only they still assumed that Celia was an alias and Kathleen was her real name, when in fact the opposite was true. Her hands had been tied: after the first revolution, as the smoke cleared and dust settled over the city, painted posters of the Scarlet children started to circulate through Shanghai to build morale. If only to prevent being suspected as disloyal, Celia told the necessary superiors that she had once been known as Kathleen Lang and had been the right hand of the Scarlet heir.

She had expected to be met with horror. Instead, she was given almost the same treatment as Oliver when he defected from the Nationalists. They figured she had walked away from the Scarlet Gang and chosen a more righteous cause. They figured that made her trustworthy. If only they knew that it hadn't been hard to pack her bags and leave the Scarlet house. She had returned to the Cai mansion for months after switching sides, staying quiet and keeping her allegiances a secret. One might have thought that it took a fight and an explosive struggle to leave, but she only needed to walk out the doors, and no one stopped her. The Scarlet Gang had long been losing control, bit by bit. Like the loose thread of a scarf, snagging and catching on every sharp object that you ran by until you looked down one day and there was nothing more around your neck.

Celia left little behind when she walked out. Her sister had been readying to leave too. Her cousin—her best friend—was already . . . elsewhere.

"Are you sure you don't know anything?" Audrey pried once more.

"Even if I did," Celia countered, jangling the keys to the shop as she tidied the front desk from the mess that Audrey had made, "I would wipe it from my brain. I don't need to know anything not pertinent to our mission at hand."

Though the Communists had accepted her as a former Scarlet, the burdensome part of that factoid was that it also revealed she was Rosalind Lang's sister. The Communists had spies in the

Nationalists—that was a fact everyone openly acknowledged. Try as they might to flush double agents out every few months, there were Communists planted in places, siphoning information about the Kuomintang that even some within the Kuomintang did not know. Like the fact that their covert branch had a weapon, a girl who couldn't sleep and couldn't age, who could make hit after hit on their enemies without tiring. Like the fact that they claimed the girl's name was Janie Mead and she was a regular agent, but the leadership of the Communists had long uncovered it was, in fact, Rosalind Lang with strange chemicals running through her veins. Sometimes Celia would receive demands asking for reports on Rosalind's actions in the city. Each time she gave the same answer: *I know nothing. I am no longer in contact with Rosalind Lang; nor will she accept my contact.*

It was all lies, of course. Celia might be loyal to the Communists, but her first loyalty was to keeping her sister safe.

Audrey stomped her foot, feigning disgruntlement. "How do you know it's not pertinent? I heard that Oliver was assigned control over Priest."

Celia's head snapped up. *"What?"*

"Oh." Audrey's lip curled. "So, gossip does get your attention after all, Miss High-and-Mighty."

"Something like that is hardly mere gossip." Celia glanced into the hallway, as if Oliver might stroll out any second. *Priest.* Agents on a task were always assigned a code name so that their superiors could speak about their progress without giving away who the agent was, in case that information got out and the Nationalists came after them. And information certainly moved around all the time. That was how their entire underground party knew that Priest was their most notorious assassin, a sharpshooter who never missed.

Celia wasn't high up enough to know who Priest was. She

hadn't considered that Oliver was either—much less to be *in control* of them.

"You seem surprised," Audrey remarked.

Surprised, with a dash of concern for her sister's sake. She was always worried about her sister, but especially when talk was moving about other assassins. Rosalind's identity had leaked here and there in certain places. Priest's was a top secret matter. If Priest went after Rosalind in an act of war, Rosalind wouldn't even see it coming.

Celia snatched the dirty rag back. "Don't you have maps to draw? Shoo."

Good-naturedly, Audrey bounced back before Celia could whack her with the rag once more. "Fine. But tell me if—"

There came a sudden crashing noise, summoning Celia's attention with a start. The browsing patron had knocked his elbow into one of the cameras. Celia would have brushed it off, but in his haste to right the structure, he pulled his arms up, revealing a thin wire from the pocket of his slacks.

"Hey!" With two long strides, Celia closed in on him. Her hand clamped on the patron's arm, securing a tight grip while her other hand reached for the wire. She tore it clean out, the rectangular device making a popping sound before it clattered out of his pocket. A spark buzzed down her finger, the electric charge tangible as it ran from one microphone end to the other plug end.

Audrey rushed to the device, picking it up and running a quick eye across it. There was a clear and obvious Nationalist logo stamped on one side: the blue and white beaming sun. Even in their espionage materials, they had the ego to go putting official identifiers on everything.

"A transmitter," Audrey said. "Thirty-second delay to whoever is on the other side, I'd guess." She looked up, meeting Celia's gaze with visible relief. Everything they had said that could have been damaging was contained within the last thirty seconds. Of course, that still didn't fix the problem of the patron holding the knowledge—

He tugged out of Celia's grip and lunged out the door.

"I've got him," Audrey declared, breaking into a run. "Get Oliver!"

"Merde," Celia muttered beneath her breath. Here she was, thinking it would be a quiet night. "Oliver!" She rushed to the back, skidding to a stop before his bedroom door. "Oliv—" Her knuckles hadn't yet made contact before Oliver was flinging his door open, looking concerned.

"What is the ruckus—"

"We had a snoop. Nationalist."

Oliver was moving immediately. He always stormed through the world as if there were warfare following right at his heels, and it was only strengthened when there really was a threat of danger. Celia wasn't far behind him, hurrying out the doors of the shop and running a scan of their surroundings. Audrey had the man down on the ground by the sidewalk. His hands were placed flat before him, holding very still while Audrey held her pistol at his head.

No one was around to bear witness at this hour. The towns-people liked to stay inside—it was too dangerous to be out and about when soldiers might patrol the night and do anything they liked.

Oliver strolled up to the situation, his hands behind his back. His collar fluttered in the breeze, one of the buttons casually loosened.

"Well," he said. "What happened here?"

"I'm not an agent," the man on the ground gasped. "Someone only wanted me to run surveillance on every shop in town to root out any suspicious actors. I didn't get anything, I promise!"

"The mere fact that you're explaining yourself to us indicates you know we are, in fact, the suspicious actors they're looking for," Oliver said wryly. "Audrey? What did he pick up?"

Visibly, Audrey held back a wince. "I was talking about Priest," she answered.

"I won't say anything!" the man insisted. "I don't know what any of it means! I can shut up. I can keep my mouth sealed like a tomb."

Celia drew closer slowly, approaching Oliver from behind and putting a careful hand on his arm.

"It's true. He didn't hear much. Nothing that would be devastating."

Oliver remained unspeaking. A strong gust of wind blew, singing out with high-pitched fervor, the sound curling around the three operatives standing in tense formation. The town seemed insistent on keening to make up for Oliver's silence.

Audrey's arm faltered, her weapon lowering. "It wouldn't be too bad if we let him go—"

Before any of them had registered what he was doing, Oliver pulled out his own pistol from his pocket and shot the man through the forehead. The shot rang loud, so quickly it might have been imagined. Celia jumped, feeling a faint splatter of wetness land on her cheek.

The man slumped over in slow motion. The nighttime rustle rushed to fill the void that the gunshot had made, the grasses underneath their feet stirring with the taste of running blood and the river nearby whistling to ask if it could be fed the body. Celia exhaled slowly, her hands shaking beneath her sleeves.

"Are our covers okay?" Audrey asked, interrupting the night. "I'm sorry—"

"We're fine," Oliver said. He wiped the spray of blood off the side of his face. "It didn't go anywhere. Don't mess up again. Don't speak of anything sensitive while others are in earshot."

Audrey looked down at her feet. She had avoided the splatter.

"I should have known better as well," Celia said kindly. "Don't feel too awful."

Though it did nothing to change the situation, Audrey gave an appreciative nod. Oliver looked like he disagreed with Celia taking a part of the blame, but he did not put voice to it. When the moon slid behind a cloud, he said, "Head back in, Audrey. Celia and I can deal with this."

Audrey nodded again, finding more energy in the movement. She hurried away without further discussion, reentering the shop and turning off the lights inside.

"It wasn't a terrible slip," Celia said as soon as Audrey left. "She used your anglicized given name, but you're already a known agent."

Neither Celia nor Oliver even possessed operative code names while they were assigned in the outskirts. There was no need while their work was relatively off the radar; no one higher up would be discussing their progress on a frequent basis.

"It wasn't a terrible slip this time, but if she gets into the habit of talking around spying ears, she's going to get herself hauled in and tortured." Oliver rolled his sleeves further, grimacing at another blot of red at the edge. He pulled a handkerchief from his other pocket—the one without the gun in it—but instead of wiping at his own face first, he gave it to Celia. "Don't go so easy on her, sweet-heart. This unit is training agents, not babies."

Celia took the handkerchief gingerly. "She's only fifteen."

"We were only fifteen once too, but we weren't careless. It's why we're alive." Oliver leaned down to move the dead man's ankles. "Now, help me out, please?"

8

He moved in that very night.

Rosalind watched him unpack his boxes, watched him inspect each item inside before setting it down in her apartment as if it were the first time he had seen that belonging. Maybe he hadn't been the one to pack them. Maybe all the many servants at his large house had been the ones to collect everything for shàoyé, and he was just now remembering he owned a golden figurine of a rooster. She couldn't comprehend how he was giving everything such a thorough once-over even while talking at a thousand miles per minute. His mouth had not stopped moving since he'd come in.

Not even once.

"—trust me on this. Information extraction is one of my best skills. We follow my lead, we shall be done with this mission in weeks—a month *tops*."

"Mm-hmm," Rosalind said, without really meaning it. She held a pen in her hand, its ink tip poised over a half-written letter.

"Futoshi Deoka oversees the branch of Seagreen Press in Shanghai, so the likelihood of him leading the terror plot is high, yes? I hear he is an incredibly tidy person. And you know what that means? A paper trail. We must direct our attention to where confidential information within the agency could be stored, because wouldn't it be under his security? Safes. Locked cabinets—"

Rosalind wondered when an appropriate time to tune him out would be. She needed to write to her sister, and she couldn't remember how to spell Manchuria in French when there was an incessant stream of nonsense swirling around her apartment. Her arm stayed positioned around her paper, strategically blocking out the scrawl of her loopy writing.

Rosalind touched the ink nib down again. *Mandchourie,* she decided, sketching a small train at the end of the paragraph to mark a section break. She continued briskly: *Now instead of a new task, I have been installed to do covert work at Seagreen Press, the Japanese paper in Shanghai. You have seen the news, I'm sure, about killings in Shanghai, which the Kuomintang think is a Japanese-led scheme originating from Seagreen. They say it is all connected: the deaths, the slowly encroaching invasion. There is little doubt that we need to start fearing what is coming from outside the country—*

A shadow fell over her paper, and Rosalind's head snapped up, her pen scratching across the page. The room was silent. Orion Hong had stopped speaking at some point without her notice.

"Oh, don't fret," Orion said, the ghost of a smile on his lips. He was looking at the stack of books by her elbow. *"The Mysterious Rider?* How very American of you—"

"Don't touch it," Rosalind snapped. Irritation flared in her stomach. Her apartment wasn't big—the kitchen and the living area were adjoined upon first entry, decorated only by Lao Lao's hand. In the bedroom, the walls were sparse and the floor space mostly taken up by books about poison. Orion was an intrusion amid everything, ill-fitting among the careful arrangements.

It wasn't that she wanted to dislike Orion Hong. It wasn't that she knew much about him or found anything to disagree with on a fundamental level other than the fact that he was possibly an imperialist sympathizer. Mostly, she disliked him only because he was here, infringing on her space and her work. She needed to rely on him for a successful mission, and he needed to rely on her, and that vital fact vexed her to no end. She hated having to depend on another person.

Orion lifted an eyebrow. "Mustn't I?"

Rosalind smacked his hand away as soon as he started to reach for the book. Somehow she had known that he would challenge her.

"Touch my desk, and I'll kill you," she said darkly. "You know what? Move anything, and I'll kill you. If you so much as *breathe* near what you should not be fiddling with, I'll—"

"—kill me?" he finished.

Rosalind turned her letter over. The ink had dried enough that she could hide the words without smearing her work. "Good of you to catch on so quickly."

Orion drew a finger along her desk. A thin layer of dust parted way, forming a straight line on the wood—a barrier, cut between the two of them.

"And if I touch *you*?"

Something in Rosalind reached a breaking point, a dam on her resentment splitting right open. Did he have to make a joke out of everything? How was he possibly the Nationalists' best spy for this mission with *this* behavior?

"Don't ever forget that you are talking to another operative," she snapped. "I will gut you alive before you even see me coming."

Orion threw his head back with a laugh, reacting with casual grace. Rosalind was *serious*. There was invisible blood soaked deep into her palms—couldn't he smell it? Each time Rosalind inspected her own fingers, it felt like there was something slick and viscous coated all the way up to her wrists. It seemed impossible that others could not sense it, that the shoulders she brushed while pushing through a crowd didn't automatically flinch away because they felt her transferring a metallic stench over to them.

"Understood," Orion said, a quirk still playing at his lips. He stepped back from her desk, sticking his hands into his pockets. "I must head out now. Don't stay up on my behalf, beloved spouse."

Rosalind cast a glance at the small clock ticking next to her. Her brows furrowed. "You're leaving at this hour?"

"Top-secret operative matters," he answered, already pushing through the sliding bedroom door.

"What are you talking about?" Rosalind called after him. "Hey! Hong Liwen!"

Orion disappeared. Rosalind drummed her nails on her desk surface. Perhaps Dao Feng had given her fake husband some other task that she was not privy to. Maybe Rosalind ought to follow him.

Silence soaked into the bedroom. With an exasperated huff, Rosalind retrieved her letter, turning the words face up again. Some of the ink at the bottom had smudged, unfortunately, but her writing was still legible. She folded the paper, then found an envelope and addressed it to Celia's location.

Rosalind would deliver it tomorrow. There was a dull ache behind her eyes when she set the pen down, but there would be no sleep. She had already forgotten what it felt like to need rest, to rise and fall with a large household in routine. Mornings with plates clinking, afternoons with the sound of mahjong tiles wafting up from the living room, nights with the household staff playing the radio loudly while they dusted off the kitchens and prepared to retire.

She hadn't enjoyed living in the Scarlet house. She had hated much of it, in all honesty. But it had been a comfort to be surrounded by noise, to know that there were living souls in the next room over who tugged her along on a constant stream of movement forward and forward and forward.

When night fell in this apartment, the quiet was always the most awful, as if darkness muffled everything it covered. Her own thoughts were the loudest noise for miles, tumbling over each other until there was only a buzz between her ears.

Rosalind rose from her seat, twisting her finger around a strand of hair. Slowly she wandered around her desk, then to the drawers, where Orion had set down the little rooster figurine amid her line of perfumes. She prodded at the golden animal, pushing it away from the precarious corner of her drawers. It would serve Orion right if his silly knickknack fell to its little rooster death, but then there would be shards on her floor. Better to save it now or . . .

Rosalind paused, giving the figurine a shake. There was something inside.

Carefully—in case she broke the rooster and was caught red-handed snooping right after she warned Orion not to touch *her* things—she prodded her fingers around its belly, feeling for some sort of opening. She was poking at the figurine with no outcome for several moments until she bumped its nose and a crack formed along its wings, letting the whole head come off.

"Now, what's this?"

Rosalind tipped out the object inside. It looked like a sheet of newspaper, crumpled tightly into a little ball. She didn't want to smooth it open in case Orion could tell what she had done, but she did lift a single corner, seeing that it was page six of an issue from *Shanghai Weekly*. Rosalind nudged the corner a little more, revealing the upper line with the date of issue: *Wednesday, 16 February 1927.*

She pushed the corner down, then returned the crumpled paper into the figurine and clicked its head back into place. She placed the rooster where it was before, as close to the edge as Orion had left it.

Shanghai Weekly. She had seen that newspaper delivered to Lao Lao's doorstep, and by nature of Lao Lao's role as a keeper of information, the old woman filed away every issue in her cabinets. She might even have this exact printing from four years ago. Rosalind tossed her hair out of her face and hurried through her apartment, clacking down the staircase and appearing in front of her landlady's front door. When she smacked her hand against the delicate wood, there was a little boy's sudden squeal and the sound of quick footsteps running toward the door.

"Xiao Ding, do *not* open the—"

Lao Lao's warning came too late. Her grandson had already opened the door a crack, one of his chubby cheeks squeezing through the gap as he peered out.

"I have come to eat you!" Rosalind declared, lunging down and swooping the toddler into her arms. Xiao Ding shrieked in delight, letting Rosalind pretend to chomp his face while she stepped into the apartment. Lao Lao appeared around the corner, breathing in relief when she squinted and recognized Rosalind.

"Oh, it's just you. Have you eaten?"

"Now I have." Rosalind handed Xiao Ding back, stomach down as if she were volleying livestock. "A little undercooked, but I don't blame you."

Xiao Ding giggled. Lao Lao took him back, muttering another warning about running off.

"I wanted to take a look at your newspapers," Rosalind said, already walking toward the cabinets in the living room. Compared to Rosalind's quarters, Lao Lao's apartment was an entirely diffe-rent world. The walls were an explosion of red and gold color, and what space wasn't already covered in auspicious character posters was decorated with picture frames or flower vases set atop the drawers and shelves.

There was also noise. Plenty of noise, mostly attributed to the two other toddlers whacking each other under the living room table. While Lao Lao tended to their wrestling match, Rosalind crouched down to examine the stacks inside the glass cabinets.

"Do you have *Shanghai Weekly* going back to 1927?" Rosalind called absently. She could only see this year's.

"I have them going back to 1911, bǎobèi. Keep looking."

Rosalind kept riffling. Minutes of careful searching passed before she felt Lao Lao's presence approach behind her.

"See it?"

"Why did it have to be *Shanghai Weekly* and not *Shanghai Monthly*?" Rosalind muttered begrudgingly in answer. At least it wasn't *Shanghai Daily*.

Lao Lao dropped to a crouch too, her elderly knees clicking. "What are you in search of? Did they catch a picture of you in 1927?"

Unlikely. In February of 1927 Rosalind was slinking off to bars in territories that were not governed by either of the two gangs ruling Shanghai, her heart thumping in her chest and her skin prickling with the thrill of her illicit activities. Now, nausea clenched her stomach and tightened like a rubber band each time she thought back on those months, but the visceral reaction was of her own making. She had no one but herself to blame.

"Dimitri Voronin, yes?" She had been the one to call out to him first, when the nights were warm and the August summer was fading. He had turned around, giving her a quick up-and-down appraisal with his green eyes, and she only thought it to be amusing, a rebuff against the Scarlet Gang's blood feud. She was not a Cai. She did not care about the Montagovs. She did not care about shunning the White Flowers.

"I know you," he had said. "Don't I?"

"Do you?" Rosalind returned, raising a drink to her lips. "Tell me what you know."

It was all fun and games until she grew to love him. Until it spun out of control, because Dimitri had been playing a careful scheme, had been guiding her hand with his arms around her, feigning a soft embrace to hide the moment his hold twisted into chains.

"I want to be your friend, Roza," he promised months later, on that cold winter night. Breath visible in the air as they walked the back alleys, circling and circling while they talked without prying eyes. "I want to be your dearest friend."

What kind of person had the decency to say those words and not mean a single part of it? What kind of person would spend all that time winning her trust until they were lovers, only to pull the rug out from under her and chase power instead?

She knew now, of course. The same kind of person who had never loved her, who had been using her to get information on the Scarlet Gang. The same kind of person who would have destroyed this city if her cousin hadn't stopped him. Knowing that he was dead didn't make her feel any better. It didn't stop the nausea of the memories or the tightness in her throat. She was one of the few who remained living after getting caught in the destructive path of her once-lover. So why did she still feel like one of his casualties?

Rosalind sighed, leafing through the next stack of newspapers. "I am not looking for my own picture. Have you heard that I was given a fake husband?"

"I heard indeed. Is he handsome?"

Rosalind rolled her eyes. She moved to scrutinize the next stack. "He's an annoyance, is what. I have a feeling he's hiding something important, but this newspaper issue might shed some light."

Lao Lao reached her hands out, taking some of the newspaper stacks that Rosalind was moving so she could see farther into the back. Neatly, Lao Lao set them down with the jade bangles on her wrists clanking a tune, keeping an orderly organization line while Rosalind dug.

"What would he be hiding?"

"No clue," Rosalind replied. "I am only suspicious."

"Shalin, you are suspicious of everyone."

Rosalind shot Lao Lao a dirty look. "I am not."

Lao Lao shook her head sagely. "The world runs on love, not suspicion."

With a snort, Rosalind turned back to the last stack at the very back of the cabinet. Love was a curse. Nothing good ever came out of it.

"Aha. I found 1927."

February was already at the top of the pile, so Rosalind flipped through the issues, scanning the dates. Lao Lao hovered over her shoulder, ignoring another squeal from one of the toddlers before a loud clatter came from the kitchen. The old woman exhaled one long breath, then rose upright slowly.

"Give me one moment—Xiao Man! Get down from there!"

Rosalind hardly noted Lao Lao shuffling away. She was too busy counting along the weeks until she finally found the right one: Wednesday, 16 February. With three quick flicks of her finger, she had turned to page six, eager to see what it was that had inspired Orion to tear out a whole page and shove it into a figurine.

"Hmm."

HONG BUYAO ARRESTED ON SUSPICION OF TREASON

Rosalind read through the article, passing over boring details about monetary transfers and invoices, before stopping at a paragraph at the end.

> "My father is innocent," his son Hong Liwen, 17, was quoted as saying outside their house last Sunday. "None of you know what you're talking about." When asked about Hong Lifu's public proclamation that their father was guilty, Hong Liwen did not offer any comment on the topic of his elder brother.

"Did you find what you were looking for?" Lao Lao called, setting the toddlers down on the couch.

"Yes," Rosalind answered. "It didn't really clear up much, though."
She didn't know what she had expected to find. Maybe an article
that said Orion was a convicted murderer who had escaped from
his cell and needed to be hauled in immediately. Alas.

While Lao Lao got her grandchildren under control, Rosalind
tidied up the cabinets, putting each newspaper stack where she had
found it. She remained deep in thought, chewing over the headline.
As incriminating as it was to have been arrested for treason, it hardly
made someone true hanjian. Plenty of Nationalist officials collabo-
rated with foreigners on the side for extra profit. It was the whole
reason the city was overrun by imperialists.

"Are you sure you don't want any food?"

"I'm fine," Rosalind called over her shoulder, heading for the
door. "I am going up now!"

With a farewell to the landlady and the toddlers, Rosalind
trekked up the stairs, frowning as she pushed back into her own
apartment. Orion had not returned, but she hadn't expected him
to. She supposed she would make use of this time while he was
out to brew some poison and stink up the apartment. It wasn't as
though she had any better way to spend her time. She never liked
being between targets because she didn't know how to pass the
nights if she wasn't creeping through the streets and watching over
someone's house. Rosalind would have to get used to it. For as long
as this current mission lasted, she wasn't an assassin; she was a spy,
which meant she was between targets for the long-term.

Rosalind reached for the dried plants she hid in the back of her
kitchen, holding up the labels to the light. She would make a non-
lethal tranquilizer. It could be useful given the stranger in her home.

With his background though, maybe she needed something
stronger.

"You won't trick me," Rosalind muttered beneath her breath,
eyes flitting to the rooster figurine when she sashayed back into the

bedroom. For the sake of their country's livelihood, the Nationalists had paired her up with Orion Hong and asked them to work together.

She dropped the dried plants into a mortar bowl. Then fetched a pestle, smacking it down with every bit of strength she possessed.

For the sake of their country's livelihood, she would work with him. She would play nice, let him into her apartment, feign a romance.

But there was no possibility that she would let her guard down even for a second.

Never again.

9

Orion walked into the double-story restaurant at a brisk pace, rolling his shirtsleeves to his elbows. Behind him, Silas Wu tried his best to keep up, nudging his thick glasses along his nose every few seconds when they started to slide down from exertion.

"I cannot believe you dragged me up for this," Silas huffed. "I'm an agent too, *not* your chauffeur."

"And as an agent," Orion replied, shooting a brief look over his shoulder to make sure his best friend was keeping up, "I need you to help me out while we pretend to drink and socialize."

Under normal circumstances, Three Bays was not his preferred locale for drinking and socializing. The crowd was too old, too full of politicians. Which meant it was his father's go-to when he had free time in the evenings, and the place where Orion was most likely to find him.

"You couldn't have worn a hat and come alone?" Silas grumbled. He wiped his shoes on the red carpet in the foyer, wrinkling his nose at the fish tanks set up by the menu boards. "I'm willing to bet no one is paying enough attention to recognize you talking to your father."

"I'm playing it safe. I've a new alias now. I cannot be a Hong."

"So you yank me along everywhere like a butler? I can't stand you."

Orion bit back his laugh, amused by Silas's stream of complaints.

Perhaps it was rude of him, but Silas would forgive the matter in minutes. Orion refused to take most things seriously, and Silas took everything *so* seriously that they evened out. That was surely how equations worked, was it not?

"Are you my chauffeur or my butler? Make up your mind."

Silas bared his teeth. He looked like a Pomeranian pretending to be a guard dog. "I'll have you know—"

"Besides, what is it that you Communists say?" Orion interrupted, clapping a hand on Silas's back as they ascended the stairs. The large wooden structure swirled in a half circle before reaching the second floor, winding around a marble fountain with a naked sea creature rising out of the water. "You have nothing to lose but face?"

Silas looked at him askance. Despite their age difference, they had been as close as brothers ever since they were both shipped off to England the same year for schooling—Orion at nine and Silas at five, living under the same roof because their fathers put them with the same tutor. Orion hadn't minded the new lifestyle. Silas, on the other hand, had grown up hating his time in the West. In his eyes, he had been sent away from a perfectly good childhood at home, so he would act out by stomping his feet during lessons, then crying at night, hoping his parents would take pity and summon him back. It didn't work. Once he was older and crying wasn't an option anymore, Silas made a task of going through his education as quickly as possible, shaving off the extra years wherever he could.

He returned around the same time as Orion. Weeks later, he had a job: an operative for the Kuomintang's covert branch. Silas had published such a scathing op-ed in one of Shanghai's top newspapers condemning the foreigners—and condemning the native elite for valuing Western education over their own—that the Kuomintang took notice. Back then, though Orion knew of the covert branch's existence through his father, it was Silas's recruitment that first gave Orion the idea to work for them too.

And here they were.

With the years they had spent together getting whacked by their tutor's ruler if they got a question wrong, and then the years after running around playing politics, Silas certainly knew that Orion wasn't misquoting from a lack of knowledge. Orion was just being an asshole on purpose.

"You have nothing to lose but your chains," Silas corrected. "Keep your voice down. This isn't a good place to be keeping up that cover."

Silas wasn't really a secret Communist. He was, if one wanted to get technical about it, a triple agent: an established Nationalist who had contacted the underground Communists claiming to defect while still holding on to Nationalist loyalties for the covert branch. Among the Nationalists he was code-named Shepherd; he had not given Orion the code name he used among Communists to prevent any chance of them finding out he was still loyal to his original faction. He had been planted for almost a year now, making slow headway toward uncovering the identity of Priest, one of the Communists' assassins. Last Orion heard, Silas was progressing well, but this wasn't a line of work where that meant anything. He could just as easily fall back to square one if a source was yanked away or the enemy grew suspicious.

Orion glanced around, eyeing the clumps of businessmen who had convened to talk outside their private rooms. There was so much cigarette smoke in the vicinity, wafting from their conversations and smothering the upper restaurant level in gray. His stomach clenched. He forced himself not to pay his surroundings any mind, to let the knots in his gut unravel.

"There's a matter I need to sort out, Silas," Orion said quietly, sobering from his previous humor. "Oliver made an appearance last night. He was searching through my father's desk."

Immediately, Silas blinked, his brows furrowing. "On the contrary, that is a matter you need to report."

No, Orion thought. He couldn't do that. What if it prompted the Nationalists to search through his father's belongings as well, wanting to understand what the Communists might be looking for? What if they ended up finding something bad?

"I will have to sweet-talk a hostess into locating my father," he said, pretending he hadn't heard Silas's suggestion.

"Or you could mind your mission instead of always sticking your nose into your father's business," Silas continued. "But I already know you're not going to do that." He paused for a moment, waving at the smoke. "Speaking of your mission . . . is it true you got *married?*"

The twitch on Orion's lips was immediate, the tension in his stomach easing a tad as it latched on to the distracting thought. Janie Mead. With her familiar face and careful mannerisms and a perennially pinched nose that conveyed a need to see Orion buried six feet underground. The more she visibly expressed annoyance at him, the more he felt the urge to annoy her, if only to hold her attention longer. She was fascinating. She was so uninterested in him, and it intrigued him immensely, partially because he swore he knew her. From where or how, he could not recall, but the feeling of having made her previous acquaintance was in his bones.

If Janie Mead's story were to be believed, she had not been in the city for the past ten years, raised entirely in America. Orion didn't buy it. But he liked a challenge, so he would not push the subject with her. He would pluck it out bit by bit instead.

"True indeed," he answered, flashing a grin. "She says her name is Janie Mead, but I can't find a single person who knows her."

Silas pushed his glasses again, nudging the very corner so he wouldn't smudge anything. "So, she's a hermit?"

"No, she's a liar. A beautiful liar, but a liar nonetheless." It was common enough among the covert branch. Orion would try not to take it personally. With a wave of his hand, he signaled for Silas to follow him farther into the second floor, where there would be hostesses to squeeze for information. "Do you know anyone who might have information about the American returnees in the city?"

"I can ask around," Silas replied. "What happened to that other girl you were dating? Zhenni?"

Orion wrinkled his nose. "We broke up weeks ago. Keep up, Silas. She liked Phoebe more, anyway."

Silas almost choked on his next inhale. It was no secret that Silas was infatuated with Orion's younger sister, not when Orion was the poor soul who had to endure the secondhand embarrassment each time Silas tried to make his intentions clear. By the time Phoebe blew out her sixth birthday candles and their parents prepared to send her abroad early, their eldest brother, Oliver, had almost finished up his studies in Paris, so Phoebe joined Orion in London instead, living right down the road. From the very moment they met as children, Silas could not take his eyes off her, no matter how much Orion made gagging noises when Phoebe's back was turned. It would have made more sense for Silas to have befriended Phoebe instead of Orion—given Silas and Phoebe were only half a year apart in age—but Silas was a wimp in all aspects when it came to Phoebe. More than a decade had passed since then, and either Phoebe remained startlingly oblivious to Silas, or she pretended to be. His sister was simply too flighty to put up with the matter.

"Jealous?" Orion asked, brow quirking. Time and time again he had smacked Silas's head and insisted that he tell her outright how he felt. Silas always refused.

"No," Silas spluttered. "Phoebe can make her own decisions."

Orion swung an arm over Silas's shoulder. "I was talking about me. Maybe if I take you from Phoebe, she'll finally notice you—"

Silas swatted him away furiously as Orion pretended to lean in. "Back, back!"

"Aw, come on—"

"You can't just play with a man's feelings like that—"

A sudden voice cut through the corridor of the second floor. *"Gēge!"*

"What the hell?" came Orion's immediate response, giving up on tormenting Silas and turning to locate the sound. "Speak of the devil and she shall appear, I suppose—Hong Feiyi, what are you doing here?"

Phoebe hurried closer, the layers of her skirt swishing with every movement. "Why are you throwing my full name around like that?" she asked sweetly. "Can I not be seeking Father's audience just as you are?"

Orion checked his wristwatch. "It's past your bedtime."

"I'm seventeen—I don't have a bedtime. Try again."

"I vehemently disagree. You are an infant."

Phoebe blew a breath up into her bangs and shook her head, disturbing all the little ringlets in her permed hair. "I am on my way out anyway. Father isn't here."

"What?" Orion exclaimed. Out of the corner of his eye, he could see Silas giving him a dirty look. Orion had dragged them out here for nothing. "Then where is he?"

"Overnight at the office, according to his dear chums in private room number five," Phoebe replied. "I did see Dao Feng along Fuzhou Road earlier though. He had a note for you."

Orion held his hand out straightaway. Phoebe was not an agent, only the winner of the world's most busybody little sister award. Where Orion had chased down his employment and Silas had been recruited, Phoebe just so happened to be in proximity to the covert branch. By virtue of who she was related to, Dao Feng trusted her enough to run messages to Orion, which meant Phoebe was looped into every single one of his missions.

Orion had protested the matter time and time again. She was not *trained*, no matter how much Phoebe liked to claim she knew martial arts. Their mother used to visit once every few months while Orion and Phoebe were abroad, and while Orion worked on his essays, Lady Hong took Phoebe out to the park, making an event out of getting air by telling Phoebe they would practice wǔshù. Phoebe would boast that she knew how to throw a punch, but then she ran away squealing if a fly landed lightly on the back of her hand. Their mother—loving as she had been—was a mere bookkeeper before she married into being the lady of the house. She had taught Phoebe nothing except how to speak loudly— certainly not fighting skills. Even if Orion had his own bad habit of involving himself in other people's business, at least he could handle the dangers. Phoebe kept wading into deep waters she wasn't tall enough to stand in. He wanted to keep her protected. He wanted her where it would be forever safe and dry.

"You're welcome," Phoebe said emphatically, passing the note. "Silas, doesn't he take me for granted?"

"W-what?" Silas stammered.

Phoebe had already moved on. "I fought to get this message here, you know. I could have sworn I was being followed into the restaurant."

Orion frowned. He lifted his gaze over Phoebe's shoulder. The second floor of Three Bays had most of its windows facing the street, letting in the loud sounds and vivid lights of every other restaurant along the block. The corpse from earlier that day flashed in Orion's head, as well as that pinprick of red, somehow marking a lethal wound despite its miniature size. Down on the street, there was a shriek—it was impossible to tell whether it signaled delight or disaster.

"How so?" Orion asked. He stepped closer to the window, pressing a hand to the glass. There were numerous people milling on the pavement directly below, oblivious to what danger might be lurking in the alleys nearby. Some in groups, laughing among themselves. Others standing alone, looking up at the restaurant . . .

Phoebe shrugged. "I saw the same man reflected in the shop windows down Fuzhou Road twice. I went home for the afternoon, and when I headed out again, I thought I saw him at the traffic lights."

Orion frowned, peering more attentively at the one man standing alone. "Green necktie?"

A pause. Phoebe's eyes grew wide. "How did you know?"

Orion didn't waste time. He snapped, "Stay here. Both of you," and dashed to the stairwell, almost colliding with a couple who were midway up.

The night was raucous around him when Orion slammed out of the restaurant, searching through the flocks of pedestrians. *There*—the Chinese man he'd spotted from the window, wearing a green necktie and a Western suit, idling by a lamppost.

The moment the man saw that he had been sighted, he turned to flee.

"Hey!" Orion gave chase, despite his flare of confusion. If the man had been following *Phoebe*, what could it possibly be for? Not the strange business with the chemical killings, surely. Had she been spotted taking something from Dao Feng?

The man sprinted into an alleyway, swinging under a laundry line. Orion hurried to follow, pushing through the surprised pedestrians and darting into the alley before the man could put too much distance between them. Though Orion was staying narrowly on his tail, he had to admit this man was running fast, and unless there was some way to slow him down . . .

Orion sighted a potted plant out of his periphery, sitting quaintly on someone's front step. Making a split-second decision, he scooped it up as he passed by. Then he threw it as hard as he could.

The potted plant smacked directly into the man's head, smashing into shards and soil clumps. Ahead, the man tripped, and with the pause that afforded, Orion closed in, grabbing his shirt collar and yanking him back.

"Who are you?" Orion demanded. "What do you want?"

The man didn't answer. He whirled around, meeting Orion head-on.

A jolt of alarm turned Orion's blood cold. The man's mouth was set in a snarl, but his eyes were entirely blank. Like he had been disturbed while sleepwalking, and still he did not wake. There was an eerie mismatch in that vacant gaze paired with such quickness—

The man kicked out. Though Orion braced, thinking he could take the hit and swivel into his own offensive move, the impact landed so hard that he skidded back three steps and slammed into the wall. By the time Orion shook his head, gasping for breath and clearing his vision, the man had run away.

Orion winced, patting around to check if he had damaged anything in the aftermath. When he seemed to remain in one piece, he rose back onto his feet slowly, his head still reeling.

"Orion!"

Silas appeared at the end of the alley. Then Phoebe, standing on her tiptoes to see over his shoulder.

"Why don't you two listen to a single thing I say?" Orion asked, wiping at his mouth. Something tasted metallic. He must have bitten himself when he hit the wall.

"What happened?" Phoebe hurried closer, glancing around wildly. Her dress settled when she stopped in front of him, each layer making her look like a wispy purple cloud that had been misplaced on the ground. "Are you okay?"

"My question is, what sort of tail are you picking up?" Orion huffed. "I'm fine. There's nothing we can do it about it now, I suppose. Tell Father to give you a guard."

Phoebe frowned. "I don't need a guard. It probably wasn't for me."

Those eyes. Orion was still thinking about them. The complete hollowness in the stare. There would be bruises on his arms and hip tomorrow for certain, but his greatest injury at present was how shaky he felt, like he had encountered some unknowable entity.

He shook his head, dropping one hand on Phoebe's shoulder and the other on Silas's elbow. At once, he pushed them all out of the alley, returning to the main road.

"Silas, let's get a drink. You—" He pointed a threatening finger at Phoebe. "Go home."

Phoebe stuck her tongue out and raised her arm for a rickshaw.

10

A city reborn is a city traumatized.

It remembers its past, every second that it took to get to this point. It sees the former version of itself and knows that it has changed, its boots no longer fitting, its hats no longer comfortable. The streets trace how they used to sprawl. No matter how it is paved over and reorganized, memories and echoes do not fade away that easily.

Trauma doesn't have to lead to destruction. Trauma can be the guiding point into something better, something stronger. Maybe a street *should* forget the sounds it used to make if the causes were factory cogs and devastating conditions.

But that matter is a coin toss, blowing either way. Dependent on the wind direction and how volatile the elements are feeling that year. Change is no easy thing. When a valley has run water down the same course for dynasty after dynasty, a momentary drought won't change its route. When water returns, it will still flow along the same rivulet carved into the ground.

This new Shanghai doesn't look that different. Still the same lights, still the same neon, still the same ships sailing into the Bund and hauling their products in, bringing people and people and more people. Put an ear to its heart, though, and you might hear the strain begin.

Put a killer on its streets, and even without really listening, the conversations start to change.

"We have been luxuriating in mess for too long. We have put up with the foreigners for too long, have let them debauch us thoroughly. We need better leadership. Maybe then the streets wouldn't be brewing criminals."

A heavy clunk of a beer bottle. A sneer at the lips. Two elderly civilians hover by a bar table, sharing a bowl of peanuts. They have seen so much. Witnessed centuries between them.

"I don't want to do this again. You force me to spit at you that you are misguided and then you do not listen—"

"What is misguided? Unity? Standing together, all of Asia, mighty as a combined power against Europe?"

"There is no such thing as an Asia combined. We are different peoples. Different histories, different cultures. You are trying to believe in a mirage that Japan is feeding out."

"What is wrong with that?"

"You don't fight European imperialism with more imperialism!"

A table behind the bar snickers. They are overhearing the debate, but they do not nudge their nose into it. This whole city has been doing the same routine for some time now: at dinner tables among parents and children, around school desks when the teachers bring it up, even between lovers when their heads are resting breathless on their pillows, gazing at one another under the glowing moon.

The first elderly man huffs. His beer sloshes, spilling onto the sticky floor. He doesn't like being told off. Once he latched on to the idea of incoming saviors with faces like theirs, it was too easy for him to sweep everything else under the rug. Isn't this what they have been waiting for? Liberation from Western rule?

"You know what your problem is?" he asks his friend. "You have your eye on the small details rather than the big picture."

"What is the big picture?" his friend returns. He cracks open a peanut. "The trouble has been with the Western foreigners for some time, but are you naive enough to think they alone carry the problem?"

"Yes—"

The first man isn't given the opportunity to finish his answer.

"*No.* The problem is everywhere. The problem is any empire that thinks it can swallow others into its rule. Europe was given the playground first, and it has hogged it. With power, it could be us too. We are not exempt."

Another harrumph. "So we should have power. Let us take power."

It is here that the conversation finally breaks up. His friend walks away from the bar counter, too fed up to continue. The first man continues eating peanuts. The first man doesn't notice a soulless set of eyes following his friend out into the night.

"Walk away, then," he mutters under his breath. "It won't stop the new order from arising."

The door slams closed. Outside the bar, the other elderly man turns around wearily, peering to see who has followed him out, his eyes weak in the hazy dark. They stand on a smaller street, an offshoot of the central entertainment district. There is no one in their immediate vicinity. Only a tree, waving with the wind. Only the moon, hanging low in the sky, ready to duck back under the horizon again.

"Hello," the elderly man says. "I don't suppose you have a cigarette?"

He doesn't think to flinch when his companion reaches into their jacket pocket.

He is too late when it is a syringe that comes out instead.

11

Morning came with a cold chill, crusting small crystals of ice at the base of Rosalind's bedroom window. Just as she'd decided that she had finished zoning out for the night and was set to "wake up," she heard a noise on the street outside and pressed her face close to the windowpane to look.

Orion waved from the pavement below. So he had returned after all. A shame that he hadn't wandered into a particularly thorny bush sometime during the night and gotten stuck permanently.

With an annoyed sound, Rosalind lifted her window, misting the glass with her breath. The clock turned to six in the morning, the first rumbles of activity starting on the streets outside.

"Hello," Orion bellowed up. He shoved his hands into his pockets, grinning widely at her. "Ready to go?"

Rosalind frowned, then slammed the window back down. Twenty minutes later, she was walking outside with a small bag slung over her shoulder, flipping open a handheld mirror to make sure her nose was powdered evenly. For the sake of appearances, she squinted into the mirror as she approached Orion, pretending to check on her alertness. It was an early hour, so it only seemed natural, except Rosalind did not sleep, which also meant she never exhibited signs of fatigue, much unlike Orion with his slouched shoulders and loose tie.

"Long night?" Rosalind asked, putting her handheld mirror

away. She didn't pause long. They examined each other for only a beat before Rosalind turned on her heel and started to walk, feeling the wind curl around the nape of her neck.

"Something like that," Orion replied. His hands were still buried deep in his pockets. A lock of hair had come loose from his combing, swinging in front of his eyes carelessly.

Rosalind held back an irritated huff, turning the corner onto a main road. The shops here were just starting to open their doors and push out their food carts, so she made a fast pivot for one of the jiānbǐng stalls. However brief, she figured it would be a reprieve from Orion's looming.

Except he followed right on her heels, hovering by her elbow. When Rosalind took her order, his arm snaked over her shoulder and dropped a handful of coins into the vendor's palm before she could even reach for her bag.

"I can pay for myself," Rosalind said sternly.

"My money is your money," Orion replied. He waved for the vendor to take the coins quickly, then steered Rosalind away, two hands braced on either side of her arms. "You won't make us have a lover's spat in public, will you?"

Rosalind's own hand twitched at her side. There were five castor bean seeds sewn into the skirt of her qipao. There was poison in the lining of almost every article of clothing she owned, given that one never knew when they might need it in an emergency. Crush up castor bean seeds and spill the powder over anything to be ingested, and internal bleeding would start in a victim before long. Quick, easy, and untraceable.

The Nationalists might protest if she did that to her mission partner, though.

Rosalind shook him off with a grumble, then stopped and put her wrapped food into her bag for later. "We wouldn't need to have a lover's spat if you would just behave."

"Behave?" Orion widened his eyes, feigning innocence. His collar was still askew, and . . . wait a moment, was that *lipstick* smeared on his neck? "I am always well behaved."

"For the love of God," Rosalind muttered, seizing him by the shoulder. While her bag was still open, she retrieved a tissue and, before Orion could protest, scrubbed at his neck, paying no heed to keeping her touch gentle. Orion winced, but then Rosalind's glance flickered up, and whatever Orion saw in her expression shut him up from speaking further.

If Rosalind was visualizing the neighborhood layout correctly, the newspaper agency was just around the next corner. The moment they walked in, the show would start. Surrounded by imperialists and hanjian, by men who believed in occupation and all the subordinates below them who wanted this country conquered until its individuality was dust.

"I need you to remember"—Rosalind gritted her teeth, making one last brutal wipe to get the print of red out—"we share a code name now. I don't care who you were before. So long as we are High Tide together, if one of us gets caught, we both go down."

If they were found out, they wouldn't be given the chance to explain themselves. Their enemies would shoot first, then hide the bodies, and no one would be the wiser that two operatives were sinking to the bottom of the Huangpu River.

Orion tilted his head, assuming an air of curiosity. "Do you question my capabilities?"

"I think that we haven't even *started* our jobs, and you were about to walk into work on our first day looking like you're cheating on me."

Orion's hand snapped up. When his fingers closed around her wrist, they were ice cold.

"As you phrased it last night—" Orion's tone was light, a smile at his lips. On a brief glance, it would have been impossible to see the flicker in his brown eyes, a split-second warning, there and gone in the time it took him to blink his dark lashes.

But Rosalind saw it.

"—I am an operative too. I have switched from cover to cover even while under my real name. I don't know what jobs they had you doing, Janie Mead, but I was rather good at mine."

He released her wrist. *Janie Mead.* Though he hadn't intended it, the use of that name reminded her how much she was hiding in that moment: a cover within a cover. She couldn't slip up while they were on this mission; she couldn't slip up in the comfort of her own home, either, with her operation partner now living there.

"If you are so good," Rosalind said, balling up the tissue in her fist, "then prove it."

"And if you want our operation to succeed," Orion returned brightly, "stop throttling me with your eyes. It's not becoming. At least not in public." He winked, then marched forward, swerving around the corner and disappearing from sight. Rosalind's mouth opened and closed. She was flabbergasted. Absolutely flabbergasted. Where did the Nationalists find someone like this?

"Hong Liwen," Rosalind demanded, recovering from her astonishment and surging forward. "You get back here."

Rosalind turned the corner, marching to fall back in step with Orion. He only gave her a sidelong smile like he was waiting for her to catch up.

"Perhaps you should switch to using Mu Liwen now," he said. "Make a habit of it early."

The covert branch had supplied him with that alias, taking inspiration from Janie Mead to make him an American-educated returnee. Rosalind, too, could come up with a new name if she liked, but there was no need. There was a reason why the Kuomintang hadn't bothered. They had most definitely filed Orion's application with Seagreen, then tossed the wife in as a bonus for the second opening when Seagreen liked the sound of Orion's fabricated background. In the office she would only be Mrs. Mu—the Mu tàitài to his Mu xiānshēng when they were addressed together. She was already Rosalind Lang pretending to be Janie Mead. She didn't need to add another layer onto it.

The office compound came into view. Though she and Orion stood some distance down the road, they had already been spotted. A man was waving vigorously, lifting his hat before signaling that he was going to step out from the security booth and fetch someone. The main building was situated at the end of a short driveway. An iron railing with an intricate gate enclosed the compound, and the booth inside controlled the gate's opening and closing, surveilling who came in and out. Try as they might to insist this was a regular workplace, it was guarded like a true imperial hub.

"We can finish this conversation later," Rosalind decided.

"Don't be difficult, darling. You're a spy. Adapt. Improvise." Orion walked off. His stroll was relaxed, and he waved eagerly when another figure appeared by the gate to greet them.

Rosalind was going to poison him in his sleep. If she didn't *actually* throttle him first.

She hurried after him, fuming.

The secretary's name was Zheng Haidi, and she seemed to know the building about as well as Orion and Rosalind did: not very well at all.

"It is through here, I'm sure," she said, opening the third door in a span of five minutes. They had taken two wrong turns to get to the production department, where Orion would be an interpreter assistant and Rosalind would be a department reception assistant, both ultimately reporting to the same higher-up, Ambassador Futoshi Deoka.

"Are you new?" Orion asked. He grimaced, narrowly avoiding

two people bustling down the hallway with piles of paper in their arms. Rosalind sidestepped much more smoothly, clearing her throat to prompt Orion to keep moving.

"Yes. I was brought in personally by Ambassador Deoka," Haidi replied airily. She was young, certainly younger than both Orion and Rosalind.

Orion cast a look back, trying to gauge Rosalind's judgment. Rosalind merely kept her expression blank. As soon as Haidi stopped and faced them, however, Rosalind wiped on a small smile, glancing around at the occupied desks.

"You will be here," Haidi said, touching Rosalind's elbow and gesturing to a smaller desk next to the department's reception. Each department they had entered and exited had been organized the same, whether it was production, printing, or writing. One large desk by the doors to deal with visitors into the department, a grouping of cubicles in the center for employees, and then offshoot doors stemming along the hallways where the higher-ups had their own privacy. There were other doors too, of course—storage units and boiler rooms and floors snaked with electrical wires that Haidi would peer her head into as if she couldn't remember which doors were dead ends and which led into the hallways that ventured deeper into the office building.

There was already someone else sitting at the larger reception desk. He looked young too, feet propped up and a book in his hands. All of his papers were shoved onto Rosalind's smaller desk. She hoped *she* wasn't the one dealing with those piles. This wasn't even supposed to be a real job.

"That's Jiemin. You'll be reporting to him if Ambassador Deoka is not around."

Rosalind nodded. Perhaps she should have tried harder to seem more amiable, but it wasn't her bright smile that would get answers here; it was her snooping and eavesdropping.

"Jiemin . . . ?" she asked, trailing off.

Haidi shrugged. "Just Jiemin. He has never given me a surname."
She indicated farther down the department, eyes on Orion next. "I
can show you to your desk over there."

"Wonderful." Before Rosalind could react, Orion leaned over
to kiss her temple. Her flinch was immediate, though she needn't
have worried because his lips never actually touched her, stopping
a hairsbreadth away from skin before pulling away.

"I will see you later," Rosalind said nicely, grasping for a fast
recovery.

Haidi and Orion walked off. It was only after she was left hovering at the reception desk that Jiemin looked up, switching which
ankle was crossed over the other. He had a necklace dangling out
of his shirt collar: a silver cross. Very unusual—at least among the
Chinese in this city.

"Hello," he said.

"Hello," Rosalind greeted back. "I am here to make your job
easier."

"Is that so?" Jiemin asked. He flipped a page in his book. "What
can you do? They didn't tell me we were getting someone new in
reception."

Rosalind shrugged. "I applied with my husband," she said. Better
to stick as closely to the cover as possible than invent her own talents. "To tell the truth, I would prefer being a housewife."

Now Jiemin looked up, crooking a dark eyebrow. He had a dusting of powder along his cheek, which Rosalind was sure she wasn't
imagining. She had grown familiar with every cosmetic under the
sun while she danced at the Scarlet burlesque club. If given a line
of glitters, she could certainly pick out which one Jiemin had used
and failed to completely remove last night.

"How very módēng nülang of you." His sarcasm was biting.
Módēng nülang—the *modern girl*, a way of life that the papers and

magazines insisted was taking Shanghai by storm. Permed hair and high heels, always hanging around Western-style cinemas, dance halls, and coffee shops. A dangerous femme fatale, cavorting freely and flitting around without a care in the world.

To an extent, Rosalind supposed she used to be one. But she was tired of being blithe and dangerous. It did nothing except box her in on what she could or could not want. Even the most modern girls held desires close to their heart that they cared deeply about.

"For you, Jiemin."

Rosalind almost jumped, taken aback by the thud of a box dumped onto the smaller desk. The man who had been carrying the box paused, giving her a once-over. His hair was slicked back with gel, his Western suit ironed at every surface. He seemed to want to say something, but when Rosalind only stared, he decided against it and walked away, returning to his desk across the department floor.

"Good choice," Jiemin said, eyes following the man. "If you let Zilin start talking, he'll never shut up about why we should welcome our Japanese overlords."

Rosalind stiffened. Was this a test?

"Shouldn't we?" she asked.

Jiemin's gaze swiveled to her lazily. "Are you hanjian?"

"Are *you*?" Rosalind replied, her tone more confused than accusatory.

At once the two of them looked around, as if realizing how foolish it was to be discussing whether they were national traitors in an office headed by a Japanese imperial effort. Jiemin sat back, turning another page in his book.

"I work for myself. We all need to get rice into our mouths somehow."

Jiemin was trying to feel out her allegiances. It had been no less than twenty seconds since he'd met her, and he was already speaking in code.

Rosalind wound around the smaller desk and sat in her chair primly.

"What a melancholy existence," she remarked, reaching for a stack of files before her. She started to sift through the various items: translations in progress, design instructions, type print stencils . . .

"Something would be incredibly wrong if we were happy working here." Jiemin put his book down and tipped backward in his chair, lolling his head to the side. "I crave melancholy in the workplace just as a Siberian weasel craves eggs." He switched to English. "More, I prithee, more."

Heaven knew what sort of people landed on Siberian weasels when they were searching for metaphors to make. Or what sort of tutors in the city today were teaching English phrases from the sixteenth century. *Prithee?*

"Okay." Rosalind widened her eyes to herself, then reached for the next file.

"When you are done with those"—Jiemin leaned over and pointed at one of the nearest cubicles, speaking in Shanghainese again—"Liza is our point of contact for distributing the files into other departments. Liza! Come meet the new girl."

Liza popped her head up from her work, a curtain of blond curls swishing over her shoulder. She was Russian, Rosalind guessed. Perhaps newly out of school—

Rosalind froze. "Oh *God*." The quiet exclamation had slipped out of its own accord, surprise rocketing down her spine so fast that she had lost control of her tongue.

The blond girl was her age *now*, but she had not been the last time Rosalind had seen her. Though she was taller, her cheeks wider, her brow matured, there was no doubt who Rosalind was looking upon.

Alisa Montagova, the last of the White Flowers.

And from what Rosalind had heard from Celia—Alisa Montagova, a Communist spy.

12

"A pleasure to meet you."

Alisa Montagova extended her hand. There was an easy smile on her face, nothing in her gaze that gave away any sense of familiarity when she met Rosalind's eyes.

"Likewise," Rosalind replied. Though she was shocked beyond belief, she managed to keep her tone level. Alisa Montagova had been a child at the time of the revolution and while the blood feud was at its height. There was no reason to eliminate her in the same way that Rosalind had been hunting White Flower merchants across the country. She could play this nicely—she was capable of that.

Her grip was delicate and relaxed when their palms met to shake.

"I don't think I caught your name," Alisa said.

Rosalind withdrew her hand. Now there was a hint of something in the curl of Alisa's mouth.

"Ye Zhuli," Rosalind answered. The name was invented on the spot, nothing more than a rearranging of someone else's—someone whom Alisa would recognize. Though Rosalind had intended only to be Mrs. Mu and leave it at that, she had to test if Alisa *knew*—

"Lovely. I'm Yelizaveta Romanovna Ivanova."

Alisa let the name ring. No one else in the room was paying attention. Jiemin had turned back to his book. Somewhere down the department, Haidi was explaining to Orion how to work the machine that communicated with other parts of the office building. But Rosalind heard the rush of blood in her ears, felt her heart skip a beat. Even as she kept her face entirely neutral, her mind was a roar of sound.

Romanovna. Alisa Montagova had taken her dead brother's name as her cover's patronymic.

"But you may call me Liza," she went on. "I know it must be easier."

Rosalind picked up a file at random. "Liza, that is so very kind of you." She skirted around the side of the table, then took Alisa's elbow before the girl could protest. Rosalind's heels were high, buckled over her ankle with a thick strap, and even so, Alisa was almost at her nose. "Come with me for a moment, would you? I would like to clarify this list with you."

Jiemin lifted his head. "You can do that with me—"

"Nonsense. Miss Liza will help me out," Rosalind interrupted. "Quickly now . . ." She pushed Alisa out into the hallway, striding three steps past the department door to leave Jiemin's earshot. There was no hesitation before she was demanding "*What* are you doing here?"

There passed a moment of Alisa feigning confusion. Merely a moment, while the office sounded like static noise and a door slammed on the uppermost floor right above them.

Then: "Miss Lang, you haven't aged a day."

Rosalind scoffed. "Don't start the act. I know Celia's your superior."

"You really should keep your voice down," Alisa said, sniffing. "If you expose me, you expose yourself."

"*Expose* you—" Irritation swept along her skin, prickling her neck and her arms where the delicate hemming of her qipao touched her. Rosalind switched from Chinese to Russian, paying no mind to her words as soon as she was confident few eavesdroppers would understand her. "Why are you installed here? I cannot imagine your employers care much about stopping a terror plot when it would do nothing to rally the common folk."

Alisa blinked slowly. It was then that Rosalind realized her mistake: Alisa had to have been planted here, yes, but who was to say it was for the same mission as her? Communist agents didn't receive assignments in Shanghai the same way Nationalist agents did. The Communists' first priority was hiding; their second priority was siphoning information. Keeping their eyes and ears shrouded safely was always going to be more important than savior acts that an ousted party could not afford to perform.

"Terror plot?" Alisa echoed. "I didn't know—" She cut herself off midsentence, smoothing down the little notch of confusion in her brow. Rosalind frowned, ready to urge Alisa to continue, before she felt a hand at the small of her back and realized why Alisa had shut up.

"Darling"—the sudden English was a jolt to Rosalind's ear— "your Russian is so much better than I remember."

There was a keenness in his remark. An unspoken accusation. Why did American-educated Janie Mead know how to speak Russian?

Rosalind turned to Orion, closing her hand around his wrist and maneuvering his touch off her.

"You always underestimate me," she said with a simper. "Don't you have a desk to set up?"

Orion's other hand came up to meet hers. Here were the two of them: looking like the picture of mutual adoration, unable to resist clutching on at every second for some contact. In reality, Rosalind knew her nails were going to leave marks on his skin after she let go.

"I did," Orion replied, making no indication that he felt the sting at his wrists. "Only I was summoned to the lobby. Apparently, I have a visitor."

Rosalind's lips turned down. "A visitor?" she repeated. "*I didn't hear that you were to have a visitor—*"

"Liwen!"

A clatter of heels echoed up the stairwell. A girl dressed to the nines hurried into the hallway, her skirts swishing at her ankles and a fur throw over her shoulders. She carried a basket in one hand and a purse in the other, though the purse was so small that one had to wonder what could possibly fit inside it. Haidi bustled out from the department doors almost immediately, looking concerned, but Orion rolled his eyes, striding forward to meet the girl.

"I guess I don't have to go downstairs anymore."

Haidi cleared her throat. "We don't allow visitors into any of the departments."

Casually, Orion waved her off. "This is just my sister. She'll be on her way shortly. *Right*, Feiyi?"

His sister nodded eagerly. Then, to Rosalind's surprise, she surged forward and shoved the basket toward Rosalind.

"For you," she said in English, her accent as British as Orion's. "I saw this gift set and just had to bring it for your first day. I know newly married couples must be too busy to cook."

With this, she turned to wink at Orion, but Rosalind could only stand there in bewilderment. Haidi clicked her fingers at Alisa and summoned her back into the department to tend to some type-setter error. Orion, meanwhile, was chiding his sister for barging in and making a scene. While the siblings argued back and forth, Rosalind's eye caught on something buried in the basket between the plastic-wrapped meat floss and jars of chili oil. Carefully, she reached in and nudged the white card open.

Hello! I'm Phoebe! So nice to meet you! Anyway, here's a note:

Glued below it, on one thin strip of paper that looked ripped from a ledger, was a line in Chinese instead of English:

Come see me during your lunch break. Usual place.

Dao Feng's handwriting. Rosalind's head jerked up. Once she started looking for it, Orion had a stark resemblance to his alleged sister—the same pert button nose, the same cupid's bow mouth—so it seemed unlikely that part was a lie. Who was she, then? Another agent? A mere messenger?

"Who did you swindle to drive you here? Ah Dou?"

His sister—Phoebe—brushed a bit of dust off her skirts. "You think I need to swindle? I called Silas."

"Oh, _Silas_."

"What was that tone?"

"Tone?" Orion looked to Rosalind, dragging her into the conversation. "Darling, did I have a tone?"

"I did hear a bit of a tone," Rosalind replied.

Orion put his hand to his heart, looking crushed. Phoebe snickered under her breath.

"It's fine. Steal Silas from me." With a glance over his shoulder to find the hallway now emptied save for the three of them, Orion gestured for the basket. Rosalind walked nearer and gave it to him wordlessly, letting him see the message. Even while his eyes scanned the paper, he continued without pause: "I have Janie anyway. She's prettier than everyone combined."

"Who's stealing Silas from you? _You're_ the notorious boyfriend-stealer, not me."

Orion stilled, his gaze flitting up quickly, observing Rosalind's reaction. Was he waiting for horror? She wasn't sure whether Phoebe was speaking in jest or not, but regardless, Rosalind's expression remained level, merely quirking a curious brow. Orion

Hong was an absolute nuisance, but on this he wasn't getting any judgment from her.

Orion's lip twitched, suddenly humored as if she had passed some sort of test. The test of bigotry, she supposed, which was a low bar for good company.

"When are you going to let that go?" Orion said to Phoebe, digging into the basket. "I didn't *steal* Henrie. I was testing his commitment to you, and he failed with shocking ease."

"Who asked you to test him?"

"Who asked you to retaliate afterward by stealing *my* girlfriend?"

"Oh, so when I wanted Zhenni, she was your *girlfriend*, but when I wasn't a threat, she was just *some girl I know*—"

Rosalind cleared her throat, cutting Phoebe off. When the two siblings jerked their attention to her, she mouthed, *Footsteps coming.*

Sure enough, seconds later Haidi appeared at the department doors, peering into the hallway to see that their little gathering was still present. She propped her hands on her hips.

"Whenever you're ready," Haidi prompted, gesturing toward the stairwell.

Phoebe mocked a curtsy. "Happy housewarming. Goodbye, dear brother and sister-in-law." She turned and pranced off, the ringlets of her hair bobbing up and down. There was something about the girl's easy manner that raised a seed of suspicion in Rosalind. She couldn't put her finger on what exactly she ought to be concerned about, but Rosalind had often employed the same tactic. No one expected a pretty face to have real thoughts.

Orion offered his arm to Rosalind, prompting their return to the department. As soon as Haidi looked away, he leaned in to speak.

"Before you ask, yes, she's my real sister."

"I can see that with my eyes," Rosalind replied, pretending as though the question had never occurred to her. "Is she a Kuomintang agent too?"

Just short of the department doors, Orion came to a sudden halt. When Rosalind shot him a strange look, asking why he had stopped, he only gave her the basket back, fussing with the crepe paper at the edges to make sure it looked nice. The white square of Dao Feng's note flashed briefly in his hand, and then it was gone, hidden somewhere inside his sleeve before anyone else could see it.

"No," he answered, continuing with their conversation nonchalantly when he finished fixing the basket. "But Silas, the rascal that drove her here? He's also covert branch—our auxiliary arm, in fact. He's been assigned part-time at a police station so we can track the chemical killing numbers coming in."

Rosalind suppressed her instinct to pull a face, knowing that they were within view of the department cubicles. Why did Orion know more details about their auxiliary support? What had she not been told?

"I suspect Dao Feng will be briefing you further on the matter," Orion continued.

"I'm sure," Rosalind said unconvincingly. Though she hadn't shown disgruntlement in her visible expression, her fingers had tightened on the basket handle. "What's this Silas's Chinese name?"

There was a moment before Orion answered. Likely mulling over how much access a different name gave her and what information would come alongside it. They had been hovering by the doors for quite some time now, but for as long as Haidi was distracted by the water dispensers across the department, no one else was paying much attention to the two of them having a full whispered conversation. The only person whose eyes would swivel over on occasion was Alisa, and when Rosalind caught the girl's gaze, she was unabashed in acknowledging that she had been caught, waving cheerily from her cubicle.

The benefits of being a married couple—prone to private murmurings across the workday. Rosalind had to admit that maybe the Kuomintang did know what they were doing when they created their mission strategy.

After a beat, Orion clearly decided that Silas's name would not give away anything critical, because he gave her a small smile and answered, "Wu Xielian."

The name was immediately familiar to Rosalind's ear. She had suspected that to be the case, given the amount of prodding she had done around the periphery of Orion's family, but to her surprise it wasn't her research that lit a bulb in the crevices of her memory. Instead, it itched at a spot farther back: Wu Xielian, the son of the business tycoon Wu Haotan. The elder Mr. Wu had worked with the Scarlet Gang—one of the inner circle who had always been at their dinners and parties—before turning his allegiances to the Kuomintang when Lord Cai shifted.

Rosalind remembered the photos he would pass around. One only needed to get a little huángjiǔ into him before he was proudly puffing his chest about his dear Xielian, working so hard while he did his schooling in England.

It had made a mark in Rosalind's memory. Her father would never have bragged about her like that.

"I see," Rosalind replied evenly. "I know of him."

Orion narrowed his eyes. "How so?"

"You know how gossip is. It moves here and there. Is he involved with Phoebe?"

A short laugh. That in itself was an answer. Rosalind tilted her head and then asked:

"Why *isn't* Phoebe an agent? All the more hands on deck rather than simply passing messages."

"Out of the question," Orion answered without hesitation. "Phoebe is someone who would accidentally pass information to the enemy because she felt bad, and I mean that in the most loving way possible."

"Hmm." Rosalind did not say anything more. By then Haidi had finished tending to the water dispensers and was heading their way, a frown pulling deeper on her face.

"I think I shall take a walk when lunch rolls around," Rosalind decided. "Do you think you can manage yourself here without me?"

Orion patted her hand. "Ma petite puce, I will do just fine."

Rosalind smiled. It was a death threat. Orion smiled back. It was a challenge. Before Haidi could tell them off, they parted and got to work.

Golden Phoenix was busy during its lunch hours, its servers bustling around with notepad paper trailing out of their pockets and trays stacked on the flat of their arms.

Rosalind pushed her way through the few patrons waiting near the register, snaking around the circular tables and making for the back. As always, Dao Feng waited for her in the same room, the door opening easily under her palm.

But when she stepped in, she had hardly gotten her greeting out before Dao Feng was asking, "Are you still in contact with Celia Lang?"

Rosalind closed the door. She took a moment to gather her thoughts, to watch the level expression on Dao Feng's face and guess if she was in trouble or not. Had they found something? Had they seen something?

The silence in the room was drawing too long. She needed to make a decision. This was not a field mission where she had to speak in tongues, nor a target to play guesswork with. If her superiors were onto her, they would not ask nicely—they would haul her in.

"No," Rosalind lied. "Why?"

Dao Feng made a noise, leaning back in his chair. "I didn't think so, but it never hurts to confirm."

"It hurts to think that I am not trusted." Rosalind took a seat. Her quip failed to provoke any humor in her handler. "What leaked?"

"It is not so much a leak as it is a thorn in our side." A waitress poked her head in suddenly, carrying a teapot. Though all of Golden Phoenix's waitstaff were on the Kuomintang's payroll in some way or another, Dao Feng still waited for her to pour the chrysanthemum tea and exit the room before speaking again.

"There are Communists installed at your workplace. We are not the only ones on the search for something."

Rosalind held very still. This she knew already, though it was hard to say whether Alisa was the only agent there or if she was one of many. Rosalind had not intended on reporting it. The Nationalists were the power governing the city now, but it hadn't always been like this; nor would it always be like this. Domestic grappling was constant. Let the powers in the city change. Rosalind didn't *care* about the Nationalists; she was using their resources to heal the wounds she had made. First and foremost, her loyalty was to herself and her sister, and when Celia was associated with Alisa, she would never report anything that might harm Celia in some way.

"Seagreen Press must be rather important if so many groups are trying to infiltrate at once," Rosalind said evenly. "Is this not good news? We can be a united force against the Japanese."

"The situation is more complicated than that."

"How so?" Rosalind pushed. "Did the Communist Party's central command issue a mission? How did *we* find out?"

Dao Feng stood up and started to walk around the room. He trailed the walls, looking deep in concentration as he hovered behind the chaise seats. Though Rosalind had entered to his interrogation, there was no sense of urgency in her handler's voice. Some of it might be attributed to Dao Feng's usual even-tempered nature.

Or he was saying as little as possible to keep Rosalind from knowing more of the situation.

She could not fathom covert intelligence. She truly preferred it when they gave her a name and shooed her off into the night to brew her poison.

"The Communists are not trying to stop the terror plot. At present, they are on the search for information. One of their own agents betrayed them and sold information to the Japanese officials working at Seagreen. Now they're hoping to retrieve the file before their secrets move higher."

Rosalind lifted an arm onto the back of her chair, skin gliding against plush velvet. "How do we know this?"

"We know everything. We have spies."

Hmm. The surety was worrisome. Rosalind pulled at a lock of her hair, winding the curl around her finger until she felt her circulation struggle.

"I gather you are briefing me about this for a reason," she said, releasing the lock of hair. "Do I need to start looking for this file too?"

"It will not be hard," Dao Feng answered in confirmation. "The file must be stored somewhere within the office. The task can be completed quickly, and you can go on with the rest of your mission. Take a peek for us before a Communist agent retrieves the file and wipes it away."

Rosalind nodded. It sounded easy enough. There were only so many places one file could be.

"Why do we want the information inside?"

Dao Feng put his hands behind his back. "Do you know about Priest?"

It was so typical of Dao Feng to answer questions with more questions.

"Yes, of course," Rosalind said. "My dearest rival."

Dao Feng shot her a warning glance. "Don't get funny."

"I'm not. It's true, isn't it? Priest is the Communist's most well-known assassin. Am I not their equal on our side?"

"I should hope not, because if we get this file, we may get Priest's identity."

Rosalind sat up quickly, her shoe dropping onto the floor with a loud thump. "Truly?"

"That's what our sources suspect. The Japanese paid big money. They were probably hoping to sell it to *us* next." Dao Feng paused. He was still lingering alongside one of the other chaise seats, his hand tapping the top of the velvet back. "If you can help it, do not let Hong Liwen in on this."

Rosalind blinked. The instinct to ask why came first; her rapid certainty that there would be no straight answer came second. Secrets on secrets—that was just how this city operated. She bent down to put her shoe on again, securing the strap more tightly.

"Understood."

Dao Feng nodded his approval. Perhaps this was a test; perhaps he wanted her to hold her tongue just to see if she could.

"Now," he said. "Tell me about your last assignment."

At the very least, this was something that Rosalind was familiar with. She told him about the explosion she witnessed, about the figures running into the grass and the police units who stopped her in Shenyang. Dao Feng was writing a note while she talked, readying a report.

"Manchuria has been invaded," he said after she finished. "The Imperial Japanese Army say it was our troops who set the explosion and used that as grounds to rush into Shenyang. The whole city is occupied."

Rosalind sat taller in her chair. "But it wasn't, right?"

"I don't believe so, but we're powerless against their press and papers saying otherwise." Dao Feng finally set down his pen. "Do you see how easy it is? Who are we to insist that we are innocent when accused? If they say that we blew up the tracks, then we blew up the tracks."

Rosalind knew where this was going. "If they say our rule is destabilizing Shanghai, then our rule is destabilizing Shanghai."

"And when they come in with their troops . . . ?"

"We do not have the means to stop them," she finished.

Dao Feng nodded. "Three new chemical deaths since the last time we spoke. The Japanese have officially entered the country. I don't think I need to go on any further about what is at stake."

He did not. Rosalind knew, just as every agent in the Kuomintang did, just as every agent was drilled again and again when they were sworn into operation in Shanghai. They could not mess up. Shanghai was the star dancer of this country—the protected darling that the foreigners all wanted a piece of. Japan was swooping in, looking to take it all for itself. Britain and France would rush to provide protection, not because they cared so much but because they wanted the city too and did not want to be locked out. If Shanghai fell, if the Japanese imperialist effort succeeded, if the Western foreigners were no longer having fun in their dance halls and racecourses and theaters, then they would withdraw, and no one would protest when the rest of China followed its flagship city, when it tipped sideways and submitted to occupation.

"I know," Rosalind said tiredly, pinching the bridge of her nose. "God, I know."

She hated that they were so dependent on their very destructors. Keep the city functioning; keep the British and the French and the Americans here and happy. What else were they to do when they had no power of their own to rely on anymore?

"You must do whatever it takes to complete your mission at Seagreen," Dao Feng went on, as if he could read her mind. He wasn't talking about the file anymore. He was talking about the terror cell. "At times like these, we have no room for morals."

"You are speaking to an assassin," Rosalind replied. Her throat tightened. "I figured acting without morals was a given."

"Forgive me for the reminder, then." Dao Feng smiled. It was a subdued expression, meant more for placating others than showing amusement himself. "You are not just our weapon, Lang Shalin. You are an agent. You are an arm in the fight for our country's survival. And if we are to survive, you must use your judgment without restraint."

Kill who you need, her handler was saying, the unspoken command between his every theatric proclamation. *Slaughter every imperialist and sympathizer in this country. So long as you can get away with it, we don't care.*

"My judgment," Rosalind echoed softly.

In her first year working, they had sent her after a Communist. A soft-spoken scholar, barely old enough to grow proper stubble around his chin, dressed in traditional robes and holding an ink nib pen. He had begged for his life when Rosalind came in through his window, and she had hesitated. What harm was he doing to the country? What did he do that the ordinary civilian was not also guilty of, disagreeing with their neighbors and throwing a fist at the big men in charge?

But Rosalind didn't trust her own judgment anymore. Someone who had once wandered too far down a dark path and gotten lost was bound to be afraid of losing sight of the lights again. She needed to be told what was right, and she didn't like to disagree.

"Don't worry," she had said quietly. She blew the poison. "It won't hurt."

She had tidied up. She had left the building quietly and gone home without a fuss, only to turn violently angry through the night, each passing hour spent unsleeping boiling her blood hotter. When she'd exploded at Dao Feng the next day, that had been the first time she'd seen him blink in surprise. Her handler took pride in expecting every possibility—and he had not expected this.

"That was *pointless*," she had spat at him. "All it served was this government's *ego*—"

"We are at war—"

"I don't *care* about your war! Why are you fighting a civil war when there are real enemies at our border?"

Dao Feng didn't bother telling her off. He could teach her how to be an agent, and he could show her how to survive. But he could never convince her to believe in a faction that she had watched fumble time and time again, that she had witnessed gun down civilians without a care in the world. In the wake of that incident, they stopped sending her after Communists. She was assigned to former White Flowers, to foreign merchants, to imperialist sympathizer officers, and she never complained again.

"Have I ever led you astray?" Dao Feng asked now. He was observing the hesitance in her expression.

"No," Rosalind answered truthfully. At least not without immediate course correction.

"Then take my word for it," Dao Feng continued. "You know how to make the right call. This mission will be successful." He reached into his pocket. "I have something else for you."

An envelope slid in front of her. Rosalind knew what it was before she even glanced at its contents, and she folded her arms, refusing to take it.

"I don't need to open that. It'll be the same as the last twenty."

It was better to let the city assume Rosalind Lang was dead, so her father knew he wasn't supposed to contact her anymore. Without knowledge of her location nor her new alias, there was no other way for him to reach her save the Scarlet channels, passing an envelope from hand to hand until someone scribbled Janie Mead hurriedly on the front and sent it through to the Kuomintang's covert branch.

If his attempts at contact had something of substance, maybe then she would bother reading the letters, or—God forbid—even set up a meeting to see how her father was doing. But they never did. It was the same boring spiel every time.

Lang Shalin, you must stop playing around and return home. If you wish not to return to the Cai house, you can come live with me where you belong. And what *is Selin playing at with the Communists—*

"Your father worries," Dao Feng said. He wouldn't pass anything to her without reading it first. Dao Feng already knew that she was correct in her assumptions.

"He worries for himself." Rosalind scrunched up the envelope. "He is troubled that he may never control me again. Perhaps if he had made a more caring effort in my earlier years, I would actually feel bad for him. But now?" She tossed the wad of envelope paper onto the table. "I have no father."

A beat of silence. Dao Feng sighed, then patted her shoulder.

"I'll be your replacement father, kid. It's okay."

Rosalind snorted. "Are you old enough?"

"Lang Shalin, I am *flattered* you would say that, but I have been in my thirties for a very long time now. No one would blink an eye when I walk you down the aisle to Hong Liwen."

Rosalind's expression furrowed immediately, intent on frowning as hard as she could at that image. In response, Dao Feng made a respectable snicker under his breath. Try as she might to be annoyed, she would have chosen her handler to be her true father in a heartbeat.

But that wasn't how it worked.

Another knock came on the door. The server brought in hot

water for the teapot. Dao Feng nudged the teapot forward to aid with the pouring, but his ever-watchful eyes were on Rosalind.

"Your mission, then," he said, bringing them back to the pressing matters at hand. "Questions? Comments? Concerns?"

"No," Rosalind said steadily. She pushed her shoulders back. "No. I understand perfectly."

13

hoebe Hong observed Seagreen Press from outside its fence, her body half-hidden behind a tree. At this angle, she was just out of view from the security booth at the front gates—it couldn't have been more perfect. As if the tree were made for her amateur spying. It would do well to wait. Maybe they would need her to return a message. Maybe she needed to go in again and pretend she had left something behind, then perform a sly exchange, like real agents did in the field, speaking in code while their items were being moved below the table.

"Feiyi."

Phoebe reared back quickly at the sound of her name, trying not to look too eager. The security booth couldn't see her, but she hadn't been paying attention to her surroundings from behind. Careless. Eyes around the city were always watching: a school friend or another daughter of a general, viper eyes and venomous jaws, ready for the slightest weakness to drag her down and spread gossip through elite society. Last month they had said she was missing from school so often because she was pregnant. The month before it was drugs. The rumors never lasted long, but they did keep her on her toes.

Thankfully, the figure walking toward her now wasn't a schoolmate. It was only Silas.

Phoebe breathed a sigh of relief. "I thought you wanted to wait in the car."

Silas came to a sudden stop, his eyes widening. "Sorry." He lifted his foot, prepared to take a step back. "You were gone awhile, so I thought to check, just in case . . ."

"Oh, it's fine, don't worry. Look—isn't that strange?" Phoebe pointed through the bars of the fence. Now that he had her approval to be present, Silas moved closer, joining her to watch three office workers walk out from Seagreen's main building. One of them was the woman from before, the stuffy secretary with the skirt two sizes too big who had practically forced Phoebe to leave. Zheng Haidi put a crate in the back of a car parked just outside the main building, then piled into the seats with the two others.

"It's only early afternoon," Silas remarked. "I wonder where they're going."

"Maybe we should follow."

Silas had already started to nod before he registered what Phoebe actually said; quickly, he tried to turn his nod into a side-to-side shake.

"No, no. Absolutely not."

Phoebe bit back her laugh. When they were children, Orion warned Silas constantly to stop encouraging Phoebe from tagging along on their outings, but it never set in. Phoebe was shipped to England early, only a year after Orion's departure. She had been assigned to live under the roof of her female tutor just down the street, but she had missed her older brother dearly, and the moment they were reunited, she started following him around everywhere. Anytime Phoebe tied her hair back and clutched her house key in her hand, bravely venturing the three-minute walk to knock on the boys' door and ask if they wanted some company on their next adventure, Silas always said yes if he was the one to answer, much to Orion's chagrin. Once, Orion almost stomped a hole through the floorboards in frustration because they were supposed to sneak into a bar, and they couldn't bring *Phoebe* into a bar.

By the time they all returned to Shanghai—Orion needed to perform damage control for their father's trial, Silas had finished his studies, and Phoebe didn't want to stay in England if Orion wasn't there—the habit had not worn off. Orion and Silas began working for the Kuomintang, and suddenly it wasn't Orion heaving a sigh because Phoebe was tagging along to their adventures; it was because Silas couldn't keep secrets when Phoebe asked him what they were up to. Silas and Orion were often paired on related missions. After a series of targeted questions, Phoebe could always know exactly what her brother was up to.

"I'm begging," Orion had pleaded once, feigning dramatics and dropping to his knees in front of her. "Stop waving your feminine wiles in front of him like that. He's not strong enough."

"I haven't a clue what you're talking about," Phoebe snorted. "He should learn to be strong."

Orion folded to his side, then sprawled right over the rug in their living room. "You're killing him, Phoebe! And *me* by proxy of having to witness it."

"Am I?" Phoebe didn't even bother holding back her gleeful tone. She stepped over her brother, her heels clicking down around him so she could go into the kitchen and fetch some yogurt. "Maybe I should become an assassin."

She tapped her fingers on the fence at present, the metal of her rings resounding along the bars. Once Haidi's car drove off and the front gates closed again, there wasn't much more to observe, so Phoebe stepped away from the perimeter. She didn't really care to follow a stuffy secretary anyway. This was enough snooping on her end today.

"Drive me back?" she asked Silas.

"Of course. Come on."

The street was peaceful while they found their way back to Silas's parked car, the afternoon breeze shaking the tree branches overhead. Phoebe peered up to observe the waving motions, then—in her inattention—almost walked right into a lamppost.

"Feiyi!"

"Don't worry, don't worry," she reassured him, straightening her dress collar. "Kind of you to be so concerned."

Silas ducked his head, fixated on opening his door. "Your brother would murder me if you ended up in the hospital after this outing. Where to? School?"

Phoebe made a small scoff as she slid into the passenger seat. It was her last year at the academy, and she hadn't been to school in weeks. They would be lucky if she showed up once a fortnight, perhaps three times a month if she decided to grace them with her presence. Her classmates were all on course for attending university after graduation, but Phoebe could think of nothing worse. Writing papers and memorizing poetry in a stuffy class-room. Ugh.

"Home, if you would be so kind," she replied. "Don't you have work today?"

Silas pressed the ignition and pulled onto the road, checking his mirrors carefully before picking up speed. His current cover was a forensic assistant at a police station, which gave him easy access to information when there were new dead bodies found and suspected to be chemical killings. Phoebe rarely heard about Silas attending his job though, or at the very least, every time she made a phone call to him, he was readily available.

"Not until the evening," Silas replied. They came to an inter-section where a tram had broken down, and Silas muttered some-thing under his breath. Without caring about the honking behind him, he steered into a side street, preferring a longer route to wait-ing in the jam.

Phoebe pressed her face up against her window. "We're going through Chinese jurisdiction?"

"It'll be easier. Unless you have a preference for another route? I can turn—"

"It's fine." Her attention dropped to the floor of the passenger seat. There was an array of paper envelopes littered there, and as Silas turned left and right to avoid running over a crate of chickens, Phoebe picked up one of the envelopes. They were all addressed to Shepherd.

Silas's eyes flickered over. "You should . . . probably put that down," he said.

Phoebe didn't put it down. "What is this I'm hearing about you being close to finding Priest?"

"I am only one of the many." Silas reached over, gently tugging the envelope away from her with one hand while he steered with the other. "I'm sure Dao Feng has multiple teams working on the matter."

"So you *are* close. Otherwise you wouldn't be acting so humble."

"I've been planted as low-level help in the Communists for long enough that they were willing to give me contact with Priest to ask recruitment questions." Silas tossed the envelope back onto the floor, then cast Phoebe a tight grimace. "It doesn't mean anything. It could go nowhere."

Entirely undeterred, Phoebe grinned, reaching over to tuck a lock of Silas's hair behind his ear. It was growing too long, starting to curl at the edges. "Have faith. I believe in you."

They turned another tight corner. Silas watched the street through the windshield; Phoebe watched him as his ears turned red.

"You're always so curious," Silas said, half beneath his breath as though he were speaking hesitantly to himself. "You should voice to Dao Feng that you want to be recruited once you graduate. You would be good at going undercover." Silas cleared his throat. "Perhaps with me. I mean, if you want."

Phoebe made a noncommittal sound. "I don't know. I quite like being free to do as I wish. Working for the government seems so bothersome."

"Is that not what you are already doing?"

"Hmm. It's just different somehow. Like—"

Before Phoebe could quite gather her thoughts, Silas pressed the brake suddenly, and Phoebe shot her hand out to the dashboard, holding herself in place to avoid flying at the windshield. The car stopped. With a gasp, Phoebe pressed back into her seat again, her heart thudding in her chest.

"What—" Phoebe's gaze flickered where Silas was looking, out his window and to the other side of the busy market road they had been moving through. There was a large crowd gathered by an alley, right between a fabrics shop and a fish market.

The conclusion came easily. No other spectacle would draw a crowd like this. All the same, Phoebe asked, "What's going on?"

Silas squinted, opening his door. He didn't step out. He only let the noise of the market flood in, removing their barrier from the confusion and ruckus. "I'll bet anything they just found another body."

"In such a public place?" Phoebe leaned closer to Silas, searching through the crowd as well. A flicker of movement caught her eye: some figure clothed in a large black coat, drawing away from the edges of the crowd and ducking quickly into a parked car. Though the car wasn't so out of place as to draw attention away from the alley, it *was* strange to park in front of a fish market. Really, it was strange for someone rich enough to own a car to drive up to a fish market at all.

The wheels screeched away. Phoebe's eyes dropped to the license plate.

"Hey," she exclaimed suddenly, draping an arm on Silas's shoulder and patting his chest rapidly. "Isn't that the car that just left Seagreen?"

Silas turned his head immediately, catching sight of the car before it could turn the corner. He nudged his glasses. "Is it?"

"I can't be certain," Phoebe replied. "But I think so."

It was too late to go chasing after the suspicious car, especially with the pedestrians and market vendors milling on the road. They sat there for a long moment, mulling over their options. Then Silas closed his door with a loud bang, muffling the bustle of the street outside.

"Eyes out, Feiyi," Silas said. "Shall we circle around and see if we can find them again?"

Phoebe clapped her hands excitedly.

The rest of the workday passed without incident.

Ten minutes before six, Rosalind shuffled her papers into a pile, and Jiemin told her that she could clock out. The rest of the production department was upstairs in a meeting with Ambassador Deoka. Orion was meeting him first, then, though Rosalind did not have high hopes that he could garner much information from the interaction, what with the rest of their department being present in discussion about type fonts.

Rosalind hitched her bag higher over her shoulder as she exited the department, taking the stairs down. All afternoon, while mindlessly sorting the papers Jiemin handed to her, she had been thinking about the file the Communists were after. One short-term goal, one long-term goal. The former was far easier. The latter required trust, building connections, getting the office colleagues to think of her as one of them, and she hated that because there was always the possibility that she would let something slip. Perhaps the Nationalists would not mind if she let Orion do all the investigating. She could just keep an eye on him to make sure he did not defect to the Japanese.

"You walk so fast, darling."

Rosalind turned around, surprised that Orion had been let out already. She hadn't even heard him come up behind her. "All in my attempt to get away from you faster."

Orion laughed as if she had been telling a funny joke. The moment his stride caught up with hers, he looked over his shoulder, inspecting the steps of the office building behind them. Then he said, very seriously: "Kiss me."

Rosalind blinked. "I beg your pardon?"

"Are we in love or not, Janie?"

Before Rosalind could rip into him for being a degenerate, she looped an arm through his and turned her head too, angling to see what he had been looking at. By the building, a clump of their colleagues remained gathered in conversation, but it was quite clear that half of them had their attention on Rosalind and Orion, watching the two as they took their leave.

"Are they onto us?" Rosalind asked.

"One asked me today if we were an arranged match who had never met before, so you tell me."

"We could have been."

"That wasn't our cover story, Janie Mead."

Rosalind stopped in her step and faked a sudden, delighted shriek. It took Orion entirely by surprise, but before he could jerk back, she had grabbed him by both sides of his face and captured his lips with hers.

It lasted no more than a second before she was pulling away, the smile on her face holding as she caught his arm again and pulled him forward. The colleagues watching them could come to their own conclusions.

"Beloved," Orion said, as they passed the gates. "What a performance. If I didn't know better, I would think you wanted to tear my clothes off."

"Oh, please." It was impossible not to acknowledge that Orion had all the physical beauty one might need to incite such a reaction. Perhaps he was used to it, the fawning and flattery in every which direction. But he wouldn't get any of it from Rosalind. "I have no desire to tear your clothes off."

"Not even a little?" he teased.

It wasn't that Rosalind didn't know what people were talking about when they whispered about such urges. Rosalind understood romance. She used to want it so badly that she sought it out wherever she looked. She would have been happy to pluck out her burning heart and wait patiently for someone to come along and take it. What she didn't understand was the immediacy. How others sighted a stranger and felt the sweaty palms and the dry throat, felt the gravitational pull to be close, close, closer. She was half-convinced that the whole world was colluding to play a big prank on her, trying to convince her that she was the unusual one. How could someone feel *any* of that for a person they didn't know? How could her stomach dip with desire unless she already recognized the shape of their smile? How could her fingers ache to reach out unless she had already memorized the lines in their palms?

Yet it had still been so easy to trick her. To pretend. She almost wished she could be like everyone else. How freeing must it be to grow attached in the blink of an eye and detach oneself just as fast. But Rosalind either loved or she did not. There was no middle ground.

"I am a good actress," she said faintly.

Orion dropped his taunting demeanor. Perhaps he heard the strangeness in her voice. Perhaps he felt the dread and the heartache that trailed after her like a dirty bridal veil. Her hand remained at the crook of his elbow, and she felt his arm tense, as if he were trying to hold her in place.

"What's the story there?"

Rosalind shook her head quickly. "No story." She forced herself to loosen the strain in her shoulders, to lift her chin and shake the strands of hair out of her face. "It is merely who I am. Falser than vows made in wine."

The tension had passed. The grin on Orion's face was back, and he reached forward to tug a curl of her hair.

Rosalind pulled away with a huff. "Don't do that. Some of my hairpins are poisoned," she warned. "What did you learn today?"

"Forget what I learned." They were on a main road now, walking parallel to the tram lines. As soon as Rosalind strode ahead, putting a few paces of distance between herself and Orion, he hurried to catch up, swinging an arm around her shoulders. "I went out with some of them for lunch and got you and me an extra assignment next week—the writing department will be short on staff for an upcoming fundraiser, so we're filling in. We'll know the whole company like the back of our hands before long, especially if we start with our own production department first." Orion ducked to avoid the awning of a stall with his tall head, barely breaking his stride even with the near collision. "Here's my thought. First we do a little chatting at work. Then we see what their nighttime leisure activities are. Soon after, we happen to run into them while they are out and about. A perfect squeeze into their social circles."

It did not sound like a perfect plan. This was a big city. "Have you learned their *names* yet?" Rosalind asked, not bothering to soften the scorn in her tone.

"Yes," Orion replied in an instant. "I might need a few of them to repeat it once or twice and perfect my pronunciation, but just about. Most of the office staff in production or writing are either Chinese or Japanese with the occasional Western foreigner. Some gate guards are Sikhs. Miscellaneous Indians and Russians and Ashkenazi Jews scattered throughout. You met one of them too, didn't you? Liza Ivanova."

Rosalind felt a flutter of panic. Was that suspicion? Did his glance last an extra beat as he turned to address the question? Did he tense the arm he had over her shoulder?

"Very briefly," she answered. "We did not discuss anything of substance."

"Oh? It didn't sound like it."

They had arrived at her apartment. Rosalind didn't want to keep spinning lies about what she and Alisa had been talking about, so she used the natural interruption to push his arm off her and rush ahead, making for the steps up.

A familiar aroma was wafting along the exterior staircase, and Rosalind sniffed as she passed the papered windows of her apartment, coming to the front door. She didn't wait for Orion to catch up; she swung the door open and found Lao Lao by the dining table, setting down the last bowl.

"I've been waiting all day to meet your fake husband. Where is he?"

Rosalind pushed the door wider and ushered Orion in. "Say it a bit louder, Lao Lao. I don't think the spies in the bushes outside quite heard you."

"Oh, so *handsome.*" Lao Lao rushed forward, taking Orion by the hands and getting a closer look at him. His face brightened immediately, soaking in the attention. "You like bamboo soup? Slow-cooked pork hock? Cumin lamb?"

"I like all those things," Orion replied. He cast a glance back at Rosalind as she set her bag on the sofa. "Janie ought to be scared that I'll divorce her and marry you instead."

"*Please* do." Rosalind pulled a pin out of her hair, letting the curls at the base of her neck tumble down her back. Quicker than Lao Lao could protest, she picked up one of the tomato dishes and walked into her bedroom. "Then I wouldn't have to put up with you." Rosalind slid the door closed with her foot.

"So finicky," she heard Lao Lao complain after her. "You come eat, then, and we'll save the rest for her when she wanders out to get a late-night snack."

Rosalind stiffened. She pressed her ear to the door.

"Does she wander out to get late-night snacks often?"

"You better be careful what you say, Lao Lao," Rosalind muttered beneath her breath.

"Ah, you know how girls are. So cautious about their work that they forget to eat and scarf down a zòngzi right before they go to sleep. It is what it is."

Rosalind stepped away from the door, breathing a sigh of relief that Lao Lao had backtracked. She stuck her spoon into the tomato with one hand and started to page through her books with the other, eyeing the notes and drawings that its authors had left behind. Dao Feng had given her these journals as guides to her poison-making. She had to admit that they were useful, but some of their findings were written in the most convoluted way, as if the Kuomintang's previous assassins had been aspiring poets instead.

"Two whistles of black tea leaves," Rosalind grumbled. "Who let one whistle become a unit of measurement?" Nevertheless, she sounded one short whistle, tipping the ground tea powder into a bowl.

She sank into her work, plucking herbs from their jars on her shelves and soaking them together. At some point she heard the sound of plates clinking in the kitchen, indicating Lao Lao and Orion were cleaning up, but she ignored it to focus on plugging in a miniature burner, angling it right under the bowl to heat the substance.

She was turning off the burner and fanning away the last of the smoke when a knock came on her bedroom door.

"One second." Rosalind found a cover—one that was designed to keep flies away from food—and dropped it over her work, pushing everything to the side of her desk. It wouldn't raise that many questions if Orion saw her making poison: it was natural enough for normal operatives to have weapons of self-defense. Still, an interest that seemed too intense might get him thinking, and if she could help it, she was going to steer away from revealing her identity as Fortune. "You may enter."

Orion slid the door open. His tie was pulled loose, the top two buttons of his shirt undone.

"Lao Lao has retired downstairs. She says the soup should be warmed before consuming again or else you'll get a stomachache."

"She would love it if I got a stomachache. Then she could say she told me so—*what* are you doing?"

"Who, me?" Orion folded onto the bed. He took his jacket off, then lay heavily on the satin pillows. "I'm sleeping. Good night."

Rosalind cast a glance at the small clock on her desk, its miniature pendulum swinging heavily to track the seconds. "It's eight o'clock."

"I am most tired, dearest. I need the rest."

"You're sleeping," Rosalind said, folding her arms across her chest, "in your outside clothes?"

"I love sleeping in my outside clothes," Orion shot back. "Makes it easy to run if we get intruders."

"At least take off your shoes. You look like a lǎowài."

With his eyes stubbornly shut, Orion kicked his shoes off to the side, letting them hit the floor at different intervals. Rosalind went to stand by the bed, looming with a silent glare. Orion didn't give up the pretense of being asleep.

She sat down next to him instead. Stared at him and tried to make him uncomfortable. When that didn't work, Rosalind said, "May I ask a question?"

"How very polite of you," Orion returned, revealing his alertness while his eyes remained closed. "Go on."

"What was your code name before this assignment?"

Orion's nose wrinkled. "Beloved, sweeten me up first before asking about such personal matters."

Rosalind knew of only a few active code names across the city. It was hardly a personal matter. If agents weren't wanted at large or infamous within the party, there was little reason they could not reveal their code names to people they trusted. Of course, the trust needed to be present first.

"I'm only curious," Rosalind said.

"As am I. What was yours?"

Rosalind thinned her lips. Orion smiled, noting through the silence that he had caught her out.

"Ah, checkmate." More firmly this time, he repeated: "Good night."

"You cannot possibly be serious."

He continued sleeping.

Rosalind thwacked the side of his leg. "Enough of this nonsense. You're sleeping on the couch."

Orion's eyes flew open. "Is my darling wife so cruel?"

"Yes." She pointed out the door. There was no chance that she was going to waste the whole night pretending to sleep in front of him. Her half-made poison needed to be transferred into a larger bowl in three hours. "Shoo."

"*Janie*," he pleaded, eyes large and wide.

"*Shoo*," Rosalind said again. "Don't force me to tell you to gǔn kāi."

With a sigh, Orion sat up. "Fine, fine, it is my marital duty to listen to you." He hopped off the bed with a casual ease, as if he hadn't been making a fuss about trying to sleep a mere minute ago. "Once again, darling, good night."

Rosalind eyed him warily as he left the bedroom, the door closing behind him. Seconds later, she heard her fake husband pushing the sofa around, creaking the floorboards as he adjusted his sleeping arrangements and moved about the various cushions.

The other side of the door finally fell silent.

"How did I get stuck with someone like this?" Rosalind muttered, rising to her feet. She took the cover off her poisons. Sniffed at the progress. Gave the bowl a shake. At least he would be out of her hair for the night.

A loud *snap!* came from the living room suddenly, interrupting her short-lived peace. Then: "Janie, is your lamp *supposed* to be plugged into the wall?"

Rosalind sighed.

14

There was one more sector on Celia's map left to be completed. The candle bled a droplet of wax down its side, landing plumply on the desk just as she reached for a ruler to measure the minimal blank space that remained on her sheet of paper.

"That's . . . not right," Celia muttered to herself. It was growing late, but her blinds were drawn wide open, letting in the light of the full moon outside. She had thought she might finish her map today, but instead she had been puzzling over the same discrepancy for the past half hour. Had there been a mistake in assignments? Was the original map where they split the sectors so outdated to the point it was missing entire grids?

Her finger traced the older version in front of her, the official government-distributed rendering that marked out fields and roads for travelers who ventured outside of Shanghai's city boundaries. Millie had the section to the right of Celia's allocated land, but she had started drawing her map from the left, which meant she had completed that edge months ago. If their new maps were supposed to align by the end of their assigned time here, either Millie or Celia had not been given the full coordinates.

Celia turned back to her almost completed map—each road painstakingly surveyed by foot and each forest patch measured with the same pace. She had already collected her information earlier in the week, aiming to finish what she thought was her last section, so why didn't the panels join up? Why was there a section of land that remained uncharted? She wasn't remembering wrong; when they were perusing the land by daylight, there had been a whole field's worth of land between these two coordinates.

Celia rose from her seat, poking her head into the hallway. "Oliver?"

No response. Celia returned to her desk quickly and rolled the maps up, putting them into a bag and slinging the bag over her shoulder. The night was cold when she barged into it, a huff of breath forming ahead of her as she tucked her ungloved hands into her jacket pockets. Their shop was situated near the very corner of the town, which meant the dense outer forestry was close by and easily traversable. The moonlight darkened and brightened and darkened again as a patch of clouds moved across its plump roundness, but none of it bothered Celia. With her focus honed, she was careful as she picked through the forest, watching for the small red markers that she had dropped in the weeks prior to mark her progress while she followed Nationalist soldiers around. There weren't any soldiers out tonight. Perhaps they had been moved elsewhere or were on assignment nearby.

The point of constructing new maps was to make the most accurate lay of the land, then illustrate a comprehensive picture of Nationalist movement with color-coded arrows and directional keys. And they had been successful: their surveys had pinpointed each Nationalist base, marking which roads were preferred by certain units and which paths were never used, so that Communist forces knew how to safely travel when the time came.

Celia paused, taking the map out of her bag and unrolling it. There was the tree line. There, creeping at a slow incline, was the rise of a slight hill. She looked down at the paper.

"You couldn't have waited an extra second for me to respond?"

"*Merde*—" Celia dropped the map and whirled around, a knife sliding out of her sleeve. Oliver reared back, his hands coming up to show peace, but Celia relaxed as soon as she recognized him.

"Don't sneak up on me," she hissed. "Especially not in the forest."

"What are you doing with a knife?" Oliver returned. His brows shot up. "Can you even use it?"

"It was a gift from my cousin." Though more decorative than productive, she carried it around for a sense of safety. "I can use it fine."

"All right. Use it on me."

Celia scrunched her nose, unable to tell if Oliver was being serious. "What—"

"Come on, what if I had been the real enemy? Let's see if you know how to use it."

"This is ridiculous—"

"Unless you can't actually use it—"

Making up her mind, Celia changed her grip on the knife, clenching the handle into her fist before pushing forward fast. She placed her blade at Oliver's throat. He peered down.

"Terrible form."

Celia almost squawked. "Excuse *me*—" Before she could scarcely blink, his arm had come up, his whole hand wrapping around her grip and turning her weapon toward her own neck. The cool kiss of the blade touched her throat right underneath her pendant, and then she too was pinned in place: her back to a tree, Oliver's forearm locking her down. The knife wasn't pressing hard enough to cause any harm, but she felt sweat break out along her spine nevertheless.

Oliver clicked his tongue. "Oops. Dead. Don't wave around weapons you can't use."

"Yes, because I would have *stabbed* you in the *gut* if you weren't you," Celia protested. She craned her head against the tree trunk, trying to tug her arm away. Oliver wasn't letting go.

"How would you have stabbed me? My arms are longer than yours. I would have knocked it out of the way."

"I would have moved *fast*—"

"And I could have stepped back as soon as you stepped forward."

The moon peeked out from behind a cloud again, resuming its full brightness. Under its glow, Oliver's eyes swiveled from the blade to the jade pendant around her throat. He finally let go of her hand, if only so that he could adjust the pendant after he had jostled it in their scuffle. With a shaky breath of relief, Celia lowered her arm so that she wasn't at risk of cutting her throat open. That was the only reason her inhale was coming slightly short. Not because Oliver was tightening the ribbon at the back of the pendant, his fingers warm when they brushed her neck.

"The chain is loose," Celia explained when the ribbon seemed to slip from his grasp just as he was finishing the knot. She kept her gaze to the side, looking off into the forest so that it didn't seem obvious how close Oliver was, hovering right in front of her as he fixed her jewelry. "It's getting old."

Oliver caught ahold of the knot before it could slip, securing it properly. "Have you considered," he asked plainly, "not wearing a pendant anymore?"

"No," Celia said. She didn't leave room for argument. He knew why she wore it, that it covered her throat and prevented hateful strangers from trying to tell her whether or not she could be a woman. She was a woman regardless; it was only unfortunate that others in this world had certain ideas about what she needed to look like. It wasn't safe for her without the pendant.

"All right."

Oliver didn't sound fazed. Over the years, Celia had gotten used to his matter-of-fact attitude, manifesting both in his easiness with letting pointless topics go and his intensity with pursuing crucial tasks to their very end.

"The more reason," Oliver continued, "not to go waving your knife around. The next victim you threaten poorly is going to loosen your ribbon even further, and what are you going to do if I'm not nearby to help you keep your jewelry pretty?"

Celia gave her eyes a small roll. "Did you follow me out here to deliver a life lesson?"

"I followed you out here because you were acting suspicious. What happened?"

Celia finally took a step back, putting distance between them so she could pick up the dropped map. When she smoothed the paper out, she tried to ignore the fact that her shoulders felt cold, shivering with a sense of tangible absence.

"From where we are standing to . . . approximately five hundred meters to the east," she guessed, "there is plenty of forestry and, crucially, a V-shaped dirt road for trucks passing through. I remember because there was a bird's nest that grew right above the sharp turn. I wondered if the eggs might fall out." Celia paused, running her finger down the edge of the map. Oliver watched the movement carefully. "That sector wasn't in Millie's map. She started farther to the right. But now I have also reached the end of my coordinates, and I have not sketched that road."

Oliver took her map. There was only the barest inch left on the paper that awaited completion, but everything remaining were meandering edges and patches of trees.

"Did you walk the road?"

Celia shook her head. "I cut along the turn and used the forest instead. Didn't want to get spotted in case there were soldiers."

"There was a mistake made during our map assignments, then," Oliver suggested. "I can send a message through and check."

"But I don't think so." Celia reached into her bag and brought out the older map—the one giving a complete overview of the land that had been split among the four of them. "Look here. It's as if the section has been entirely snipped out. There are no roads."

For a very long time, Oliver remained silent, staring at the map. Then:

"It is common enough for maps to have errors," he said carefully. "Sometimes if there's nothing for large distances, it's easy to miscalculate and represent it as smaller than it really is."

Celia nodded. "I've encountered that. It's an easy fix to adjust the scale bar at the bottom. But here . . . it's *not* nothing. There are roads. You can't adjust the scale on a road and call it a day."

She watched Oliver chew through the matter, his jaw clenched tight and glowing silver by the moonlight. Oliver was not an easy person to please and an absolute terror to get some sort of empathy from. For that reason, though Celia wouldn't admit it to anyone for fear of sounding terrible, she took particular pleasure in plucking a smile from him.

The corner of his mouth twitched. Her chest warmed.

"So the roads are new," Oliver concluded. "When was our reference map drawn?"

Celia flipped to the back, searching for the print information. "1926."

"Then let's find out what else is new."

In the quiet of the night, the two of them started to pick through the forest, their shoes coming down cautiously on the undergrowth. There were a few prickly plants that Celia swerved fast to avoid and, a few steps ahead, Oliver tried to flatten them first with his boots so Celia had an easier path forward.

"There's the sharp turn," Celia announced after considerable distance, pointing ahead. The trees had been cleared on either side of the gravel road. The V of the turn shone under the white of the moon.

"Let's go left," Oliver declared.

Celia did not hesitate to follow, but she did raise her eyebrows, wincing as a particularly sharp stone pressed through the bottom of her shoe. "You don't want to split up and check both directions, just to be sure?"

"That would be silly. You can see how the right starts to bend at an eastward angle." Oliver hastened his speed, and Celia hauled her bag higher up her shoulder, the maps inside crinkling. "It will soon enter a ninety-degree bend. Meaning it must connect to the dirt road that begins at the edge of Millie's map."

"Meaning it doesn't lead to any unknown destination we want to investigate," Celia finished, catching on to his logic. "I see."

Oliver kicked one of the rocks underfoot. "You agreed with me so easily. I'm honored."

"Of course. I'll agree with logic."

"Usually I have to boss you around a little before we get there."

Celia sighed. "You just like bossing me around. We only met because I snapped at you in that alley and your little ego wasn't able to stand it."

"My little ego can always stand being snapped at by you, sweetheart. Look, up ahead—is that on our maps?"

Celia wasn't quite tall enough to see what Oliver was pointing at. She frowned, pushing onto the tips of her toes, but then the ground rose and leveled the smallest amount, and she caught the barest glint of silver among the trees.

"What is it?" she asked. "A shed?"

"Too big," Oliver answered bluntly. "I guess it's not on our maps, then."

It took some time before they were approaching the structure, but at that point it was quite clear that the distance had messed with Celia's perception. It was not a shed. It was a whole warehouse, built with high ceilings and a large wooden door to the side. The dirt road ended here, as if it was constructed specifically to lead to this location.

"Wait." Celia reached for Oliver's arm, holding the two of them still. They listened: to the swirling wind, to the rustling leaves, to the animals and critters that populated the heaving, breathing forest. Somewhere, afar, a train was passing by, the steam-fueled shriek of its whistle echoing into the clearing.

"No cars out front," Oliver said quietly. "This is an empty location."

"You think it's military?" Celia whispered back.

"It has to be." The train whistle died away. The breeze slowed, settling the world. "But whose?"

Oliver walked toward the wooden door, undoing the heavy metal latch. It swung the other way and hit the stopper with a loud, egregious *clang*. Celia flinched, but then Oliver pushed at the door, and that sound was even louder, rumbling until the whole entrance was wide open and the cavernous inside opened its mouth.

"Did you bring a flashlight?"

"I must confess that when I slipped out into the night, I didn't think I would need a flashlight." Celia entered the warehouse, trying to peer through the darkness. A shelf, and a box, and . . .

An electric hum started behind her. Seconds later, the overhead bulbs flared on, throwing the whole space into brightness. Celia spun around, her eyes wide.

"Found the light switch," Oliver declared, a finger still hovering over it. "See any faction flags?"

The walls were smooth metal. An even allotment of beams held the high ceiling up, interrupted by bulbs dangling every few feet. But no faction flags, nothing that might indicate if this was abandoned Communist possession or forgotten Nationalist property or something else.

It was a strange setup for a warehouse. No windows. No other exit except for the front, though there was a smaller door on the other side that looked like it led into another room.

And in the center of the warehouse . . .

"What *is* that?" Celia demanded.

It looked like an operating table. Cold and clinical and long, gleaming dull silver. If it weren't for the buckles down the side, it might have looked like something stolen from a hospital. But the blood spatter along the edges, rusted into the leather of the straps, told another story.

Oliver's brows were drawn tightly as he approached the table, reaching out to tug one of the straps. For a very long moment, he stayed unmoving, turning the buckle over. There was something handwritten on the surface of the table too. Scientific formulas, scribbled in pencil.

Celia inched closer, her gaze shifting between the odd find and the way Oliver was staring at it. He had adopted a peculiar expression. Recognition.

She touched his elbow. "Have you been here before?"

Oliver blinked. He tore his gaze away from the pencil scribble. "Why would you ask that?"

"Believe it or not, I do know how to read your face," Celia replied. *"Have* you?"

"No." Oliver's answer came quickly. He didn't elaborate. When he nudged one of the straps, brown-red flecks shook off from the leather. "Let's poke around. See if there's anything else."

Though Celia opened her mouth to argue, Oliver was already walking off, and it was a lost cause to convince him otherwise. She followed his lead in searching the warehouse, pushing around wooden crates and sifting through the shelves. Whoever had owned this warehouse, they left behind beakers and test tubes and the occasional Bunsen burner, its pipes hanging off the table edge. Some of the crates on the floor were padlocked, others emptied. Some shelves were spotlessly clean; others were coated over with a sheet of dust. It was hard to tell whether this warehouse hadn't been in use for years or if someone had been around that very day.

"We should take a crate," Celia suggested. "Crack it open with a hammer."

Oliver didn't reply. He was staring at the table again.

"Oliver."

His attention snapped back. By the time he looked at her, his expression had smoothed into indifference.

"Yes, sweetheart?"

Every alarm bell in Celia's head went off. These few years, she let Oliver keep plenty of secrets out of necessity. It wasn't hard to recognize the signals that arose when he was doing it: the quick topic pivots, the vague answers, the minute flicker of his dark eyes. But what was he doing keeping secrets *here*?

"What is it?" she demanded. "Tell me."

"Tell you what?"

A hot impatience flushed into her cheeks. She marched toward him, but he didn't move, calm while she tipped her head up at him. "Are you intent on acting the fool?"

"Are you intent on getting us in trouble?" he asked. There was only composure in his tone. He didn't hesitate before touching her face, swiping a thumb along the ridge of her warmed cheek. Celia had moved close enough for the gesture to seem natural, and she shifted back abruptly, her face heating further. Before she could say anything more, Oliver was pushing one of the crates back, aligning it with the dust so that no one could tell it had been moved.

"We should go," he said. "If this is an active Nationalist warehouse . . . We get soldiers sniffing around us often enough—we don't need to inform them that we're nearby and snooping on their business too."

"There is something *in* these crates—"

"But we can't dig around without making a mark." One of the

bulbs overhead flickered. Oliver looked up. The line of his jaw tightened, sharp and devastating and exactly how a deadly agent ought to look. "This has little to do with us anyway. How shall we report this warehouse? 'Might want to take note of the facility. We can take refuge in it to heat up our food over an abandoned Bunsen burner while marching to war'?"

Celia tore her gaze away and stared at her shoes, hiding her peeved expression. She suddenly could not stop thinking about everything Oliver kept from her. All his visits to Shanghai, those full days when he would simply disappear with no one the wiser to what he was up to.

"Come on, sweetheart," he said, striding for the light switch. With a casual flick of his finger, the warehouse fell into thick darkness. "Until it concerns us, we can just draw this location onto our maps and leave it be."

"Fine." Celia didn't mean it. Not in the slightest.

When Oliver turned around to check if she was following, she offered him a slight smile and let her fists curl in determination behind her back.

15

Orion watched his wife lock up their apartment the next morning, craning his neck while he adjusted his shirt into place. He had wrinkled his previous night's outfit beyond saving. This new selection was far more comfortable. The collar tucked against his vest. The sleeve cuffs rolled up once so that the length was just right.

He was quite fond of silk. Before he was sent off to England, his mother used to pick out his outfits every day, matching a nice shirt to a pair of trousers and adding a small tie or a pin. It was always his favorite when she chose silk, because she would pick him up and nuzzle her face into the sleek fabric, then release him for a short second when she pretended that he had slipped out of her grasp. She always caught him again to his delighted squeal, *"Māma, hold on tighter!"*

He missed her. After he was sent abroad, it was never the same even when she came to visit. She took the journey without his father because his father needed to work. And each time she stepped into London with her host of household staff, a parasol clutched in her hand, Phoebe needed her more, needed some momentary sense of parental affection that she had almost been too young to remember before being shipped off.

Orion had spent eight years in England. He hadn't been allowed to pack his bags and return home until after he received word of his father's trial, and by then his mother was gone. Before Orion and Phoebe had finished crossing the ocean to get back, she had fled into the night with nary a note nor a goodbye.

The circumstances of her absence haunted him. Whether he had done anything to cause it. Whether she had truly left on her own, or if someone had taken her, or if—God forbid—his father had done something. Being three and a half years older, Oliver had finished his education in Paris and returned to the city long before Orion did, had witnessed their father's descent, had described their mother's alleged disdain growing in that period. It didn't matter that General Hong was later cleared. Their mother had already walked out the door, unable to bear his traitorous reputation—or at least that was what Oliver had claimed before he left too.

"Ready to go?"

Orion blinked, returning to the present. Janie Mead was looking at him, waiting for them to take the stairs down.

"After you." Orion ushered her ahead, following a step behind. Once he returned to her side in the courtyard, he held his arm out in front of her. "Feel this."

Janie dropped her keys into her bag, her eyes narrowing. "Must I?"

"Feel it. Come on. It's silk." He waved his arm around. The grass was wet with dew, brushing against his ankles while they strolled through and pushed out into the driveway. Perhaps it had rained sometime during the night, though he hadn't observed any sounds while asleep on the living room couch.

With a sigh, Janie reached out and pinched a segment of his sleeve, acting as if he had coated poison onto the fabric.

"Delightful," she said, in a tone that signaled the very opposite of delight.

Janie Mead didn't bother speaking for the rest of their walk to the office, though Orion attempted several more topics of conversation. By the time they were nearing the gates of Seagreen Press,

Orion gave up on trying to win a genuine reaction from her. She looked to be in her head. She looked to *live* in her head, in fact. There were two types of people in the world: those who hid their wreckage on the inside and those who wore it on the outside. Orion was everlastingly afraid that a single frown from him would appear a cause of concern and incite others to dig into his troubles. Janie Mead, on the other hand, clearly did not share the same burden. If she was angry, you knew it. If she was distracted, you knew it. Hell, one glance at the pinch of her full lips and Orion knew that he would need to call her name twice before she responded, and even then, she would be annoyed to be disturbed from her reverie.

"Ready?" Orion asked quietly, stepping through Seagreen's gates.

In near unison, the two of them waved at the guards out front. As soon as they passed security, Orion offered his arm to Janie. This time she took it without complaint, her fingers settling gingerly into the crook of his elbow.

Her hands were so delicate. No calluses on her palms, no roughness at her nails. Even an agent in administration would have been given some training from their handler; even Silas, who mostly did informational spying, knew how to throw a punch just in case any mission reared an ugly turn of events.

Where had they found someone like Janie Mead?

Before he had quite gathered the words to ask, they had reached the third floor, entering into the production department. Janie immediately halted, her nose wrinkling at the group of people standing around the reception desk. It looked like some impromptu social event was being hosted right over her work space. Perfect.

"What is this?" she muttered beneath her breath.

"I'll introduce you," Orion said happily. He put his hands on her shoulders and started to push her forward, despite the reluctance in her step. Out of his periphery, he sighted movement by the cubicles, but it was only another colleague peering to see who had come into the department before turning back to her work. Liza Ivanova—the one whom Janie had been in such heated conversation with. He needed to dig to the bottom of that.

"I've already met one of them," Janie Mead said, keeping her voice low so the group wouldn't hear her as they neared. "Zilin, the man on the right. Jiemin practically accused him of being hanjian."

Oh? Orion tried to cover his surprise. Like yesterday, Jiemin was not paying any attention to what was going on around him. He kept his feet propped up on Janie's desk, far more invested in his little book. "And you didn't think to tell me?"

"Not enough basis," Janie returned immediately. "Someone else's word alone cannot mark him as suspicious."

"Yes." Orion nudged his mouth closer to Janie's ear, getting his last retort out before they reached the group. "But accusing someone else of being hanjian without basis certainly is suspicious—ah, ohayō, how is everyone today?"

Orion had done his rounds, meeting every colleague in the department yesterday, intent on making a good first impression. They were all around the same age, late in their teens or newly in their twenties. It made sense: when the imperial effort prepared to send representatives, they searched for fresh blood out of school. Fresh blood who had not yet seen enough of the world, who wanted so badly to impress their elders and perform their duty to the country. It was the same on the other side, wasn't it? If Orion had been older and wiser, maybe he wouldn't have shoved himself into the covert branch, put himself at the mercy of following his handler's every instruction. Maybe he would have sought more options to achieve what he wanted. There was no use regretting it now—he was a spy, and he was good at it.

"Hello," the girl on the far left said in English. She beamed, waving at Orion and extending a hand to Janie Mead. "You must be the lovely wife."

Janie reached out to shake, her red lips curving into a smile. Orion watched her—adopting a loving expression even while his gaze sharpened. He supposed he should be glad that Janie Mead *knew* how to act wonderfully sociable and still chose not to when it was the two of them alone. Perhaps that meant he was in acquaintance with the truest version of her, that he need not worry she was hiding something.

Somehow, he doubted it.

"Darling, meet our colleagues." Orion smoothed his hands from Janie's shoulders to her arms, pivoting her inch by inch to introduce the people around them. "This is Miyoshi Yōko. Ōnishi Tarō. Kitamura Saki. And . . . Tong Zilin, is it?"

Zilin frowned, seeming unimpressed that his was the only name Orion had snagged on. It was surely the easiest, so he knew it was a deliberate move on Orion's part.

"Correct," Zilin said. He turned his attention to Janie, nodding at her wrist. "Did that come from Sincere?"

Orion felt the jolt of surprise from his wife when she looked down, as if she had forgotten what was there. A thin bracelet sat looped below her sleeve, dangling with a silver charm.

"I cannot remember," she answered. Janie Mead spoke in such a peculiar way. It wasn't that she was not fluent in English; she sounded like she had been well educated in some Western society, where she had picked up their mannerisms and speech patterns, where she had learned the precise way they added a quick rise to the end of the questions. Even the best tutor wouldn't care to nail in the miniature habits.

But her accent sounded drawn out. Feigned. Not American.

Janie looked up, pretending to ask Orion if he might know, and Orion shrugged.

"I may have gifted it to you. I have simply lost track over the months," he said.

No matter. Orion could keep listening until he heard what the discrepancy was. English was the common tongue in the office. Their Japanese colleagues were not fluent in Chinese, and most of the domestic Chinese hires would not know Japanese, so Janie Mead couldn't hide from him forever.

"Hmmm . . ." Without asking for permission first, Zilin grabbed Janie's wrist, examining the bracelet. Orion frowned immediately, wary over the gesture, but it would be impolite to make a commotion, especially when Janie was letting him take a look, unperturbed.

"I was eyeing one in the window just like it for my fiancée," Zilin continued. His accent had the slightest lean into British, but not as strongly as Orion's. Perhaps he had spent fewer years there, or he had picked it up from a British tutor without leaving the city. "But I didn't have time to go in and buy it before our picture started."

Tarō leaned up against the reception desk, an eyebrow lifting. "Which picture? I thought you weren't one for the theaters."

Zilin finally let go of Janie's wrist. He puffed his chest. "Those ones from Italy. They play on Sundays."

"Those films are fascist propaganda."

Orion stiffened, a breath of horror snagging in his throat at Janie's proclamation. It was valid enough to say. Shanghai's theaters were open to taking pictures from every corner of the world, and the current Italian market was notorious for pushing in a selection extolling the achievements of fascism. The theaters would play it without complaint; it was up to the viewer whether they wanted to watch two hours of documentary footage about empire-building. There were fascist branches in the Kuomintang too. The films certainly had an audience.

But silence had swept over the group. Some things were known by all but unspoken for the sake of propriety.

Saki chuckled lightly, waving her hand and breaking the tension. When Orion relaxed, he realized belatedly that Janie must have felt his grip tighten on her arms.

"Oh, that's an exaggeration," Saki said lightly. "The same critics would probably denounce our paper too."

"Right," Janie replied without missing a beat. She reached for a file on her desk, raising her hand for a small hello to Jiemin. "Please excuse me now. I must tend to a meeting in five minutes."

Orion let go of Janie as she moved, but his eyes continued tracking her while the conversation among their colleagues pivoted direction. Ambassador Deoka had summoned her for a meeting in the morning, simply to meet the new hires. Orion had already seen the ambassador yesterday and discerned nothing of note from their exchange, except maybe that Deoka dyed his hair too often and was drying out his forehead. Perhaps Janie would pick up more.

Orion turned over his shoulder. Janie walked out the doors of the production department. Then she stopped, leaning against the wall outside.

"Do excuse me as well," Orion said quickly, bowing his head in apology. He spun around and followed her out the doors, coming into the hallway. Janie Mead didn't stir. She was staring into space when Orion neared and touched her elbow.

"Hey." His greeting echoed. "Are you okay?"

"I'm fine," Janie said. She couldn't have sounded more like she was lying if she tried. Her words were void of emotion. As if she were reading off a script. "Where is Deoka's office?"

Orion did not answer her. He tried again. There was something that he could tug from her—there had to be. "Give me this first: *Are you okay?*"

Janie's eyes flickered up sharply. There seemed to be a reprimand in that single look. He knew, of course, that *okay* was too vague a question for the expression she was wearing. All the same, where else could articulation start? If they couldn't find okay, how did they slide into *terrified*? How did they unravel *enraged*?

For a moment, Janie remained quiet. Then she looked over

Orion's shoulder, and he turned too to follow her line of sight—to watch Yōko waving her arms around excitedly, the group by the reception desk throwing their heads back with raucous laughs before dispersing to get to work.

"They're not all bad, I know," Janie said, her voice as soft as the brush of a feather quill. "But when they are here only because their empire is trying to swallow us up, it's *so* hard not to hate them."

That last part came out with vehemence, spat more than said. When Orion swiveled back around, he felt an electric shock run down his spine, felt it dislodge something within him. She should know better than to say such things out loud. And yet she had said it anyway, had let the words take shape instead of swallowing them in.

Orion, biting down on the back of his teeth, hurried Janie a few steps away from the doors. He couldn't decide if it was bravery or stubbornness. He couldn't decide if the buzz that had started at his ears was admiration or fear. For so many years, he had survived where he was and kept his family name untarnished by playing it safe and staying unopinionated. It was not that he didn't have national loyalties; he wanted freedom and autonomy as much as anybody off the streets. He would pick up his gun for this country if the occasion arose one day. Their current mission was a matter of national protection—if he didn't believe in it, he wouldn't be here.

But it was dangerous to voice it. Dangerous to bring it out into the light rather than keep that belief tucked deep in your chest. Better to say you follow instructions from the top in the fight for national dignity. Better to play at being a soldier, doing what you were asked, and if the government decided to switch who was an ally and who was an adversary at the expense of the people, there would be no hurt cut deep into your heart.

Orion's mouth opened and closed. Though there was no one watching them, he reached out and brushed a lock of Janie's hair out of her face.

"I understand," he said shortly. "I do, Janie."

More than he wished to. He knew exactly what she felt because it was the same rage he'd had toward his father when the hanjian accusations came rolling in. It was the insistence that there was a mistake, tracing the evidence back with a shaking finger and that breath of relief when, indeed, it did not line up—when it could be proven that his father was not a traitor. Orion cared too much about keeping the waters calm around him, could easily play pretend and smile while he was on a mission, but resentment lurked heavy in a corner he tried not to reach into. It had been there since those early years when his tutor brought in language instructors, when they forced in the British accent, the perfect French, then Japanese as the political stage started to change. It had grown heavier as he read the papers, the headlines about foreign business ventures controlling the country, different imperial efforts taking root.

Hatred did have a home in him, however weak the hearth was.

Janie pulled away. Her eyes flickered down the hall, avoiding Orion's gaze. "Where is Deoka's office?"

Orion pointed along the corridor, then gestured left with his hand. He felt unsettled. Something about Janie Mead was persistently intent on unsettling him.

"Third door," he said, his volume returning to normal. "Don't forget to bow first."

Janie nodded her thanks and hurried away.

Rosalind felt like a bobblehead as she nodded her thanks, hurrying away with Orion's watchful eyes on her back.

She didn't give herself time to grow unnerved—or even more unnerved than that conversation with Orion had already made her. She raised her fist and knocked on Deoka's office door.

"Enter."

With a deep breath, Rosalind turned the handle, then stepped in. Ambassador Deoka was sitting at his desk, fingers clacking down on a typewriter. Remembering Orion's reminder, she performed a small bow, folding her hands at her lap. The door clicked closed after her.

"Hello," Deoka greeted in Chinese. He didn't slow his typing. "Name?"

"My surname is Mu, production department reception assistant," Rosalind replied easily. "I was told to report in."

"Ah, yes, Mrs. Mu." Ambassador Deoka finally stopped typing, reaching under his desk and pulling open a drawer. Though it took him no longer than a few seconds to find what he needed and bring it forward, Rosalind's mind worked in rapid-fire, viscerally imagining what he might retrieve: a pistol to shoot her, a bomb to release, a dossier that exposed every wrong she had done as Rosalind Lang, each hit counted on her name.

Instead, it was only a map of the office building.

"I must give you this," he said. "Production stores a lot of its excess material, so the marked crosses are the appropriate filing rooms. Don't put anything anywhere else, understand? I don't want a mess in my building."

Rosalind moved forward, hand outstretching. Just as she took the slip, Deoka's phone rang, and she jumped, dropping the paper.

"My apologies, my apologies," Rosalind rushed to say.

Deoka didn't look bothered; he merely nodded to excuse the blunder. As he began to speak rapidly over the phone in Japanese, Rosalind crouched and scurried a few steps to pick up the paper from where it had fallen on the floor.

She paused. There was a crate by the corner, looking dark and out of place with the office's beige color scheme. With a quick flick of her eyes at Deoka and finding him to be facing away, his chair turned to the wall and his attention fixated on whatever he was animatedly explaining, Rosalind leaned over and made a quick scan of the crate's topmost surface.

SHIPMENT INVOICE A29001
September 25, 1931

From:
Warehouse 34
Hei Long Road
Taicang, Suzhou, Jiangsu

Weekly issue—Seagreen Press.

Taicang, Rosalind thought. *Isn't that where Celia is assigned?* Her last letters had been postmarked with that location. Why was there a printing factory all the way out beyond the city? Surely there were cheaper options nearby.

Before Deoka could spot her wandering interest, Rosalind stood up, pretending to dust off the map. His phone call was finishing, and she hurried in front of his desk as he was hanging up, her hands folded in front of her with the paper clutched tightly.

"I will distribute materials accordingly," Rosalind assured once she had his attention again. She inclined her head, surveying his desk subtly. Some note cards, some scattered files, nothing else as suspicious as those crates—and if the invoices were correct, they were nothing but shipping boxes. "Is there anything else?"

Ambassador Deoka waved his hand. "No, no. Back to work, please."

Rosalind faltered for a second, almost taken aback. She didn't know what she had expected in this meeting, but she was surprised. Perhaps some more interest on Deoka's part regarding her presence at the office, even an iota of suspicion. He only looked eager to return to his typing.

"Yes, sir."

Bizarre. Truly bizarre. She hadn't expected a laughing villain twirling his mustache, but this was almost *too* normal.

She backed out of the office, opening the door just as Zheng Haidi was preparing to come in. Haidi offered a slight smile, extending her arm to give way and usher Rosalind out first.

"Thank you," Rosalind murmured. Once she stepped past, Haidi entered the office, the door closing after her. For a moment, Rosalind remained there, her eyes narrowing as conversation began inside. The walls were too thick for her to hear anything. She could press her ear against the door, but anyone walking the hallways might catch her. It wasn't worth it. With a sigh, Rosalind proceeded back to the production department, smoothing out the map in her hands.

There were four levels, two red crosses on each floor.

It didn't look insidious. Even the layout of Seagreen Press could not hide mysteries: each room was straightforwardly accessible, marked clearly for its function.

Rosalind turned the corner and entered the doors of the production department, making for her desk. Jiemin looked up briefly when she returned but said nothing. She took a seat, set the map down, and glared at it in concentration, like she could unveil secrets she had not previously seen if she just stared hard enough.

"Darling!"

Rosalind gasped, startled by Orion's sudden appearance before her. Jiemin cast her a funny look, wordlessly asking why she wasn't used to the sound of her own husband's steps, and she pretended there was a mosquito over her shoulder, thwacking around the air to play off her reaction.

Orion paused. "What are you doing?"

"Annoying little flying insect," Rosalind said. She smacked Orion's arm, committing to the act. "Ah, there we go. I think I got it."

"Ouch," Orion said quietly, rubbing his arm. "Can I speak now? Is the insect gone?"

Jiemin had turned back to his book. Rosalind nodded, and Orion leaned in, whispering into her ear.

"I did some asking around. Many of our fellow colleagues are going to Peach Lily Palace tonight."

Rosalind frowned. She knew the name. Peach Lily Palace was a dance hall. When it opened on Thibet Road five years ago, the venue had been in direct competition with the Scarlet burlesque club, and Rosalind had been asked to reinvent her routine for the sake of keeping the Scarlet club fresh and new.

Now the Scarlet club had gone under, transformed into a restaurant, while Peach Lily Palace remained operating. A handful of the Scarlet dancers had jumped ship to Peach Lily Palace even before their proper shutdown. Dancers weren't exactly needed when club owners started getting involved in civil war instead.

"We absolutely must go too," Orion finished.

"*Tonight?*" Rosalind replied in a whisper. A sweat broke out at the back of her neck. Would the old dancers recognize her? Or was it so absurd to imagine her still alive that they would think her a mere doppelgänger?

"It will be fun." Orion brushed her hair along her neck. Whether he knew that she was nervous and was easing her reaction, or it was merely a coincidence that he chose that moment to play with her hair, she could not tell. He was clicking his tongue in approval, already moving to return to his desk. "Tonight it is."

16

Alisa Montagova had made an endearing setup of her living space, a tiny safe house apartment located two floors above a dance studio on Thibet Road. Though there was hardly enough room for a bed, a stovetop, and a small door that led into a smaller washroom, she had decorated well. The walls were covered with photographs. A sketched poster of Moscow sat right above the entranceway.

Alisa had been born in Shanghai, and she had never left Shanghai, so in truth, Moscow was some fantastical land in her mind that she had no particular attachment toward. Her cousin Benedikt, however, sent postcards all the time detailing every nook and cranny he encountered, and she supposed that painted a vivid enough picture to love. As a former White Flower, he had been hiding there since the Nationalists took over Shanghai, but at least he had his husband, Marshall, for company.

Alisa sighed, flopping onto her mattress. Benedikt and Marshall were safe, or as safe as anyone could be. She had gotten used to having the two of them around while she was growing up—seeing them around the house almost as often as she saw her brother. They hadn't only been Roma's best friends; the three of them had made up an image of the White Flowers for civilians to gawk at on the streets—the heir and his two right-hand men, unshakable and formidable, just as gangster rule was.

Then the White Flowers dissolved. Then Roma was gone, and Benedikt and Marshall were forced to flee before the Nationalists hauled them in as enemies of the state. Once they'd slipped into the Soviet Union, the Nationalists had a lot more to be worried about than chasing alleged rebels into a neighboring territory, but it did mean that everyone Alisa called family had been driven out of Shanghai.

She had been so young when revolution came. She had had no stake in the city back when the Scarlet Gang was aligning with the Nationalists and the White Flowers were being dragged in with the Communists, division lines drawn along every conflict broiling within the city. She couldn't have known how this would all pan out. When soldiers swept the city and the Nationalists took over as their official government, marking the end of the White Flowers' reign and her father's iron fist over half the city; when her father disappeared, and she didn't join her cousin in fleeing because she wanted to find out what happened to him.

She had been too young. She had joined the Communists willingly, knowing it was the only faction that would take her, but she never could have fathomed how long this civil war would last.

Dusk was falling. The window above her bed showed the sky darkening and bruising into a faint violet that cast shadows along the room. For a moment, Alisa let herself bask in her exhaustion, slumped on her bed in her work clothes. Then, with a bounce, she got up again, charged with sudden energy.

"Perestan'te shumet'!"

The old man's voice rang with an echo from downstairs. Alisa shifted on her floorboards deliberately, stomping an extra time for good measure. He was always yelling through the ceiling and telling her to stop making noise, though it wasn't as if she could help the terrible construction of the building. Until she was evicted, she was staying right here. And if she *was* evicted, there were plenty of other White Flower safe house apartments in the International Settlement that went unoccupied, forgotten and abandoned amid the takeover in the city, lost in the paperwork that one would have to sift through first.

"Hey! Girl! Don't you hear me up there?"

Alisa put on the phonograph at her windowsill, drowning out the old man with music. She kept hopping around in her own interpretative method of dancing. There was a problem that had been plaguing her at work. The typeset didn't align right on one of the stamp presses, but some of the papers had already been printed. Either they could fix the first batch by hand or adjust a new overlay. . . .

The phonograph stuttered, and Alisa frowned, going over to fix its tinny tune. She had purchased the device secondhand from some shabby store in Zhabei, so it was old, almost falling apart. Alisa didn't know why she lived as if she were barely scraping by when she had the means to be a well-to-do person in this city. She had plenty of savings from her family, and Seagreen distributed wages in cash every week. On top of everything, she didn't even pay her own bills. Each month, the statements arrived at her door-step with her accounts already balanced, paid off by an anonymous donor. She wasn't one to look a gift horse in the mouth: though she had a suspicion about who was doing it, she was perfectly fine letting them stay in the shadows with their helping hand in case it wasn't safe to initiate contact.

Alisa supposed she was just dedicated to keeping up her cover as an office worker. She was a spy, yes, but she was also installed at Seagreen Press out of her own interest. Two years ago, the Communists decided they didn't need so many scattered agents merely running errands and risking capture, so they streamlined operations by presenting her with a list of workplaces that they wanted surveyed long-term. International politics couldn't go ignored. This civil war involved only two parties, but the foreigners always needed to be watched in a place like Shanghai. Alisa had scanned down the list and made her selection, and since then her days had passed by happily designing fonts for the most part and, on occasion, keeping her ear perked for intelligence from Japanese officials that might concern the Communists and their plight of survival. When Celia was on assignment inside the city, Alisa reported to her; when Celia was assigned outside city borders, they skipped her in the chain of command, and Alisa reported directly to a higher superior every month.

It was a quaint living, strangely enough. For as long as the war did not press into Shanghai, for as long as the city's sleeping agents were not needed in active action, Alisa Montagova could spend her time eavesdropping and doing something useful that wasn't hiding—at least not entirely.

Alisa finally shook the phonograph into playing smooth music again, adjusting the latch at the side. The busy road below her third-floor apartment was a whole world of activity, clumps of rickshaws moving in and out of view like birds taking flight.

Alisa narrowed her eyes. She pressed closer to the window. It was only of late that an actual mission had come knocking. One of their own had defected for money and passed confidential intelligence on to Seagreen Press's officials, and she needed to retrieve the file containing the information to figure out exactly which of their secrets had leaked. The problem was, the building was enormous, with hundreds of files moved around day in and day out, so it wasn't exactly easy to find *one* unless it just so happened to be blazoned with a COMMUNIST PARTY SECRETS label.

Of course, there was the problem of those Nationalist agents appearing at Seagreen too, both of whom clearly had some other mission unrelated to Communist intelligence.

And both of whom were currently walking below her window

on Thibet Road, heading toward the dance hall that operated right across from Alisa's apartment.

"Miss Rosalind, *what* are you up to?"

Alisa turned off the phonograph immediately, clutching her coat and fetching her bag off the hook on the wall. The music came to a halt. The floorboards creaked noisily with her rapid movement. The elderly man downstairs started yelling again.

With a devilish smile, Alisa hurried out of her apartment, walking extra hard just to be a pest.

It had been a long time since the city saw Rosalind Lang, a long time since they stopped sketching her on the posters plastered around the Concessions to remind its people of the elite who had fallen.

Still, Rosalind kept touching her face absently as they approached Peach Lily Palace, as if she could wipe off her features and slap on something new. There was little chance she would be recognized. But if she was . . . her present cover could be at risk.

"Earth to Janie Mead."

Rosalind looked up, wrinkling her nose at Orion. "What happened to only using our aliases?"

Orion ran a hand through his hair. It was especially loose tonight—whether on purpose or because he had run out of pomade, Rosalind was uncertain. At least it suited the rest of his look: the black shirt with three of its top buttons undone, the deep green vest with gold detailing stitched around the hem, the long black coat fluttering with the breeze, and the gold rings on his fingers, which caught the light of every flashing neon sign.

"My apologies, beloved," he corrected. "It will not happen again."

Rosalind rolled her eyes, holding her tongue as the dance hall attendants opened the doors to Peach Lily Palace, welcoming them in. Faithful to its moniker, the hall had a floral scent, a mixture of the smoke machine onstage and the natural perfume of its patrons, who mingled around in their bright qipao and clean pressed suits. Where Orion was dressed like he had rolled right out of his father's bank vault, Rosalind had picked the most modest thing in her closet: long sleeves and a high collar. The last thing she needed was to stand out and start encouraging rumors that Rosalind Lang was alive and well, socializing in the city's dance halls.

"I see them," Rosalind said. Peach Lily Palace was big, far bigger than the Scarlet burlesque club used to be. Its ceiling was outrageously tall, painted white and carved with patterns that trailed down the walls until it reached the banisters of the second level, where patrons could stand for a better view of the stage. On the lower level, it wasn't only the show floor that served as entertainment; there were also gambling tables at the opposite end, near the bar and away from the stage. That was where some familiar faces were flocked: Yōko, Tarō, and Tong Zilin.

Rosalind made another brief inventory of the space, of the chandelier hanging from the stage and the various other light fixtures shining across the hall. That was something different too: Peach Lily Palace was well illuminated, every face cast in a warm, golden light as they mingled about. At the Scarlet club, Rosalind had accidentally ruined her shoes numerous times by stepping in spills she didn't see until a second too late.

"Come on," Rosalind said.

Just as she started forward, Orion grabbed her arm to stop her. "I—I have to go tend to something first."

Rosalind frowned. "What?"

"I'll be back." Without any more explanation, Orion walked away in the direction of the stage.

"What?" Rosalind demanded again, flabbergasted. "You can't just slip off. What is wrong with y—"

There was no use. He was already gone, merging into the crowd of patrons and inserting himself into a circle of people. Rosalind's vision was good, but she didn't waste time eyeing the well-dressed group to determine who Orion was seeking out. Knowing him, he had sighted some former lover he had slighted in the past.

Rosalind gave a small, irritated huff, then marched toward the gambling tables on her own. Unbelievable. They were one combined unit, and the first thing he did on a critical task was wander off.

"Mrs. Mu!" Yōko exclaimed when she spotted Rosalind. "What a coincidence to see you here too."

"Oh, I'm here all the time," Rosalind said airily. Tarō and Zilin were three steps away, peering over the shoulders of the seated players. "What are they playing? Poker?"

"Five-card stud, it would seem," Yōko answered. "Zilin claims he always knows the best time to fold."

"He must be omniscient if that's the case." One of the players shuffled, the red and black colors flashing under the lights, spades and hearts and aces and diamonds, faster than the eye could catch.

Yōko made a noise of consideration. "He *is* pretty good at intuition," she allowed.

"You cannot intuit something like this." Rosalind walked a step closer. "It's all fortune. The cards have been decided already. No amount of skill and timing can change his hand."

"Ah, what a short game!" Zilin whirled around suddenly, patting Tarō's shoulder too hard and exaggerating his surprise upon seeing Rosalind. His cheeks were blotted with red. He was drunk. "Where's your husband, Mrs. Mu?"

"Somewhere nearby, I'm sure." Rosalind made a search of the crowd. Orion had entirely disappeared. "You know how he is. A people pleaser, always flitting around."

"One would think it's most important to please your own wife first."

Barf. Rosalind didn't bother with a reply. Her eyes were fixed

- 173 -

on the stage as a troupe of dancers hurried on, getting into position before the jazz band started their next set.

She squinted. Was that . . . ?

It *was*. Three of the dancers were familiar faces. Girls who had worked under Rosalind at the Scarlet club.

And when the opening notes of the saxophone swept through the hall, prompting the girls to begin, Rosalind recognized their steps immediately. They were using *her* routine—the same routine she had taught them.

She almost laughed.

"Fancy a drink?" Zilin asked the group, his voice startlingly close to Rosalind's ear. She smoothed down her sneer before she turned around, looking ever the pleasant picture. Yōko and Tarō seemed enthusiastic about the question, so Rosalind nodded along with them.

Zilin pointed up the stairs to the second level bar. Tamping down any appearance of hesitation, Rosalind followed, trailing after her colleagues while they spoke of the bets they could put down at the other tables later.

Orion, where the hell are you? she thought angrily. He was the one who had bragged about his information-extraction skills. Meanwhile, Rosalind was already itching with annoyance. She wasn't fit for this kind of work. The only reason she had been good at getting money out of men at the Scarlet club was because they thought she was joking when she was rude, and they were always inebriated.

Yōko and Tarō were perfectly alert tonight. Only Zilin teetered around drunkenly, so Rosalind doubted she could get away with pressing all three about their motives in Shanghai and their opinions on Japanese imperialism and the pan-Asianism movement.

"I was almost afraid to leave the house today," Rosalind started, thinking that she might as well try.

Yōko turned around on the stairs with a gasp. Tarō prodded her to keep moving, furrowing his brow at the roadblock in his path.

"Why?" Yōko asked, her whole face creased with concern.

Rosalind made a casual shrug, like the topic of conversation was merely at the edge of her mind, something she thought to mention only to fill the silence. "I read the newspapers a lot. Haven't you heard about the murders? There is a serial killer out and about."

"Serial killer is a little dramatic," Zilin offered from the top of the stairs. They reached the second floor, and Zilin hiccuped before snapping his fingers at the bartender. The bartender ignored him, too busy serving the people already clustered around him.

"How is it dramatic?" Tarō asked. "There *have* been a series of deaths with the same pattern. That's the very definition of a serial killer."

Zilin waved off Tarō's words, clearing at the air around him as if the claim had made a tangible stench. "We are in foreign territory. We are protected." He pushed forward, trying to get through the people, but he was still calling over his shoulder, trying to continue the conversation at loud volume. "It's not as if we are gangster-ruled anymore. Maybe we should have been afraid when it was a bunch of lawless crooks leading us, but now we have order. We have Western innovation."

Rosalind's hands curled, nails digging into her palms.

"Western innovation can fend off a murderer?" she asked dryly. Zilin did not hear her. He was at the bar already.

Yōko sighed. "I'm going to try the one downstairs instead. Ōnishi-san? Mrs. Mu? Care to join me?"

Tarō nodded, but Rosalind had had enough. She needed a moment to breathe.

"I will meet you there," she said. She sighted what looked like a washroom's exterior sink, so she started in that direction. "I must use the water closet."

Yōko and Tarō disappeared down the stairs, leaving Rosalind to her leisure. She sidestepped the bar crowd and trailed her hand along the second-level banister as she walked, watching the dancers on the stage and the couples twirling on the show floor below. Orion was still absent.

At the sink outside the women's washroom, Rosalind peeled her gloves off and washed her hands, just for something to do. She stood there for a few minutes with the cold water running on her skin, letting her mind rest, letting the music and the hubbub reach her ears and bounce right out.

When someone approached from behind, she felt their presence long before their voice cut into her thoughts.

"You brought up a rather intriguing conversation, Mrs. Mu."

Rosalind turned the tap off. She took her time drying her hands, throwing the used towel into the basket beneath the sink.

"I can hardly remember what we were talking about," she said, finally grabbing her gloves and turning around. Though Yōko and Tarō were not around anymore, she and Zilin both continued speaking English. They could have switched to Shanghainese or any Chinese dialect, but Rosalind had a feeling that her colleague enjoyed staying in an imperial tongue.

"The deaths," Zilin slurred, as if she truly needed the reminding. The new glass in his hand was nearly empty already. "All the deaths in the city, brought to those who deserve it."

Rosalind froze. "I beg your pardon?"

"They deserve it!" Zilin was raving now. He threw his glass down. It bounced on the plush carpet, the last few droplets of alcohol splashing into the threads before the glass rolled to a stop near the edge of the wall. "They are only happening in the Chinese parts, are they not? Only in those grubby alleyways and filthy housing blocks. If we rebuilt those areas, it would not be happening. If we hauled those people out and took their shabby shops down, there would be no killer. Let the French Concession in! Liberté! Égalité! Fraternité."

It felt like her limb was moving on its own. Her hand rose, and then it was slapping Zilin's face as hard as it could manage. She did not regain control of herself until her palm was stinging and Zilin was rearing back, a red mark on his cheek.

Damage control, she thought. *Now.*

"My greatest apologies," she gushed. "I don't know what came over me." She started to put her gloves back on. "I just . . . I have terrible experiences with the French, you see. All that égalité business stirred a beastly part of me."

"Mrs. Mu." Zilin's voice had changed. It was sharper, a hint of amusement slipping in, like he knew something she did not. "Where did you say you were educated?"

Rosalind's glove stopped halfway up her hand. She backtracked her last few seconds and found her mistake. *All that égalité business.* For crying out loud, she had slipped into her real accent.

"America," she answered.

Zilin did not look like he believed her. He was smiling now.

"Our higher-ups are going to be interested when I tell them about your thoughts on our foreign collaborators," he said slowly. "Unless . . . you have other thoughts you would like to tell me in private. It might persuade me."

The corner of his lips quirked, albeit sluggishly in his drunkenness. He wanted her to shut him up. He wanted her to shut him up using means fitting for dance halls and seedy venues, where girls were hired for dance partners and late-night companions.

Rosalind finished pulling up her gloves. When she set her arms down again, she brushed her fingers against her pocket.

"Come with me, would you?" she said sweetly. Fine. She could play that game.

Zilin followed willingly. He needed no persuasion to enter the women's washroom with her, waiting while she knocked on the stalls and checked that they were empty. She didn't even need to persuade him to come closer when she turned to face him.

It made it all the more easy for her to pull a cloth from her pocket and suddenly press it to the lower half of his face.

Zilin cried out, but she was already moving with the momentum. Rosalind slammed his head into the wall and pinned him there; her wrists braced around either side of his face, fingers laced together in her effort to keep the poisoned cloth over his mouth and nose.

Zilin bucked. Rosalind held firm.

"Don't struggle," she purred. "You know who I am, don't you? If you love the Concession so much, you must have heard of me."

He tried again, this time trying to surge to the side. Rosalind pressed harder, her heart hammering against her chest.

"You have heard of me. Of course you have. They call me Lady Fortune—no matter how much I insist that it's just Fortune." She leaned closer. "Do you know how many people have gotten away from me?" A bead of sweat was dropping down Zilin's temple, landing on her pinkie. *"Zero."*

His eyes were bugging so ferociously that they were close to exiting their sockets. If he had tried—really tried—with his full strength, it was possible he could have pushed Rosalind off. But she had fear on her side. She had roused panic and a bone-deep sense of dread in her victim, and that—that was as deathly paralyzing as venom.

"It doesn't matter how much you suck up to the foreigners," she continued, her voice low. He was not struggling as hard anymore. The poison in the cloth was kicking in. "It doesn't matter how much you pretend to be distant from the rest of us, frowning on everything that keeps us alive. I was always going to catch up to you."

Rosalind clamped down on the cloth as hard as she could, forcing him to breathe deep, breathe in the poison. This was out of necessity, she assured herself. This was an effort to shut up the sources that would have leaked her identity. But a righteous fire was burning in her veins. If she glanced into the mirror, she wondered if she would see a glow cast around her skin, a furious zeal coming from the inside out as her anger took the reins. Retribution for her country. Vengeance for her city. That was how she was redeeming her name.

At last Zilin's eyes closed, his body turning slack. Rosalind stepped back immediately, letting him fall to the floor with a sickening crunch, arms and legs splayed at awkward angles. Slowly, the anger started to ebb. Slowly, she started to take inventory of her situation again.

She had a dead man on the washroom floor. She was the last person seen with him. And the dance hall was at full occupancy, which would make it exceptionally hard to dispose of her evidence.

"Merde," Rosalind whispered.

She needed to lock the door, formulate a plan.

Which was exactly when the door opened, bringing someone in.

17

Orion pushed through the crowd, coming to a natural stop by one of the poker tables. At first he didn't say anything. He merely pretended to observe the game, arms crossed over his chest.

Then he dropped into one of the emptied seats, drawing the attention of the man on his right.

"Why have you been so hard to get ahold of recently?"

His father's gaze flickered to him.

"You know where to find me," General Hong replied, giving a smile that did not reach his eyes. "You're a young adult now. I have no business checking in on you and your daily affairs."

"I didn't ask to be checked in on," Orion retorted. "It would simply be nice if you were home once in a while. Oliver made an appearance the other day. Did you know that?"

Gauging from the way General Hong turned to look at his son, he did not know that.

"I beg your pardon? You didn't think to tell me this earlier?"

"As I said"—Orion leaned back, letting a woman reach over the table to shake the dealer's hand—"you have not been easy to reach."

"Liwen. You can easily send a note to the office."

"*Yes*, well . . ." Orion trailed off, unable to find the right words. This whole time, he had been speaking English while his father used

Shanghainese in reply. It felt easier somehow. To adopt a foreign tongue for difficult matters, to blame that foreignness for the conversation's friction. The version of him who spoke Shanghainese with his father wouldn't give him attitude like this. That version of him, who had trust and love and belief for a father he admired, seemed to exist only in the past.

"I didn't want to put it in a mere note. I wanted to explain it to you directly. Oliver broke into the house and was searching for something in your office."

General Hong frowned.

"I kicked him out, obviously," Orion continued. "But pray tell, why would my brother show up like that?"

Someone at the table won the round. The chairs rocked with celebration, bodies shaking with uproar and feather boas flying around in disarray. Orion ducked to avoid an arm that was waving around his head, glaring up at the two people who stood behind him. His father, meanwhile, sat still; there was no one who dared motion too forcefully around *his* head.

"I don't know," General Hong answered evenly.

Orion's mouth opened and closed. "How could you not—"

"You should have reported it immediately. Then we could have checked the perimeter. We could have found him. He is a traitor. There is no sense in protecting him."

"I wasn't *trying* to protect him," Orion hurried to say. The insistence tasted sour on his tongue. He could say that he wanted Oliver arrested, could claim before a podium that he wanted his defector brother to be executed as enemies opposing their government ought to be, but he would only be mimicking the words of his father, echoing back the speeches that he had heard so often they had erased all thought of his own. Of course a part of him was keeping his brother out of trouble; otherwise he would have pulled the trigger when he saw Oliver that night.

"Father." Orion spoke quietly, so that only General Hong could hear him using the address. "Why would Oliver risk himself like that—"

"If he shows his face again, you tell me promptly—understand?"

Orion's fists curled at the interruption. By now he should have been used to running into wall after wall when it came to his father. General Hong never cared to communicate properly anymore, only in bits and pieces, making small handouts when he deemed Orion worthy enough to know something. On the matter of Oliver, though, Orion was not certain if his father was choosing to obscure information, or if General Hong didn't want to look the fool and reveal that he too was in the dark.

"Why don't you ever *do* something?" Orion hissed.

His father's expression remained level. "What would you like me to do?"

I don't know, Orion thought. Go back to how it was. Travel back in time and not mess up. Pluck his head out of the sand and look at how they were now, because he had been caring once before; he had been loving once before. It was only that he chose not to be anymore, and that dissonance was worse than if the warmth had never existed to begin with.

"Never mind." Orion pinched the bridge of his nose. "Forget I said anything."

General Hong peered at him. "What's wrong with you? Are your headaches starting again?"

Orion moved his hand away, almost taken aback. In his first few weeks as a spy, he had gotten into trouble while chasing someone and hit his head on a bad fall. It almost disqualified him permanently for agent work when the Nationalists asked after his progress and he could barely leave the house to make any. He had been plagued by headaches for months after, bouts of dizziness that came and went on a whim. On particularly bad days, it was as if the whole world was closing in around him: his lungs seizing, his thoughts swirling at a thousand miles per minute.

Silas had been his saving grace. If Orion went off the grid, Silas got involved in his missions to keep him on track, working double assignments and reporting extensively when Orion could drag himself out of bed again. As time passed, the painful attacks lessened in frequency, until Orion wasn't seeing stars every time he lifted himself up too quickly. The headaches hadn't come in a while now—these days, as a remnant of the old injury, they usually arose only if he pushed himself too hard with physical exertion. He didn't know his father still remembered.

"No. No, I'm fine." Orion got out of his seat. There was nothing more to be said about his brother, he supposed.

"Will you be home tonight, then?" General Hong asked absently, just before Orion could make his farewell.

"I'm on an assignment right now," Orion answered. "I haven't been home in days."

"Ah, is that so?" General Hong lifted his hand, signaling to the dealer that he would take cards this round. "Very well."

It was impossible to tell what he meant by that. Orion would exhaust himself trying to figure it out. All he could do was incline his head and excuse himself, pushing away from the poker table and wandering off in search of his wife.

Rosalind lunged for the dropped cloth in a panic. Just as she was rising, fist clutched tight to prepare for another fight, she recognized who had come in and exhaled sharply with relief, dropping her murder weapon again.

Alisa Montagova folded her arms. "Right here?"

"I wasn't exactly given plenty of options to work with," Rosalind shot back. "Lock the door."

Alisa did as she was told. Rosalind didn't bother asking the girl how long she had been watching, or how she knew to follow, or what she was even doing here at Peach Lily Palace. In this day and age, one had to expect spies everywhere.

"The back exit has been barred for months," Alisa said. "You can't move him out that way."

Rosalind crouched down delicately, digging through Zilin's pockets. She didn't find anything particular: his wallet, keys, two playing cards that were folded at the corners. So he was cheating at his poker games. How expected.

"Suggestions, Miss Montagova?"

"Ivanova," Alisa corrected, whip-quick. While Rosalind rolled her eyes and continued frisking the line of Zilin's clothes to make sure she wasn't leaving evidence behind, Alisa Montagova was deep in thought, rubbing the palm of her hand against her chin.

She walked forward after a long moment, looming over Zilin's body.

"Why don't you pass it off as one of the chemical killings?" Alisa suggested.

Rosalind frowned up at her. "Because I don't know what chemicals the killer is using. This also isn't Chinese territory."

"So serious." Alisa bounced into a crouch too. She wasn't wearing heels like Rosalind, so her feet were completely flat, bringing her closer to the ground. "It's not as if the policemen are very good at their jobs. Just use that"—she pointed to the pin in Rosalind's hair—"to make the injection wound, and they will mark it off as one."

Rosalind reached into her hair, sliding out a pin. It was thin and sharp, a perfect piercing mechanism. Then her eyes narrowed. "You came up with that plan rather quickly."

"I am an agent for a party that has gone entirely underground," Alisa shot back. "If I don't think quickly, I die. Now, do you want my help or not? If you evacuate the dance hall, there's a window at the back of the main stage that I can haul him through. It will look like he was killed in the alley."

As soon as Alisa finished outlining the plan, a wisp of an idea started to unfurl in Rosalind's mind. The dance troupe was still running their routine downstairs. If they had started ten minutes ago, then their first costume change was likely fast approaching.

"How can I trust you?" Rosalind asked. She rolled Zilin's sleeve up.

"Same way you trust me with your identity. Same way I trust you with mine."

On the other side of the women's washroom door, a burst of voices neared with sudden gusto. The knob jiggled—once lightly and another time more vigorously—but when it wouldn't open, the voices gave a bad-tempered grumble and moved away.

"We have no other choice," Alisa continued.

Rosalind muttered a curse under her breath, then pointed a finger at Alisa. She wanted to chide the girl like a child, but it was jarring to see a face as old as her own, to tell her off when Alisa had caught up in age. Alisa lifted her chin, looking eager for a lecture. It would probably serve as her daily entertainment.

No time.

Rosalind yielded, taking a deep breath and twirling the pin in her hands. Before she could feel the push of nausea in her throat, she stabbed down, sinking the metal half an inch into the soft of Zilin's inner elbow. When she pulled the hairpin out, there was a thin coating of red over the silver. She cupped her hand beneath the tip, catching a droplet of blood before it could hit the floor. Alisa grimaced in disgust, and Rosalind shot her a silent look of scorn, asking Alisa if she wanted to do it instead.

Alisa, at least, had the self-awareness to look adequately reproached. She shot to her feet and shuffled to the sink inside the washroom, turning on the tap and gesturing for Rosalind to go ahead. Careful not to jostle the body, Rosalind rose too and stepped over him, putting her hand under the water. In three quick swipes, Rosalind had the blood cleaned from her pin and off her glove, shaking away the excess water before it could soak the fabric. Then she slipped the pin back into her hair, its jewels catching the light of the mirror.

"Be careful lifting him," she warned. "He's heavy."

Alisa nodded. She gave a salute. "Ne volnuysya, I have it handled."

"How can I not worry?" Rosalind muttered. Alisa Montagova was a thin girl and Zilin was almost six feet tall. Still, Alisa was right: there was no other choice.

Rosalind took the two playing cards off the floor, scrunching them into her fist. Everything else needed to stay on Zilin's body to make the sight look normal when he was found. His cheating hand, however—Rosalind ripped the thick cards, shredding the spade and the diamond into pieces. When she tossed the paper bits into the nearest toilet stall, Alisa was watching, a small smile playing at her lips.

"It's on you now." Rosalind tugged her sleeves straight. She opened the door. "Be safe."

With her jaw gritted tight, she cast a silent prayer for luck and slipped out.

18

Outside the washroom, Rosalind paused for a moment, taking in the stillness of the second level. *Danger*, her brain warned, and she tamped it down with a vexed *I know*. It felt like the dance hall had gone quieter, before she realized it was only the music downstairs hitting a lull so it could launch into its next set.

Rosalind urged herself to move. She walked along the second level with her eyes trained forward and her gait casual, taking no time to peer down onto the show floor. She didn't want to risk Yōko or Tarō seeing her and asking where Zilin had gone. It was a guess, but she proceeded in the direction of the stage, circling around velvet chairs and chatting couples until it seemed like she was above the dancers. There had to be a way down for maintenance. . . .

Rosalind sighted the red partition screen. She pushed it aside, her gloved fingers giving only a light nudge. Ah—success.

"Maybe I'm not such a bad spy after all," Rosalind muttered, hurrying down the narrow stairwell. She emerged in a hallway with a frightfully low ceiling, which meant she was either behind the stage or in a basement level under it. The details didn't matter. There was only one door in sight, so Rosalind entered.

The first thing she noticed was the array of costumes dumped on the floor. Then: the vanity mirrors set up in a row, its table space bursting with cosmetics. Five changing cubicles stretched down the length of the dressing room, the curtains of each one roped neatly.

No one was present. Rosalind strode near the cubicles, reaching out to undo the ropes and pull the curtains shut one by one. They were heavy and cumbersome, hanging down a tall rod and sweeping onto the floor like the skirts of an overconfident debutante. When the first rustle of activity came from the hallway outside—the voices of showgirls returning for a costume change—Rosalind slipped smoothly behind one of the cubicle curtains.

The main door to the dressing room flew open. The girls started to complain about how much they hated the next routine, how the lights were too bright, how the feather boas itched. Rosalind reached into her pocket. When her hand met only air, she pressed along the lining of her dress, and came up empty too.

"Damn," Rosalind whispered, peeling her gloves off. She was out of poison. "If you can't be a good spy, can't you at least be a good assassin?"

The curtain twitched. One of the showgirls stepped in. Before she could scream, Rosalind clapped a hand over the girl's mouth, the other one coming around her neck.

"Don't struggle." Rosalind pressed her thumb and her index finger onto the showgirl's pressure points. She was an echo of herself from only minutes prior, but this time her voice was gentle even while her fingers pushed hard. "I promise you'll have a bigger headache if you struggle."

The girl looked familiar. The set of her eyes, the pencil-thin eyebrows. Her name seemed to hover at the outer periphery of Rosalind's memory, but then her head lolled as she fell unconscious, and Rosalind wiped her thoughts away before she could dwell further. If she knew her once, that was in the past. If she knew her once, that was Rosalind Lang's life and not Janie Mead's, and she couldn't slip up from being Janie Mead.

Rosalind exhaled shakily, letting the showgirl slump to the floor.

It didn't sound like the girls outside had heard the struggle. With a regrettable wince, Rosalind moved the showgirl so she wouldn't tip over and hit her head. Then she eased the costume out of the girl's hands and put it on instead.

An orange dress, decorated with furs along the shoulder. The bottom cut off like a leotard, paired with fishnets. It had been a while since she had changed with such speed, counting the beats inside her head to time their next stage appearance. She was finished before the voices outside were done, waiting for the moment they looked around to count their numbers and pause, yelling, "Daisy! What's taking so long?"

Rosalind picked up the orange top hat from the floor. She pinned it to her hair, undid the low bun at her neck, and stepped out. No one paid her any attention; no one noticed she was an entirely different girl while she pretended to adjust the strap of her dress, her face inclined away. The sparse minutes between changes were too frantic, too busy, and she became one with their unit as they pushed through the hallway and up three small steps, down another passageway, and into the wings of the stage.

The stage was built low, raised just two steps higher than the rest of the show floor. And it was from here, tucked in the shadows, that Rosalind finally caught sight of Orion again, leaning against one of the dance hall pillars.

He looked like he was here to enjoy the show. He had abandoned her on their task while they were under a joint code name, while their mission was at a turning point, to enjoy the show?

What is wrong *with him?*

The music switched into their cue, and someone nudged her from behind, moving the mass of dancers out from the wings. In her sheer disbelief, she forgot to resist, reverted four years and fell into old habits to keep the show going. But Rosalind had pulled on a costume only to trigger an evacuation, to get close enough to the only thing in this dance hall she had observed that could incite enough chaos: the smoke machines onstage.

There wasn't enough time, though. She would look too suspicious lunging for them now. The piano keys merged with the trumpet, and Rosalind's eyes moved to Orion again. She recognized this song—in fact, this exact lineup of songs—from the Scarlet burlesque club. She had a better idea.

Rosalind followed the last of the dancers out smoothly. Her mind shut down. She felt the hot lights and the eyes from the crowd; she felt the glittering chandelier overhead chase geometric refractions along her cheeks. Her gaze stayed on the chandelier for one beat, two beats, three. The music soared into a lull, letting the showgirls take their position, letting Rosalind find her place on the right side of the stage, plainly in Orion's line of sight.

She caught his gaze. She held it, waiting, waiting . . .

But he didn't recognize her.

When the song took its fast melody and Rosalind fell into the steps of the routine, she could tell in the way that his stare stayed politely intrigued, in the way he tilted his head and swept his eyes up and down, following the line of her arms when she extended them, the length of her legs as she slid across the stage.

Dancing was no art in Rosalind's mind. It was a carefully calculated series of steps, a persuasion that could be used to sway minds and change thoughts. It was as scientific as any chemical reaction, only the variables at work were colors and limbs and movement. That was how she remembered the routines even years after learning them: one flourish after the other in a formulaic input and output.

The saxophone took its solo. The first line of dancers scattered off the stage and dispersed onto the floor, seeking targets who would give generous tips. At the Scarlet club, they used to split their earnings with management at the end of the night. Funny how it worked—Rosalind had been familiar with the idea of pinning down a target and carrying out a mission long before she had turned assassin.

The second row of dancers fanned out. Rosalind, with Orion's eyes still on her, made a beeline right for him, waiting for the moment he caught his blunder, waiting for that glazed stupor to sharpen.

It didn't. Not even when Rosalind stopped in front of him. Not even when she set her hands on his shoulders and smoothed them down, stopping on his chest, because all he said was, "Listen, I'm a married man—"

"I *know*, you blockhead. You're married to *me*," Rosalind interrupted. Her demeanor switched, a quick snap from alluring showgirl to furious wife, her hand seizing the loose collar of his shirt. "You abandoned our task for *this*?"

The mist in his eyes finally cleared. Recognition sank in, his lips parting as he reconfigured the sight onstage with the girl he had been partnered with. For a long second, Orion was at a loss for words.

"I really did have business to take care of," he finally managed. "And now it is taken care of. Why are you wearing a dancer's costume?"

The music was changing, signaling a return to the stage. Rosalind spared a glance over her shoulder. "We can discuss this later. Give me your pistol."

Orion jerked back. "What?"

"Your pistol," she demanded again, holding her palm out. "You brought it, yes?"

"*Yes*, I brought it, beloved." He reached into his inner coat pocket and took it out hurriedly, pressing the gun into her open palm and closing her fingers around it before anyone could see what they had just exchanged. His words grew more and more frantic, matching her hiss. "Why didn't you bring yours? And don't tell me you don't own one—I would laugh until the pigs started flying."

The dancers were turning back. They took little steps, mimicking the motions of woodland animals ambling in the wild. Rosalind was the only one who stayed unmoving. That had been her metaphor. That had been the instruction she used to teach the girls their choreography.

"I don't own one."

"Why not?"

"Drop it."

"Clearly you *need* it—"

"I don't. Like. Carrying. Weapons," Rosalind spat. There was a volatile anger curling in her gut. Something about Orion Hong ground her gears to an intolerable degree. "Now get ready to run."

"*What?*"

Rosalind turned around, aiming the pistol at the chandelier on the stage. Right before any of the girls reached the steps to the stage, she fired one bullet after another at the glass chandelier on the high ceiling.

She didn't like weapons, but she had once belonged to the elite of a vicious gang. She knew how to use them. She knew how to shoot, even if her aim wasn't perfect.

The chandelier broke on the fourth bullet and crashed to the stage.

"Go!" Rosalind snapped.

The dance hall erupted with chaos, movement bursting in every direction. Rosalind caught a flash of orange at her periphery, and she tucked the gun into her costume, hiding it from view and spinning to follow the rest of the dancers. There was too much going on for anyone to notice that she had fired the bullets. While other patrons rushed to bottleneck the front entrance, the dancers fled for immediate safety, and Rosalind was quick to join them in hurrying around the stage and into the dressing room.

As soon as the door closed after them, Rosalind broke from the crying girls, heading for the cubicle where she had left the other dancer. Daisy. She did remember the short-haired showgirl. But like everyone else in the city, Daisy was older, a changed version of herself. When Daisy woke up, she would think it unfathomable that the same Rosalind from four years ago had attacked her.

Rosalind pulled the curtain tight. She changed fast. The zip of the costume came down, the hat dropped to the floor, her bun was pinned back. When she put her qipao back on, it almost snagged on the gems in her hair, but she pulled the collar up quickly and looped the fabric off the sharp points, the lace sitting tight around her neck again.

How much time had passed since the chandelier fell? How long would it take to evacuate the dance hall? How long did Alisa need to drag the body?

Rosalind poked her head out from the cubicle, eyeing the overhead lighting. The moment she saw there was only one large fixture on the ceiling, decorated with an elaborate seashell design, she withdrew Orion's pistol again and pointed. Before the girls had scarcely caught their breath and stopped crying, she had shot the lights in the room, blanketing them in absolute darkness.

The girls started to scream, reaching a fever pitch. Fortunately for Rosalind, that gave her the opportunity to rush out from the changing cubicle and charge for the door, ramming into multiple bodies on the way. It didn't matter; they couldn't see her. She was back in the hallway in no time, looking around furiously to determine which direction was—

Orion skidded around the corner. "Jesus, Janie, where did you *go?*"

"What—I thought I told you to leave!"

They couldn't stand around arguing like this. Before Orion managed a retort, Rosalind grabbed his wrist and hauled him with her, hurrying away from the back of the stage and through the dance hall, avoiding the large shards of glass. They burst out the doors with a mass of other patrons, swallowed into chatter and conjecture immediately.

"Was it a shooter? I thought I saw a shooter among the showgirls!"

"Don't be nonsensical. How could a showgirl do that? It must be poor installation. It happens in these places."

A cold wind blew onto Rosalind's face. The Frenchwoman beside her was near hysterical.

"Mr. Mu! Mrs. Mu!"

Orion whirled around, seeking the echoing voice. Yōko and Tarō were pushing closer from the other side of the crowd, waving frantically.

"Janie, hide the pistol."

Rosalind bit back a curse. The pistol was crammed shallowly in her sleeve, barely concealed from anyone who looked directly at her. Thinking fast, she reached for Orion and wrapped her arms around his middle, tucking herself into his chest as if she couldn't bear to hold herself upright anymore. While her arms were hidden under the fabric of his coat, she took the pistol and slid it back into his inner pocket, safe and out of sight.

A breath of relief whispered out from her lungs. As soon as the weight of the pistol settled into Orion's coat pocket, she felt him relax too, and he settled his chin atop her head.

"Good," he whispered, quietly enough that only she heard him. For a moment, Rosalind didn't move, her cheek pressed to the smooth fabric of his shirt, the contact humming with warmth. Remaining these extra few seconds was a necessity—a matter of avoiding suspicion. All the same, she had to admit there was an unexpected sense of safety that came with being wrapped up like this, secreted away from the world and hidden in a hollow that would snarl before it let its cherished subject be taken away.

"Thank goodness we found you two." Yōko finally pushed through the crowd, coming to a stop before them. Rosalind pulled away almost reluctantly, sliding her arms out from underneath Orion's coat as Tarō caught up too. "Did you see how any of that happened?"

"Not at all," Rosalind replied. "I ran into my husband again just after you left. Next thing we know, there's screaming from downstairs and we needed to hurry out."

"So incredibly bizarre," Tarō agreed. "Who would have thought a place like this would be the site of such chaos."

"Indeed." Orion's agreement came with an aggrieved air. Yōko and Tarō didn't seem to catch his tone, but Rosalind glared at him in warning, which he ignored. "Who would have thought?"

A blare of sirens came down Thibet Road. Police, arriving to survey the scene. Just as their flashing lights pulled up outside Peach Lily Palace, Rosalind caught movement at the mouth of one of its alleys and spotted Alisa, waiting there for her attention.

She looked casual, completely at ease. When she finally caught Rosalind's eye, she nodded once, then disappeared with the crowds along the sidewalk.

Rosalind put her hand on Orion's elbow. "Qīn'ài de," she said. "Let's go home now."

Orion nodded tightly. Yōko and Tarō bade them farewell, though the two were more distracted by the sirens. With her grip tense, Rosalind gave another tug on Orion's elbow, and he finally turned to follow her away.

They had ridden separate one-person rickshaws home, so there had been no chance to talk. As soon as the runners let them off outside Rosalind's apartment building, scurrying away after taking their coins, however, Rosalind felt the air grow thick. She stepped in through the building doors and trekked across the courtyard. Orion's heavy footfall was a dull echo on every stair up.

They reached her apartment. The door opened. The door closed.

"You better start talking before I blow a gasket, Janie Mead."

Rosalind whirled around, throwing her gloves onto the couch seat. "That is so *rich* of you," she returned. "Please don't forget that you were the one who slunk off without explanation."

"Walking off for a few minutes was enough reason to smash a whole chandelier without consulting me first?" Orion exclaimed. "What was going through your head?"

"If you want to be consulted, maybe you should be around as active events are happening."

Orion made a noise of disbelief. "You are *so* hostile for no reason—"

"Hostile?" Rosalind echoed. "Because I was fulfilling our task? Maybe you should adopt some more hostility—"

"*How* was crashing the chandelier helping our task?"

Rosalind fell quiet. Sooner or later, someone would find Tong Zilin's body. It would summon the authorities, and the authorities would come sniffing around Seagreen Press. Orion would hear about it then—how Zilin had been killed tonight. Perhaps he would put it together. Or perhaps he would consider it too absurd that it had been by Rosalind's hand. He didn't know that she was an assassin. He didn't know that she was Fortune, plucking cards out of men's pockets and shredding whatever luck they thought they had on their side.

"You will have to trust me," Rosalind said plainly. She was being unfair, but he also hadn't communicated why he slipped off, nor told her why he had disappeared that first night. Why should *she* give up her secrets?

Yet Orion wasn't backing down.

"This is ridiculous," he said, pacing a small circle around the living room. "Someone could have gotten hurt."

Rosalind scoffed. "And?" For once, Orion Hong was not carrying a conversation merely with light jibes. Of all matters that he decided to take seriously, why choose this? Where was this version of him at other times?

"Don't tell me you are that callous—"

"So what if I'm callous?" Rosalind snapped. "I don't *care* if some rich patron gets a little scratch. I don't *care* if the dance hall has to rebuild and use its precious funds for renovation. I care about hauling this forsaken country off its knees, and I'll do whatever that asks of me. Won't *you?*"

The apartment fell silent. Rosalind's voice had risen louder and louder in volume as she spoke, and now her final demand boomed across the living room with an echo. It seemed to trigger something in Orion, because he surged forward, his jaw tightening with each long stride. Rosalind stepped back in an attempt to keep their distance, but she had scarcely taken three steps before her shoulders hit the wall. As much as she tried to look unruffled by Orion's threatening proximity, her heart was thudding in her chest.

"I—" he said forcefully, "—am doing my best."

Rosalind swallowed hard. With no less than an inch between them, she watched Orion's throat bob up and down too.

"All I can do," Orion went on, "is my best. Some of us don't have the luxury of working only for the cause, of being national heroes. Some of us need to care about ourselves, too."

The hitch in his voice took Rosalind's attitude down a small notch. There was something too raw there, utterly different from his usual easiness.

"I'm not asking you to be a national hero." Her words came out quietly this time. "It doesn't take a national hero to smooth over the cracks in one city."

Orion stepped back, putting space between them at last. There was a flicker in his eyes—a crinkling of his brow that Rosalind caught before he looked away. Acknowledgment. Surrender. As if somewhere deep within him, he thought Rosalind was right, even though Rosalind was only being harsh to steer his attention away from the *why* of the evacuation tonight.

"What would have happened if you were caught?" Orion asked. "What would you have done if the glass slit a foreigner's throat and they didn't let us leave until they found the one who'd fired, and then the Nationalists threw us to the wolves instead of bearing the scandal to save us? What then? Do you wish to be a martyr, Janie Mead? Because I do not."

When Orion looked at her again, Rosalind didn't avert her gaze. She stared, brazenly.

"That is a meaningless hypothetical," she said. "It didn't happen."

"And if we're going to continue working together," Orion countered, "I need to hear your answer. I will not condone recklessness. I have too many people to protect. A family name to uphold."

Rosalind's fists tightened. The unspoken part of his statement hung in the air: *I have too many people to protect—do you?*

No matter what Rosalind did or how she behaved, the only person she could damage in this city was herself. Her sister already wore the label of the enemy. There was no one else Rosalind cared to look out for. But she didn't know if that was better or worse than constantly trying to hold other people on her shoulders, bearing burdens without the same courtesy returned to her.

"As I said—meaningless." She pushed away from the wall. "They have us bound in matrimony and in code name. Do you think they would separate us that easily? You're stuck with me until the end."

Orion drew a rough hand through his hair. The dark strands fell forward, like slashes cut into his stricken expression. He didn't look at her. Perhaps he didn't want her to see the loathing that would be in his eyes. Dao Feng had practically stated up front that he trusted Orion most to carry out this mission and Rosalind most to keep an eye on him. He wouldn't allow an agent transfer at this point.

"God," Orion muttered. "Whatever."

Before Rosalind could ask what *that* was supposed to mean, Orion pivoted and walked into the bathroom, the door slamming after him. Seconds later, she heard the sink run, water splashing loudly against the basin. The conversation between them was over, though it had achieved nothing. Outside, there came the hoot of an owl, its call surrounding the apartment. Night was thick and heavy, permeating the windows with a darkness that seemed tangible, that could be grabbed and molded into shape if she opened the window and reached out.

"Good night, I suppose," Rosalind muttered. She drew the blinds, pulling them down firmly. By the time Orion emerged from the bathroom, Rosalind had already closed her bedroom door.

19

"Lock the doors! *Now*. Come on, get a move on!"

There was a bang from the front of the shop, then Oliver's voice, yelling loudly enough to reverberate into the bedrooms at the back. Celia scrambled from her chair, twisting her hair out of her eyes and shoving it down with a pin. In the hallway, she passed Audrey and Millie hauling out a long set of chains, which Celia could only guess was for the front doors.

She hurried into the shop. Oliver was at the entrance, pulling the dead bolt into place. It *was* closing time, but why was he moving so frantically? He hadn't even been on shift today; he was supposed to be in town making final perusals for their completed maps.

"Sweetheart, give me a hand."

Celia strolled over. "What happened?"

"Nationalist soldiers nearby. They might be looking for us."

"Might?" Celia echoed. She reached for a wad of tape by the front desk, supplying the roll to Oliver as soon as he pressed a sheet of newspaper up to the windows.

"I can't be certain. I saw their trucks rolling into the area."

Goose bumps prickled along her arms instantly. Once Oliver had a hold on the tape, Celia moved to help him with the newspapers, passing him each sheet. They had run over their evacuation plan many times, but this didn't seem to qualify for a full evacuation, only the precautionary measures: cover their windows, lock their doors, make the shop seem temporarily abandoned. If the Nationalists were sniffing around without any suspicion in mind, they would pass the shop without much thought. If, somehow, the Nationalists had gotten wind of their presence here and actually moved their forces around the shop, then it was time to run.

"Are they driving into town?" Celia asked. A thought occurred to her. "Or are they going to the warehouse in the forest?"

Oliver shot her a quick look, pausing with one hand propped against the window. Then, remembering that time was of the essence, he held the roll of tape up and ripped a piece off with his teeth, taking the square out of his mouth and sticking down a newspaper corner.

"You're still thinking about that?" Oliver asked. "There's no reason for us to believe it's a Nationalist base."

"I know." Celia passed over another sheet. "All the same—" She paused, her eyes latching on to the new sheet in her hand. A jolt of surprise sprang down her spine. The text was all written in Japanese . . . except for the larger title splashed on the frontmost page in both English and Japanese.

SEAGREEN PRESS 青海新聞

"Oliver," Celia said suddenly. "Where did you get these newspapers?"

Oliver looked down briefly. He didn't understand why she was asking. "Nearby, I'm sure. Around the dress shop?"

"Was someone selling them?" Celia pressed. When she made a quick scan, it seemed the other sheets already pasted onto the window were written in Chinese. Those were the usual large publications commonly found around these areas. So where had *this* one come from?

"No. They were tossed in those newspaper stands on the street corner." He frowned, gesturing for her to pass over the next sheet. "What's the matter?"

"Seagreen Press," Celia said emphatically, pointing at the paper heading. Alisa's covert workplace. And last she had heard from Rosalind, also the location of *her* newest assignment. "That's a Japanese company writing for its citizens in Shanghai. Why would its papers reach all the way out here?"

Oliver paused, taking the issue in Celia's hands. Recognition flickered in his eyes.

"What are you suspecting?" he asked.

There was certainly some sort of suspicion forming in her mind. Celia just hadn't quite put everything into its right order, hadn't tidied up the edges of a complete conclusion.

She turned around.

"Hey!" Oliver called after her. "Where are you going?"

"Don't worry. I'll take the back door. No one will see me."

"What? That didn't answer my question!"

Celia kept walking. She heard Oliver shout at Audrey and Millie to finish newspapering the windows before pattering after her, hovering over her left shoulder, then her right shoulder as he tried to force some answer out of her. They were both already dressed in dark clothing, so Celia only grabbed a pair of gloves from her room before she was wordlessly stepping out the back door, perking her ears for the sound of trucks in the distance. Their heavy wheels ground along the town gravel paths in an unmistakable manner. It could only be military vehicles rapidly heading their way.

"Are you going to brood, or are you going to come with me?" Celia asked, setting off into the night. Though Oliver caught up quickly, his stomps communicated that he was displeased with having to play follower.

"I'm not afraid to drag you back to the shop."

Oliver pulled a branch aside. He had always possessed the talent of issuing threats with the most cordial delivery. Even now, while they picked through the forest, his words bore an undercurrent of danger, like he would need only the lightest trigger to act.

Celia cast a glance back so that Oliver could see her doubtful expression. As soon as their eyes met, she turned back to navigating their path, a smile twitching at her lips.

"Yes, you are."

It was all a guise. The tall, scary Communist agent with the scarred knuckles and the jaw cut from marble—who once didn't move for three hours because the neighboring shop's cat had wandered in and taken a nap on his foot. The terrifying de facto leader among their group—who sometimes stayed up till odd hours fixing the buttons on Audrey's blouses with a needle and thread because Audrey didn't know how to sew.

Oliver made a noise of protest. "How dare—"

"Shhh," Celia interrupted, both because she had heard something and because she took joy from telling Oliver Hong what to do. He could hide it from the others. He could boss them around and let them believe in a certain level of cruelty. But Celia knew better. And she supposed she only knew better because he let her in, because he let those real flashes slip through, aware that there was the possibility she might use it against him and risking it anyway.

She didn't know how to feel about that. She had never been handed a responsibility so big before: protecting someone's trust. Someone who wasn't family, someone who had no existing obligation to her.

The moon disappeared behind a cloud. Celia slowed, head tilted to the wind.

"I was right," she whispered, peering through the dense trees. "They're going to the warehouse."

Though it had been some time since their first nighttime excursion through the forest, it wasn't hard to find that suspicious

V-shaped road again. Now there were trucks rumbling down it, one after the other in neat file.

And there was only one destination at the end of that road.

"Celia, hold on."

Just before Celia could creep forward again, Oliver reached for her arm, holding her in place. The moon emerged from behind the clouds and illuminated the grimace on Oliver's face. She deciphered it immediately.

"You did report the warehouse," she stated. There was nothing in her tone that asked for confirmation; she was as certain as the skies were dark, and she was only saying it aloud so Oliver knew she had caught on. "You reported it, and they told you to investigate alone in case it turns out to be a critical Nationalist secret."

"Sweetheart—"

"Don't *sweetheart* me," Celia commanded, throwing her arm out of his grip. Maybe that was why she didn't know how to feel about Oliver. She had his trust, but she didn't have his secrets. He might put his very life into her open palm without hesitation, but he could not answer a question truthfully so long as the cause—and their superiors—dictated he keep quiet.

"There are some things that I need to figure out first before I go putting you in danger with the knowledge," Oliver said calmly. "It's nothing you need to worry about."

She recalled that look of recognition on his face when they were at the warehouse. Her question about whether he had been there before and his quick switch of the topic.

What are you hiding from me, Oliver?

Celia marched forward. If he didn't tell her, then she'd find out for herself.

"*Celia.* Come back here!"

She did not. She walked until she had the warehouse in sight, and only then did she duck behind one of the prickly bushes, watching the trucks park around the foreboding warehouse. It was uniformed Nationalists who piled out from the cars, carrying crates in their arms, moving in and out of the warehouse quickly. She didn't see any leader among them. Only soldiers, mostly unspeaking. Their manner had a peculiar air. Not fear, nor unease as they passed each other by. The first thought that occurred to Celia was *absence*. The soldiers up ahead were moving in the same way that people sleepwalking did.

Celia turned around. At some point, Oliver had begrudgingly followed, coming up behind her to watch quietly. They couldn't go any closer or they would risk being sighted, which was unfortunate. She wanted to see their faces.

"Doesn't this scene look off to you?" she whispered.

Oliver remained standing, his arms crossed over his chest. "Hard to say," he reluctantly replied. "It could be—"

A flash of metal caught the moonlight from behind him. Celia didn't think; she dove up and threw Oliver out of the way, the two of them landing upon the prickly undergrowth just as a bullet rang through the night. Celia gasped, her hands clutching on to whatever fabric she could grasp of Oliver's jacket. Oliver, meanwhile, snapped to alertness the moment they hit the ground, his arm coming around her waist to brace their movement.

The bullet struck the place where he had been standing, spraying bark everywhere upon impact. It would have been a headshot.

"Are you okay?" Oliver demanded.

"I'm fine, I'm fine," Celia hurried to reassure him.

Oliver muttered a curse. "Stay down," he instructed, angling his body to deposit Celia smoothly onto the forest floor and pulling a pistol from his pocket. He waited for the next flash of metal, then fired—on his third bullet, there was a human cry ringing into the night.

They had underestimated the Nationalists to think that they could slink around spying on an enemy faction's activity. There must have been soldiers stationed around the perimeter too, watching for intruders.

"This way," Celia said tightly, springing to her feet and grabbing ahold of Oliver's arm. The gunshots would have echoed down to the warehouse, and they needed to get out of range before other soldiers started searching. They plunged deeper into the trees, twigs snapping beneath their feet and branches scratching at their faces. Celia kept listening, waiting for a shout, waiting for the sound of pursuit.

At a considerable distance away, Oliver slowed and gestured for her to do the same. They took in their surroundings carefully. The moon was at the apex of the sky now. The tree leaves bristled above them. The thicket murmured beneath them. It was quiet.

It seemed they had gotten away.

"Dammit, Oliver," Celia cursed, catching her breath.

"Damn *me*?" Oliver returned, his eyes wide.

"Yes, damn you!" She adjusted her blouse collar, brushing off the bits of bark that had gotten stuck on her clothing. "If I knew you were investigating this, maybe I would have known what to expect! Maybe we would both be sitting happily in the shop right now."

"Please, in what universe are you willing to sit around happily even if I had given you information?"

"It wouldn't hurt to tell me what instructions you're under. You don't have to give details, just don't *lie* to me."

If the point of keeping secrets was to protect each other, then Celia couldn't see the logic here. She could accept not knowing who Oliver was meeting with each time he went to Shanghai. She didn't need to be given the ins and outs of his private missions. But she would not be kept in the dark about matters that she had *asked* to know—that she was already involved with when *she* was the one who discovered the discrepancy that led to the warehouse.

"I've never lied to you," Oliver insisted. He pointed a threatening finger at her, stopping only a hairsbreadth away from her nose. "And that is the last time you go throwing yourself in my path, understand? What were you thinking? You could have been shot."

Celia's mouth dropped agape. "You *would* have been shot if I hadn't done that! Are you serious right now?"

"That's the risk I take on as an agent. That's the risk I am willing to bear while fighting for the nation. If I get shot, I get shot. *You* don't put yourself in *my* firing line like that."

"Oh, sure," Celia spat. "Nation over everything, right? Even your life."

A howl moved through the forest. They both stiffened, trying to determine the source, whether it was mechanical or human. Neither—it sounded more animal, fading away after a few seconds. The wind blew softly. Celia and Oliver looked at each other again. Slowly, he withdrew his menacing pointing, though his arm didn't return to his side.

"Yes, Celia," he said, almost tiredly. "Nation over everything."

She knew that he meant it. When someone like Oliver said those words, it was not a catchphrase for pretty pamphlets and performative battle cries. He put his very heart into its intent.

Then his hand curled around her face, the motion gentle while his thumb brushed a soft graze over her cheek. Celia froze, blinking rapidly to register what was happening. He had never done this so blatantly before. There had been the casual nudge on the shoulder, the brush of their fingers while passing a cup of tea. There had been playful taps on her chin. Or rough inspections if one of them was hurt, quick fix-ups with bandages and antiseptic. Never this—never contact that had no other explanation, none save for a certain want.

"Nation over everything," Oliver repeated, his voice firm. "But not you, sweetheart. Never *your* life in exchange."

Her mind rang with the screech of a broken radio. White noise:

humming between her ears while she searched desperately for something—anything—to say. Then, like someone had changed the channel, it was not tenderness that formed her response but blistering anger.

"You're so damn selfish," Celia said, jerking away from his touch. "Have you ever stopped to consider that I value your life just as much? If you want to protect me, don't you think that I want to protect you, too?"

Oliver visibly inhaled, taken aback for a flash of a second before he composed himself. It was enough to give an answer: the notion had never occurred to him. How little he thought of her. How little he thought of whatever it was that existed between the two of them.

Celia turned on her heel and walked off, nothing more to say.

20

A few days later, Rosalind had to admit that Deoka's map of the building was coming in handy.

The filing rooms were usually staffed by one or two assistant secretaries, picking their nails at the desk or wolfing down a plastic tub of noodles. Rosalind never had to do the filing herself; she set down the folders from production, then whoever occupied the small room would chirp "Otsukaresama deshita" and wave her off. Rosalind had no clue what the phrase meant, but they all said it, so she figured it was a signal that she had done enough and could leave her colleagues to it.

"It's an equivalent to *thank you*," Orion answered quickly, in the midst of rushing to a meeting when she'd asked him. "Not the literal meaning, but I'll explain after work if you wish." He kissed her temple briefly, then hurried off.

They hadn't spoken about their argument. They had merely gone to sleep in separate rooms and risen the next morning pretending like everything was fine, which meant everything did not feel fine. It wasn't as if Rosalind and Orion had ever been the best of friends, but now something was even frostier. Orion's jokes were half-hearted; Rosalind's jabs felt overly laced. He didn't carry through with any of his teasing, and she couldn't follow through with any remark that had a pinprick of truth to it. When they left the house this morning, Orion had run back inside after forgetting his hat and she had rolled her eyes to scoff a short "Typical." Except the word had snagged halfway in her throat, and she sounded like she might have choked on something, much to Orion's concern when he reemerged.

She watched him exit the department. She turned back to her work, chewing on her bottom lip.

The afternoon passed routinely. Rosalind moved back and forth across different filing rooms, piles funneled from one location to another. While Orion continued his people-pleasing and information collecting, Rosalind was sniffing her nose around the rooms and thinking about Dao Feng's other instruction: the intelligence file.

On her final run to distribute a pile of folders marked for room number eighteen, her eyes stopped on a trash can in the corner, and her attention snagged immediately. The secretary had his back turned, running an eye along the newly delivered materials to make sure Rosalind had brought the right ones, and without thinking, Rosalind asked, "Is that a Communist flag in the trash can?"

The secretary turned around. "Pardon?" he said in English.

Merde. Rosalind realized her mistake as soon as the words left her lips. She had said gòng dǎng out of habit. She was repeating the term that Dao Feng threw around, that others in the covert branch used when referring to the Communists. Only Nationalists shortened it like that. Condensed it up with a thin layer of disparagement. Everyone else said gòng chǎn dǎng.

"The Communist flag," Rosalind repeated, switching to English too. Thankfully, English was far plainer as a language, so there was less chance of giving away her identity with a simple term. Provided that she controlled her accent, at least. She could only hope that this secretary had switched to English because his Chinese wasn't as good. Perhaps he had missed the small nuance. "In the trash can, over there."

She pointed. The secretary leaned in.

"Now, would you look at that," he said evenly. "Indeed it is. I wonder how it got there."

"You don't sound the least bit puzzled," Rosalind observed.

The secretary only shrugged. He tapped something on his typewriter, dark eyes glancing along the reference numbers pasted at the front of the folders. "This is the Communist room. By my invention, anyway . . . We're not allowed to call it such officially, but the higher-ups brought it onto themselves for sorting the building by topic. Deoka probably wanted to dispose of hate mail in specific trash cans."

In one flourish, the secretary swept the folders into his hands and ordered them until they were the same height.

"You must be one of the new hires," he went on. "I don't think I've seen you here before."

"Yes," Rosalind said, ignoring the fact that she probably couldn't be considered *new* anymore with the time that had passed since she started. She had hardly made any progress with getting to know her colleagues. Orion, meanwhile, was going around greeting everyone by first name. They were a combined agent rolled into one anyway. If Orion became the friendly face and Rosalind became the eyes in the shadows, she was perfectly fine with that delineation of roles.

The secretary cleared his throat. Rosalind had been staring at the discarded flag again.

"My surname is Mu," she hurried to supply, recovering from the pause. "The reception assistant in production. You are . . . ?"

"Tejas Kalidas." Tejas turned the folders sideways, making them the same width too. "I would shake your hand, but then the folders would fall out of alignment again."

Rosalind inclined her head. "That's quite all right." She stepped back, over the door's threshold again. "I will be on my way unless you need anything more."

"That's everything." Tejas put the folders underneath his desk. With a wave, Rosalind made her exit, still thinking about Tejas's flippant remark. The filing system in the building was organized by subject, each room collating together materials that were alike. *How curious.*

Rosalind descended the stairwell, so engrossed by her pondering that she almost bumped into a colleague coming up. She apologized quickly, shaking her focus back on track. There was one more envelope she had to collect from room five on the second floor, and then her tasks for the day were complete.

"He hasn't been here for days. I'm concerned."

Rosalind slowed on the second floor, catching the wisps of conversation funneling out from a break room. Some instinct told her to listen, to muffle the click of her heels and pause.

"It isn't entirely unlike him to refuse communications."

"Yes, but it is unlike him to fail to report to the higher-ups. When has Tong Zilin ever risked seeming incompetent?"

Rosalind's breath snagged. One male voice and one female voice. So Tong Zilin's disappearance had been noticed. She crept closer to the wall.

"Do you think we need to go check up on him? He still has some of our papers, doesn't he?"

"No. He moved his work along last Thursday. Didn't he? It landed on my desk."

"Someone else did that, I guess. It wasn't my hand. And he finished it all?"

"It looked fine to my eyes. The only thing now is—"

Without warning, something clattered with a startlingly loud sound at the other end of the hallway. Rosalind winced, internally cursing the clumsy colleague who had just dropped their lunch tin. The conversation in the break room halted. There would be no telling what sort of *work* Zilin didn't pass on.

But if Tong Zilin was guilty of collaborating with the terror scheme—and he most likely was, given his beliefs—then these two in the break room were probably involved too. Pass along a missive with kill instructions, write up the report on attack procedures, take a phone call with officials in Japan: they didn't have to get blood on their hands, but they were guilty all the same. What was worse, being the cog or the blade of a killing machine? Didn't they both perform the very same function if they were one part of a whole?

Rosalind backed up quickly, resuming a natural walking pace right in time to collide with Haidi as she walked out from the break room. With a feigned jolt of surprise, Rosalind cried out, hands flying forward for balance. Haidi, meanwhile, scrambled to order the clipboards under her arm, half of them knocked askew.

"Oh, do excuse me. I was in such a hurry that I didn't watch where I was going," Rosalind breathed. She reached out, hoping to help with the clipboards and snoop on what they were.

But as soon as her fingers neared the one clipboard that was slipping, Haidi clasped her grip around Rosalind's wrist, keeping her away. It was like a band of metal had been closed over her skin. Though Rosalind froze, alarmed by the response, she suspected that even if she had tried to tug her arm back, she would not have managed.

"I have it under control," Haidi said. She gave a kind smile, entirely incongruous with the hold she had over Rosalind's wrist. "Thank you for the gesture nonetheless."

Haidi let go, then shuffled the clipboards back into neat arrangement. She inclined her head and hurried off. Seconds later, another colleague—the male voice from before—poked his head out from the break room, going in the other direction. Rosalind couldn't recall his name, but she was sure Orion could once she pointed him out.

Ouch, Rosalind thought, rubbing her wrist. It had turned a bloodless white because of Haidi's death grip. What sort of vitamins was that girl consuming?

Displeased, Rosalind fetched her envelope from room five quickly, grumbling under her breath. Jiemin didn't look up when she returned to her desk. Half the department had been summoned away for various meetings, some with Deoka in his office and some upstairs with the writing department.

"Here you are," Rosalind said, putting the envelope in front of Jiemin. "I'll help you with those now." She took a section of his work pile.

"Do you know where they go?" Jiemin asked absently, turning the page of his book.

She didn't need to know where they went. She was only looking for more work to give herself an excuse to move around. A plan had occurred to her at some point between the second and third floor.

"I will ask Liza." Rosalind was off before he could question her. She approached Alisa's desk calmly, the folders clearly in sight so that any onlooker would know why she was there.

"Hello," Alisa greeted pleasantly. "Do you need direction?"

Rosalind leaned in. Though she didn't mean to pry, she could not help the automatic survey she made of Alisa's work space: a framed photo of a fat cat, a to-do list in her small handwriting, a copy of *Yevgeniy Onegin* tucked behind her three mugs, the novel in its original Russian cover surrounded by a border decoration.

"I have a proposition for you, actually. It's very important that you hear me out first."

In an almost imperceptible change, Alisa sat up straighter in her chair. She cast a wary glance around, speaking again only when she had confirmed the other cubicles nearest to her weren't occupied.

"I'm listening."

Rosalind pulled the building map from inside her qipao, unfolding the paper with one hand and smoothing it out atop the folders. She pointed to number eighteen: that small door down the hall, near the stairwell. With a mere glance at the walls outside, it would be hard to guess that there was a whole filing room in there, supervised by a secretary sitting bored at his desk.

"I know you're looking for a file. Plans that your defector passed on. I think it's in this room."

Alisa's head tipped up suddenly, shooting her a disbelieving look. Whether it was because Rosalind knew of Alisa's objective at Seagreen or if it was because of her hypothesis that this was the location they were looking for, she wasn't sure. She kept pushing on.

"You're trying to steal it back, so let's work together. If I distract the secretary guarding the filing room and you get it, I want a copy of whatever it says."

Alisa made a thoughtful noise. At the very least, it was not immediate refusal, which meant that she was considering it.

"You know what the file is, it would seem," she said. "I would get in trouble for letting a copy circulate."

"But what matters most is taking the plan away from the Japanese, yes?" Rosalind returned. "Why not combine our forces to achieve exactly that?"

Alisa's cheeks turned gaunt as she bit down on them. She was chewing on the proposition, quite literally. "I don't think my superiors would be happy about the Kuomintang getting the information."

"Your superiors don't have to know." Rosalind flicked her hand, waving the matter off like a fly was whizzing around her face. "Don't tell me you don't keep other secrets from them."

Alisa gave her a wry look. Rosalind returned it in an identical manner.

Some few seconds later, Alisa sighed and said: "I suppose after one impromptu collaboration, we are already in deep water together." She huffed. "If anyone asks, though, I gave you nothing."

"Of course."

She had been banking on Alisa's lack of loyalty, and she had played her cards right. It wasn't that Rosalind expected Alisa Montagova to be any less efficient of an agent—she had simply guessed that Alisa worked for the Communists because they were the only faction willing to take someone of her identity when civil war broke out, and a job was merely a job, not a life-and-death commitment. They were both rather similar as far as their stances toward their respective political factions went. Neither cared about the faction itself, but they took on the burden for the sake of what that faction could provide.

"You said you would distract the secretary," Alisa said, bringing Rosalind's attention back to the situation at hand. "How?"

Rosalind hadn't thought that far. She peered through the department. "I shall figure it out as it unfolds. Allons-y."

Without further debate, they departed from the cubicles, Rosalind handing half of the folders to Alisa as if they were distributing together. Alisa was quick on her feet, following Rosalind's lead.

"I cannot begin to imagine where the file might be once you are inside the room," Rosalind said as they left the production department. They passed two open office doors. She kept her voice low. "All I know is that this filing room should be the most likely location compared to the rest of the building."

"If you can get me in without being sighted, just leave the rest to me," Alisa answered.

Rosalind nodded. They continued forward.

But just as they were coming upon room number eighteen, there was the sound of another door opening, and then a small burst of voices coming into the corridor. Among them, Orion sighted her instantly and headed over with an unspoken question in his eyes.

Just my luck.

"Hello, dearest." He put his hand to the small of her back. "What are you doing?"

Rosalind forced a smile. "Only some tasks. For my job. Which I am currently working at."

Alisa rolled her eyes. Orion did not look convinced. Behind him, there were two others from the department, peering over curiously before walking back to their desks.

The idea struck her like a thunderbolt. A distraction.

"Storm off," Rosalind instructed under her breath.

Orion's brows flew up. "I beg your pardon?"

"Storm off," she repeated. "Toward the stairwell over there, as closely as you can without descending. You're mad at me. Get mad."

To his credit, Orion did not waste another second idling in confusion. He threw up his arms and crowed, *"Unbelievable!"* before stomping off.

Rosalind waited three seconds, pretending to be shocked. Then she hurried after him, letting her heels clack loudly on the linoleum floor.

"Am I wrong?" she yelled after him. It wasn't hard to summon the guise of anger. Acting was easiest when there was a true basis to it, after all. "No matter where we go, you cannot stop associating with that girl! I saw you talking to her again last night!"

Orion paused near the stairwell, heeding Rosalind's instruction. It took him a moment to catch on to the track of Rosalind's fabricated argument, but he played along easily when he whirled back around, pretending that he had found more to say and couldn't storm off anymore.

"That's absurd. It wasn't anything."

"It didn't look like it." Rosalind jerked her hand by her side, indicating up. He needed to be louder.

"If you're going to accuse me of something"—Orion's volume increased, seeing her cue—"WHY DON'T YOU COME RIGHT OUT AND SAY IT?"

"Whoa, whoa, what's going on here?"

The question pierced through the echo of Orion's voice, still bouncing around the stone walls of the stairwell. Tejas had poked his head out from the filing room, and in sighting Rosalind and Orion, he shuffled over, taking it upon himself to break up the fight.

"Yell any louder and you're going to summon Deoka," Tejas warned. "And he won't take kindly on being disturbed."

"It is hardly my wrongdoing," Orion said. "Why don't we ask my wife what issue she takes with my social life?"

Rosalind laughed bitterly. She didn't have to force it; it came entirely of its own volition. "Your social life? Did you not swear *vows* to me? What happened to dedication and commitment?"

"You're imagining things."

"I wouldn't be if you would only communicate what you get up to!"

They needed more time. This wasn't enough for Alisa to make a good search. Before Orion could find some other direction to take the argument, Rosalind caught Tejas's elbow and dragged him toward Orion.

"Look at that," Rosalind instructed, pointing at Orion's neck. "Tell me that isn't the mark of infidelity."

Tejas squinted. Orion flinched back self-consciously.

"I . . . don't see anything, Mrs. Mu," Tejas said. He tried to step away. Rosalind put her hands on his shoulders, forcing him to remain in place.

"Is this some sort of loyalty pact among men?" she demanded. "It's right there. Look closer!"

There was nothing there. Only Orion's unmarred tanned skin, golden under his white shirt collar. But Rosalind didn't mind being the unhinged wife developing hallucinations if it served a purpose.

Tejas sighed. It would seem that he had given up trying to bring some sense into the argument, because when Rosalind wouldn't let him go, he said: "You know what? Yes. I see it. Horrible. Mr. Mu, how could you?"

Orion's mouth fell open. "*What*? This is ridiculous—"

Someone cleared her throat behind them. When Rosalind and Tejas both turned around, her hands finally releasing him from her death grip, they found Alisa standing outside the filing room, looking angelic and innocent with her work pile in her arms and her head tilted curiously, as if she had been waiting there the whole time.

"Mr. Kalidas, these are for you. If you would be so kind as to relieve me from having to witness a domestic spat."

"*Please*, relieve me as well," Tejas exclaimed, striding to Alisa and taking the pile from her. He returned to the filing room, slotting papers into the shelf by the entranceway, and Alisa caught Rosalind's eye briefly, giving a nod before turning on her heel for the main production department.

Excellent. Alisa was even better than Rosalind thought. It was time to draw this show to a close.

"You know what," Rosalind said. She looked around, pretending she had just noticed where they were, growing embarrassed that this was a public argument. "We can talk later. I have to get back to work."

"Wait, stop."

Orion grabbed her wrist. Her genuine confusion drew her to a halt.

"What—"

"I'm sorry." Before she could stop him, Orion had taken her into his arms, wrapping his embrace around her tightly and propping his chin over her head. She had already known how stark their height difference was from their little pocket-slipping stunt outside

Peach Lily Palace, but again she startled at the easy way he slotted her against his chest. "Let's not fight."

What . . . sort of act is this? "Um." She brought her arms up awkwardly, patting his back. "It's . . . it's okay."

"You mean it?" Orion asked. "You are not merely saying that?"

Was Tejas even in hearing range anymore? Rosalind pulled away the smallest distance so she could check. The hallway was empty. She supposed Orion was only pulling the final curtains. She reached up to tap his cheek.

"Don't upset me in the future and it will be swell, I suppose."

"Okay," Orion said simply. "I'm sorry. I really am. Some things I figure aren't important enough to tell you. It's not that I mean to keep secrets."

Rosalind blinked.

"Oh," she said. Her usual improvisation seemed to have stopped working. All she could come up with was another: "Oh."

Orion put a finger under her chin, tipping her face up to him.

"I am forgiven?"

"Well," Rosalind said. "You hardly give me a choice with such sincerity."

Orion gave her a bright smile, liquid and honey and beautiful. Despite knowing it was a show, Rosalind couldn't help giving him the smallest smile back.

21

Phoebe stuck her spoon into the yogurt, digging directly from the large tub. She was the only one in the household who ate things like *yogurt* anyway, so it wasn't as if anybody else would mind.

The front door opened and closed. Her father came in, a briefcase swinging at his side.

"Bàba," Phoebe greeted. "Ah Dou said he brought your mail in and put it in your office."

"Wonderful." General Hong paused at the entrance of the kitchen. "Is school not in session today?"

"No," Phoebe lied easily. She didn't bother elaborating. She didn't need to. Her father took her answer at face value and nodded, already making his way up to his home office.

The house fell quiet. She could hear the clock in the living room ticking, its echo slithering along every smooth surface. Ah Dou was out shopping. The maid was away this week, visiting her rural hometown.

Phoebe needed to find something to do today. Silas wouldn't be coming around until the evening, so there were plenty of hours to kill. If only she were older—then she could really embrace the socialite life. Instead, she was hovering in her awkward years, seventeen and too young to be taken seriously, too old to be told what to do. It was the same ambivalence with her family status:

known well enough that she could coast by on her last name, not quite powerful enough for her to disregard what she said and how she behaved.

She wandered into the living room. Stood there like a polished statue.

"Feiyi."

Her head shot up eagerly. Her father was calling her from upstairs.

"Yes?"

"Come here, please."

Phoebe tossed her hair over her shoulder. Her shoes were loud on the staircase, clacking all the way up and coming to an abrupt stop where her father's office began. He waved her in; she entered only once she had the invitation.

"Ah Dou mixed in some mail that was meant for you," he said. There was a small envelope in his hands, her name printed primly at the center. When Phoebe took the envelope, she flipped it around curiously, looking at the postmark printed along the top.

"Who is sending you mail from Taicang?" General Hong asked, observing the same thing.

"I haven't a clue," Phoebe replied.

Her father handed over a letter opener. It was silver-plated, engraved with their family name at the base. "Open it."

Phoebe took the letter opener carefully, not wanting to slash herself by accident. She made a quick cut across the envelope, then took out the contents.

General Hong frowned. Phoebe turned the paper this way and that to read both sides.

"A church pamphlet asking for orphanage donations," she said. "Establishments in this city are truly taking new strides to run their advertisements."

"How peculiar."

There was a tone in her father's voice. Phoebe smoothed the pamphlet down, running her eyes over the church's address.

"Should I be concerned?" she asked.

"I'm sure it's nothing." He brought his trash can up. Phoebe dropped the papers in, both the envelope and the pamphlet, trying to shake off the chill that had swept over her neck. "Run along now."

Phoebe nodded, taking her leave.

"Hey."

Rosalind looked up, her scribbling pen coming to a stop. She had been taking notes, copying out a roster of every employee at Seagreen Press. Under the guise of wanting to learn everybody's names, she had extracted an office-wide list from Jiemin, which—in her ever-humble opinion—she thought was a rather smart tactic.

"Hello," Rosalind replied, keeping her voice cool. She tucked the roster away, then switched to Russian before speaking again. "I almost wondered if you had stolen off with the file." Hours had passed since their little stunt with the filing room; it would be time to clock out soon. Jiemin was away from his desk. At the far side of the department, Haidi was leaning over Orion's cubicle, talking through a higher-up's agenda for the next week. "Let's see it."

Alisa slid something out from under her arm. Though it looked like a regular department folder, Rosalind opened it to find a smaller one tucked inside, stamped with a red CONFIDENTIAL.

"So," Alisa said. "Does your *husband* know about this?"

Rosalind shook out the second folder and retrieved the thin notepaper inside. It was written in Chinese, which meant she didn't have to waste time translating—she could read and copy at the same time. *Mobilize in the south. . . . River bypass . . . Mountains . . .*

A frown pulled at her lips. Wasn't this supposed to be about

Priest? This looked like a regular report on Communist movement.

"It's not his mission," Rosalind answered, still scanning the plan and rummaging for blank copying paper in her drawer. "Keep your voice down. I'm not entirely certain which languages he speaks. And what's with the emphasis?"

"Emphasis?"

"You took on an emphasis. As if to imply that he is not my husband, whom I love with every bit of my heart."

Alisa gave Rosalind a knowing glance. "Come on," she said. "I remember seeing you around with Dimitri Petrovich. You had a different way of looking at him."

The words on the notepaper immediately blurred, swirling and colliding as Rosalind's vision did a violent tilt. She felt her blood turn to slush. Then to ice, sharp points cutting gouges into her veins. "You saw . . . what?"

Dimitri Petrovich Voronin had become a rising favorite among the White Flowers after Roma Montagov's position took a turn for the worst. It made sense that Alisa would want to keep an eye on her brother's potential usurper; it made sense that, of all people, Alisa might have recognized Rosalind around the city with Dimitri while others hadn't, that Alisa had once caught sight of a happier Rosalind, who lived in ignorance and cruised by on faith.

But the thought of being associated with that other version of herself was horrifying now. *That* Rosalind was an enemy, someone she had to push farther and farther into the recesses of her mind, someone she could never think about too much lest she make a return. The Rosalind who was here today would never reacquaint herself with her former remnant; she was too busy trying to fix that girl's damn mistakes.

"I spied on everyone back then, don't worry," Alisa said. "It was only out of my own curiosity. I always kept my mouth shut." A beat passed. Alisa looked down, playing with the hem of her shirt.

"Maybe I shouldn't have. Maybe my brother would have stopped Dimitri earlier if I had told him what I saw."

Rosalind swallowed hard. She forced her vision to focus again. Her heart to beat again. It was nice of Alisa to leave the other half of the blame unspoken: Dimitri nearly destroyed the city because Rosalind had helped him. Dimitri acquired power amid revolution and set death and destruction on the city in the form of man-made monsters because Rosalind had found victims for him.

"And maybe I should have said something too," she determined quietly. "Maybe then your brother and my cousin would still be alive." When the printed words before her were legible again, she picked up her pen and started to copy them onto her own blank paper. "If there was an onus on anyone, it is on me, Miss Mon— Ivanova."

Alisa stayed unspeaking. She didn't look saddened as Rosalind did. Her expression was one of thoughtful contemplation, as though Alisa were considering something that Rosalind was not privy to.

"Don't be too hard on yourself," Alisa said eventually. "Juliette wouldn't want that."

Rosalind swallowed hard, busying herself with the second half of the notepaper.

Below are code names of Communist-aligned agents infiltrated into the Kuomintang:

Lion.

Gray.

Archer.

There was no time for her personal lament anymore. Rosalind tilted her head curiously.

"Have you read over this yet?" she asked.

"Of course," Alisa replied. She barely held back the clear *duh* that wanted to follow. "I saw the list of double agents. Given that only the code names are provided, I doubt your Nationalists will be able to do much with the information."

Unless they already have suspects, she thought. Rosalind folded up the notepaper, sliding it back into its small folder. That was the end of the missive. Though there was nothing about Priest, at least the Kuomintang would be interested in those three double agents. "Here. All yours."

Alisa took the file back. "Are you clocking out now?"

"Not yet." Rosalind rose from her seat. "I have a meeting with Ambassador Deoka before the day's end."

It wouldn't have been her job under normal circumstances, but after seeing how efficient she was in distributing her folders, Jiemin had given her his remaining tasks. Which included reporting in to Deoka and giving him the department report that Jiemin had written up.

Alisa nodded. Just before she turned to go, however, she hesitated.

Oh no, Rosalind thought. *Alisa Montagova*, please *don't apologize. . . .*

"If I upset you by bringing up Dimitri—"

"It's fine," Rosalind cut in at light speed. "It's . . . it's been a long time."

Four years. Whole lifetimes passing by. The city rebuilding under her feet. The streets repaved and cast over for new buildings to rise up with their chrome plating and silver inlays.

"A long time," Alisa echoed quietly. "But not for you."

Rosalind blinked in surprise; Alisa was already walking away, returning to her cubicle. Indeed—whole lifetimes had passed by, and Rosalind was still nineteen.

Before she could start thinking about her other misfortunes, Rosalind gathered the day's department report and made the trek to Deoka's office. When she knocked, it was clear through the muffle of the door that he was on the phone, but he called for her to enter anyway. Rosalind pushed her head through the door hesitantly. Deoka spotted her and waved for her to proceed.

He was speaking English. ". . . yes . . . yes, I know. They are only routine drills, so it shouldn't be a problem to enter through Zhejiang. They will be passing through Shanghai, but we can locate soldiers in the periphery of the city."

Rosalind tensed just as she was presenting the report. Thankfully, she recovered before a tremor could shake along the paper. Deoka turned to her and mouthed his thanks when he took it.

"Ah, it is no difficulty," Deoka continued on the phone. He thumped his hand on the heavy hardwood of his desk. "Listen, listen. China is a child who needs discipline. You will see no reason to challenge our acts. We are like a parent who spanks a naughty, spoiled child—stern yet sympathetic."

Don't react, Rosalind commanded herself. She forced herself to look elsewhere in the room, to the map of China pinned to his wall, but it only made her angrier to see the country laid out before him like some show prize. *Don't react. Leave. Now.*

If she lobbed a wad of spit at the ambassador right this moment, she was sure it would come out molten. As fast as she could, Rosalind made her exit, closing the door after herself with a click that took every muscle of control.

Rosalind pressed up against the wall, exhaling into the empty hallway. A *child* who needs discipline? That was a complete and utter *joke.* They had the longest continuous history of any country in the world. They had been around for dynasties upon dynasties.

And yet . . . and yet. When did imperialists care about history? All they wanted was to crush its conquests to dust: all the better to sweep them nicely into shape.

An echo of footsteps rang from her left, signaling movement coming up the stairwell. Rosalind didn't want to be sighted lingering, so she smoothed her hands down her qipao and headed back to the department. Jiemin had returned when she sidled into her seat again. The pen on her desk was almost out of ink: it had left a few smears on the wooden surface when she'd put it down. Jiemin leaned over without looking up from his book, passing her a tissue for wiping.

"Thank you," Rosalind said.

Jiemin turned a page. Rosalind rolled her eyes, wondering what could be captivating his attention.

Some of the street stalls liked to publish bootleg translations of crime fiction coming in from the West, those mysteries and whodunnits where the final chapter always unveiled the bad man. Maybe she ought to read some too; maybe it would help develop her spywork. The problem with this mission was that Rosalind wasn't trying to catch people in a whodunnit. She knew the *who*: people in this very building. Sooner or later they would isolate the names that were responsible. It was more the *for what purpose* and, for crying out loud, *why chemicals?* Was a gun too commonplace? Did they want the League of Nations to think the Chinese parts of the city had a stray needle problem and that was why it needed to be colonized? One would have thought they could better achieve their aims at destabilizing the city if they made it seem like gangsters were wreaking havoc again. If an imperial power was pushing at the borders, trying to invade, wouldn't it be more convenient to bring back the blood feud? Pretend that rival gangs were tearing the city in two again?

Rosalind leaned back in her chair, chewing on her lip. Dao Feng had given her this mission with the Kuomintang's hypotheses and guesses neatly packaged, but they had to know too it didn't make sense.

This was what they had confirmed: agents of the Japanese imperial agenda were killing civilians in Shanghai; these agents were targeting areas not under foreign control; these agents were injecting chemicals as their preferred weapon of choice; these agents were coming out of Seagreen Press.

It sure as hell gave the killings an easily identifiable pattern. But if the Kuomintang thought this was an attempt at laying the groundwork for an invasion, why did that need an easily identifiable pattern? One serial killer in the city was hardly a good enough reason to invade.

Then again, it wasn't like they needed a reason anyway. Manchuria was invaded because of a measly train track explosion.

Rosalind sighed. Maybe the Kuomintang were right, and maybe the Kuomintang were wrong. Maybe there was something else going on beneath the surface, and maybe there wasn't. Her job wasn't to care. She was their spy, not the brains of the operation. She just needed to follow instructions and get information. One part was already complete: she had found this file in record time. The rest couldn't possibly be any harder.

She retrieved the office roster from her desk drawer and got back to copying names.

22

"'ll meet you at home," Rosalind said to Orion, five minutes before the workday was set to end. She leaned over his shoulder, putting her mouth closer to his ear. "I have to see Dao Feng."

Orion looked surprised for a brief moment before nodding and reaching for something on his desk.

"Can you give this to him while you're at it? I've been meaning to send it through."

He didn't make any effort to cover the words from Rosalind when he passed her the folded note. It fell open, reading:

> **Oliver made an appearance in Shanghai. He's on the hunt for something. Be wary.**

"Your brother?" Rosalind blurted.

Orion turned around in his chair. "How do you know my brother?"

"It's as if you forget that your family is famous." Rosalind tucked the paper into her pocket, evading the question. "I'll pass it along. Anything else?"

"That's all." His chair squeaked as he leaned back, tapping her fingers in farewell. "Good luck."

A jolt shook along her hand. Rosalind made a quick fist to smooth away the effect, thinking little of it.

The sun had set minutes prior, and the air outside was turning brisk. Though it was a perfectly ordinary time to be leaving the office, she found herself glancing over her shoulder every few seconds as soon as she strolled through the main reception and out the front doors, kicking gravel while walking through the compound. Even once she left Seagreen Press's gates behind her, there was a watchful sensation creeping along her arms.

Rosalind crossed the road. At the intersection, she tried to hail a rickshaw, but it ran right past her, heading for a man on the opposite corner. There were no other rickshaws in sight. No matter. Rosalind pivoted on her heel, biting back her sigh. She could walk. Golden Phoenix wasn't far from here anyway. This was a prime time to be out and about, enmeshed in activity from every side, strangers brushing arms, eyes meeting once and then never again. Darkness approached at a steady pace, purpling the clouds. It was at this time that the streets and shops turned on their nighttime lights and threw open their evening services, when Shanghai turned from a city inhabited by people to a city inhabiting its people.

In the beginning, shortly after Rosalind was yanked back to life, the only way she could mark the passing of the days was the tangible shift that swept through at this hour. Yesterday and today, today and tomorrow—it was no longer the act of waking and rising that split the difference between those concepts, but how the smell in the air was suddenly turned new at night.

She circled around a tram light, turned past a parked car. When Rosalind was some distance into an alley shortcut, she heard an echo behind her. She paused. Looked over her shoulder the barest fraction.

She continued walking, and the echo resumed.

This time of the night was a picture to wander through, but wandering had its drawbacks. She was being followed.

"A single break," Rosalind muttered. "That's all I ask. It's not much!"

She picked up speed, swerving into the next alleyway. With her breath held, she skittered against one of the building awnings, pressing to the wall and holding herself quiet.

Seconds passed. Minutes. When Rosalind heard nothing more, she stepped out cautiously, her heels light on the concrete.

Then a bullet tore through the night, skimming her arm.

"Oh, *jeez*—" Rosalind broke into a run, bolting down the alley and making a quick pivot left. Her arm burned, her coat sleeve frayed and singed where the bullet had traveled. Though she clutched her fingers to the wound and drew startled yells from a strolling couple she barged between, the blood ran merely for the length of one alleyway before it stopped. Her coat rustled, jostling the file inside its lining when she removed her hand from her sleeve, her fingers wet.

Rosalind slowed on a busier street, furiously searching the alley that she had just run through. Multiple pedestrians gave her curious looks, swerving past her on the sidewalk and eyeing the rip in her sleeve. Rosalind wanted to yell for them to move away. To take shelter in case more bullets came tearing out from the dark and struck a target who wouldn't heal like she could.

"What do you want?" Rosalind whispered into the night. "Who are you?"

The chemical killer, her mind guessed first. It had to be. Why else would someone be shooting at her?

Suddenly a pair of hands grabbed her from behind.

"Hey—" With a vicious jerk of her elbow, Rosalind tugged her arm away, shoving her foot back in the same breath. Whoever the attacker was, they staggered away with a grunt, and Rosalind spun around to face them. Black hat. Black gloves. Loose black clothes. The only distinctive feature was a blue scarf, thick around their neck and looped enough times that nothing of their face was visible.

When the attacker moved forward again, they brought their gun out, and Rosalind glanced around in panic. Another bullet narrowly grazed her ear. Rosalind didn't know where the shot had landed, but she didn't want to test its mercy again. It was bound to hit someone, especially in the dark, when people couldn't even see that there was a fight going on.

"Enough," Rosalind hissed, catching the barrel of the gun. She forced the weapon away, tearing it out of the attacker's gloved hands, but the attacker didn't seem to care. In that pause, her attacker threw a punch at her stomach, and as soon as Rosalind flinched, they reached into the lining of her open coat.

The turn of events was so surprising that Rosalind didn't stop the attacker from ripping into her inner pocket and plucking her copied file away. At once, the mysterious attacker swooped for their gun and ran off, tucking the stolen information close to their chest before disappearing around the corner.

Rosalind was left to heave for breath on the sidewalk, winded and sore, unable to believe what had happened. She had been pursued for the *file*? At the very least, she had expected the killer that stalked the city.

"Bèndàn," Rosalind muttered, rubbing her stomach with a wince. Even without a copy, she had the short lines memorized. She touched her ear.

Who had that been? A Japanese agent taking their information back? A Communist agent securing the information that was theirs to begin with? Another Nationalist with an alternate mission?

Before the attacker could come back and Rosalind could actually receive an answer to her questions, she hurried away.

Orion opened the door to the passenger seat, sliding in smoothly and closing the door after him.

"You're early," he said. "Well done."

Silas shot him a glare from the driver's seat, pulling on the steering wheel and merging back onto the road. "For the final time, I am not your chauffeur. Don't praise me as if I should preen."

"I'm not praising you to see you preen." Orion glanced into the back, seeing the seats cleared and empty, save for one small paper bag. "I'm praising you to get a smile. Let's see it."

Silas bared his teeth rudely. He eased the vehicle to a stop at the red lights.

"This is the first time you've asked me to fetch you after work. Where's Janie?"

"With Dao Feng," Orion answered, digging into his pocket. "Can you take us to this location?"

In his hand, he unfolded a piece of paper, revealing an address written in cursive handwriting. Silas leaned closer to read the words before the lights flashed green and his attention returned to the road, his brow still furrowed down.

"That's Chinese jurisdiction. What business have you got there?"

"That's what we're going to find out. This is from Zheng Haidi, Seagreen's lead secretary. She said she had some burning information to offer me."

Silas seemed concerned—or at least more concerned than usual. "Does she suspect something of your identity?"

"That's the thing." Orion kicked his feet up on the dashboard. Without looking, Silas reached over with a brutal thud, whacking Orion's legs back down before he could get good footing. "Ouch—I don't think she's reporting to me as if I am a Nationalist. She said it concerned Janie."

Silas cast a look at the address again, then ducked his head at the windshield, reading a faraway street sign. When a rickshaw beside them surged ahead, Silas took the opening in the traffic and turned.

"And it's tonight?"

"In two days. At noon. I want to see the location first, lest it be a trap."

"A secretary setting a trap," Silas muttered. "What a line of work we do. Have you heard from Phoebe?"

Orion peered at the back again. He suspected that paper bag contained Phoebe's errands—as usual. "I cannot go two days without hearing from my demon sister. She said something about making cakes?"

"Muffins," Silas corrected. He paused, glancing away from the road briefly and catching Orion roll his eyes. "I called ahead to say I would be over with the jar of jam she wanted, but I got almost a minute of ringing before your father picked up instead."

"Did you have a nice chat?"

"I hung up immediately. What's wrong with you?"

Orion laughed, though he swallowed the sound when Silas pulled near the curb, coming upon the address. Turning serious, he pressed against his window, counting the numbered buildings before waving his hand for Silas to brake properly in front of a shabby hotel. They had arrived at the location.

"See anything?" Silas asked after a beat.

"It doesn't look like a secret Japanese base, if that's what you're asking." Orion turned away from the window. "But appearances can be deceiving. I suppose we shall find out."

Silas thinned his lips, starting the ignition again. "Your house now?"

Orion shook his head. "My apartment with Janie. I'll leave you and Phoebe to your muffin nonsense."

With a huff that baking muffins was not nonsense, Silas pressed on the accelerator and pulled away from the hotel.

———

"I was ambushed."

Dao Feng looked up as Rosalind barged into the private room, his brow furrowing immediately. *"What?* Are you all right?"

"I always am." Rosalind took her coat off and tossed it on the table, glancing at her left arm. The qipao sleeve underneath was burned too, expensive fabric curling with damage. "I saw the Communist file. Their deserter sold out three of their people, who—get this— are planted with *us.* Double agents."

"Oh?" Dao Feng had been getting out of his seat, but seeing that Rosalind was perfectly fine, he settled back down again, fingers drumming on the red tablecloth. "Nothing on Priest?"

"Nothing on Priest," Rosalind confirmed. "Only on Lion, Gray, and Archer."

Though he made no visible movement, there was a flash of surprise in Dao Feng's eyes. Surprise—then confusion.

Rosalind leaned forward, reaching for the teapot. She poured herself a cup, the little leaves swirling around the liquid.

"Do you recognize the code names?"

"There have been mutterings about a Gray in Zhejiang," Dao Feng replied, looking deep in concentration while he absorbed this new information. He reached for his briefcase, taking out paper and a pen. "He is of considerable infamy, so I'm struggling to comprehend how he could be planted in the Kuomintang without us knowing of his true Communist identity."

"Well, I don't think the information will be under wraps for long." She paused, taking a moment to sip her tea and consider how she would word what she was saying next without giving Alisa away. "I believe the Communists have retrieved the file too, so all our spies there will surely hear about the code name leak soon. Give me a sheet. I'll copy out the rest of what I remember."

Dao Feng stopped. He had been in the midst of starting his own note. "Do you not have the file?"

"Did you not hear me when I walked in?" On usual days, Rosalind didn't show her handler this much attitude. But she was tired and bloody, and it was possible there was a shard of something that had gotten stuck under her skin when it healed over because her shoulder hurt a little when she moved it. "I was ambushed. Someone took it. God knows who."

Dao Feng made a thoughtful noise. He didn't look fussed to have been snapped at. If Rosalind tried to get crankier, Dao Feng wouldn't get angry in response. He would only take her attitude and turn it into some lesson until Rosalind was bored to the point of calming down.

"Press lightly on the pen. It's running out of ink." He rolled the extra stationery toward her teacup. With an unintelligible grumble, Rosalind snatched the pen before it could clink against the ceramic and started to write, ignoring Dao Feng when he finished with his own note and loomed over her shoulder to watch her put down character after character. The moment she finished, he took the sheet and folded it up, joining it with his report and pushing both papers into a thin envelope.

"Can you drop this off?" he asked. "I am needed at another meeting elsewhere."

"If I must," Rosalind answered begrudgingly. There was a postal collection box around the corner from Golden Phoenix, a tall red entity that she passed each time she walked into the restaurant's alley entrance.

Dao Feng sealed the envelope. It was addressed to Zhabei, so Rosalind had to guess it was going to a command office there or to the house of a covert branch superior—either way, the information would move securely. No one had the power to go messing with official government correspondences anymore. Not like how the Scarlet Gang had forced the postal service to a halt while tracing down her letters to Dimitri, at last pulling back the veil on her treachery.

Rosalind shook her head quickly, clearing her mind. That cursed conversation with Alisa was really getting to her.

"One last thing." Rosalind took out the note from Orion. "From my husband."

Dao Feng scanned the short sentence, then gave a heavy sigh. It probably wasn't Rosalind's imagination that she spotted two extra wrinkles appearing at the corners of his eyes.

"Both of you are intent on delivering burdensome information today," Dao Feng muttered. "I will walk out with you."

They packed up—Rosalind gathering her coat and downing her cup of tea, Dao Feng picking up his briefcase and putting a hand on Rosalind's shoulder as they stepped out of the private room.

"You must keep those code names to yourself," he warned as they walked through Golden Phoenix. "It will be a danger should the other party know you hold anything that could uncover them."

"I know. Don't worry," Rosalind assured him. "My lips are sealed."

They exited through one of the side doors—Dao Feng held the plastic covering out of the way, letting Rosalind enter the alley first. She breathed in, filling her lungs with the night air. When Dao Feng ducked out too, he paused just outside the doorway, lighting a cigarette.

"I'm off," Rosalind declared. "You know how to find me should you need anything."

Dao Feng nodded, waving while he inhaled the smoke. "Get home safely, Miss Lang."

With a mock salute, Rosalind walked off, holding her coat tighter around herself. She was paranoid, suddenly, that she would pick up a tail again—with good reason, after the night she'd had. Her nerves were on high alert when she returned to the main thoroughfare and turned the corner for the postal collection box.

"You're strong," she whispered to herself. "An agent, a dancer."

She carried poison now. Fast-acting poison, sharp-bladed poison. She was not defenseless.

Rosalind pushed the envelope into the box, heard the *clunk* of it joining the loose mail inside, and bobbed up on her toes, pleased that she was done for the night.

Then a familiar shout rang out from the alley behind her.

Rosalind whirled around. "Dao Feng?" she exclaimed. "Dao Feng!"

Tā mā de. Her panic roared to life, stinging her heels as she ran back the way she had come, almost slamming into the alley wall when she didn't turn the corner fast enough. Her wrists sang with pain, smarting from the shock of barely catching herself against the bricks. She didn't pay them any mind. The alley had turned entirely silent.

"Dao Feng!"

Rosalind's eyes grew wide at the sight before her. Dao Feng was collapsed. He lay by the door into Golden Phoenix, having not moved a step from when she'd left him. And at the other end of the alley, another shadow was slipping away—the very same shadow with the dark clothing and the distinctive blue scarf wrapped tightly around their face.

The attacker disappeared. Rosalind remained rooted where she was. She couldn't comprehend what she had just witnessed: that very same pursuer from earlier having returned for another attack and leaving her handler lifeless on the ground. Weren't they only concerned with the file?

Had they *followed* her here?

Rosalind broke out from her stupor. She lunged forward.

"Please, please, please—" Rosalind crashed onto her knees beside Dao Feng. Rough concrete pressed sharply into her skin. "Please, please don't be dead—" She put her fingers to his neck. A pulse beat on. Weak and irregular, but there, nonetheless.

"Dao Feng, can you hear me?" she gasped.

She ran an inspection along his middle, searching for the site of the injury. She could stanch it. Hold it down until help arrived. Her heart was pounding so loudly in her ears that she could hear nothing else save her own breathing. But Rosalind saw no clear wound. No bullet hole. No signs of a stabbing. Perhaps the light of the moon was too weak. But what could *possibly* take a grown man down—

Her eyes latched on to his arm. Dao Feng's sleeves were pushed to his elbow. And right at the crook, there was a dot of red.

A sob echoed into the night. Rosalind didn't register that it was her making the noise until a second joined it. The chemical killings. It was here. And she was wasting time by crying instead of saving her handler.

"Help!" Rosalind screamed. *"Help!"*

23

Hospital lights always gave Rosalind a sickly feeling, even when she wasn't there for a problem of her own. The blue-white tint in the bulbs cast the whole corridor with a ghostly atmosphere, compounded by the fact that Rosalind was the only one sitting in the row of orange chairs, her legs crossed and her fingers tapping nervously against her lap.

"Janie!"

Rosalind leaned forward in her seat, tracking the figures as they came up the steps. Guangci Hospital was located on Route Pere Robert, otherwise called Saint Mary Hospital by the foreigners. Its wings were big, the rooms spacious. Each footstep echoed twofold, reverberating up and down the smooth walls. On her way in, she had passed the gardens, which spread so vastly around the hospital that the trek seemed endless, her heels sinking into the soft mud as she passed shrubbery and religious statues.

"Hello," Rosalind greeted tiredly. She dabbed her eyes, moving from inner corner to outer corner. By now they were certainly dry, yet she needed to check nonetheless. She had already scrutinized her reflection in the hospital windows and fixed her cosmetics, cleaning up the smudges as if nothing had been out of place to begin with. Other people didn't need to witness her weaknesses. Even she didn't want to see herself going through them, so why would they?

Orion walked to the seats, followed by his sister, then by a boy

Rosalind hadn't met before. She would guess this was Silas Wu.

"He's alive," Rosalind said before anyone could ask. She knew what they must be wondering.

"And stable?" Orion asked, dropping down next to her.

"For now. They wouldn't tell me much because I came in afterward to avoid suspicion on my identity." Rosalind gestured to the seats on her other side. "Don't you want to sit?"

Phoebe shook her head, signaling that she would stand. The boy hovering behind her smiled politely when Rosalind turned her gaze on him.

"I'm Silas," he offered, giving an awkward wave.

"The auxiliary unit to the mission—I know." Rosalind extended her hand. She wanted to be nicer when this was her first time meeting Silas Wu, but she barely had the energy to lift her arm, never mind do it with enthusiasm. "Janie Mead."

"Lovely to make your acquaintance." Though Silas shook her hand, he darted a quick glance at Orion in the process, his grip wary. If Rosalind weren't in emotional upheaval, she might even laugh over the fact that Silas seemed afraid, as if waiting for Orion to tell him off for touching her.

"She doesn't bite," Orion said, noticing the same hesitation.

"Yes, I do." Rosalind took her hand back, then curled her arms around her stomach. She turned to Orion. "I called an hour ago. What took so long?"

Her dear husband looked just as weary as Rosalind felt when he blew a breath up at his hair, getting the one strand out of his eyes. "I went home to tell my father first and get the news moving up the chain of command." He jerked a thumb at his sister. "Then I picked up a tail and a tail's tail; hence their presence."

"*Hey*," Phoebe and Silas countered in unison.

"I'm concerned too," Phoebe added. "I wanted to make sure Dao Feng is all right."

The nearest door thudded. Rosalind sat up straight, craning her neck to check if someone was coming, but it was merely the wind moving through the hospital and shaking the infrastructure. They wouldn't let her into the wing where they were keeping Dao Feng, but the door between the hallways had a glass window built into the middle. She had been peering through it every ten minutes.

"He's not all right," Rosalind said, leaning forward in her seat. She felt pinpricks of pressure starting at her eyes again. *God*. This was intolerable. She hated caring about people. The worst part was that she never even knew when she had developed genuine warmth for a person until they were put in trouble and distress reared its ugly head. Wasn't worrying about Celia enough? Why did her heart have to go making other ties too?

"You said over the phone that it was a chemical killing attempt," Orion prompted. There was disbelief in his tone.

"Yes," Rosalind replied. "The doctors told me that much before they slammed the door in my face, worrying that I was a journalist." She pricked her nails into her leg. The sting kept her alert. "I just don't understand. Golden Phoenix is French territory. Since when has the killer hit there?"

The hospital fell silent around them, Rosalind's question booming loud. Phoebe gave a small sigh. Silas began to pace.

"Why were you meeting Dao Feng tonight?" Orion asked a few moments later.

Dao Feng's instruction whispered into her mind immediately. *If you can help it, do not let Hong Liwen in on this.* But at this point Rosalind wasn't sure which direction her secrecy was supposed to extend. Dao Feng had been taken out of commission. What good was keeping secrets from Orion when he was her only remaining mission ally?

"He asked me to fetch a file out of Seagreen," Rosalind answered plainly. "There was Communist information sold out to the Japanese.

I'm sure rumors were already moving among the Nationalists about what the contents read, so we wanted to take a glimpse. At the very least, I got that intelligence moving before Dao Feng was—" Her throat closed up. She couldn't say it. He almost hadn't survived. If she hadn't heard his shout. If the restaurant owner hadn't hurried out when she'd screamed for help. If the car hadn't been called fast enough . . .

Orion nodded, assuring her without words that she didn't have to continue. Phoebe walked a small circle around the hospital corridor. Silas, his eyes tracking her absently, stood with his chin propped in one palm.

"As of this moment," Orion said when Rosalind remained quiet, "the Nationalists aren't quite sure what to do with us. They'll have to go through a few bureaucratic hurdles of clearance before Dao Feng's covert agents are placed under someone else. We're without a handler."

Rosalind blinked hard. She couldn't sit here anymore. She needed to move, or at the very least incline her head away so no one could see her expression. As Orion continued, she stood up, wandering over to the plastic newspaper stand opposite the seats.

"The only thing my father warned was that we keep a clamp on the news that Dao Feng has been injured. Once our political adversaries receive word that the covert branch is vulnerable, they will strike for sure."

Rosalind started to riffle through the topmost newspaper issues. They hadn't been updated in a while. Or perhaps the news had merely been running the same headlines for some time, in bold font, tall font, vivid black font. Some were from foreign presses in Shanghai, others from domestic papers.

MANCHURIA INVADED

JAPAN INVADES CHINA

JAPANESE SEIZE MUKDEN IN BATTLE WITH CHINESE

INCOMING WAR?

NORTHERN TERRITORIES UNDER OCCUPATION

"None of this," Rosalind muttered under her breath, "makes any goddamn sense."

The attacker who left the scene of the crime was the very same attacker who had chased after her earlier that night. They had pursued her for the file; they had tried to kill Dao Feng. So why not kill her, too?

"Were you there?" Phoebe asked suddenly.

Rosalind looked up, noting that the question was directed at her. "No," she said. "I ran back when I heard Dao Feng shout."

"How did *Dao Feng* of all people get bested?" Silas muttered.

Rosalind was wondering the very same thing. She had never been able to get a good hit on him during their training sessions. *Never.* Just as she was wondering how someone had known to take the file from her. Just as she was wondering how these two matters were related: the file thief being the very chemical killer terrorizing the city under Seagreen Press's instructions. Her head was hurting. When she fought the attacker, they hadn't seemed vicious. It was hard to explain. She hadn't *seen* the act committed on Dao Feng, after all. Had it been two different people? Had the figure with the blue scarf seen who attacked Dao Feng, then?

Rosalind crossed her arms, suddenly very cold. Another gale of wind moved through the hospital corridors. She felt watched. She felt entirely out of her depth, barely kicking to keep her head above water.

The door slammed. This time, it was an actual doctor coming through.

"You're still hanging around?" he asked, spotting Rosalind.

Phoebe hurried toward the doctor, clasping her hands together and taking over the show before Rosalind could say anything.

"The patient is my father," she breathed, the words running together so smoothly that Rosalind would never have known she was lying. "Please, I came over as fast as I could—"

"Even family relations cannot enter at the moment," the doctor interrupted, yanking off the stethoscope around his neck. He brushed by, looking harried. "The patient is in precarious condition. He'll be watched and the room under strict regulation until the toxins leave his system."

"There must be something you can tell us," Orion added, rising from the chair. "His recovery, or . . ."

The doctor was already moving down the stairs. "All I can tell you is *go home*. There is no fast recovery in a case like this."

Rosalind kicked her shoes off and tossed her coat onto the couch. It was creeping near two in the morning, a citywide fatigue thickening with the hour. Even if she never slept, the exhaustion of the day's events was catching up to her.

"Take the washroom first if you wish," she said to Orion, collapsing onto the couch and resting her forehead on her knuckles. She closed her eyes.

Orion shut the front door with a heavy thud and slid his shoes off beside hers. Though she couldn't see him, she felt his gaze shift to her, watchful while she rested.

"So, what are we going to do?"

Rosalind's eyes opened with a flutter. "With the washroom?"

"No, beloved." Orion shed his own jacket. He gave a deep sigh, then reached for the dimmer switch on the wall, lowering the brightness of the overhead bulbs so Rosalind wasn't squinting painfully. "With the disastrous state our government has found itself in."

"What *can* we do?" Rosalind asked. "We cannot pause the operation at Seagreen without inducing suspicion. Tomorrow is that fundraiser we are filling in for, no? We can only proceed onward until we have a new handler to report to."

"Heaven knows when that will be," Orion muttered, drawing nearer to the couch. Suddenly, before Rosalind could stop him, he dropped to a sudden crouch and reached for her elbow, pulling her arm toward him.

"Hey—" Her complaint died on her tongue. She glanced down, swallowing a curse when she realized what held his attention. Her qipao sleeve had been covered by her coat on their way home, but now the rip was stark. It was also soaked with blood from where the bullet had grazed her skin.

"You're injured," Orion said, alarmed.

"It's not as bad as it looks—"

Orion was already marching into the kitchen, calling, "I'll get a cloth. Hold still."

Merde, Rosalind thought frantically. *C'est une catastrophe.*

In that moment, Rosalind made a split-second decision. She wasn't ready to explain her healing. She didn't want to scramble for an unbelievable lie, have Orion lift the fabric and turn a suspicious look on her, knowing that there was no reason there should be a tear in her sleeve and blood drying underneath but no mark. They seemed to have come to such a precarious peace—something nearing an understanding. It would be a shame to lose it.

While Orion rummaged around the kitchen counter, Rosalind pulled a pin out of her hair—luckily, she hadn't worn her poisoned ones that day—and took a deep breath. Then, before she had time to flinch, she pressed the tip of the metal to her arm and re-created the wound, running an exact gouge through the damaged sleeve fabric.

The new injury burned like hellfire. She swallowed her scream, wiping the metal off quickly and shoving the pin back into her hair just as Orion returned with a wet cloth in one hand and bandages in the other.

"Wrap quickly," she instructed. "I . . . I hate the sight of blood."

Orion looked like he didn't believe her, if the frown he made was any indication. He sat down on the couch and gestured that he was going to unloop the top buttons on her qipao. When Rosalind turned her neck for him to go ahead, he had her collar loosened in seconds.

"Practice," Orion said jokingly. She didn't think he was joking all that much. Still, she didn't chase the conversation thread; she opted to watch him work, wary for the first sign of abnormality. As carefully as he could, Orion was peeling her sleeve down, wincing once the wound was exposed. The blood smelled noxious, like melted metal mixed with something burning.

"The bandage," Rosalind prompted, her heart picking up speed.

Orion adjusted the fabric of her qipao, bunching it around her arm so it wouldn't fall any lower. "I ought to clean it first—"

"I'll throw up on you," she threatened. "Don't think I won't."

He didn't listen. He examined the wound. "What did you say this was again? A stray bullet?"

"No," Rosalind corrected quickly. "Something in their fist when they tried to hit me. I swerved. Maybe a blade."

Orion made a vague noise. He brought the wetted cloth up and dabbed at the wound, cleaning away the dried flecks around the gash. Rosalind could already feel her skin stitching itself back together. Her agitation ratcheted her pulse to a rapid staccato, the sound pounding in her ears. It felt too much like her panic earlier that night. It felt like cold sweat at her neck and a bone-deep terror shaking her from head to toe.

"Cover it up," she seethed through her teeth. *"Now."*

"All right, all right." Orion pulled a strip of the bandage free, wrapping it gingerly around the wound. One inch, then another, covered by the dull white. The moment the gash was fully covered, Rosalind breathed a long sigh of relief. Orion must have taken the sound as comfort that the blood was out of sight, because he made a careful effort to spread the layer of bandages farther down, also covering the dried blood he hadn't managed to wipe off.

"You're lucky you have me," Orion said, winding the bandages to make a second layer. "It would have been impossible to wrap this on your own."

I wouldn't need to wrap it on my own, Rosalind thought. She watched him detach the bandage from the rest of the roll, tucking the end away carefully. His face was tight in concentration, a tiny bit of his tongue poking out. Rosalind almost smiled, but then Orion looked up, asking, "What?"

"Nothing."

"You were smiling."

"I didn't smile. Yet."

"Then you admit . . ." Orion trailed off, his hand tightening around her elbow. Only a minuscule fraction of a second passed before Rosalind gauged something was wrong, that there had been a dip in his voice before he stopped speaking. Her immediate assumption was that her bandage had slipped, that he had inevitably made the freakish discovery.

But when Rosalind looked down, her heart in her throat, the bandage was still in place. She blinked—once in her disorientation, then another time to actually see where his attention had gone.

Oh.

With her collar undone, the front and back of her qipao had separated along the shoulder seam. The fabric had folded low along her spine.

Her scars were in the open.

Rosalind held very, very still. For whatever absurd reason, she was afraid of his reaction, preparing for horror or disgust or some combination thereof. It didn't matter what he thought—the logical part of her maintained that fact stringently—and yet she had frozen, hovering in wait.

He loosened his grip around her elbow. She watched him lift that hand and touch his finger to the top of the nearest scar, smoothing along the raised tissue.

"Who did this to you?" Orion's voice was violently quiet. "I'll kill them."

All of Rosalind's nervousness dissolved, transforming into a short, delirious laugh. "It was a long time ago," she said. "There is no marital honor to defend there."

"*Janie.*"

The name had always sounded strange to Rosalind, but now it felt entirely wrong. Like Orion was chiding someone else for taking the matter so lightly. She almost wished he had her real name. Maybe it would make their partnership easier. Maybe she would trust him more. But she supposed that was the point—the Nationalists didn't want them trusting each other. They wanted her to keep an eye on him and report him at the faintest signs of traitorous behavior.

Rosalind tugged her qipao up. She put the top button back in, if only to hold the two sides together again, hiding the scars from view. "Drop it."

"If someone is hurting you—"

"I said *drop it.*"

Rosalind shot up from the couch. Orion did the same, following the two steps she took across the living room and hurrying in front of her to block her path.

"Look," he said seriously, "I know we're not actually married, but I'm not going to stand around if—"

"Leave it *alone*, Orion."

"Who would *do* something like that?"

Rosalind gritted her teeth. What was it like to sound so disbelieving? To live in a world where scars were only from injuries and mortal enemies?

"You really want to know?" She gave him a push. She had only intended to move him out of her way, but then he looked so taken aback that she pushed him a second time, forcing him to stumble against the hallway arch.

"My family," Rosalind spat. "My family did this to me."

They had whipped her. They had forced her to her knees and punished her, refusing to relent until her blood had soaked the burlesque club floor and she had passed out from the pain.

Orion's lips parted, a soft exhale breathed into the room. His stunned reaction gave Rosalind the immediate urge to hide, but there was nowhere to go. She could only reel back, cradling her hands close to her chest in case they went rogue and pushed him again—and again and again, until he was miles away.

"Why?" Orion whispered.

A simple question. As simple as life. Had she deserved it? She had caused misery by betraying her family—that much was certain. Even after they'd caught her and whipped her bloody, she hadn't given up Dimitri's identity.

Of course you deserved it, her mind liked to whisper during her quietest nights.

I hadn't known what I was doing, she would always try to refute. *I chose wrong. I wasn't beyond saving.*

All she had wanted was love. Somehow, she had gotten cruelty from every direction instead.

"Trust me," Rosalind said. "If there was something that could have been done, I would have done it myself. I am not defenseless."

Orion shook his head. "I don't think you're defenseless. I am incensed on your behalf, as someone who has grown to care about your general well-being. There's a difference, beloved."

Rosalind swallowed hard. She curled her fists tighter against her chest. As much as she was attempting an easy demeanor, her hands gave off a tremor and her cheeks felt hot.

"How nice of you." The words came out frosty. She couldn't help it. She was *trying* to sound kind. She tried so hard to be kind, and still, *still*—

"I'm not being nice. I'm covering the barest minimum of human decency." Orion seemed to give up, pivoting and walking into her dark bedroom. Once he entered the room, however, he dropped onto the bed and folded his arms at her, his expression wide and frank. He wasn't finished. He just had to do a dramatic location change first.

"Is that why you're working for the Nationalists?"

Rosalind didn't follow him into the bedroom, but she did walk up to its doorway, leaning against the frame. With greater distance afforded between them, her face was allowed to cool, her pulse allowed to steady. Orion hadn't even bothered turning on the ceiling lights over the bed. There was a single shaft of illumination coming in from the window, bleeding the streetlamp's white glow atop him.

"What?" she said. She forgot what he had asked.

"The Nationalists," he prompted again. "Do you work for them because you have nowhere else to go?"

"There are plenty of other places to go." Rosalind thought about the girls on the streets. The girls that were in abundance at every corner. "Restaurants. Bars. Dance halls."

"But no other place for the ambitious." Orion leaned back, ever casual in his disposition. He always lounged in such an uninhibited manner that one would think he owned the bed, owned the whole apartment. Some people simply had a flair for belonging in every space they entered, other people's bedrooms included. "No other place for the savior types."

Rosalind scoffed. "Then you speak of every agent. Of course we all have nowhere else to go. Who would allow themselves to be shuttled from one assignment to the next for the rest of their lives if they had a perfectly good home waiting?"

A long moment passed.

"Someone who believes they have a duty to fulfill," Orion answered quietly. It was hard to tell if his eyes had turned watery or if it was merely the dark playing tricks. Before she could make a conclusion, Orion tipped backward onto the bed, bouncing as he settled on the mattress.

"Are you talking about yourself?" Rosalind asked. She took a step forward.

"No," Orion replied in an instant. "Not myself."

Oliver, then, Rosalind guessed. Celia's smile materialized in her mind too. She supposed she had no argument. Those self-sacrificing agents did exist—people like Celia, people so dedicated at their core. Rosalind couldn't find that greater dedication in herself. And when she looked at Orion . . .

She had no place to say that he *wasn't* dedicated to a belief, but she did recognize something of herself in him.

"You have a home, do you not?"

At some point, Rosalind had started walking into the room, though she didn't fully register it until her knee bumped into the bed. Orion glanced to his side, and, finding Rosalind to be nearby, he reached for her wrist and gave a short tug.

Rosalind folded herself down next to him. There was no reason for them both to be lying along the bed's short side—half their bodies sprawled off the edge—when they could have easily adjusted, yet they remained without complaint.

"I have a home," Orion agreed. He turned his face toward her. "But it is not good."

Rosalind kept her eyes trained on the ceiling. She knew she

was being observed. She felt it, like a phantom touch.

"Is it big and glamorous?" she asked. The Scarlet house prodded at her memories. Maids and cooks and servants leaving one after the other as the family coffers ran drier and politics turned more dangerous. "Are there rooms that should be filled sitting empty and forlorn instead?"

"Yes."

Orion returned his gaze to the ceiling. Together they might have made a still-life painting, rendered as symmetric shadows that stared up into nothingness.

"I tried to hold on," he continued softly. "But that only made it fall apart further. Now preservation is all I have left. It's not a home, not really. It's an image I've trapped under museum glass, put on display for my visitation every so often."

He cared enough to make the preservation effort, at least. Rosalind didn't know if she had simply never made the attempt or if she had never possessed the power to put her home under a glass case. She had always been the afterthought, the tacked-on side cousin. She was not the heir. She didn't have the family name.

She didn't have the right to preserve its golden years. Those golden years had never been hers.

Slowly, Orion sat up. He peered at Rosalind, who blinked in his direction.

"What are you thinking?" he asked.

She reached to touch her bandaged arm. Though she grasped the injury site carefully, she could feel that the wound had already smoothed over underneath. It was a waste of bandages. A waste of time and attention that could have been used elsewhere.

"That Tolstoy was wrong when he said every unhappy family is unhappy in its own way." Rosalind let go of her arm. "We're all the same. Every single one of us. It's always because something isn't enough."

Orion reached for her bandage with a *tut*, readjusting the part she had moved. She wondered at what point he would make the realization that she didn't merit the fuss. Sooner or later he would. They all did.

"*Anna Karenina* is hardly a novel to take a life lesson from."

"Just humor me, Orion," she said, her voice faint.

A sigh. She couldn't interpret what that meant. She only felt the brush of Orion's fingers against the top of her ear, tucking a curl of her hair back before he got to his feet.

"Good night. Don't sleep on that arm."

When Orion exited her bedroom, closing her door after him, Rosalind almost wanted to call him back. There was something nice about their conversation, even if it had started tense. There was something about breaking through that initial wave of righteousness and anger, settling on understanding instead. But calling him back required effort, and Rosalind had none remaining. All she could do was turn onto her side, pressing down on her arm, and stare into the darkness, hoping that Dao Feng would survive.

"Did we go after the head of the Kuomintang's covert branch?"

Papers rustle in the room, rapid leafing and booklet searching. "No."

"Then why is he in the hospital for an alleged chemical killing?"

The room turns colder. The night outside is vibrant with neon, and with only a desk lamp inside, the red and gold bleed in through the window, leak along the lotus wallpaper.

"I—we didn't do anything tonight. Our killer is—"

"I know. Go see what this is. Report back."

The door closes. The building shudders. And the night carries on, taking no side in this plot unraveling in the city.

24

I n the morning, Rosalind stirred her coffee tiredly, poking her nose around the break room cupboards. She spotted a carton of milk near the back, but it took only one sniff to know it was sour. *Yuck.* Only Westerners were going to change these out, and there weren't enough of them here to use the communal spaces. At least the office provided milk to begin with. She gathered that most of her Chinese and Japanese colleagues weren't accustomed to drinking it like she was, pouring a generous dollop into her coffee every morning as a pretentious Parisian twelve-year-old. Tea leaves, on the other hand, were well stocked in every cupboard, from fresh tins to freeze-dried packets.

With a grimace, she dumped the sour milk into the sink. The liquid swirled and swirled, draining down the metal basin. Rosalind would have wasted another minute merely staring at the hypnotic motion if she had not heard footsteps heading her way. She tossed the carton. Turned around with a completely changed demeanor, then picked up her mug, taking a sip right as Alisa Montagova walked in.

"Hello," Rosalind greeted cheerily.

Alisa stopped in her step. She glanced over her shoulder, a look of utter fear crossing her face. "What?"

"I was saying hello. I cannot say hello?"

"Not like *that*. What happened?"

Rosalind supposed there was no point beating around the bush about it. "Did you tell your superiors that I had a copy of your file?"

"No, of course not," Alisa answered at once, reaching to open a cupboard. She fetched a pink mug with cat ears on the rim. "I don't have a death wish."

"Did they say anything at all about Nationalist agents at your workplace?"

Now Alisa's frown was growing deeper. "I imagine my superiors *know* the Kuomintang are installed here too," she said, "but my job is to keep an eye on what missives reach Japanese officials. I'm to stay one step ahead of Japanese interference in Party affairs, not aid our civil war. There's no reason to mention it. In fact, it's dangerous to give me information in case I'm captured."

Rosalind leaned against the counter, thinking. She believed that. There was no reason Alisa would report more than she needed to.

"Someone robbed me of my file copy last night," Rosalind explained, dropping her voice. The corridors outside allowed for eavesdroppers, so she needed to be careful. "No less than half an hour later, my handler was hit by the chemical killings, and I saw the same mysterious person lingering nearby."

Alisa took the information in coolly, but a little notch appeared between her eyebrows, like a crescent moon.

"Is he dead?"

Rosalind shook her head. "He survived, but he has not awoken." She clinked her little spoon against the side of her mug. "I wonder if it was a mimicry. If it was a Communist hit, not Japanese."

That was what she had spent last night mulling over. Why had the same attacker appeared once to steal the file and again as Dao Feng lay unconscious in the alley? The Japanese didn't know that Rosalind had taken it. Their spy networks were not good enough to have heard it by some whisper—that much she was certain. On the other hand, the Communist spy networks *were* good enough for the task to have leaked.

Either that, or a Nationalist had done it.

"There's no way it was us," Alisa stated without hesitation. "We wouldn't be foolish enough to go after your handler. Do you think we would risk active warfare within the city? Our numbers are low enough as it is."

"But I cannot think of any other explanation," Rosalind returned. "It is not hard to mimic the chemical killings—we know that from experience."

Dao Feng had been targeted in French territory. Just as Alisa had left Tong Zilin's body on Thibet Road, in the International Settlement. It did not fit the modus operandi of the other attacks: those bodies were littered across Chinese jurisdiction, targeting the nameless and masses.

"He's in the hospital?" Alisa asked.

Rosalind nodded, setting her mug in the sink.

"Then that means there are real doctors looking at his injuries. Doctors who can see it *is* chemicals that tried to kill him, not a mere pinprick made on his arm as our mimicry was. Come on, Miss Lang. Use your head."

Alisa did not pour herself any coffee. She dug into the very back of the cupboards and pulled out a box of orange juice instead. She looked content with her explanation; Rosalind was still chewing on the thought.

"Can you do some digging?"

Alisa paused, her orange juice midpour. "I beg your pardon?"

"Around the Communists," Rosalind clarified. "Find out if it was your people that plucked the file copy from me."

"Da ladno," Alisa muttered under her breath. "Absolutely not. I'm not sticking out my neck like that."

"It could be linked to the killings across Shanghai. Don't you want to put a stop to it? To innocent people dying on the streets?"

"Sure," Alisa answered plainly. "But you just said you think your handler's attempted killing was mimicry."

"I don't *know*. That's why I'm looking for answers anywhere I can."

Alisa took a deep drink from her mug. With her cheeks puffed out, she shook her head vigorously. "Forget it," she said after gulping the juice down. "I'm not turning double agent for you."

"I'm not asking you to turn double agent. I just want a little investigating."

"Are you going to pay me?"

"*Pay* you? You are definitely not lacking any money."

"Ummm . . . you don't know that. My brother could have been an extravagant jewelry buyer who blew through the family budget years ago."

Rosalind massaged her temples. "Alisa Montagova, I swear to God—"

A loud shout rang through the second level. At once, both Rosalind and Alisa exchanged a frown, then hurried into the corridor to see what the disturbance was. A commotion came from the stairwell; then a host of uniformed police constables appeared in view, proceeding onto the third floor.

"Oh, no," Rosalind muttered, hurrying away.

"Hey, wait," Alisa hissed. "Where are you going?"

Rosalind didn't respond. She hastened up the stairs right after the clump of constables, pausing by the department doors in time to see the uniformed inspector stop by Jiemin's desk, declaring, "We're going to need to question your department. We're investigating the murder of one Tong Zilin."

Gasps shot through the office cubicles. While muttering and whispering began among her colleagues, Rosalind observed the inspector carefully, then ran her eyes along the constables that had accompanied him. The Shanghai Municipal Police used to be deeply infiltrated by Scarlet payoffs and bribes; even with the Scarlets merged with the Nationalists, old habits died hard. The police force was still run by guānxì and underhanded exchanges all through the International Settlement. Most constables were simply lazy men holding a title, turning a blind eye to businessmen and keeping the city in line just well enough for its politicians to hold the stage and its foreigners to profit. What did they care about justice? They only wanted cases closed so they could go home.

"What is going on?" Deoka appeared at the doors of the department, his hands behind his back. Rosalind inclined her head and moved aside, though Deoka hardly noticed her presence as he walked past. "We don't look kindly upon disturbances. . . ."

"It shall not take long, Ambassador," the inspector replied. "We have evidence that suggests Mr. Tong's colleagues were the last people to see him alive. It may help us put together what happened."

A quiet smattering of footsteps sounded up the stairs. Alisa had arrived too, coming onto the third floor to witness the scene. With the more the inspector talked, the more the whole department shifted in their seats. Rosalind saw glances exchanged and shaking hands steadied in laps. She saw terror upon parted lips and noses twitching in distaste. Which reactions were markers of guilt? Which of the faces before her were shocked because they had been partners-in-crime with Tong Zilin while passing on instructions from above, resting easy at night thinking there would be no consequences and now doubting what had been certain?

"All right," Deoka said, extending an arm to welcome the constables toward the cubicles. "So long as you do not disturb our work."

Rosalind took a step forward, catching the inspector's attention. Out of her periphery, she saw Orion shoot to his feet, concerned that she was about to do something rash. And he didn't even *know* that she was the one who'd killed Zilin—what little faith he had in her.

"Mr. Tong is dead?" Rosalind gasped, feigning shock. "Why, I saw him just that night with—" She turned around, eyes landing on Alisa and lifting her hand to her mouth as if she needed to stop herself from speaking.

The inspector nudged two of his constables out of his way, coming nearer.

"Go on."

"Oh, I'm not sure . . ."

Alisa marched in Rosalind's direction, her eyes wide. "What are you doing—"

"Please," the inspector prompted, "do continue."

Rosalind skittered a step away from Alisa, her arms tightening around herself. "Well, I thought I saw Liza Ivanova talking to Tong Zilin outside of Peach Lily Palace. It must have been some days ago. But that couldn't possibly have anything to do with his death, right?"

From the cubicles, Orion was visibly trying to catch her attention, trying to figure out what she was doing. And Alisa—Alisa was so taken aback that she said nothing. She could only stare at Rosalind with her jaw agape, thrown by the betrayal. They both knew that Zilin's body would have been found outside Peach Lily Palace, which was not public information. Throwing that little tidbit around was as good as being caught red-handed.

The inspector was already moving, waving a few of the constables along. "Liza Ivanova, if you could come back to the station with us and answer a few questions, that would be ideal. Ambassador, I don't think we need to have any conversations here after all."

"What—" Alisa resisted for the briefest second when the constables started to lead her away, but she must have figured it was better to seem scared and cooperative. As the inspector walked toward the door, pausing to give Deoka his farewell, Alisa glanced back once more, her brows furrowed in sheer stupefaction. It was her word against Rosalind's now, Alisa seemed to realize. She resolved her expression into blankness, following the police out.

The department remained idle for a long moment. Then Deoka clapped his hands. "Back to work! Come on!"

At the front desk, Jiemin turned back to his book. At the cubicles, the assistants took their seats once more and the interpreters ducked their heads into their sheets, scrambling to look occupied while Deoka walked past them to exit the main department and return to his office. Only Orion scraped his chair back, coming to Rosalind and putting an arm around her to give her an embrace, pretending she needed the reassurance. In reality, he was using the maneuver to put his mouth against her ear and whisper, "Why did you do that?"

"Tell the truth?" Rosalind murmured into his neck.

"No." Orion's grip tightened on her shoulders. "Tell *me* the truth, darling. Who is Liza Ivanova?"

Rosalind tipped her head up, a small, scheming smile twitching at her lip. "She's working for the Communists." From outside the windows of Seagreen Press, there was the loud bang of a car door closing. "But I think we can give her a push to bring her into our task."

Phoebe twirled in front of her full-length mirror, tilting her head to get another angle on her long skirt. This belt didn't fit perfectly, but her other one was silver, and she wasn't going to match *silver* with the gold hem. Maybe she would get another but in green. Or perhaps pale pink. Or maybe . . .

The phone rang downstairs. She heard Ah Dou's slippers shuffle along the second-floor landing as he hurried to the living room. Phoebe continued rummaging through her closet, trying to complete her outfit for tonight. She rarely associated with her schoolmates, given her horrible academy attendance, but she heard they would be at Park Hotel after nine, and she loved making appearances. Dip in and dip out, let them see how she was flourishing without contributing any more information to add to gossip. Her father called her naive when she insisted she wouldn't need those ties. He always said the city was run by those who knew the right people and those who held information on the right people— even if she didn't care to learn in school, she needed to go if only so her cohort would remember her name.

It was the only way she could make something of herself, allegedly. Phoebe didn't know how much she believed that, but she *did* want to make something of herself. So she supposed she would keep those social circles running outside the academy.

"Phone for you, Miss Hong."

Phoebe hurried to her bedroom door, opening it to find Ah Dou standing patiently. "For me?"

Ah Dou nodded. "Careful with the floor. It's a little slippery."

"You clean too often," Phoebe said, breezing by him. "Take some more rest!"

Her sock-clad feet were light on the stairs, hurrying down with nary a sound. She was always refusing to wear her slippers, which was probably what encouraged Ah Dou to clean so often, else she would be turning all her white socks gray. Obviously he was the one who would have to deal with that when it came to laundry day, so his precautionary measures were understandable. Despite Ah Dou's warning about the clean floors, she still almost slipped near the living room table, narrowly catching herself by grabbing onto the phone cord.

"Hullo?"

"Stop answering the phone in English. How many times have I told you that?"

Phoebe rolled her eyes, tipping backward onto the couch and

tugging the cord over. She dragged her legs up, resting her chin on her knees while she propped the receiver against her ear.

"If Father's colleagues want to gossip about our upbringing, they can do so freely," Phoebe replied. "What can I help you with, gēge?"

Orion, on the other side of the line, breathed a sigh. "I have a favor to ask of you. I would do it myself, but Janie and I must attend a fundraiser for Seagreen tonight and fill in for the writing staff."

"Ooh." Phoebe perked up, thudding her feet back onto the floor and adjusting her skirt. "Do tell. Shall I accost a politician? Seduce a pretty girl? Decode a telegram?"

"I worry about what goes on in that mind of yours." There was a rustle on Orion's end, then a feminine voice snapping at him. Phoebe made a little smile, guessing it was Janie telling her brother off. As he deserved.

"Tell Janie I say hello," Phoebe said.

The rustling stopped, bringing Orion's attention back to the phone. "Janie already thinks I'm enough of a menace without you adding fuel to the fire. Be ready at the door in half an hour. Silas is picking you up to begin the operation."

"Operation!" Phoebe crowed, her excitement rising. "You still haven't told me what I'm doing. If you build this up as a whole thing and it turns out I'm only fetching some package . . ."

Orion sighed again. The sound was almost loud enough to be a groan. "It's your lucky day, mèimei. How do you feel about taking part in a jail break?"

25

As soon as Orion finished his phone call, Rosalind started prodding him, urging him to hurry lest they run late for the fundraiser. If they missed the preliminary speech, then their article would be missing its opening remarks, and if they were only doing this to get a higher footing at Seagreen, then they would need to do the job well.

"Hey, hey, don't frown at me," Orion said, hurrying out of the bedroom with only one arm shoved in his jacket. "You're the one trying to break Liza out of the police station, and I'm the one spending precious time finding resources for your plan."

"You're sending your sister," Rosalind returned. She reached for the other sleeve of his jacket, providing her help since he clearly needed it. "It is hardly the royal battalion. Besides, if you hadn't signed us up for this assignment, I could do it instead."

Orion lifted his brows. He smoothed his jacket down. "You could single-handedly break into a police station?"

Rosalind didn't hesitate. "Yes."

"Beloved . . ." Orion trailed off with whatever other nonsense was waiting in his mouth. Now that his jacket was on, his next task appeared to be struggling with his cuff links.

Barely holding back her insult, she whacked his fingers out of the way and plucked the links from him. "Every day you come closer to driving me off the deep end. Let me do it."

Orion offered his wrists without protest. Carefully, Rosalind folded his sleeve cuffs down, then set the link in, delicate with her touch so that she wasn't wrinkling anything. When she finished, Orion was watching her, visibly holding down a smile.

"What?" she demanded.

He shrugged, but the smile only grew wider. "You're acting like a real wife."

Rosalind narrowed her eyes. "No 'thank you,' only sarcasm. So ungrateful. What would you say if I were really your wife?"

"That's easy." Orion popped his collar, then opened the door for her. "I would kiss before I spoke."

Rosalind felt her face burn. She marched past him, her shoulders rising to her ears, and stomped out the door.

The fundraiser was being held at a mansion on Bubbling Well Road.

Rosalind took a sip of her drink, reading through the notepad in her hand. The champagne was flat and bitter, leaving a bad taste in her mouth after it went down. She smoothed her tongue along the back of her teeth, grimacing. Maybe it was all the smoking she'd done when she was sixteen, burning out her taste buds. Maybe the fundraiser head, Mr. George, was providing cheap, flavorless champagne because his accounts were running dry and he was only fundraising for this charity so he could embezzle the money away. Both were likely explanations.

"I see another colleague I can talk to. How is the note-taking?"

Orion returned to her side, a new drink in his hand. The fundraiser had finished with its speeches, so the event had turned to socializing. Under the garden lights, his hair looked like it had been brushed with gold. Rosalind passed her drink to him too, freeing her hand to flip through the notepad. A woman was trying to push between them politely, and without looking up, Rosalind stepped aside, opening a path through the grass.

"We have everything we need. Whenever you're ready."

They had wanted to kill two birds with one stone: report on the fundraiser and make progress with their mission by talking to the few other Seagreen colleagues who were in attendance tonight. Rosalind had been writing everything they needed for their article; Orion had been doing the people-pleasing.

"Give me a few minutes, then," Orion said. "I need to—"

Rosalind snapped her notepad closed. A middle-aged man appeared before them suddenly, giving a nod to the conversation partner he had departed from. He was dressed in a Nationalist military uniform. The medals of a general hung from his jacket. It didn't take Rosalind long to decipher the man's identity, especially when Orion fell quiet.

"General Hong," Orion greeted, snapping out of his surprise to fake unfamiliarity. "Fancy seeing you here."

"A pleasure to see you again," General Hong returned. They shook hands briefly, a rapid series of questions passing through their frowns: *What are you doing here?* thrown from father to son and then *Business, of course!* conveyed in return.

General Hong shifted his attention to Rosalind. "This is . . . ?"

"My wife," Orion answered. "Remember?" Another unspoken exchange happened over Rosalind's head. Did his father not *know* about his mission?

"Ah, yes," General Hong said in a manner that indicated he had not in fact remembered. "Why have I never seen your lovely wife before?"

Rosalind kept her expression blank. He probably had; she must have walked past plenty of Nationalist generals when she still lived in the Scarlet house.

"You two chat," Orion said abruptly, prodding Rosalind forward and returning her drink to her. "I have a colleague to greet."

Before Rosalind could protest, Orion had disappeared. She considered calling him back, but he looked as if he was using the excuse to slip away, unwilling to have a conversation with his father while she was hovering around. She recognized that tone—it was the same one she used to take on when her father started proposing his wild ideas, like moving cities or quitting business. A level volume, careful to signal her displeasure without taking it too far to be a brat. Careful not to rock the boat, even though each word screamed: *Why can't you be better?*

"I only returned to the city recently," Rosalind answered once Orion walked off. She watched him pause near a Frenchwoman from production and launch into lively conversation. "I am yet to completely reacquaint myself with everything here."

"I remember now," General Hong said. "An American returnee, is that right? Did you have supervision there?"

Rosalind's jaw tightened. It was a simple enough question, but there was a thorny reminder laced into the words. Her current undercover persona should have been one of flippancy: some careless girl who had come of age amid the parties and debauchery in New York. But that was too close to someone else she had once known, and she couldn't play the role thoroughly enough. The real Rosalind thought going to big parties was only fun if you enjoyed getting your pockets picked.

"Plenty of supervision," Rosalind replied easily. "Where else would I have acquired such nice manners?"

General Hong didn't laugh.

"You have known Liwen for long?"

"Not long." Rosalind faltered. She wasn't sure if he was asking under the guise of their fake marriage, or if he was genuinely asking how long she had known his son. "He is . . . good at his job."

It wasn't a lie. In fact, it was the only entirely truthful thing that she could think to say.

But General Hong tilted his head curiously. "Oh?" he said. "No need for exaggeration, dear."

"It's—" Rosalind scratched her wrist. She tried for a smile. "General Hong, it's not an exaggeration. I do mean it."

"Then I suppose he has you fooled. He cares little past anything trivial."

Rosalind held in a sharp breath. "General Hong—"

He was not finished. "You'll see soon, I suppose. He will jump from girl to girl, embarrass you plenty, and then take boys to bed too. What do you defend him for? I don't know why he is intent to work this job when he cannot take it seriously."

So they were talking about Orion as Orion now, not as his cover. Rosalind would be lying if she said she had never doubted his abilities too, but it was a whole other matter to hear it said aloud and from his own father, no less. Almost instinctively, Rosalind's gaze moved to where Orion stood talking with the Frenchwoman. His father, too, peered over his shoulder to examine the scene a few paces away.

"He has never known how to do anything but play, and we indulged him while he was young. Now he is my remaining heir, and he won't partake in society responsibly. He *has* to go be the hero. He *has* to take covert role after covert role."

"General Hong," Rosalind said very faintly. "Why are you telling me this?"

"I warn you out of generosity," he said. "So that you can protect yourself."

You warn me for control, Rosalind thought in correction. It was always about control: over the narrative, over what he thought was his to order around. He didn't think Orion ought to play a covert role when that forsook the role of being the dutiful heir to an elite family, the second son who was his father's last chance of leaving a legacy after the eldest turned out to be a disappointment.

"Please excuse me." Rosalind tipped her glass, where there was a mere gulp of liquid remaining. Indicating that she was going to fetch another, she extricated herself smoothly, stepping past the general and walking away.

I don't need your warning, she wanted to call back, but her eyes were pinned on Orion nevertheless, watching him talk to the Frenchwoman with a heightened sense of wariness. She didn't walk toward the refreshments. She moved closer to her husband, coming within earshot of his conversation. Orion hadn't noticed her approach. In fact, he hadn't glanced over in a while, as he had earlier in the night each time he thought one of their colleagues was acting suspicious, meeting her eyes from afar so that Rosalind could make a note of it with her pen too.

Orion lifted his hand, touching the woman's shoulder. Rosalind listened harder. It didn't sound like they were talking about politics or governments or the usual topics that gauged a colleague's relationship to the terror plot. They were speaking French, discussing . . . *jewelry?*

"—these diamonds don't suit your complexion as well as they could. You need a ruby or two to complement your natural blush."

His hand moved away. He glanced up at the same moment, making the briefest flicker of his eyes. Though he sighted Rosalind, he did not acknowledge her. Rosalind almost couldn't believe it. That she had been defending him to his father, and now he was doing precisely what General Hong had accused him of, flirting unabashedly *right* in front of her. Hot irritation swept down her neck, so intensely that her skin itched.

The Frenchwoman spotted Rosalind too. Unlike Orion, her attention did not immediately swivel away. She turned fully in Rosalind's direction.

"Isn't that your wife?" she asked him. Her lips quirked up. "Perhaps you should tend to her."

"It's no matter," Orion replied. His eyes locked with Rosalind's again. It was only then, seeing the easiness in them, that Rosalind realized what was going on. Orion thought she had no idea what he was saying. The Frenchwoman was smirking because she thought Rosalind was standing there cluelessly, some laughingstock at the mercy of monolingualism.

Don't say anything, she ordered herself. *Ignore it. Turn around and get a drink.*

"Rumor has it that you were arranged to be married. Is it true?"

Orion scoffed. "Don't listen to rumors. We only have an understanding. My wife won't stop me from admiring others—"

Oh, forget it, Rosalind decided viciously, marching forward. He already knew she spoke Russian. What was one more language on top of that? It was his own fault for assuming she didn't speak a language that most of the elite in this city learned.

"Sans blague! You should have told me earlier that you were running low."

Rosalind swept in front of Orion, plucking the champagne flute out of his hand so that the glass clinked against her own. She didn't know whose eyes grew wider: Orion's or the woman's. Rosalind turned to the woman.

"La musique crée une sympathique atmosphère de fête, non? Aimes-tu le jazz?"

There was no chance to respond; nor was it a real question. Rosalind's tone was laced with venom, hardly hearing the music she was speaking about. She inclined her head. "Pardon. Let me go fetch a refill."

And with her throat burning with pettiness, Rosalind pivoted on her heel and marched away.

They had one job. *One job,* and Orion couldn't pay attention.

She slammed the emptied glasses down on the refreshments table. Out of the corner of her eye, she thought she saw General Hong hovering around again, but by the time she turned to look, he was being summoned away to the far side of the garden.

"Janie."

Rosalind sniffed. She inspected her nails. "Oui?" Now that she had shown her hand, she did not care to soften her blow. Without waiting for Orion, she tucked her notepad close to her chest and turned to go.

"Attendez."

Rosalind, civilly, halted on his instruction. She watched Orion cycle through a host of expressions, not bothering to conceal a single one as he walked closer. He spun through disbelief to shock to understanding—and settled, at last, on intrigue when he finally stood before her.

"Darling," he said slowly. He was still using French. *Ma chèrie.* "What else are you hiding from me?"

"That depends." Rosalind's posture had taken on the stiffness of a predator, ready to pounce. "How many foreign women are you going to embarrass me in front of?"

"Am I only limited to women?"

Rosalind reached out, intending to land a slap worthy of his insolent remark, but Orion caught her arm before her palm could strike. He grinned. Across the garden, though the Frenchwoman had been watching before, she now averted her eyes, hurrying away to find another conversation partner. *That's right,* Rosalind thought. *Flee.*

"Unhand me," Rosalind instructed.

Orion did not unhand her. "Jealousy is a good look on you."

"It is not *jealousy*," she hissed. "You are supposed to be married to me, do not forget. If you insist on public philandering—"

"*Philandering!*" Orion exclaimed. "I was only speaking to her—"

"And what did you garner?" Rosalind demanded. "Do we think she's a part of the scheme?"

Orion loosened his grip on her wrist, only so that he could slide his hand along her arm, the movement almost sensual. He leaned in, bringing his lips near her ear, bringing the heat of his breath and the warmth of his skin.

"I apologize," he whispered. He had switched back to Chinese. "I promise you have my whole heart, until its last beat—"

Rosalind shoved his chest. "It's time to go. Get the car." She turned, treading through the grass in the direction of the mansion's front gates. Though she had a head start over Orion, he caught up easily, striding on his long legs.

"Come on," he insisted. "Don't get mad, beloved—"

Rosalind held her hand up, the notepad crinkling under her other arm. "Don't speak to me."

"*Janie*. It meant nothing! It was mere foolishness!"

He continued on and on until they got to the car, though Rosalind didn't grant him anything in response. His pleas only proceeded to grow more ridiculous. When she slammed the passenger door after herself, Orion went as far as to ask if she would like to hit him to make her feel better. Though she figured hitting him probably *would* make her feel better, she only tossed the notepad to the floor of the car and folded her hands in her lap, commanding, "Drive, Orion."

He watched her warily. "Are you truly upset?" he asked, pulling out of their parking space. His tone had switched. As gravel scattered beneath the car, making loud popping noises, it seemed to occur to him that Rosalind might not be exaggerating an act.

Rosalind bit down on her molars. She heard her teeth scrape together. "Your father decided to offer me a warning just then," she said. "Said that I ought to protect myself from you and your trivial nonsense."

The car fell into silence. Orion tightened his grip on the steering wheel, watching the intersection that was rapidly approaching. They were driving down a residential block, so the streets were mostly emptied.

"You know"—Orion stepped on the accelerator—"it does get tiring sometimes. That I only joined the covert branch to help my father's standing within the Nationalists after he was accused of treason, but he thinks I'm doing worthless work and wasting my energy every time I go undercover. And guess what? Now the Nationalists think we're *both* Japanese spies! There's just no winning."

A pang struck Rosalind's heart. So he knew that the Nationalists didn't fully trust him. Much as she didn't want to relate, she felt a tangible echo of his frustration. An old echo, but an echo nevertheless. She'd spent tireless nights organizing her father's logbooks, scouring his receipts, trying to keep his affairs in order. She knew how it felt to pull the strings behind her father's arms so that the Scarlet Gang didn't think him useless, so that he didn't get it in his head that he was not needed and move himself and his two remaining children out of the city into the countryside. Rosalind almost wondered what would have happened if she had let him. If she hadn't been resolute to remain in Shanghai, if she and Celia had packed up their bags obediently and removed themselves from this treacherous urban game. Perhaps they would have been better off.

"And are you?" Rosalind asked, point-blank.

"Am I what?" Orion returned, squinting out the windshield. He paused at a corner, then turned. "A Japanese spy? Darling, I think *you* have more cause than I do."

Rosalind jerked back into her seat. The audacity to turn it on *her*. "I beg your pardon? *You* speak Japanese. *Your* father was accused of being hanjian."

It was a low blow right after he had been truthful, but she

needed to say it. She needed to fling out the hit and hear what he had to say for himself. Maybe then she could finally figure out why Dao Feng had been mistrustful enough of Orion to plant her at his side.

The car stopped suddenly, right in the middle of the road. Orion had stepped on the brake, and Rosalind slid forward, narrowly catching herself before she slammed into the dashboard.

"Fine," Orion snapped. "And yet Janie Mead isn't *your* real name. Why has no one in this city heard of you? Why can you speak Russian?"

"I was educated abroad." Rosalind stuck her nose in the air. "Both of those oddities are perfectly natural."

"No one is teaching you how to speak Russian in America."

This was ridiculous. He was derailing the topic intentionally. And perhaps it would have worked . . . if Rosalind had not learned the exact same techniques in operative training.

"Why are you making this about me?" Rosalind tapped the steering wheel. "In fact, why have you stopped the whole car in an intimidation tactic? I only asked a simple question."

"And it is insulting that you would even ask." In a huff, Orion triggered the ignition again. The car rumbled to a start. When he reached up to fix the rearview mirror, Rosalind's eyes shot up too, then did a double take.

There was another car hovering some distance behind them, at the edge of the road.

"Orion, wait," she demanded.

"What?" His voice was still acidic, a quiver in his lip and a deep furrow in his brow. Somehow, the genuine anger in his expression made him seem more real. Like a regular person she might have something in common with instead of a covert agent who valued sordid affairs over their mission.

"We're being followed."

All the hostility in Orion's expression dropped. He looked at the rearview mirror properly, his foot coming down on the brake again. "What? Who—"

They weren't afforded more time to react. Before their very eyes, a projectile flew from the other car and exploded beneath their vehicle with a booming sound, throwing them right off the road.

26

Alisa shook the bars of the holding cell, testing the limits of her captivity. She supposed it was too much to ask that one of the bars be secretly made of dough to allow for her easy escape. No luck.

With a grumble, she stepped away from the bars, pacing a small circle in the cell. They were leaving her here overnight, insistent that they hadn't finished asking their questions and that they needed to report up to the commissioner of police first. She knew how this would work: if they couldn't find any conflicting information, if no one important made a call, then they would pin her for the crime. Never mind any of the logistics. Never mind motive or alibi or anything else a usual court of law wanted to look at. They would just make her guilty.

Well, to be fair, she *was* guilty in some sense, but that wasn't the point.

Alisa marched to the bars again, then smacked them repeatedly. All the other holding cells were empty. There was no one to witness her useless antics except the one constable that stood on guard by the door.

"Dammit, Rosalind," Alisa muttered under her breath. She knew this hadn't been done out of malice. It wasn't as if Rosalind would have been caught for murder even without casting the blame on Alisa; even if Rosalind *had* been caught, she was the one walking around arm in arm with Orion Hong, whom Alisa had recognized in an instant despite his false name. One phone call from his father, and Rosalind's slate would be clean.

So what was the point of this? Alisa propped her foot up on the wall. Was she too trusting? She supposed she had a problem of being too trusting. She rarely found it within herself to hold much of an opinion about anything. She liked hearing other people's opinions. She liked being an invisible set of eyes acting as a spectator over the city. Now look where she was—dragged into visibility only because she had decided to give someone of her past a helping hand.

Alisa huffed. She was so never going to be charitable again.

A loud bang sounded on the door into the holding cells. Alisa glanced over warily, hurrying to the bars again as the guard there startled too, peering through the glass slab.

"What was that?" she called.

The guard didn't answer. He kept peering through the glass, watching to see what the sound was.

Then, suddenly, the glass shattered with a flare of light, and he stumbled backward, his hands flying to his eyes with a cry of pain. Alisa blinked in shock, shuffling away from the bars. The moment the light faded, an arm reached through the glass slab and opened the door from the inside, giving it a push. Two people entered the holding cells—a girl and a boy. The boy surged forward and held a cloth to the guard's face. The girl headed for Alisa, pausing in front of the cell with her hands on her hips to observe how the bars worked.

Alisa recognized both of their faces, though from different avenues. The girl—she was the one who had shown up at Seagreen Press the other day as Orion's sister. She matched the description of Phoebe Hong that floated around the city: short and made of energy, a mass of gel in her hair to keep the finger waves at the front, the rest of her ponytail trailing down her green dress. The boy, however . . . Alisa had met him at an underground Communist meeting. Beneath his thick glasses, his eyes were wide and doe-like, his mouth pinched in ever-present concern. The first time she'd seen him, he had been making the exact same expression while taking instructions from a superior.

What was a Communist agent doing running around with a Nationalist's daughter?

The boy dropped the unconscious guard, then headed for the cell too, coming up behind Phoebe with a set of keys in his hand. Just before Phoebe turned around to address him, he raised a finger to his lips, directed only for Alisa. The gesture was easy to understand.

Don't tell. She doesn't know.

Alisa nodded.

"See," Phoebe said to him. "I told you that would work."

The boy tossed her the keys he had retrieved from the guard's pocket. "I was never in doubt. We must hurry if we are to leave before the main office is staffed again."

In confusion, Alisa watched Phoebe unlock the cell, then drag the bars wide open.

"Your saviors have arrived," she declared. "I'm Phoebe, by the way. I hope you're Liza, or else this is going to be really awkward."

Alisa tilted her head curiously. She said nothing. She took in the situation and drew an utter blank as to why this chain of events was happening.

"Well?" Phoebe prompted when Alisa remained unmoving. "Come on. Do you want to go or not?"

The car crashed against a thick tree.

Though Rosalind braced as best as she could, her head still

slammed hard against her window upon impact, sending shock waves of pain through her temple. The world was loud with screeching as the metal around them settled. With a cough, Rosalind clambered to her knees on her seat, trying to squint through the darkened rear windshield. A trickle of blood dripped into her eyes. She wiped it away.

"What the hell was that?" she demanded.

Orion winced, pulling himself onto his knees to peer through the car's damaged rear as well. He didn't look too hurt, save for a few shallow cuts from the flying glass.

"Those are Japanese military flags," Orion observed, sounding aghast when he spotted the parked vehicle. He touched his jaw. A bruise was blooming. "Have our covers been blown?"

"Impossible." Rosalind, too, saw the flags that fluttered at the head of the military vehicle where the explosive had been fired from. But it didn't make sense. "If the Japanese knew we were agents, why not chase us out of Seagreen? Why attack us in the dead of night, and like this, no less?"

The two of them waited, tense, observing whether it could have possibly been a misfire, an accidental release of a military weapon kept inside one of their transport vehicles. Then a round of gunfire echoed into the night, and they both dived low, avoiding the bullets that pierced through what remained of the car's windows. New glass shattered in every which direction.

"Stay down!" Rosalind and Orion shouted in unison before looking at each other in surprise. Another round of gunfire flew at the car. They pushed out from either side of their doors at the same time.

Rosalind snapped the heels off her shoes, rolling behind a tree nearby. There was no way the residents in the neighborhood had not heard the first explosive go off and even less of a chance that they were not hearing this gunfire echo through the night. But there would be no help coming. The country—as much as Shanghai always forgot—was at war, and if strange noises were tearing down the streets outside, a civilian's best chance of survival was to stay in and stay out of sight.

Rosalind smacked the two shoe pieces against the tree, triggering the mechanism inside. At once, thin blades pushed out of each heel, sharpened and coated with a barely visible purple dust. If they were forcing her to get messy, then getting messy it was.

From her right, there was a return of gunfire, hitting the front windshield of the military vehicle. While Orion fired at their opponents, Rosalind hurtled forward, arms raised to meet the men who piled out of the car. She counted five, all dressed in black, blending into the night. Three were holding weapons. Two had rope in their hands.

Rope? Rosalind ducked at the first encounter, avoiding the soldier with a length of rope pulled long in his hands. Despite her immense confusion as to why they were holding *rope*, she moved fast when the soldier lunged, using her blade to slice the length in two and then spinning to make a shallow cut on the man's arm.

"Janie, take him *down*," Orion hollered from afar. "He is coming from behind—"

The man, indeed, had followed after her once she skittered away. But the moment he reached out again, he tripped over his own feet. In seconds he was twitching on the ground, froth rising to his mouth.

Rosalind flipped her blades in both hands, refortifying her grip on each. She sidestepped one of the other men as he aimed his gun in her direction, then sank to her knees and stabbed his thigh before he could adjust his stance and point the rifle down. She did not need to be particularly wily or cut critical wounds into her adversaries. The blades were coated with a fast-acting poison that would do the job for her.

Rosalind pulled the blade out.

"Janie!"

A bullet skimmed by her shoulder. Rosalind gasped, whirling around; she would have taken another bullet to the face then and there if she hadn't thrown herself to the ground, her wrist striking hard against the pavement and one of her blades skittering away. The man lunged toward her, holding his rifle up for a brute-force weapon rather than taking the brief second to reload, but before he could swing a full arc and strike Rosalind, Orion appeared behind the man, slamming his pistol into the man's head.

The man dropped. Orion swore viciously, wiping blood from his nose. He must have been struck at some point.

"Up you get, beloved. Can I borrow a knife? I'm out of bullets."

Rosalind lunged for the blade she had dropped, then tossed it to Orion. "It's poisoned. Stab smart, not hard."

There were two remaining men who were also taking inventory of their winning chances. A second passed. Rosalind flipped her one blade nervously. Without waiting any longer for their opponents to recover, she lunged at the nearest man, hauling him close by grabbing an end of his rope.

"Your left! Down!"

Rosalind ducked without hesitating, missing a swing from the second man and getting out of the way for Orion to lunge at him. She spared a quick glance over. Right as the first man's rope entangled with her arm, she yelled, "From behind!"

Orion avoided the hit aimed for his shoulder blade. He was eerily smooth on his feet. Though Rosalind had called out a warning, it was like Orion knew to move before he had even turned to see the attack coming. Rosalind, in her distraction, lurched to the ground, rolling to avoid slamming against concrete. Her opponent followed, but from her angle, she was afforded the opportunity to kick up, directly at his chest. When he staggered back, Rosalind did not bother clambering up too. She only stretched with her arm and plunged her poisoned blade through the man's shoe.

He fell.

Elsewhere, Orion finally disarmed their last opponent, throwing his rifle away and slamming an elbow into his neck. With one hit, it was done. The man joined the others on the ground as a heap of limbs. The residential street settled into stillness.

Rosalind got to her feet heavily, dusting her hands off. Her legs hurt like hell, scratched and lacerated from raw contact with the gravel. The slit down the side of her qipao offered plenty of maneuvering room so long as she did not care about modesty, but it didn't offer much combat protection. No matter—the cuts would be gone soon.

"Those were not Japanese people," Rosalind declared, breaking the hush of the night.

"I know," Orion replied. He was short of breath. "Their faces . . . Chinese, I'm almost certain."

The rumble of more heavy military vehicles sounded in the distance. Rosalind and Orion both whirled in the direction of the noise and sighted three identical trucks coming their way, each flying the imperial army's flag.

Where were the reinforcements coming from? Why were they coming after Rosalind and Orion at this time of the night?

Rosalind eyed the bodies on the ground. And *why* were they flying the Japanese imperial flag?

Orion returned her blade. "We cannot fight that many more. We need another plan."

"I know." Rosalind clicked the poisoned blades back into her shoe heels. She lifted her left foot, then her right foot, turning her high heels into high heels again before settling her gaze on the military vehicle those first five men had tailed them with.

"Get the wheel," Rosalind commanded, pointing at the vehicle.

She hurried quickly to the car they had crashed, throwing open the damaged door and fetching the notepad she had tossed on the floor. If their covers were still intact, she would not be losing their precious quotes from the fundraiser.

"What?" Orion asked.

"The wheel," Rosalind emphasized again. "Let's go."

Orion finally understood. They could not fight three more incoming cars, and the explosive had totaled their borrowed Nationalist-supplied car. If they were to flee, the only option was stealing their enemies' transport.

"There's another pistol in that glove compartment," he called to her, already moving for the military vehicle.

With the notepad in hand, Rosalind leaned for the glove compartment, thudding her palm against the latch and snatching the extra pistol out as soon as the compartment fell open. Their attackers' reinforcements were getting closer, almost pulling up on the scene.

Rosalind ran for the military vehicle, then swung herself onto the high step and into the passenger seat. These vehicles were void of doors. When Orion got into the driver's seat and stomped down on the pedals beneath the wheel, the other vehicles arrived, seconds away from blocking them in. With no time to spare, Orion yanked on the stick shift and put them into reverse with a deafening screech on the road.

"How good a driver are you?" Rosalind asked, tossing the notepad onto the floor and clutching her seat tightly.

"Adequate, I *suppose*," Orion replied, turning onto the main thoroughfare. He made a smooth operation of winding in and out of the other cars that were rumbling along during the late hour, but they still weren't losing their pursuers. Some of the other trucks were turning onto the smaller side streets to remain in parallel pursuit.

"Drive into the alleys," Rosalind instructed.

Orion looked hesitant. "The vehicle is big. There will barely be space—"

"Which is exactly how we lose them." Rosalind held back her shriek, almost flying off her seat when Orion slammed the brakes to perform a fast pivot. She threw a glance behind them. "Other way! Other way! There's a car there!"

Orion muttered something unintelligible in French and did another sudden pivot, pulling their vehicle in the other direction. Unfortunately, the alley he had turned into was not entirely aligned with the one they had been trying to enter before, and the side mirror by Rosalind broke off, smashing to bits against the alley wall.

"ORION!" Rosalind screamed.

"I AM DOING MY BEST, BELOVED."

"YOU ARE GOING TO GIVE ME A HERNIA."

Orion swerved hard on the wheel again, navigating a tight corner in the alley. Rosalind tried to visualize what streets were upcoming. They would be approaching Chinese jurisdiction soon, and then the alleys would *really* grow too small to drive through.

She was still holding on to the extra pistol. Her finger looped around the trigger, securing her hold. It was hard to see in the night, and especially hard when these alleys did not have the lighting of the main streets, but when Rosalind peered through the back to eye the nearest truck on their tail, there was movement in its front seats. Rosalind would bet anything that the men inside were loading up their weapons to shoot. If there was another projectile in that car, she and Orion were doomed.

The problem was that their own back window was situated too low to get a good angle: firing from there would only get a few shots at the ground. Rosalind looked to the side of her seat. She was right-handed. The vehicle was driving too close to the alley wall for her to even try aiming backward from here.

Orion's side, on the other hand . . .

"Orion, lean back."

"What?"

She was already climbing into his lap, hooking her legs around his seat and holding his shoulder with her free hand to remain steady. Before she could block his sight, Rosalind stuck her arm out his window, shooting at the nearest vehicle in pursuit. The first bullet shattered its windshield. The second bullet struck its front tire. The third—Rosalind didn't even know where that one went. She only knew it stopped the vehicle in its tracks and jammed up all the others hurrying after it.

Then the pistol was empty.

"DAMMIT!"

"Oh my goodness, not so close to the ear," Orion complained, lurching the wheel to turn another corner.

Rosalind gripped his shoulder tighter, trying not to get thrown right out of the vehicle with the abrupt motion. "Apologies for the volume," she bit out. "Would you like me to blast your ear off to fix it?"

"Must you be so violent, darling? Kissing it better would be perfectly fine. There's a spare magazine in my jacket pocket, but these pistols are just impossible to reload."

Rosalind intentionally whacked his head with her elbow as she reached into his jacket, rummaging for the spare magazine. True to his word, she needed many precious seconds to determine how to reload the pistol, and by the time she had pushed the slide cross-bolt lock from left to right, then pulled the slide to the rear, there were vehicles on their tail again, merging in from the other alleys after the main one had been blocked. This time, the vehicles were shooting back.

"Keep driving south," Rosalind instructed. "Into Chinese jurisdiction."

"We have to lose the nearest trucks before then," Orion returned, flinching when a bullet struck his side mirror. "Or else we can't shake them when the alleys are even smaller."

Rosalind finally had the pistol loaded again. She would have to do this sparingly. Her teeth gritted, she stuck her arm out and returned fire again. One bullet slowed the nearest vehicle down. Two bullets rendered it unmoving. The jam was instant, but they couldn't give the pursuers time to recover.

"Turn here!" Rosalind bellowed.

Orion did not hesitate. He pulled the wheel and made the fast pivot into an alley filled with clotheslines and cobbled pavement. With two vehicles following them now, having pulled in from different alleys, Rosalind shot at a large flowerpot balanced upon a balcony railing, raining ceramic tiling and soil chunks onto their pursuers' path just as Orion turned again, rumbling back onto a main road. Chinese jurisdiction. The street stalls were out in full flare tonight.

"That alley, over there!" Rosalind pointed to a dark path beside a small-scale cinema. The moment Orion pulled in, the vehicle's wheels shuddering and screeching with effort, he killed the engine immediately, and the two of them held still—entirely still—as if their movement inside the vehicle might attract attention too.

On the main road, their pursuers rumbled by at high speed. A long moment passed after the last vehicle disappeared. They did not turn back.

Rosalind breathed out, dropping the pistol and slumping as if all the energy had been yanked from her spine. She hardly cared that she was still atop Orion; he leaned into her too, resting his forehead upon her collar, palpable relief emanating from the two of them that they had gotten away and could afford a moment to rest.

"Good shooting," Orion breathed, his exhale hot on her neck.

"Thank you," Rosalind returned. "Good driving."

Orion lifted his head. He grinned up at her, though for whatever reason, he had closed his eyes. "I know you don't mean that. But I like it when we work as a team anyway."

She liked it too. Some deep, innermost part of her.

"Janie," Orion said suddenly.

Rosalind started with alarm. "What's wrong?" Her first instinct was that he had sighted more pursuers, only his eyes were still closed . . .

"I don't mean to worry you, but I might be incapacitated for a moment."

Rosalind didn't like the sound of that. "That is quite frankly the most worrying thing you could say."

"I'll be fine, I promise." Despite his assurances, his breathing was coming more shallowly. Under her palms, she felt his heart rate picking up too. "I took a bad fall a few years ago. I landed quite gracefully and handsomely, I assure you, but my head didn't like being knocked against concrete. Had bad headaches for months. Each time I would be fully convinced that I was dying."

A small wheeze. Orion seemed to consider his own words.

"Janie, I might be dying."

"You are not dying," Rosalind said firmly. "How is it still happening after years? Have you seen a doctor?"

"The best doctors that the Nationalists have to offer," he answered, breaking off with a wince. Visible pain flashed in his expression, his eyes squeezing tighter. "They said there's nothing they can do. It comes back sometimes if I exert myself too hard. I don't know why."

He was trembling. Rosalind still had her legs clamped around his seat, so she could feel each shudder that went through him.

"Hey," she said. She didn't know how to fix pain. She wasn't very good at being a gentle, calming presence. But she did know how to soothe panic. "You're okay, do you hear me? You're not going to die. If you die, I'll personally punch you in the chest repeatedly until you resuscitate."

Orion pressed his head into the seat—pressed hard, as if he were trying to absorb himself into the leather backing. He let out a weak laugh, though the sound was swallowed by the sharp inhale he made afterward, ragged and terrified.

"You're okay," Rosalind repeated more kindly. "You're going to be okay, I promise." She smoothed his hair away from his forehead. As soon as he felt her touch, Orion shifted forward, leaning right onto her shoulder. Rosalind blinked, recovering quickly to sink one hand into his hair and settle the other at the back of his neck. He went around the world so tall, so confident; it was a surprise that he was capable of folding himself small, capable of seeking comfort in a girl like Rosalind.

The most frightening part wasn't that she had found herself in this position. It was that it felt natural.

"I'll list out every form of punishment I'll deliver you if you die," Rosalind whispered into his ear. "Just focus on my voice. Ready? First we'll start with my favorite: putting you in a hundred layers of clothing. None of it silk. Horror. Then in the afterlife, we'll roll you down a hill, and you won't even be able to stop yourself, and I'm going to have so much fun laughing at how ridiculous you look. . . ."

On and on Rosalind went, blabbering without registering what she was saying. It wasn't her actual words that mattered, only the constant stream of nonsense, drawing Orion's attention away from his panic so that he wasn't thinking of the pain, so that he was distracted until the pain itself eased.

At a certain point, she could feel that his pulse was returning to normal. She could feel the tension draining from his shoulders, the tightness in his posture easing until he wasn't bracing for another wave of head-splitting agony.

Orion finally lifted his head off her shoulder, his eyes fluttering open. Midsentence, Rosalind stopped her nonsensical chatter, looking carefully at him. He stared back with eyes that had gone entirely dark, his pupils blown to such proportion that his brown irises were nowhere in sight.

"You're stopping there?" he asked, his voice still faint. "I was really getting a visual picture for being skinned alive."

"I can get more descriptive anytime you like," Rosalind replied. She held his gaze, waiting to gauge how he was. Orion looked shaky but otherwise seemed to have overcome the panic, even if some of the pain remained.

"See?" she said quietly. "Didn't I promise that you would be okay?"

Orion nodded. "You did." He shuddered out a breath. "Thank you."

Nothing of their behavior before had felt strange, but now the gratitude unnerved her tremendously. Rosalind played off her non-committal response by clambering off his lap, where she had been situated this whole time, and dropping onto the other seat with a heavy thump.

It didn't feel like she had done him something worth thanking. Making world-ending promises and sticking by them was the only way she got through the day sometimes. Focus on one task, get it done. Focus on one target, think of nothing else until they were dead. Promising Orion that it would be all right if he pushed through was a tactic she had learned by trying it on herself first.

She wasn't as kind to herself, though. Maybe she ought to be.

"I meant to tell you . . . ," Orion started. Color was returning to his face rapidly, etching away at the pale bloodlessness and bringing in a pink flush. He reached into his trouser pocket, then brought out a chain between his fingers. Rosalind didn't comprehend what he was holding until she saw what dangled at the end of it: a very, very small key.

"This was around the Frenchwoman's neck," he explained. "She's Seagreen's point of contact for informants who wish to offer the press their thoughts confidentially. There's a small lockbox under her desk that she brought out for Haidi once, and I saw her take the key from her neck to unlock it. It's as good a place as any to hide confidential information about a terror scheme. I figure if I drop the key beside it afterward, she'll only think she lost it on her own."

Rosalind's mouth opened and closed. And opened and closed.

Then she smacked Orion's arm.

"Ow!" Orion protested. "I'm still fragile!"

"You couldn't have told me?" Rosalind exclaimed. "You just took my philandering accusations like that?"

"Beloved, there was hardly a point when I could show you what I had slipped into my palm. I didn't want to look suspicious lest she start wondering when she had lost the chain."

Rosalind huffed, shaking her head. His logic was sensible, but she was still aggravated. After the night they'd had, she needed at least eight hours of staring at a wall before she could stop sulking.

"There was plenty of time before we got shot by a projectile," she insisted. She could hardly wrap her mind over *that*, either. Rosalind reached below her seat, searching for the notepad that had slid around during the pursuit. "That had to be an international violation of some sort. We are not at war yet. Why are they pursuing us through the city and coming at us with guns?"

Orion rubbed at his temple. Rosalind kept a careful watch on him out of her periphery, but he didn't seem to be experiencing any new tension, only smoothing away the previous waves.

"But those were not Japanese people," Orion countered. "So, all in all, *what* just happened?"

Rosalind found the notepad. As she reached, however, her hand also nudged what felt like cloth. With a frown, she tugged out the notepad . . . alongside a hat. She peered at it curiously, scrutinizing the fabric using the one alley light that illuminated the inside of the vehicle.

"Is that a hat?" Orion asked, leaning forward.

Rosalind turned it around. At its front, there was a red five-point star stitched into the fabric. Instantly, the past hour made sense.

"Red Army uniform," Rosalind answered. She looked over at Orion. "Those Japanese flags were merely a disguise. We just fought Communist militia."

The alley around them felt abruptly cold. Uncomfortable in the same way that battlefields were. Surrounded by vast, vast land, where anything could happen at any moment.

Their attackers had not been the Japanese at all. This had been domestic warfare.

"Now the question is"—Rosalind dropped the hat, her fingers buzzing with the contact—"did the Communists just come after us because we're Nationalists or because of something else?"

27

"So, are you an enemy of the nation?"

Their hostage—Liza Ivanova, allegedly—looked up with a quirk of her brow.

"What is an enemy, really? I've certainly never disrupted the nation's livelihood, if that's what you're asking."

Phoebe crossed her legs under her skirts, rearranging the thick fabric. She made herself more comfortable on the couch, jostling against Silas, who was sitting primly next to her. They were waiting at his house, a modest manor tucked in a relatively secluded section of the International Settlement. Silas's parents were out of the house on a business trip, so there had been no trouble bringing Liza in. The staff who were in the vicinity doing kitchen chores or bedroom cleaning knew to avert their eyes and keep their mouths shut about whatever was going on with the hostage situation.

Well, Liza wasn't a hostage, per se, especially when she was just sitting on the other couch, flipping idly through a magazine, with the freedom to get up at any point she wished, but it made Phoebe feel more official to use such terms.

"I meant—are you working for the other side?" Phoebe clarified, casting Silas a look to show that she was being careful with her wording.

"Sides are interchangeable," Liza replied, her easy tone unwavering. "Do you have bread? I'm starving."

Silas stood up immediately. "I'll get bread," he said. Beneath his breath, intended more for Phoebe as he passed, he added, "I've never met anyone who talks in circles so much. My goodness."

He padded into the kitchen. Phoebe returned to her interrogation, despite the lack of preliminary information they could get out of Liza. It wasn't as if Orion had been particularly helpful on his phone call, either. All he had said was that Liza worked for the Communists and warned Silas that she might recognize him, so he would need to maintain the guise of being a double agent in the midst of betraying his friends.

"Have we met before?" Phoebe asked. "I feel as though we must have met before. How old are you?"

"Seventeen," Liza replied. She flipped to the last page of the magazine, then stretched for a literary journal on the coffee table. "Though I gather that we are of different social circles."

"Nonsense. I know all the seventeen-year-olds in Shanghai." It was a huge exaggeration, especially in a city so dense, but when Phoebe exaggerated, she held fast to it. "I knew your face was familiar."

Liza didn't look marginally convinced. "My brother was well known around the city. You might be recognizing him."

"Oh, I know all about famous brothers, too," Phoebe said with a pout. She drew her legs up onto the couch, hanging lopsided off the edge. "The papers will ramble on and on about Oliver and Orion, but no one ever remembers *me*."

Liza said nothing. Phoebe felt like she had lost the thread of their conversation, or perhaps she had clutched it too tightly and somehow managed to pulverize the whole thing in a ham-fisted grab. With a toss of her ringlets over her shoulder, she tried again.

"Who's your brother?"

Liza's gaze flickered up, the first glint of sharpness entering her dark eyes. In the kitchen, Silas was closing a cabinet door, and the sound seemed to jolt Liza to look around, to remember where she was.

"You'll find out soon enough."

"What is that supposed to mean?" Phoebe pushed herself upright again, returning to a proper sitting position before Silas came back with bread on a plate. He passed it to Liza, and Liza took it with a *thank you*, her expression carefully controlled. From outside the house, Phoebe thought she heard voices wafting nearer, approaching the driveway.

"Janie must know, then?"

Liza took a bite of the bread. She shrugged. "I don't know. Does she?"

"Feiyi, come on, you're both only going to tire yourselves out," Silas warned. But Phoebe was insistent. She knew how to play the annoying-girl game. She was the reigning champion of annoying girls.

"How did you get into this line of work?"

"How does anyone get into this line of work?"

"Let me speculate," Phoebe said, tapping her chin in thought. "You mentioned a brother. An important brother. He must be a Nationalist—you work the opposite side to keep him safe. In a game of hide-and-seek, you choose to hide and watch others walk right past you unknowingly, gathering information from the shadows so that you can protect him."

Liza snorted. After one bite, she was picking at the bread instead of eating it, rolling up little bits of the dough. "Please don't quit school anytime soon for detective work."

Phoebe scowled. Silas, having returned to the seat beside her, smoothed her hair back over her shoulder in a placating gesture.

"Fine, so it's not family," she said. "A lover?"

Liza mimed a gag. "I have always been mightily uninterested in all matters of romance and whatever else lovers do."

"Then the only option left is money," Silas supplied. With Phoebe's hair tidied, Silas leaned back into the couch, but the motion took him farther away from her. She frowned. Was he afraid of disturbing her skirts? She shuffled closer, pressing herself to his side again.

"Or," Liza said plainly, "the only option left is wanting a job in politics. I'm Russian—relatively speaking, the Communists are willing to trust me, so I work for them. How did you not begin at the easiest starting point?"

A loud knock came at the front door. Phoebe bolted up, waving for Silas to stay put. It was easy for her to shuffle into the foyer in her frilly socks, gliding along the clean floors like she was skating. The voices outside were midargument, loud enough to be wafting into the house.

"—identities have leaked."

"You don't know that."

"Yes, Orion, because it was a *coincidence* that we were attacked—"

Phoebe opened the door before Janie's knuckles could come down to knock a second time. She peered at her brother, then her brother's fake wife, and pulled the door wider, welcoming them in with a flourish.

"We've been expecting you."

"I gave you these instructions, scamp," Orion sighed, stepping in. He kicked off his shoes. "Janie, the stage is yours. What did you mastermind this plan for?"

As soon as Janie Mead came in too, Phoebe made a quick glance at the path outside, checking for intruders. There was no movement to be concerned about, but there was a rather large mosquito crawling up one of the entrance pillars. Hurrying to get back in, Phoebe scooped up a pebble from one of the large plants sitting nearby and threw it at the mosquito.

There—squashed. Nasty things. Phoebe skittered back inside, returning to the living room. Janie and Orion were standing before

Liza, while Liza remained sitting, still picking casually at the bread. Silas gestured for Phoebe to come closer, but she shook her head, opting for a better view by the hallway.

"Bread?" Liza offered the roll.

"You're not going to yell at me for framing you?" Janie asked.

Liza nodded her chin at Orion. "Does your husband know yet that it was you who killed Tong Zilin?"

Orion reared back with a look of utter disbelief. *"What?"*

"Ah," Janie said. "There's your revenge."

Liza smiled. Orion seemed astonished that Janie was not denying it. All the while, Phoebe and Silas exchanged a glance, left out of the loop. They hadn't even known what they were breaking Liza out of the holding cells for. Had it been accusations of *murder*?

"Why didn't you tell me?" Orion demanded. "Is *that* why you crashed the chandelier at the dance hall? Oh my *God*, Janie—"

"Can we," Janie hissed with a lower volume, "resume this conversation another time?"

Orion bristled visibly. Liza looked like she was trying to hold back her laugh.

"Don't stop on my behalf," she said. "I have nowhere else to be. Except jail, apparently."

"You're welcome," Phoebe called from the hallway.

With Orion temporarily mollified, Janie smoothed down the fabric of her qipao, turning back to Liza. "Look. It won't be hard for us to clear your name. In return, however, I want the same thing I asked for earlier. The Communists assigned you to Seagreen— you're the one most connected to these two avenues and the most likely to get answers. Why that file was yanked away from me. Why my handler was hit. Why they just came after us with guns blazing and a length of *rope*."

Silas sat up straighter. Phoebe finally stepped into the living room properly. "What? Are you okay?"

Orion gestured for Phoebe to sit, pressing a finger to his lips. "We're fine. We got away easily."

Meanwhile, Liza only slumped in her seat, a frown deepening on her face. She had a very delicate nose, which twitched while she considered the matter. Although it was quick, Phoebe caught Liza's gaze darting once to Silas. The Communists thought Silas defected. Silas was, in fact, playing a very balanced game as a triple agent, and he needed to maintain the guise in front of Liza in case it leaked. Though Phoebe pretended not to notice, she saw him jerk his head in a minuscule motion, urging Liza to leave him be.

"You think it has to do with your investigation at Seagreen?" Liza asked. "That people on my side are involving themselves in the terror plot?"

Janie threw her hands up, but it wasn't to signal her rejection of the idea. It was a movement that radiated with bewilderment.

"It has *something* to do with it, but I can't figure out what. Get me answers, and my husband will make the right series of calls so that you're not a fugitive anymore. Though I'm sure you would have plenty of fun being a fugitive."

Liza got to her feet. Slowly, she dusted her hands of bread crumbs, then stepped away from the couch. Despite the many eyes pinned to her every movement, she was casual as she walked out of the living room.

"If I were more spiteful, I might just run off into the countryside and live as a fugitive forever." Her voice bounced back, loud with the echo in the foyer. "But not only am I kind—I am the bigger person. You'll hear from me soon. Goodbye."

The front door opened, then slammed after her. The house stayed unmoving for a long moment. Then Orion turned to Janie.

"She is so strange. How do you know her?"

"That's too long of a story." Janie tightened her hold on something close to her chest: a notepad. "She's only strange because she was raised that way. The world moves for her. She doesn't move with the world. She knew there was never any real trouble—or at the very least, she knew that I was going to get her out of it."

Phoebe peered closer, trying to read what was scratched at the back of Janie's notepad, but then Janie caught her eye, and Phoebe started to attention.

"Thank you for your assistance, Phoebe. And you, Silas."

"Oh, anytime," Phoebe exclaimed. "If you need anyone to tail Liza Ivanova, let me know. I have a feeling she and I could be the best of friends."

Orion shook his head. He picked up the chunk of bread that Liza had left behind, then tossed it in the trash can on his way to the front door. "I knew she reminded me of someone. I'll walk you home, Feiyi."

28

I f Celia missed anything about Shanghai, it was the marketplaces. Out here, in the more rural parts of the country, the selection was pitiful—only the most common vegetable types, each variety smaller than average.

"Be glad there's food at all," Celia mumbled to herself, sifting through the qīngcài bunches. Once she found one that wasn't as yellowed as the rest, she brushed the dampness off her hand and hauled her shopping bag higher up her shoulder. The morning was rising slowly, drawing the wash of dawn over the rickety stalls. There were only three other townspeople at the open market this early, so she took her time walking around, her flat shoes padding down on the rough dirt ground. Her wardrobe choices were entirely transformed while she was undercover, and then toned down even further whenever she was outside the shop. Cloth and cotton fabrics even if she was wearing a qipao. No silk, and certainly no designed lace.

Celia's gaze flickered up, watching two new shoppers enter the marketplace. She went alert immediately, entertaining the possibility that this was an agent pair, but then they parted at the entranceway, as if their side-by-side appearance had been mere coincidence. Overhead, a bead of water dripped along a stall and landed with a splat on Celia's shoulder.

She turned to the seller and paid, hurrying to leave. It wouldn't do good to dawdle, not knowing what sort of people could come sniffing around. She was still on edge after seeing the soldiers at that warehouse. Though she and Oliver had gotten away, though they had returned to the shop and shut the door to silence, waiting and waiting for a sign of pursuit and hearing nothing, it didn't mean they were in the clear, especially not after one of the soldiers had been injured by Oliver's bullet.

She had spoken very little to Oliver since that night. It wasn't that things had soured between them—Celia was too much of a people pleaser to ever manage sour. All the same, she didn't linger long in the rooms he entered, didn't seek him out when there wasn't any need. If she was around him too much, she would be tempted to shake him by the shoulders until he divulged every secret he was keeping from her, and that probably wouldn't go down well. Oliver had to come clean on his own terms for it to mean something.

If that's even possible. Celia had never been very good at making demands. Something about it had always felt fundamentally wrong to her; she could never rid herself of the feeling that being difficult would drive people away. Still, on this, she needed to stand firm.

Celia glanced over her shoulder. The two new shoppers remained at the market as she exited. Good. It was only her paranoia then. Just to be safe, she still chose a different route back to the shop, walking the longer main road through the town.

She passed a dress shop. Then halted in her step.

To her left, there were three metal-lined newspaper stands, laid out with a cover in case of rain. Oliver had said he'd picked up that issue of Seagreen Press near a dress shop. Was this the one? The displays remained nearly full. When Celia walked up to the stacked piles and did a preliminary flip through the topmost issues, it looked as if they were updated weekly, which meant nothing should have been changed since Oliver was last here.

Celia dropped to a delicate crouch. For good measure, she

sorted through each of the piles, trying to see if Seagreen Press was buried underneath. It was not here. There were only the usual publications from Suzhou and some of Shanghai's news, all written in Chinese, as would be expected around these parts.

Had that one issue been a fluke? What kind of publication accidentally delivered a single issue on a fluke?

Something about the incident nagged at Celia incessantly. Rosalind's last letter said that Seagreen Press's existence in Shanghai was to cater to its Japanese residents. Up here, outside the city without foreign influence, what purpose would a foreign newspaper serve?

Who was the one keeping these stands in order anyway?

Celia looked up. Along the road, there was a dress shop, a glassware shop, and . . . *ah*. A bookstore. She straightened at once and hurried to the shop, pulling her qipao skirt above her ankle before she crossed the threshold. A small bell chimed, signaling her arrival.

"All the deliveries go through the back!" a voice called.

"Good thing I'm not making a delivery," Celia replied.

An old man popped his head out from the shelves, pushing his thin wire-frame glasses higher up his nose. He returned to the front desk with slow, patient steps.

"Ah, my apologies, xiǎojiě. I have come to expect the delivery cyclist at this time. What can I help you with?"

This was the first time she had come into the bookstore despite the months they had spent undercover around these parts. There was no use making too many local connections when it only increased their chances of being tattled on if the Nationalists came sniffing around. Celia looked around, eyeing the well-kept shelves and neatly dusted ledges. 紅樓書店, the sign above the door read. *Red Chamber Bookshop.*

"Do you"—Celia pointed over her shoulder to the road outside—"do you run the newspaper stands over there?"

The old man nodded. "Are you looking for something?"

"Sort of." Celia hesitated, trying to determine how to word her request without sounding odd. "I saw something there the other day. In Japanese? My . . . my niece is learning the language, so I wanted to fetch it for her."

For a moment, the old man stroked his beard, looking like he didn't comprehend what she was talking about. Then he clicked his fingers. "Oh. I remember now. That was a mistake, dear. The delivery person gave me the wrong box. It was supposed to go to another location—I saw newspapers and put them out with the rest without thinking."

A wrong delivery?

Celia pulled her grocery bag higher onto her shoulder. "Do you know where it was supposed to go instead? It would be useful for me to obtain one."

"I wouldn't know but—hey! Li Bao! We've got a question for you."

At the other end of the shop, the back door had been propped open with a cinder block. It made it easy to spot the man—Li Bao—pulling up on a bicycle and tugging his cap off. The old shop owner bustled over, chiding him for being late.

Three baskets hung off the bicycle at different places. They were filled to the brim with packages and smaller boxes.

"A question?" Li Bao barked. He took the toothpick out of his mouth.

"About the misdelivered box." Celia needed to jump in before the old man could divert the topic with his reprimands about timeliness. "You brought something here that was meant for somewhere else . . . ?"

Understanding lit up in Li Bao's eyes. "Oh, yes. It was going to Warehouse 34 out on the dirt roads. I brought it to shop number 34 instead."

The warehouse teeming with Nationalists. The soldiers hauling those crates. There was no doubt about it.

"They were waiting on it too," Li Bao continued. "Their overseer gave me a whole earful about being irresponsible. Thankfully, I had another box of theirs and it tided them over, but *phew*."

"Another box?" Celia asked. "Also newspapers?"

Li Bao put the toothpick back into his mouth. "*So* many. And they were unpacking it right in front of me, shoving the papers into a different crate that they wanted shipped off that very day. Don't know what's wrong with those stuffy military people."

This didn't make sense. None of it made sense.

"Kuomintang, right?" she confirmed anyway.

Li Bao gave her a strange look. "Who else?"

Nationalist soldiers were taking Japanese newspaper deliveries, then putting them in other shipments and sending them back out? *Why?*

Celia inclined her head. "Thank you. This was plenty helpful. I might go inquiring for a copy."

Before the old man could offer further thoughts, she excused herself and exited the bookstore. She walked back to the photography shop in a daze, mulling and mulling and mulling some more. Millie and Oliver were on shift at the front desk when she walked in through the doors, so deep in thought that she almost tripped on a costumes trunk that had been left out.

"Any good finds?" Millie called.

"Only yellowed qīngcài," Celia replied. She caught Oliver's attention, then tilted her head toward the back. Miffed as she was about his handling of the warehouse mystery, she needed his opinion on the latest development. "Help me in the kitchen for a second, Oliver?"

Oliver abandoned the camera he had been fiddling with and followed her promptly. She waited until they were alone in the kitchen, until she had set her bag down on the counter, before she started to speak.

"I need to go back into the city to warn my sister."

Oliver took the egg carton out. He placed it above the cabinet. "What happened?" he asked evenly.

Celia tried very hard to keep her voice calm. To keep moving, distributing the groceries to their rightful places while she spoke.

"I traced where those Japanese newspapers came from. Seagreen Press? They were supposed to go to *that* warehouse." She slid the peppers away. "Oliver, the people behind Seagreen Press are responsible for a series of ongoing killings in Shanghai."

"I know," he said easily.

Celia held back her sigh. Of course he did. "You know?"

Oliver made a small grimace. "My brother is your sister's current mission partner. I found out a few days after their assignment began."

"He's *what*?" Celia leaned on the counter, absorbing the information. This wasn't relevant to her current concern, but she was caught on it, nonetheless. "I thought they sent Orion in for high-society tasks . . . and seducing women to divulge if their husbands have Communist sympathies. What's he doing investigating the Japanese now?"

"He's well trained for information extraction and fluent in Japanese. I suppose they think he's the most qualified. It's Lady Fortune that I'm curious about when it comes to sending agents in. She's hardly a spy."

But she is *trusted,* Celia thought. More trusted—she would guess—than Orion, even if they each had a sibling on the other side. Rosalind *had* said the Nationalists assigned her with another agent whom she was watching carefully. She just hadn't clarified who he was. It was so typical of Rosalind to leave his name out; she most definitely thought she was saving Celia from the obligation of reporting to Oliver how his brother was faring.

"Either way," Celia said, returning from their tangent, "if—and it still remains an *if*—this warehouse is the very root of a Japanese imperial scheme that the Nationalists have sent my sister and your brother to investigate . . ."

". . . why are their own soldiers at the warehouse?" Oliver finished, a frown pulling at his lips.

Celia shook her bag out, having cleared it of groceries. She let the silence draw long as she folded the fabric into squares, smaller and smaller until it was a little shape that she could put on top of the cabinet.

"How soon can we leave?" she asked.

29

Shortly before noon, the office was undergoing a hubbub of activity, various assistants wheeling in boxes from the cars parked beneath the building. While Orion cupped his mug of tea and let it brew in his hands, he wandered around to the department windows, peering down at the cars in the compound. New shipments, they said. Printings straight from the factory.

Ambassador Deoka was down there, directing the movement. As was Haidi, standing at his side. The two of them exchanged a few words before Haidi nodded and bowed, setting off toward the front gates as if she were going on a leisurely stroll. Orion glanced at his wristwatch. They were meeting in fifteen minutes. Did Deoka know? Had Deoka sent her? If Haidi had something to say, why not find a meeting room in the building? Why go so many streets away?

The Frenchwoman's lockbox had been a bust. Orion was one of the first people to show up at the office this morning, before Janie had even finished pinning her hair up, just so he could rummage around. With the department empty, he had made a direct line for the Frenchwoman's desk and unlocked the box, only to find nothing except letters from other expatriates reporting unruly neighbors on foreign territory. Useless.

They were rapidly exhausting their routes of investigation. If Orion were a less confident young man, perhaps he might even start worrying.

Well—he was a little worried. Just a little.

His wristwatch ticked, marking ten minutes to noon. He set his mug down on his cubicle desk, picking up his jacket from the back of his chair. When he passed the front of the department, Janie looked up and tilted her head at him curiously, but he only waved, leaving through the doors before she could ask. Once he had attended the rendezvous to see what Haidi had to say, maybe he would have a better explanation. Maybe he would have something useful for their investigation.

I have information about your wife that concerns you, Haidi had whispered to him. *People like you want information, don't they?*

Orion hadn't forgotten what Janie had tried to brush aside the previous night. Her ease when it came to taking out one of their colleagues. Her ease when it came to *hiding* it, tamping down the matter of murder like it was nothing.

"So?" Orion had demanded once Phoebe departed. His sister had asserted that she could walk up the driveway by herself, which left Orion and Janie standing under the streetlight at the corner of the road, Janie staring at the wrought-iron gates wrapped around the Hong mansion and Orion trying to peel her apart with his intense scrutiny.

"So . . . ?" Janie echoed, playing daft.

"Tong Zilin," Orion pressed. Earlier in the night, she had used the excuse of finding a better time to explain; with Phoebe departed, it was only the two of them, an empty street, and a long, long walk before they reached home. "Is it true?"

Janie tugged her bracelet, a thoughtful expression on her face. Orion was so tired that he was seconds away from keeling over and taking a nap on the sidewalk. Janie, on the other hand, seemed perfectly alert, even if she kept refusing to look directly at him, which was odd.

She started to walk. Orion followed, hovering at her side

persistently as she picked up speed. It wasn't until they were some distance away from his family home that Janie said:

"He caught on to a slip in my cover. I had to make a split-second decision between being exposed or shutting him up."

"So you killed him."

He saw Janie's shoulders stiffen. Her pace sped up further. "Are you disapproving?"

"No, of course not." Orion's hands had been dirtied too after his years working as an agent, but it was a rare occasion. Like when they were being pursued at high speed by mysterious entities firing projectiles at their vehicle. "I only want to be kept informed."

That earned a noise from Janie, one that Orion didn't entirely know how to read. Some mix between acceptance and curiosity. A low hum at the base of her throat, purring outward. There was a lot about Janie Mead that Orion didn't know how to read.

"I panicked," Janie said plainly. "I thought it was easier to keep it to myself. That's how Dao Feng trained me."

"That's how Dao Feng trained you when you ran solo." Orion sidestepped a puddle, moving onto the road for three paces before returning to the sidewalk. He resisted the urge to take Janie's elbow, to spin her so she was facing him and he could pry everything she hid out into the open. "We are High Tide together now, are we not? We are one combined unit now, are we not?"

Janie did stop then, as if she had read his thoughts.

"I ought to have told you," she stated. "Yes. You're right. It was careless and dangerous, and if you had needed to cover for me, it would have been easier if you'd known the true extent of what happened."

Orion almost couldn't believe what he was hearing. She sounded sincere. Was she . . . admitting to wrongdoing? Who was this girl and what had she done with the operative he'd been sharing a roof with for weeks?

"Good." He wanted to push his luck. "Are you keeping any other secrets from me, Janie Mead?"

She turned to face him properly, searching his gaze under the glow of the streetlights. The night blew a sudden cold breeze between them, but Janie hardly flinched, too busy considering the matter he had put forward.

"One," she said quietly. "But I don't want to tell you yet."

And like that, she surged ahead again. As if she hadn't admitted that she might drop another bomb on him any one of these days. He didn't know if it was better or worse that he knew now to brace for impact.

Who are you, Janie Mead?

In the present, Orion shouldered through the main doors out of Seagreen Press, winding around the activity outside. He passed Ambassador Deoka with a nod. Though Ambassador Deoka nodded back courteously, Orion felt the official's gaze follow him all the way to the front gates.

"Count your days," Orion muttered aloud, hailing a rickshaw. "You will not be here for long."

If the hotel had a name, Orion was having trouble finding it when he walked in, looking around to ensure his location was correct. What sort of facility didn't have a sign out front? The lobby inside was nice enough: a fish tank in the corner and a glass panel installed over the front desk, protecting the receptionist at her chair while she filed her nails. Still, there was no doubt that this was Chinese territory. The walls had none of the veneer that the foreign hotels had, none of the decor and shimmering gold that came as a result of money exchanged for jurisdiction.

"I'm looking for Zheng Haidi," Orion said, approaching the desk.

The receptionist checked the logbook, already open to a page in front of her. "Room three, ground level. Hallway on your left."

Orion's arms were prickling. When he walked down the hallway and approached room three, he didn't knock first; he just walked right in, taking inventory. Better to get this over and done with—if he thought too long about anything, he might mess it up.

"You're early!" a high-pitched voice exclaimed from the settee. Haidi jumped to her feet, her hair loose at the nape of her neck.

The hotel room was arranged as any ordinary room would be. A bed, the settee, a table. Large windows, thin curtains—*hmm*.

"Is that a problem?" Orion asked, striding to the windows. He peered onto the street outside, holding the smile on his face. "You're lovely in the light as always, Haidi, but I didn't get enough sleep and I have a mild headache. You don't mind, do you?" He tugged the curtains closed before she could answer.

From the settee, Haidi blinked rapidly, taken aback.

"Not at all," she replied after a beat. "I trust you didn't have too much trouble finding this place."

Orion leaned back against the wall. He folded his arms, then crossed one ankle over the other. The curtains were pulled, so no photograph evidence of a setup. What else did he need to watch for? Wires? Microphones?

"Nothing I cannot navigate." Subtly, Orion ran his eyes to the side, inspecting the adjoining bathroom. Nobody was hiding inside. "You said you summoned me here for something important. What's the matter?"

Haidi took a moment to pour from the teapot on the table. Orion hadn't wasted any time before getting to the topic, and with her face inclined down, he could not tell if Haidi was reacting with neutrality or displeasure.

"Come sit, won't you?"

Suspicion took root in his gut. He didn't show it—he walked to the long seat and dropped down, elbows propped on his knees in casualness.

"I made a discovery the other day," Haidi said, "and I thought it pertinent to tell you. The last thing I'd want to see is my colleagues dragged down into terrible schemes."

Orion laced his fingers together. If he had learned anything from so many years socializing and schmoozing around people with ulterior motives, it was how to pick up their tells. Haidi was making a concentrated effort to look directly at him. When her words slotted in one after the other, it sounded more like she was reading off a script. Like she was reciting words that had been carefully fed to her already.

This is a test, Orion thought frantically. But of what? From whom?

"That's kind," he said carefully. Haidi shifted closer and set a hand on his arm. He reached for the tea, nudging her off. "But you said previously it had to do with my wife. I gather there is nothing of my wife that I don't already know."

Haidi's eyes flickered to her purse, which sat at the end of the settee. In his catalogue of observations, Orion filed away the knee-jerk reaction.

"Certainly," Haidi said. "Tell me, how well do you really know her?"

Orion didn't like this one bit. No matter how many times he emphasized the word "wife," Haidi was not letting up, which meant this was an intentional task. Under usual circumstances, he would hardly fight a clear seduction. But this had to do with Janie. If Haidi was poking around to see where Orion stood with her, then Janie was being suspected, and Haidi was trying to determine whether Orion was to be looped in with her or considered innocent. High Tide was one unit. Orion would never be so foolish as to separate himself from her.

Only . . . it was true that he knew nothing about Janie. And though he didn't know who Haidi was working for, she had to have *some* information to be doing this.

"I suppose I married her quite fast," he allowed.

"Ah, of course." Haidi leaned in, her perfume swirling under his nose. Orion almost sneezed. "I suppose you were taken by surprise, weren't you?"

She trailed a finger along his jaw. He held back his flinch. If he lurched away with visible distaste, he would lose access to the information she had. But if she kept going, Janie was going to kill him. With her bare hands.

Orion did the only thing he could.

He faked a nosebleed.

"Oh—" One of his hands launched up to pinch his nose; the other one slipped into his pocket and opened his penknife, slicing his own index finger open. When he touched his nose, it looked as if it was running with bright red, smeared along his upper lip. "Could you grab a wet towel, please?"

Haidi jolted to her feet, her eyes wide. "Yes, of course. Hold on."

She hurried away into the bathroom, jostling around the cabinets noisily. Orion already knew that there were no towels in there: places like these would hardly supply free amenities. When she emerged, she gave a harried, "I'll ask the receptionist," and slipped out.

Immediately, Orion lowered his finger from his nose, scrunching his fist tight to trap the bleeding. With his uninjured hand, he opened Haidi's purse and peered at what was inside.

A gun—interesting. A hair ribbon. Some loose-leaf paper.

Orion shook the contents around, digging to the bottom. Something made of glass clinked as it rolled around, and he dug in to find a small vial filled with green liquid. He set it down and reached for the final object he had observed: a photograph.

"Hm . . ." He brought the photo closer. The subject was a Kuomintang politician standing over an outdoor podium. Orion didn't know where exactly it was, but it looked like one of the public gardens in the settlements. He gathered that Haidi wasn't carrying the photograph around for the politician. Far likelier was the fact that Janie stood in the background, perfectly caught in the frame. She was wearing a dark qipao, a ribbon looped around her wrist. For a second or two, Orion only observed her smile in admiration.

Then his gaze dropped to the handwritten description at the bottom.

Juewu Gardens, 1926.

"What?" he murmured aloud. Five years ago. He had been seventeen. Janie should have been even younger. So why did she look almost the same?

The rapid clatter of footsteps neared the door from outside, and Orion put the photograph where he had found it, snapping Haidi's purse closed and scooting to where he had been on the settee. When Haidi returned with the towel, he squeezed his finger hard, letting a rivulet of blood drip down his arm and stain his sleeve.

"Here, here," Haidi said quickly, hurrying close.

Orion took the towel from her, pressing the cold cloth to his nose. In the same motion, he stood up just as she was sitting down.

"I think it's best if I go," he said nasally. "I'll see you at the office. I'm sure you can tell me anything you want there. Zàijiàn!"

Before Haidi could protest, Orion was slipping out, closing the door after himself. He took the towel away from his nose as soon as the handle clicked, wincing at the cut on his finger. What a mess. He wiped his nose as well as he could, then hurried out of the hotel, ducking his head from the receptionist.

Outside the building, he tossed the towel into the first trash pile he saw. There was still a smear of blood on his lip when he wiped, but no one paid him any mind while he walked down the road, weaving between shoe shiners and fortune card readers. The cool air was helping clear his mind, even with the noise on Shanghai's main thoroughfare streets. With the sun beaming down at the center of the sky, the city was rumbling at the height of its daytime activity, and Orion sank right into it, holding his hand up to stop the bleeding.

He watched a fight begin near the vegetable market. He tossed a few coins at the sleeping bodies slumped outside the shops. Each step on the pavement set off another wave of thoughts roaring through his head.

By the time he had been walking long enough for a thin layer of sweat to gather down his back, his thoughts were no clearer about the past half hour's events. All he felt in the dip of his chest was worry and bafflement. Most of the latter emotion was directed entirely toward his pretend wife and what information she could possibly be hiding from him that was hauling their cover into crisis.

Orion slipped into a public phone booth, grimacing when the dark green paint job on the door chipped off into his palm. He dusted his uninjured hand to clean it, then lifted the phone receiver and dialed.

"Hullo?"

"Do you have a moment?" Orion asked. "I need your help."

"You're needing my help a lot recently," Phoebe replied over the line. She sounded very pleased. He could practically imagine how she was sitting at that moment: holding the cord of the telephone, her head hunched into her shoulders like a little gremlin catching the first scent of treasure.

"Yes, well, you did offer it yesterday."

On the other end of the line, Phoebe had most certainly sat up straight.

"Am I stalking Liza?"

"I want you to observe her," Orion corrected. He hesitated a moment, then said, "Janie is keeping something from me. Something big. And I'm certain that she and Liza knew each other prior to Seagreen."

A tap came on the glass of the phone booth. Orion turned around to find an old man gesturing for him to hurry up, and he made an apologetic gesture, holding up his hand to indicate a few more minutes.

"I checked Seagreen's records," he went on. "Liza Ivanova lives in an apartment opposite Peach Lily Palace. Run into her accidentally, offer to help in her task. You're the only one among us officially unaffiliated with the Nationalists, so you'll have a better chance at playing the neutral card. Somehow, we need to uncover what Liza and Janie have on each other."

Phoebe considered it for a moment.

"I must ask . . . ," she said, "why are we off investigating a Communist operative to find out about your own wife? It sounds rather complicated. Can you not ask Janie directly?"

"Ask her what secret she is keeping from me?" Orion snorted. "Because that would go well." He shook his head. "There's something hidden there. I know it. Can you do it?"

The old man had started tapping on the glass again. Orion gestured more forcefully, bidding patience while his sister mused on the task. It was a mystery why she was even pretending to think about it. There was no doubt that she was trembling on the other side, waiting to agree.

Phoebe cleared her throat. "You can count on me," she declared.

30

At the end of the workday, Rosalind made her own way home, seeing as Orion had never returned to the office. She was rushing, a laundry list of developments prepared in her head to report back to him. Ambassador Deoka had made a stop among the cubicles to deliver an announcement. She had talked with several colleagues in the break room afterward, all of whom they needed to add to their arrest lists as contributors to the terror plot.

"You have been hard at work to ensure our issues run smoothly each week, and your work has been recognized," Ambassador Deoka boomed. There were men standing with him wearing pleasant smiles. Perhaps sponsors, or investors. "Seagreen's second anniversary is approaching, so there will be a function in celebration. It will be held at the Cathay Hotel next Friday at eight o'clock. I hope to see each and every one of you there in celebration."

"I'm so very glad Cathay was the location chosen," Hasumi Misuzu from the writing department said, bustling around the second-floor break room right before clock out. "If I have to spend prolonged time in Chinese territory, I might kill myself. Or personally raze the ground so they can fix up the hideous architecture."

Ito Hiroko from production didn't even care that Rosalind was listening in on the conversation, blank-faced. "Calm down. There's no need to do any razing. We can brighten it up easily under firmer governance. Mrs. Mu, wouldn't you agree?"

Rosalind put her cup in the sink. She said what they wanted to hear. "The city slowly rots. Loose governance and Western governance are equally dangerous."

Misuzu and Hiroko both nodded.

"It is time for Asia to come together," Misuzu suggested.

"Surely, surely," Hiroko agreed. "Under one great empire."

To them, these opinions were nothing worth hiding. If they were a part of the terror plot, it was only another administrative task they needed to complete—sending along reports and shredding what remained, passing on numbers and forgetting the rest.

At last freed, Rosalind turned onto her street, breathing out and loosening her shoulders. She had stayed overtime to finish up the conversation in the break room, and now the sky was dark, hazed with deep violet. None of the lights outside her building were on yet, so she stepped into relative darkness, making her way up the exterior stairs. When she unlocked the door to the apartment and entered, only the washroom light was illuminated.

"Add Hasumi Misuzu and Ito Hiroko to our lists," Rosalind called in lieu of a greeting. She tossed her bag onto the couch. "Even if they're not guilty, I'd love to see them arrested and tried merely for being staunch imperialists . . ."

Rosalind trailed off. Orion had come to the washroom's doorway, leaning out to indicate that he was listening. He was in the midst of shaving, half his neck still covered in foam.

And he was shirtless.

"Hello," he said.

". . . hello," Rosalind replied with some pause. "Is there any reason you're half-naked?"

"My shirt got blood on it. Didn't want to get foam on it too."

Rosalind resisted the urge to massage her temples. "And how, may I ask, did your shirt get blood on it?"

"Funny story, actually." Orion retreated into the washroom to resume his task. Rosalind followed him in, sitting on the counter while he peered at the mirror, his chin tilted up. "First: that lockbox was a dead end. Second: Zheng Haidi, our delightful secretary, summoned me to a hotel room today. She had plenty of questions about you. About us."

Questions? Rosalind frowned, folding her arms.

"What did you tell her?"

"Beloved, I could hardly get a word out with the speed she was trying to drag me to bed."

Rosalind lurched off the counter, her fists clenching. "Is she out of her mind? I'll—"

"Hold on, hold on," Orion warned, rinsing off the straight razor. "As much as I adore the sound of you jumping to threats, this was no ordinary attempt at inciting an affair. She was assigned, Janie. I just wonder who she is working for. Whether it is Deoka who suspects us and why we haven't been kicked out of his office if so." He brought the razor to his neck again, then winced. "I sidled out of there by cutting my finger open and pretending my nose was bleeding. Hence the stained shirt."

Now that she was looking, Rosalind noticed the index finger on Orion's right hand was wrapped, the bandage reddened. Human skin was so fragile. *Mortal* human skin was so fragile, one sharp slash away from spilling blood and guts and secrets out from its casing and onto the cold linoleum floor.

"You aren't concerned."

Her eyes flickered up to his face, startled out of her inspection. "Of course I'm concerned. If she's asking questions, then our covers are under suspicion."

"I meant about me," Orion clarified. "I was bracing to defend myself. I had a whole speech prepared that I didn't do anything to instigate this, and you didn't even raise your voice."

Rosalind put her hands on her hips. "Do you think of me as some all-controlling harpy wife?"

"Yes."

Her glare had the force of a physical punch.

"I'm kidding, I'm kidding," Orion hurried to tack on. He wiped off the rest of his foam and took a step toward her. "Thank you for trusting me."

"Don't overplay it," Rosalind said, her frown returning. The washroom smelled like him now, a mix of spice and mint. "But . . . it was silly of me during the fundraiser to take your father at his word and jump to conclusions when you haven't shown me reason to believe him. Or at least *that* much reason."

Orion looked amused. He hadn't expected this.

"A little reason."

"A little reason," Rosalind agreed.

"For what it's worth"—Orion propped his arm on the wall, caging her in—"maybe I do like seeing you jealous."

Rosalind rolled her eyes, opting not to reward his shameless behavior with a response. His proximity was supposed to be some sort of tactic to make her flustered, she guessed, but she was only concentrating on the fact that Orion had missed a spot right by his jaw.

"Give me the razor."

He blinked. "I beg your pardon?"

She touched the curve of his jaw, where there remained stubble. His skin was warm, radiating with energy.

"You didn't do a very good job, but that's expected with your injured hand. Give me the razor."

Although Orion looked hesitant, he did slowly reach for the straight razor. "I . . . don't know if I want you holding a blade so close to my throat."

Rosalind had to resist the twitch at her lips, trying to look like she was taking this very seriously. "What?" she asked, forcing a scowl. "Do *you* not trust *me*?"

"I never said that." His throat bobbed up and down. His chest rose and fell, accompanying the deep breath he took in. "Okay. Yes, I trust you plenty. Please, I accept your help."

"Wonderful." She took the blade. Rather roughly, she grabbed ahold of his jaw with her other hand to position him, her fingers splayed along his neck. One finger rested right on the soft spot where his pulse was pounding.

"Relax," she breathed, running the razor down carefully. "Don't get so flustered."

"I'm not flustered," Orion protested.

"Mm-hmm." Rosalind proceeded with her task. She could feel Orion watching her. He was trying very hard not to exhale, which Rosalind knew because she would feel the air on her face if he did.

"You're allowed to breathe," she whispered.

"Stop it. You're actively trying to make me nervous," Orion returned.

With a laugh, Rosalind stepped away, finished with her task. She rinsed the razor in the sink and tapped the droplets off, setting it to the side. When she turned around, Orion still hadn't moved, standing by the door with a doltish look on his face.

"What?"

"Do that again," he said.

She looked at the sink. "Wash the razor?"

"No, beloved. Your laugh."

Now Rosalind really was going to start getting flustered. She blew a dismissive breath, then brushed by him, exiting the washroom and stretching her arms. "Put on a shirt. Didn't you have somewhere to be tonight?"

"Yes. Headquarters wants to speak to me." A shirt went on.

"While I'm there, I'm going to push them to assign us a new handler as quickly as they can manage. We cannot keep operating like a headless chicken, especially if Seagreen Press is onto us."

Rosalind reached for a notepad on the coffee table. "All right. I'll be here doing my housewife things."

Orion emerged from the bathroom, his brow already quirked up. "Housewife things? Like sitting on the couch?"

The paper under her fingers made a crisp sound as she flipped, stopping on the first blank page. "I choose to interpret domestic tasks in my own unique way."

With a small shake of his head, Orion said his farewell and exited the apartment. As soon as the door closed after him, Rosalind let out her smile.

Phoebe lugged her basket close to her chest, peering around the driveway to confirm that Silas's parents had not yet returned from their trip. It was no matter if she had to greet them, but she liked summoning different versions of herself best suited for different people so that they would adore her at her utmost potential, and this late at night, she was low on energy.

She knocked on the front door. An old housekeeper answered and, recognizing Phoebe, let her in wordlessly.

"Silas?" Phoebe called, kicking her shoes off in the foyer and proceeding down the hallway. "I've brought you extra muffins. Pay attention to me, please."

His house was built so that the bedrooms and living areas were emphatically separated, placed in different wings of the manor. It was often difficult for Silas to hear her arrive because sound didn't carry well between the wings, but he would keep his door propped open when he was expecting her. Though Phoebe hadn't given him any advanced warning today, she was still surprised he didn't emerge from his room to greet her. Frowning, she walked farther ahead and knocked directly on his bedroom door. "Silas?"

The door opened. When Silas appeared, however, he quickly pressed a finger to his mouth, warning her to stay quiet. There was another voice behind him. Phoebe's scowl was immediate, taken aback as to who was in his *bedroom*, but she realized seconds later that the voice was too grainy and distant to be a visitor. Silas was playing a recording.

"Who is that?" Phoebe whispered, entering the room. There was a phonograph on his table, spinning a disk inside.

"Priest," he answered distractedly. "It's the only way she will communicate with me. Written messages are too easily opened and spied upon."

Phoebe set the basket down. *"She?"*

"Oh." If they had been speaking Chinese, there wouldn't have been any difference between pronouns. But Phoebe had opened with English, and so Silas had followed, making the differentiation in his speech. "I only assume, with the sound of the voice. I could be wrong, knowing how they're learning to alter sound now."

He sat back at his desk and resumed whatever he was writing while the recording played. It was as if Phoebe weren't even in the room. When she tuned in, the voice did sound distorted, pitched lower than a natural speaking tone.

"—proceed down this route if you want our trust. First and foremost, remember—"

Phoebe harrumphed. "I shall take my leave, then."

"Wait." Silas looked up so fast that his hair fell in front of his glasses. "You only just got here."

"Yes, well, your focus seems reserved for this girl on the airwaves. I was going to ask if you wanted to drive around with me tomorrow, but never mind."

"It's my job to investigate," Silas said nicely. "I was assigned to her. The more I get to know her, the likelier it is that I unroot her identity. And of course I can drive around with you tomorrow."

Phoebe still held her frown, crossing her arms. There was a note of something in Silas's tone. Not vengeance, not outrage. *Admiration.*

"You ought to be careful," Phoebe said. "Priest is a Communist *assassin.* What if she finds out you have been in allegiance to your original side all along and comes after you?"

The recording ran to a stop. Silas set his pen down. "It will be fine. I—"

He was interrupted by the sound of the phone ringing. In the hallway, the housekeeper called out a summons, but Silas was already moving to answer it. Phoebe trotted after him, ever watchful as he picked up the receiver.

Central command, he mouthed in explanation some seconds later.

"What are they saying?" Phoebe whispered.

"Yes," Silas answered into the phone before he could mouth another explanation. "I'll be there immediately."

He hung up.

"What happened?" Phoebe demanded. Silas was already hurrying back into his room, fetching a jacket.

"Anti-Japanese riots outside of Seagreen, and they can't reach Orion or Janie," he answered. "Someone might use this opportunity to destroy evidence. I'm off to keep an eye on it."

"I'm coming too."

Silas paused. He might have thought to argue, but then he cast one look at Phoebe and sighed. "Okay. Let's go."

31

I n a noisy apartment some few blocks away from Seagreen Press, no call can come through. While the keeper was not watching, a young infant yanked the telephone line out, and it will not be discovered until morning.

The apartment upstairs is still. Calm. Unknowing to what transpires nearby—movement and chants bellow through loudspeakers, a mass of people moving down the road. These few months have seen similar incidents blooming across the foreign settlements. It always begins small. Someone on the other side, performing an incendiary action: a lone imperialist shouting slogans, a soldier resorting to brutality upon a routine search, an argument inside a tram. Then it erupts. Then the locals make use of their numbers and form their mob, and with their fists combined, they become a fighting force. They finally find some sort of power.

Outside Seagreen Press, the mob has gathered out of a delayed vexation. They have already burned three Japanese businesses on their way here. They shake the front gates, turn their loudspeakers to the air.

"Boycott all Japanese products!" they shout. "We are not Japan! We will not be made into Japan! We will not be swallowed into your empire!"

Two mission agents—or one mission agent and an aspiring mission agent—run onto the scene.

"Is it bad that I almost want to join them?" the girl with the ribbon in her hair whispers.

"No," the boy answers. "But we are more powerful than that. We don't need to pick up a torch when we can manipulate the war's fire before it starts."

They circle around the road, keeping a careful eye on the building. Though the mob is strong, there is no telling who could blend among their numbers with other intentions. A soldier with instructions from his government, perhaps, told to destroy evidence; a fellow employee at Seagreen, warned by their higher-ups that Nationalist spies are planted among them and that now is the time to burn it all. The two agents at the periphery watch for danger, for anything explosive that could be thrown over the gates. Much as they hate to be providing protection, Seagreen cannot burn. Then they could prove nothing. Then whatever plot grows there would only find another place to flower, and they would have to start from ground zero.

While they govern the scene, they do not see movement behind them.

A killer, sitting at the edge of a building rooftop. A killer, slowly clambering onto their feet and hopping down to the pavement, getting to work before the mob can fully dissipate, before the road is no longer thunderous with noise.

"Hey," the girl says suddenly. She tips her head up at the sky. Night is heavy and watchful, a roiling swath of dark being held back by the streetlights. When the police sirens roar in from the end of the street, they are almost drowned out by the crowd. "Do you hear that?"

"The sirens?"

"No. The screaming."

She rushes away before the boy can respond. A sinking feeling has gripped her spine, some sixth sense telling her what the scream was. It is innate to expect the worst of the dark. Night draws out the miscreants of the city; night should be feared for what it can easily hide.

The killer trails around the corner, moving away in the same second that the mission agents enter the alley behind Seagreen. The breeze scurries near too, the same gale of wind swirling away from an executioner's hands and into their lungs.

"There are so many," the girl gasps. "Why are there so many?"

The sirens have arrived at the other side of the compound, police loudspeakers fighting back against the rioters. The two pay it no heed as they hurry through the civilian bodies, counting four, five, *six*. They turn around the dead's arms, still warm, freshly robbed of life. Each looks the same: a weeping wound at the inside of their elbow.

"Something has changed," the boy says.

He looks over his shoulder, feeling a shiver skate up his spine. He almost thinks the killer might still be watching. When he examines the scene again, something is lying next to one of the bodies, and he goes to pick it up. A glass vial, incredibly cold to the touch. He holds the object up to the light, and green liquid swirls around inside.

He shows it to the girl. "They're starting to get careless."

32

Seagreen Press closed for a few days while the police surveyed the alley out back and cleared the bodies. When Rosalind returned to the office, she was jittery, impatience raging in every part of her body. She hated inactivity; she'd rank it first on a list of useless ways to be spending her time.

"You'll have a meeting with Ambassador Deoka in ten minutes," Jiemin told her when she sat down at her desk, morning sunlight drawn across her chair. "I have stock to manage, so you must report in for me."

Sometimes, Rosalind wondered whether she would still work as an operative when—*if*—the country eventually settled into peace. Or maybe she would end up chasing some other life-and-death route. Maybe she had developed a compulsion for fixing broken things. National anger fueled every operative, but the crack that it drew in each of them seemed to grow longer for some and shorter for others. Broken things called to broken things, tried to slot their shards together in the hopes that they would fit. If the country wasn't crumbling anymore, what suitability did she have for its care?

Rosalind nodded. "I can do that. What am I reporting on?"

Maybe that was why she had been so drawn to Dimitri Voronin. And afterward, even if the city hadn't almost fallen, even if Rosalind hadn't lost so many of those she loved, even without a single iota of motivation, maybe she was always supposed to become this foul killing thing by nature of her being.

"Here. Let me find it. I've got everything ordered for you already."

Jiemin bent down to rummage through his drawers. Rosalind waited patiently, eyeing the other notes on his desk.

It would do good to interact with Deoka more. In their time away from the office, she and Orion had put their heads together and debated the names on their lists to confirm what accusations they were giving to the Nationalists. She had been surprised at how easily they agreed on each point, but it made sense. This had been their joint effort, after all. Each name was only jotted down after a brief meeting of their eyes and a minuscule nod of Rosalind's approval to Orion or vice versa.

"All that's left is finding out who is actually dirtying their hands doing the killings," Orion had said the night before, putting the pen down.

"And confirming that Deoka is the mastermind," Rosalind added—at the very least, the assigned mastermind with instructions from his government. It was easy to make the call based on what they observed. Finding the evidence that would stand up in a court of law was harder.

"Which one first?" Orion asked. Without hesitation, he turned sideways along the couch and dropped his head into her lap, looking up at her. Rosalind only sighed. At this point, she was so used to him nudging into her personal space that she didn't mind anymore.

"Both at once," Rosalind returned, reaching for a lock of his hair. She had meant to give it a firm tug in an attempt to irritate him, but instead she found herself wrapping the lock around her finger, curious if the curl would hold.

"Information anywhere it will come," Orion said. "I like it. There's the plan, then."

Now, across the department, the Orion outside of her memory gave her a wave as her wandering attention caught his gaze, that same lock of dark hair falling forward. He blew her a kiss. She ignored him.

They needed to meet with Silas soon and push their intelligence together. He had been busy while Seagreen went under. After reporting the alley bodies to the police under his auxiliary undercover identity, he had stayed with them to siphon information about the newest killings, which meant no contact until the coast was clear lest he be exposed.

Six whole bodies, Rosalind thought with a shiver. Without a handler giving them direction, their only option was to put their group thinking to work. What had changed? The killer had certainly been littering bodies here and there without caution, but this was a mass hit—and in the French Concession, no less. Had Dao Feng's attack not been mimicry after all? Was he simply the beginning of an altered modus operandi?

"I do appreciate your flexibility," Jiemin said, drawing Rosalind's thoughts back to the present. "All you youthful workers"—he finally found the right pile of paper in his drawers—"you live to make me look withered and decrepit."

Rosalind eyed him. "How old are you, exactly?"

"Eighteen."

Rosalind extended her hand to receive the papers. "I'm older than you. Watch your back before I steal your job and get paid more."

Jiemin didn't look humored—he only gave her the papers and swayed back into his chair as if he needed to seriously consider whether Rosalind would steal his job.

"It is the way of the world," he sighed beneath his breath.

Rosalind shuffled through the pile absently, familiarizing herself with what she was reporting in on. Five minutes passed, and when she glanced at the clock again, her eyes swiveled back to Jiemin, who had started writing something by hand. In English, too, if she wasn't mistaken.

Subtly, Rosalind inched forward in her seat.

"Jiemin," she said, resuming conversation. "Will you be at the function? The one at Cathay Hotel?"

He didn't look up as he responded. "Quite unlikely."

"Why not?" Rosalind tilted her head, trying to read the text script. *Dear Bosses* . . .

Jiemin suddenly folded the paper into thirds. Damn. He had already finished writing. "Why skip an exhausting social function?" He put the letter in an envelope, then shuddered with revulsion. "I have better ways to waste time than climbing the corporate ladder."

"Don't be such a spoilsport." She leaned in his direction, pretending to give him a jolly thump on the arm. There was some likelihood she could catch hints of the letter if it slipped from his grasp. . . . "You're not alone in your distaste for the corporate world. The rest of us simply know how to take advantage of small joys when they arise. There will be free food."

Unfortunately, Jiemin was already sealing the envelope, smoothing down the vertical length until it was laid flat.

"All the world's a stage," Jiemin said plainly. "And all the people merely players. While I admire how others choose to perform their piece, I have a different exit and entrance."

He started to write the address. An ordinary name, an ordinary street, Zhouzhuang Town, Kunshan City, Jiangsu Province . . .

Hold on, Rosalind thought suddenly, backtracking several mental paces. *Zhouzhuang? Why did that sound familiar?*

"You should get going." Jiemin's voice coming again almost startled her. "You're expected on the hour."

"Of course," Rosalind said. She got out of her chair, her thoughts still moving at breakneck speed. For a fleeting moment, she latched on to something that Celia might have once said to her, and the connection snapped into place. Celia was in Zhouzhuang often. Rosalind didn't know why.

The meeting with Deoka went quickly. Perhaps it was because half of her was zoned out, but the ambassador didn't seem to notice. She reported in; he gave her her tasks. There was nothing to indicate that he suspected her or that their mission was at risk of being compromised.

"Anything else?" Ambassador Deoka asked.

Just as Rosalind was set to take the dismissal, an item in the corner caught her attention, and her eyes leveled on the mysterious crate again. It looked the same as last time. Out of place amid the otherwise refined decoration and certainly out of place as far as task delineation went, because why would Ambassador Deoka himself need to be receiving the newspapers being shipped in? That was production's job.

"I was wondering whether our report on the fundraiser was to your satisfaction?" she asked, buying time. Maybe if she looked closer at the shipping label . . .

"It was perfectly fine," Deoka replied. "You may return to work."

Rosalind bowed her head, then exited the office. There was no point inciting suspicion by trying to get at the crate when it wouldn't offer answers.

In the middle of the corridor, though, Rosalind stopped suddenly, her heels squeaking on the wooden flooring. But it *was* a different crate from the one she had seen last time, wasn't it? Even though she had been too far away to read the text on this one, she realized the shipping label had been pasted onto the side instead of the top.

Seeing Jiemin write that letter had given her an idea. Instead of returning to the production department, she took the stairwell down to the first floor and walked into the mail room.

"Mrs. Mu," Tejas said in greeting when she entered. "What can I help you with?"

Rosalind blinked. "Don't you work upstairs?"

"I take shifts wherever needed, so I'm here today." He wheeled his chair along the desk, then laced his fingers together. "The company tries to avoid unnecessary extra hires."

"Fair enough," Rosalind muttered. She cleared her throat. "Can I see the logs of all shipments going in and out? We have a problem up in production, and I need to track where a package is coming from."

Tejas turned in his chair, glancing at the first shelf in view. "I would have to go rummaging for anything past June—"

"From June until now," Rosalind interrupted.

With a thoughtful noise, Tejas stood up, wandering deeper into the mail room. He shuffled around for a few minutes—moving packages readied to be shipped out and packages readied for internal distribution across Seagreen—before returning with a clipboard.

"This should do, I believe."

"Thank you," Rosalind said gratefully, taking the clipboard. She flipped open the first page and scanned down the logs, focusing on the incoming packages. A prickling sensation was starting at her fingertips. A hum across her nerves, right at the precipice between knowing she was onto something and not quite realizing what that something was yet.

It was easy to search the deliverer's line for the same address she had seen on the shipping label the first time: Warehouse 34, Hei Long Road, Taicang. Each time, Ambassador Deoka was noted as the recipient of the shipment. They were relatively frequent deliveries too. The same line was logged every week or so.

Rosalind didn't know what to do with that information. While Tejas got distracted by something clattering at the back—a package that hadn't been balanced well enough on its shelf—Rosalind stood there by the doorway, gnawing on the inside of her cheeks. There was *something* here. She knew it.

She traced a finger along the entire registry on one of the crates. *Warehouse 34. 19 September. 13.59 lb.*

Rosalind stopped. She tapped that column, her attention zeroing in on the crate's weight. It was a rather specific number. When she looked at the other crates, they were all the same.

Rosalind started to look at the outgoing logs instead. She didn't search for a familiar location. She ran her finger down the boxes that marked how much each package weighed and found more that were the very same number. Nothing would have identified those entries as the very same crates that came into Seagreen Press if not for the weight.

Which meant, sometime after the crates came in, they always went back out. All to an address in the International Settlement near the major commercial district: *286 Burkill Road*. Seagreen Press was an intermediary for whatever was in those crates, and she was willing to bet it wasn't just newspapers.

Rosalind set the clipboard down just as Tejas was returning from the back of the mail room. Her heart was pounding against her ribs, close to tipping out of her body and landing with a splat on the floor.

"You found the problem?" Tejas asked, taking the clipboard back.

"Yet to be determined," Rosalind replied. "But I certainly found something of note."

Many streets away, nearer to the heart of the city, Phoebe was pulling Silas out of his car, insistent on having backup. They had parked beside a stall selling flowers. The seller inched forward, ready to advertise a bouquet, but he seemed to decide against it and darted back in fright as soon as he sighted Phoebe singlehandedly yank a boy from his seat, her earrings clinking on either side of her head with her vigorous movement.

"Come on," she commanded. "I need you to keep watch."

"Phoebe, this is a bad idea." Silas pushed his glasses up, peering at the apartment building half a block down. "I can't believe we've been driving around these few days as a stakeout. I really believed you were curious about observing architecture!" He tried to stand his ground. "Orion is reckless putting you up to this."

"He isn't putting me up to anything. I offered." Phoebe clasped her hands together, her silk gloves gliding against each other. "Please, please, please, come with me. I would be ever so afraid, breaking into an apartment by myself."

After so many days of fruitless driving, Phoebe had accepted that there was no chance she would fulfill her mission that way. It was time to get her hands dirty. She had promised Orion she would find intelligence for him.

"Can't I convince you to partake in a different outing instead?" Silas pleaded. "I'll buy you cake. Or pastries? You like pastries."

"No! We have to do this." Phoebe separated her clasped hands, clutching at her skirts instead. "Do you want to watch me beg?"

"*Phoebe—*"

"So help me, I'll get on my knees right in the middle of the street, and then you will have to answer for my virtue—"

"Fine, *fine*," Silas hurried to say, unable to withstand her theatrics. There were two red blots deepening on his cheeks. "Let's go."

Phoebe beamed, her manner switching to happiness in the blink of an eye. The apartment building across from Peach Lily Palace had its entranceway tucked between a shoe shop and a dance studio, leading up a narrow set of stairs. They approached the door cautiously, but no one was around to keep watch or stand guard. Phoebe supposed that was to be expected around these parts. She clattered up, Silas following shortly behind. On the first landing, there was an old man—another resident—squatting by a metal basin to shine his shoes.

"Hello," Phoebe said, stopping in front of him. "Is there a Liza . . . uh—" She cut herself off, racking her head for what Liza's full name was. Orion had told her. She knew he had.

"Yelizaveta Romanovna," Silas supplied into her ear at a whisper.

"Yelizaveta Romanovna!" Phoebe repeated. She cast Silas a brief, grateful look. "Is there a Yelizaveta Romanovna here?"

"The Ivanova girl?" the man grunted. "Upstairs. So damn noisy all the time."

"Thank you." Phoebe skittered around the man and resumed her climbing. When Silas didn't immediately follow, she turned over her shoulder and gestured for him to hurry. Hesitantly, he circled around the man too, taking the steps two at a time to catch up.

"Phoebe," he said. "What if she's home?"

"Unlikely," Phoebe replied. "Once the Municipal Police discovered she was missing from her cell, they surely would be sending regular inspections to her apartment to see if they could catch her here. She wouldn't risk coming back. In fact . . ." When Phoebe came upon the door on the third floor—the only door on the third floor—she reached out with her gloved hands and turned the handle. It opened easily. "I was betting they wouldn't lock up after looking around, either."

Silas looked increasingly worried. "I thought you said Orion sent you here to *find* Liza."

"He did. But I think there are better ways to get answers."

Phoebe nudged open the door, entering the apartment. The first thing she noticed was the shabby flooring, squeaking upon her entrance as if the panels had once suffered water damage. The walls looked lumpy and thick, painted over and over again with each new occupant. Behind her, Silas winced with every step they took past the door, looking like he wanted to call the police on her himself.

"Stand guard, would you?" Phoebe instructed. She was already browsing the small space, eyes scanning the shelves and the compartment above the bed. "Yell if you hear anyone coming."

Silas, heeding instruction, stood sentry by the door, though his whole disposition twitched with nervousness. Left to her own devices, Phoebe trailed a finger along Liza's desk. An inkpot. A poetry collection. A bulging picture frame that did not contain a photograph but instead a Russian magazine with a title that Phoebe couldn't read.

She picked it up. "How strange—"

"Come on, put that down."

Phoebe whirled around with a scream. By the door, Silas also spun, startled by the noise. Somehow, Liza was standing in the room, her arms folded.

"Silas, I said to watch the door!" Phoebe shrieked.

"I was!" he claimed. "I was standing right here!"

Phoebe took a step back, her legs knocking into the desk. Her eyes were wide on Liza. "Oh my God, you're a ghost."

Liza burst into laughter. "No." She pointed to the wardrobe. "I was in there. But you should see the looks on your faces."

With the wardrobe door open now, Phoebe caught sight of pillows and papers strewn inside, where Liza had clearly made herself comfortable. There was no way that Liza was in there constantly, but it did give her a hidey-hole in the event that officers came poking around the apartment again.

Slowly, Phoebe's heart started to return to its normal rate. By the door, Silas looked like he still needed medical attention. His eyes stayed pinned on her, silently entreating that they leave while knowing that Phoebe would dig her heels in if he actually said anything aloud. Smartly, he remained quiet.

"You find too much joy in this," Phoebe huffed to Liza.

Liza waved her fingers. "Set that down. Did your brother send you?"

Phoebe put the frame down. She frowned. "Why does everyone say that? Maybe I'm just a busybody."

"Maybe you should put your busybody antics to real use instead of sniffing around people like me." Liza jumped onto her bed, crossing her legs. "Wu Xielian, close the door, please."

Silas didn't hesitate for a second. He closed the door, both hands braced upon it even after there was a click.

Liza splayed herself on her sheets. She looked like a starfish, her hair acting as an extra limb that stuck straight up. "I suppose you're here to get a progress report, then. I've been entering different liaison stations all week, rummaging around their information. Nothing of note so far, but there's one more prominent location."

Phoebe was a little taken aback. She hadn't expected Liza to communicate so easily.

By the door, Silas cleared his throat. He asked, "Se Zhong Road?"

It clicked. Liza was trying to figure Silas out. As far as she had been told, he was an agent on her side, and yet it looked as if he had remained mum to their superiors about all these occurrences among the Nationalists.

"Indeed," Liza said. She bounced on the mattress again, tumbling off the side and returning to her feet. "You're familiar with it?"

Silas seemed to sense the trap. He swiveled a glance at Phoebe, stuck between two acts: either pretend that Phoebe knew about his alleged betrayal, or look concerned that Phoebe was about to catch on. He opted for neither. He only kept his expression neutral.

"I wouldn't say familiar with it. I've heard some things."

"That works nicely then." Liza reached under her bed, tucking something into her hand. "Do you two want to help?"

Phoebe and Silas both stared at her, unable to believe what they were hearing. Then:

"Really?" Phoebe asked, at the same time that Silas said, "Absolutely not."

Phoebe turned to Silas, her gaze pleading. "Silas—"

"Stop that," he protested, holding his hand up to cover her large eyes from him. "We are not aiding this!"

"We need to know what happened to Dao Feng!" She hurried in front of him, taking ahold of his wrists. "We need to know if it was a domestic hit. We need to know why my brother was attacked. He's in danger! How can we sit back and do nothing?"

"We're not doing nothing," Silas insisted. He gestured toward Liza. "A skilled agent is at work on it."

Liza grinned happily, taking the compliment.

"*Silas*," Phoebe whined.

"*Phoebe!*"

Liza snorted off to the side, muttering something about being glad she would never have a lover's spat. Overhearing her, Silas turned even redder than before.

"We have to," Phoebe insisted again, ignoring Liza. "Please?"

A second passed. Silas was working through intense internal conflict.

"Fine," he sighed eventually. "Only because you're just going to do it alone if I refuse." He turned to Liza. "What are we to do? Stand watch?"

"Oh, no." With a flourish, Liza revealed what was in her hand—a box of matches—then tossed it at Silas. "You're handling the explosives."

33

Alisa had told the two annoying Nationalists—or rather, the two annoying . . . whatevers—to meet her by the location, thinking it too suspicious if they exited her building at once. It would give her time to fetch the explosives.

She was actually just fetching firecrackers, but she loved nothing more than giving people a little fright and anxiety.

She watched the hand on her old pocket watch pass a full minute, then slinked out from the building, blending into the crowd on Thibet Road. Her precautionary measures kicked in. While she inspected a cart full of turnips, she pulled a jacket from her bag and slid one arm in. When she passed over a few coins to buy a single tomato, she grabbed the other sleeve with the same motion, changing her outerwear's color. As soon as she turned around, her bag slid down her arm and landed with a hard thud on the ground. Feigning a tired sigh, Alisa reached down, using the pretense of retrieving her bag to hide her hand as she reached in again and pulled out a hat rimmed with false hair. She ducked her head, all her blond curls falling forward by the push of gravity, easily scooped up at once and shoved under the hat before she straightened.

Alisa turned to peer at herself in the reflection of a pharmacy window. If anyone was watching her, they just lost her before their very eyes. Perhaps she should dye her hair black and cut it into a bob for real. The style was starting to fall out of fashion in this decade, though. A shame.

"How much?"

The boy on the small plastic seat jerked his head up, taken by surprise at Alisa's sudden inquiry. She had approached from behind, avoiding the busy rickshaws rumbling around the intersection of Fuzhou Road and Shandong Road. At the sidewalk right outside the Tai He Pharmacy, the boy had set up a stall to sell painted toy horses, hawking to the pedestrians moving about the intersection corner.

"Which one?" he asked, gesturing to the horses.

Alisa shook her head. "I want the firecrackers."

"Shhhh!" the boy hissed immediately, looking around. What was he acting so surprised for? Everyone knew he was infamous for being Fuzhou Road's explosives kid. The toy horses were only a front. "You trying to get the police to come?"

Peeved, the boy pulled a black cloth bag from behind, opening the top for Alisa to peer inside. "I only have a few left for today. Take it or leave it."

She handed over a wad of cash. "Enough?"

"Eh. It will do if you don't yell again."

They made the exchange, and Alisa continued on her way, hugging the cloth bag to her chest. She headed east, following the main roads where the crowds were congregated. The farther she walked, the thinner the streets turned, the pavement growing rough and the smell of wet laundry wafting under her nose.

Alisa stopped outside an ordinary-looking brothel. Though the first floor functioned as intended, the upper levels were also a Communist liaison station, going undercover to avoid detection by the Kuomintang.

Phoebe and Silas were already waiting, peering at a newspaper around the building corner. She walked up to them, giving over the bag.

"Wait five minutes, then light them," she instructed. "Catch their attention first, then lead them away for some distance. There are only six people working on the upper levels of this facility—I need them distracted."

"This is the crudest mission task I have ever been given," Silas muttered. He peered into the bag.

Alisa clicked her tongue. "So long as it gets the job done. Ready?"

She didn't wait; she didn't quite care. If they were going to help, then they really ought to be flexible.

Her feet quick, she passed through the first floor of the building, climbing the stairs hidden near the kitchen. There was a reception desk to greet visitors coming onto the upper levels, and Alisa prepared a small smile.

"I have an appointment with Rabbit," she said. There was no agent code-named Rabbit. It was only a catchphrase to prove that she was welcome here. She leaned on the front desk. "I don't suppose you can put me in contact with someone?"

The woman behind the desk peered at a calendar, checking if she was expecting anyone today. Surprise visits to liaison stations were rare and, subsequently, suspicious.

"I don't know how much I can help—"

The first firecracker went off. From the upper levels, the bang sounded just like gunshots, and the receptionist shot to her feet, asking Alisa to please hold.

A door opened down the hallway.

"What is that?" a man bellowed, hurrying out. He was followed by two others, their faces equally harried. There was a third floor above them, so Alisa had to assume the other two operatives were there. On the ground, the firecrackers grew louder. If this was an attack, then the first priority of business was evacuation. She watched the receptionist hurry down the stairs first, then the three men, urgent in their need to see what exactly was making the noise.

Alisa, as soon as she was left alone on the floor, darted into one of the offices. She didn't have anything specific she was looking for, so she didn't waste time sifting around the stacked boxes or piles of folders. She hurried for the desk instead—which took up half the office—and made a quick scan of its contents. Rosalind had been insistent that Communists had come after her and Orion Hong. That they might have taken the file back from her, that they might have attacked her handler afterward.

"How am I supposed to get information about whether we're pursuing Nationalists without outright asking?" Alisa muttered to herself.

Nothing caught her eye. Time was ticking.

Then she saw the telephone hooked to the side of the table, and an idea occurred to her. Maybe she *could* outright ask. It wasn't as if these were true war plans out in the countryside. The level of confidentiality couldn't be that high within their own network.

Alisa picked up the telephone. As soon as the operator answered, she deepened her voice.

"My apologies. My last call dropped, and then I was summoned away for urgent business. Could you reconnect me with the previous line?"

"One moment, please."

The operator didn't seem to consider anything amiss about her request. It was normal enough for calls to drop.

A click came over the line. A few seconds of silence, then a gruff voice, barking, "Wéi?"

Alisa worked frantically to place it. It was nobody whom she had spoken to personally, for sure. Had she heard it broadcast on the radio before? Was it someone high up?

"Wéi? I cannot hear you. Speak up!"

She took a shot in the dark.

"Uh—hello. What is our next move on pursuing those Nationalist agents?"

The response was immediate. Whoever the last caller dialed on this line was, he didn't even notice Alisa's awful imitation of what she thought middle-aged men sounded like when they talked.

"Did my message not go through? Pivot into observation. It's too dangerous. No more pursuit after the last time was a failure. Shred the memo. The assignment has been transferred to covert."

Click. The man had hung up. Alisa put the receiver down quickly, her heart racing. *No more pursuit after the last time was a failure.* Then it *was* the Communists. They really had gone after Rosalind and Orion, unless there happened to be other Nationalists pursued through the city too.

But . . . *pivot into observation. It's too dangerous.* What had any of that meant? What was *dangerous* about Rosalind and Orion?

Alisa perked an ear to the window, listening. The firecrackers had stopped. The building would be returning to normal operation soon.

"Wait," Alisa whispered. She picked up one of the files on the desk.

```
Memo: 4 Bao Shang Road
(Contact made under the guise of being
Kuomintang agents. Do not contact
again; subject is suspicious.)
```

She flipped it open.

```
Transcribed by ███████████
```

```
"I saw it all happen through my window.
I live on the sixth floor, so high up,
good angles into the alleyways behind.
Late at night, █████████████████████
████████████████████████████████████
```

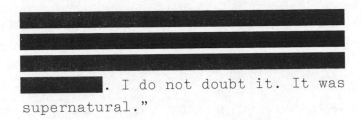. I do not doubt it. It was supernatural."

Alisa nudged the file back the way she'd found it. They redacted these memos so heavily because the agents reading them already knew what the matter was, minimizing the chance that a pair of snooping eyes would stumble onto the details, which was exactly Alisa's aim.

"Number four, Bao Shang Road," Alisa memorized aloud. Before the rightful owner of the office could return, she hurried out and returned to the front desk, as if she had been waiting there all along. The receptionist emerged from the stairs first.

Alisa clutched her hands together innocently. "Is everything okay?"

"Only some troublemakers," the receptionist answered. "You needed something?"

The other three entered the floor then too, muttering among themselves with their curiosity. One by one they disappeared back into their offices, doors closing in a series of thuds. No one called out in suspicion. No one yelled out in accusation that someone had been rummaging around the liaison station.

Alisa nodded. "I need an address for the active operation in Taicang."

"Hey."

The moment Alisa called out from behind, she watched both Phoebe and Silas jump six feet into the air, with Silas almost falling off the restaurant step he had been crouched on. As he hurried to stand, his hand whacked a lantern hanging overhead, taking it right off its hook, and though Alisa was about to call out a warning, it was Phoebe who caught it smoothly before it could hit the ground, saving the flame inside.

"You take far too much pleasure in doing that," Silas huffed. "Were you successful?"

Alisa sat down on the step too. The restaurant was closed, either recently out of business or on its off-hours. Phoebe hung the lantern back into place.

"Partially," Alisa answered carefully. "I think we did go after Orion and Ros—Janie." Alisa coughed, pretending the accidental slip had been a strange noise in her throat. "But . . . for whatever reason, they've decided not to pursue it further."

"And the other items Janie wanted?" Phoebe asked. "The file? The handler?"

Alisa shook her head. "I don't know. I'll keep digging, I suppose."

Silas looked confused. Phoebe, too, pulled a face, winding her finger along her necklace.

"I don't understand," she said. "But maybe it's just me."

"No, it's not just you," Silas reassured her. "That also does not sound right to me."

Alisa shrugged. "I'm only telling you what I found."

"And there was nothing else?"

Alisa considered telling them about the memo. But there was nothing particular about the information anyway. She may as well investigate first, and then give Rosalind the information directly if it was pertinent.

"Nothing." Alisa stretched her neck, then pivoted to go. "Oh"— she turned over her shoulder, already walking away—"and I got you this: 240 Hei Long Road, Taicang."

"What is that?" Phoebe called after her.

"Your other brother," Alisa answered. "In case you ever need him."

———————

Hours later, Rosalind was working herself into a sweat, exhibiting the most amount of physical activity she had performed in weeks: buttoning up her new qipao. Orion had been summoned to local headquarters again. The apartment was all hers. When she returned home to find a qipao delivered at the door, she figured she might as well try it on before the function at Cathay Hotel. Most of her nice clothes had frayed over the years—if not by wear and tear, then by bloodstains.

"How many buttons can you put on one article of clothing?" Rosalind muttered. She glared into the kitchen mirror, jostling the glass surface when her elbow knocked into the gilded side. The buttons were so *miniature* for no reason. Her own fault, she supposed. Her vanity had won out when she got the qipao fitted while Seagreen was out of action. In the selection process, she had chosen the one that was most formfitting, with a high collar and no sleeves. Deep green fabric and yellow flowers stitched in by hand, the design pulled together by a series of small buttons at the back.

The final button went in. Rosalind breathed out a lungful of relief, her arms almost numb when she lowered them to her sides again.

Then she glanced down, seeing the necklace she was supposed to be trying on too, and swore out loud. At the same time, the door to the apartment opened, bringing Orion in.

"What are you cursing about—"

He stopped. Stared. Kept staring.

Rosalind peered at the mirror again. "Did I grow an extra head? What are you looking at?"

"I—nothing, nothing." Orion shook himself out of his daze. He unwound a black scarf from his neck and tossed it onto the coffee table. "Did you—is your—are you—" He cleared his throat. His words seemed to have escaped him, and Rosalind quirked a brow.

"Do you need any help?" Orion finally managed, nodding to the necklace.

"Please," Rosalind said. She held the chain out, and Orion walked behind her, their fingers tangling for a moment while she passed the pearls.

He drew his arms to her front and settled the chain at her neck. "I absolutely must inquire something," he began solemnly. "Did you dress up so nicely just for me? If you had told me earlier, I would have made a dinner reservation to celebrate the occasion."

Rosalind scoffed. Though she could hear the humor in Orion's tone, she wouldn't be surprised if he were half-serious. "I'm trying on the qipao for Friday. The day I dress up to dine with you is the day something has gone very, very wrong in my mind."

Orion held back his laugh, pressing his lips together. "Oh?" He opened the necklace clasp. "So was that an imposter at our wedding meal?"

"Yes, I hired an actress," Rosalind deadpanned. "I have too much trouble digesting whenever you're around. The stress you give me shuts down my intestines."

Orion secured the clasp. The pearls hung nicely at her collar, not too high, not too low. Rosalind took a long look in the mirror, examining herself for any detail to be improved. When she didn't find anything, she hummed her approval. Over her shoulder, Orion stayed unmoving too.

"We really missed an opportunity, you know," he said. His fingers reached for the edges of her sleeveless qipao, tracing the lace there. She suppressed a shiver. "If we had entered Seagreen only engaged, we could have faked the ceremony too and invited everyone."

Rosalind considered the idea. Her reflection tilted her head when she did; her lips turned down on either side of the glass.

"Shuǐxiān," she said suddenly.

Orion blinked. "What was that?"

"Daffodils," Rosalind repeated in English, in case he had not understood. The Chinese language didn't have an exact name for the flower—its literal translation was "water goddess," because the yellow and white blooms were said to scatter evil spirits. "I would have liked daffodils in my bouquet."

Once, she used to dream about things like that. A Western-style wedding, with white veils and a long dress train. Some old church in Paris, the pews filled with only a scattered handful of people, the air smelling like summer warmth and a meadow of flowers.

But that wasn't her future anymore. If she were to encounter any meadow of flowers, it would be on the battlefield during war, the ground watered with crimson and growing with bloodred petals.

"Why daffodils?" Orion asked.

Rosalind hesitated. It was hard to say it aloud. But she wanted to answer truthfully. "I . . . well, I saw them in my mother's wedding photos."

She had stumbled onto the album without her father's permission, found it tucked in one of the farthest corners of his office when she was rummaging around for his stock receipts. The cover had been plain, no description or markings, but had opened to her parents grinning at each other, looking so happy even with the blurriness of the aged photograph.

She had always known that her father hated her birth, hated how her and her sisters' arrival into this world had taken her mother away from him. All the same, it was bizarre to see it confirmed, bizarre to see a moment frozen in time that captured him like she had never seen him before. Some part of her did not care if she never spoke to her father again. Another part of her persistently carried a fantasy of being appreciated in the end, that he would blink awake with a start and realize that his children were still here, still clutching at survival every day and in need of help.

"You don't talk about your past much, Janie Mead."

Rosalind shrugged. "What is there to talk about? It's shadows and gloom."

"You know plenty about me when my whole past is splashed in the newspapers." His voice had turned quiet. Without being asked, Orion started helping her remove the necklace, her fitting finished. "Give me some crumbs, at least. What was your favorite childhood food?"

Rosalind considered the question for a mere second. The apartment was suddenly drafty, bringing a proper shiver down her spine. "Croissants."

"How French."

"Our French tutor bought them for us." Not a lie. He did buy them—in Paris.

"Our?" Orion echoed. His head lifted, catching her gaze in the mirror for a fleeting second before turning back to the necklace clasp. "You have siblings."

"Sisters," Rosalind allowed. "One is dead. The other is far away."

A quiet exhale, behind her. "I'm sorry."

Rosalind hadn't felt heartache for Kathleen in some time now. The real Kathleen, the one who hadn't turned fifteen years old before influenza took her life. Rosalind's grief had grown muted, appearing only when the memory of that hospital room flashed in her head once in a blue moon. She saw herself clutching Celia's hand when the doctors rushed in, the two of them frightened and trembling and wondering what was going to happen. If she was entirely honest, what she mourned the most was how life had been while Kathleen was alive.

"It's okay," was all she said aloud. "What is family for if not to love us and then break our hearts?"

The necklace detached. Orion set it onto the kitchen table beside them, each pearl clinking down on the wooden surface. When it came to real heartbreak, Rosalind wasn't thinking of Kathleen.

She was thinking of Juliette.

The final image she had of her cousin was in that safe house after revolution had broken out. Rosalind had been in a world of pain, her family's punishment still fresh and raw, the whip marks on her back still bloody. She wanted to take it out on the world. She wanted to resent everyone she loved—just to feel something other than helplessness.

Is this the last time I'll see you? she had asked her cousin. A single moment of vulnerability breaking through her haze.

I don't know, Juliette had answered, as quiet as a grave, as grave as the quiet. If Rosalind had stayed a moment longer, the tears would have fallen from her eyes. She had left without looking back.

She should have looked back. Just once more.

"You're the eldest of your sisters."

Rosalind turned around to face Orion, pressing her back to the mirror and feeling the qipao's silk lining graze against the raised edges of her scars. Orion wasn't posing a question this time. He was making a statement.

"How did you know?"

"You remind me of Oliver sometimes." Orion looked pleased to have been right. "The seriousness. The world on your shoulders."

At that moment, a fading beam of sunlight found its way through the window. It bounced right off the metal of a frying pan, and suddenly the kitchen was as bright as a golden spotlight. Rosalind and Orion both squinted, bracing against the radiance in their periphery, but it didn't interrupt their conversation. Something unexplainable had already wrapped around them like a protective layer, comforting and secure.

Even if she closed her eyes against the piercing gold, she could re-create the image before her in her mind's eye, not a detail to be spared. The kitchen with its tidy tables. The walls in pale green.

Orion with his gaze on her, lashes half-lowered, dark as though they were dusted with soot. It was entirely unfair how lovely he was in every light, like he had been drawn to life with a tape measure in hand, each proportion perfect and unrelenting.

She wondered if he knew who Oliver's mission partner was. If he had ever seen Celia in the field before and whether he would make the connection if the two of them were placed before him.

"Do you miss him?" Rosalind asked.

Orion widened his eyes, those dark lashes turning up.

"Of course," he said. He knew exactly who she was talking about without missing a beat. "I hate him for leaving. That doesn't stop me from missing him. It is the same with my mother. But no matter how much I tear myself apart trying to figure out why they would go, it doesn't bring them back."

Rosalind felt her heart twist. She tugged a pin out of her hair. "You don't have to justify yourself." Her heavy mass of hair tumbled down her back. "You feel what you feel. You'll drive yourself mad otherwise."

"Ah." Orion put his hands in his pockets. "There's another tell that you're the eldest. The wisdom."

Rosalind shook her head. She was only the eldest by a few minutes anyway. There was hardly time to gather that much wisdom. Still, it was nice to be assigned that label. It was nice, for once, to be someone worldly and knowing rather than foolish and irresponsible and easily tricked.

At last, Rosalind pushed off the wall mirror and wandered away, breaking the bubble that had formed around them.

"I found the most curious information today," she called as she entered her bedroom, leaving the door half-open so that Orion could still hear her. She didn't realize that their conversation had almost dropped to murmurs until she resumed normal volume again.

"How so?"

"I looked into Seagreen's logs when the mail room attendant wasn't watching too closely." It was much easier to unloop all the buttons at her back than it was to close them. One after the other, they popped loose as soon as she gave a firm tug. "There's a shipment that keeps getting sent to the office, addressed directly to Deoka. A crate, allegedly containing our weekly issues. Isn't that curious? He hardly has to burden himself with menial tasks like checking the quality of each issue."

Rosalind stepped out of the fitted qipao, rolling her shoulders around as blood rushed back to all the places it had been pinched out of. With a quick inspection of her closet, she pulled out another qipao, this one far more casual, more suited for street strolling.

"You said *allegedly*," Orion called from the living room. "What do you think is actually in them?"

"Why don't we go find out?" Rosalind changed quickly, then grabbed a set of earrings off her vanity. She slid the door open fully, standing in the threshold as she stabbed sapphires into her earlobes. "286 Burkill Road. That's where the packages are being sent. The boxes could have instructions. They could have murder weapons. They could have correspondences. Either way, they keep shipping *something* to an alternate location, and what could be more suspicious than moving work items off the work site? If we're trying to find evidence for Deoka as the mastermind behind the terror killings, there must be something important here."

Orion craned over his shoulder. He had seated himself on the couch in the time that Rosalind was changing.

"When did you get home?" he asked suddenly.

Had he not heard what she just said? This could close their whole mission, and he was asking about her clock-out hour instead?

"Five thirty?" she guessed. "What does that have to do with anything?"

"You waited." He rose to his feet. "You waited for me to get back. You could have easily made a detour to Burkill Road yourself after leaving Seagreen."

She could not keep up with Orion Hong. If he wasn't chiding her for not telling him enough, he was surprised that she was treating him as a trusted partner.

"You're so very right," she said, heading for the door. "I should have gone eons ago. Why have I bothered waiting for you—"

Unmoving from where he stood, Orion snagged her by the arm as she passed, stopping her in her step.

"It was not a critique." He smiled. "I'm just pleasantly surprised."

Perhaps Rosalind should have been a little surprised at herself too. It hadn't been a question that she would wait for him to come along. She had known he would return shortly, so it was only sensible.

"Your life is mine as mine is yours," she said, very seriously. "We are bound in duty if not in matrimony. I won't make the same mistake twice."

Orion's smile had turned into a wide grin. She didn't know what was so amusing about all this—did he like the idea of their mutual death? She had always known he was a little off the rails.

"It's cold outside, beloved. I'll fetch you your coat," Orion said, heading for the bedroom. "Burkill Road, off we go."

34

The tram was moving slowly, inching along its tracks at a snail's pace. They were entering Nanjing Road, which meant there was activity in every direction, rickshaw runners and pedestrians surging onto the roads on a whim, scaring even the toughest tram operator. Rosalind peered out the open window, eyeing the road ahead. Men in business suits reading their newspapers by the fading sunlight; elderly women with their shopping baskets; pickpockets moving through the crowds with lightning-fast fingers.

The busyness would start turning residential as soon as Nanjing Road transitioned into Burkill Road. Sincere and Wing On loomed ahead like two dragons guarding their hordes, shoppers moving in and out of the department store doors as their protective underlings.

From her side, Orion suddenly put an arm around Rosalind's shoulder. "I think we're being followed."

Rosalind didn't visibly react. "We're on a tram, dear."

"Okay, let me rephrase. A fellow passenger is keeping an eye on us a bit too closely for my comfort. The man reading *Shanghai News*. He got on when we did."

Carefully, Rosalind lifted her eyes to make the search. There were two long rows of seating, one on each side of the tram, so she sighted the man opposite them immediately. He was pressed right up against the operator's box, holding his newspaper over half his face. When her gaze remained on him too long, his eyes shifted up, locking with hers for a fraction of a second before he turned back to his paper. He was Chinese, dressed in a Western suit. Unless they decided to outright ask, it was impossible to know whether he was Deoka's man, a Communist agent, or some mysterious third party.

The tram stopped, letting new passengers on.

Rosalind said, "On my mark, let's get off."

"We're still three stops away."

"You want to be followed to our location?"

Orion grimaced. "Right."

If Deoka had sent him, their covers were about to be blown mere steps away from the end. They were so close. Rosalind waited, eyeing the last passenger squeezing onto the tram. Up front, the driver pulled on the bell, giving a warning for the pedestrians ahead.

"Now. Go left."

At once, Orion and Rosalind stood, taking separate exits and pushing past the newly boarded passengers. Rosalind's feet hit the pavement hard; a second later, Orion exited from the front of the tram.

The tram lurched away. The man reading *Shanghai News* had not reacted fast enough to follow them off.

"Here I was," Orion said, "thinking that we were having a lovely evening date."

Rosalind started to walk. They weren't far from their destination, or at least not far enough to justify getting onto another tram. "You don't start all your dates throwing off a tail?"

"I'm divorcing you immediately if that's your idea of fun."

Rosalind's lips twitched. "Watch your step."

Orion almost tripped on the tram tracks despite her warning. She released a burst of laughter; Orion gave her a half-hearted glare. For the rest of their walk, the two were watchful for more pursuers, but the night was setting in, and the dark made it easy to blend in with the strolling crowds.

Eventually, as they came to Burkill Road, the frantic commercial activity lessened. Rosalind and Orion observed the numbers, counting up. 278 . . . 280 . . . 282 . . .

"Does this location look familiar to you?" Rosalind asked under her breath.

Orion shook his head. "I've never been here before."

There was the address: 286 Burkill Road. It was a single residential building, unlike the commercial shops on either side. Rosalind might have guessed it to be a hotel if not for the front door, heavy and foreboding. Perhaps an apartment complex, then, with the units inside shared. She shifted closer, waving Orion along. In case they looked suspicious lurking around, she made a show out of peering into the saloon windows next door, pretending to be searching for someone.

"What do we do now?" Orion muttered. "Stake it out?"

The front door to 286 Burkill Road opened. A woman exited, her purse swinging on her arm. Rosalind turned quickly to get a better look, but the woman was a stranger.

"Why don't we just go in?"

"What?" Orion demanded, as if he might have misheard her. "Why would you say that?"

Rosalind reached her hand out wordlessly, prompting Orion to take it. Much to his credit, he didn't hesitate despite his complaining, their fingers intertwining before Rosalind tugged him forward, climbing the three steps to the door. She didn't give him any time to doubt the plan. Rosalind pushed through the front door and took them into the building.

It was dark inside, one exposed lightbulb hanging from the ceiling. A set of stairs to their left only led to a second-floor door, so it was hard to say what the rest of the building looked like.

Nevertheless, Rosalind's shoes had sunken into a circular rug upon entering, and there was a small table with a telephone at the back. This didn't look like a building hallway, one that would split into separate apartment units. This looked like the foyer of a house.

Suddenly, a door opened from the side, bringing a man into the foyer. Though he had been deep in thought, muttering something to himself, he stopped short the moment he spotted Rosalind and Orion. He stared at them. They stared back. When he spoke, it was in Japanese.

Rosalind squeezed Orion's hand rapidly, spurring him into action. He reacted fast, answering the man with a smile and gesturing toward Rosalind as if he was explaining that she had wanted to see something in here. Rosalind tried her best to look as though she were following the conversation. The light was flickering, turning even dimmer. It was very likely that they could pass for Japanese.

But the man's tone had started turning sour. Orion let go of her hand. He was trying to placate the man, assuaging him—

Rosalind reached down in a blur, snapping a thin blow dart gun out of her qipao lining and putting it to her mouth. Before Orion had noticed that the man was reaching for something in his back pocket, her blow dart landed on his chest. The man paused, looking down.

He crumpled to the floor with a thud.

"What was he saying?" Rosalind asked. She dropped the blow dart gun beside him.

Orion needed a moment to gather his thoughts. He stared at the man, blinking once, twice, before surging forward to check the man's pulse and turn him over. There was a pistol clutched in his hand, almost fully drawn. Orion had been seconds away from getting shot.

"That this isn't a place for visitors. Come on. Let's see what he was hiding."

Orion hurried into the side room, making a cautionary sweep before prompting Rosalind to enter too. Inside, as he locked the door after them, Rosalind needed a moment for her eyes to adjust to the darkness before she could see the shapes and outlines in the candlelit office. Thick velvet curtains were drawn over the windows, blocking the night outside. There was an air of clamminess despite the tidy desk and clean painted walls. As if at any second, the ceiling might start seeping with water.

"I see more crates," Rosalind stated. They were stacked by the corner, identical to the ones that had been in Deoka's office. When Rosalind crept closer, her eyes adjusted to find a similar shipping label affixed to the top, though these were signed with Ambassador Deoka's name as the sender.

Rosalind searched around for something to pry off the crate top. "I'm going to open it," she said. "This might be the only chance we have to see what's inside." On a cursory glance, however, the desk had been cleared of anything she could use, and there was nothing else within reach. Orion shrugged too, patting around his pockets and coming up empty.

"I can offer you a gun if you want to shoot it open."

The walls seemed to shudder at the very thought of a bullet being fired within these quarters. It would probably set fire to the stifling air. With no other option, Rosalind pulled a pin out of her hair, inserting the sharp end into a slit along the crate's top and pushing down.

"Any luck?" Orion asked two minutes later.

"It would be nice to get some help," Rosalind muttered, wiping a thin layer of sweat off her forehead. "I'm guessing they don't usually use a thin pin to open—"

Just as she gave the metal one hard push, there was a thunderous knock on the door. Rosalind jumped, so startled that she lost her grip on the hairpin. Though it finally pried open the crate and popped the top component right off, the pin snapped backward in an abrupt, uncontrolled motion, drawing a short red scratch down her arm.

"Tā mā de," Rosalind muttered. Her hairpin clattered to the floor.

"You did it," Orion said.

She had also just poisoned herself, but she supposed that was a problem to deal with when it started setting in. The door jiggled, pushing against the lock. One voice shouted a question. When neither Rosalind nor Orion answered, that one voice turned into multiple, surrounding the foyer. Given that there had been a man left unconscious out there, it was only a matter of time before the other occupants of this building knew that something was wrong.

Rosalind winced, making a rapid search of the crate. They were running out of time. Inside, the topmost layer was an issue of Seagreen's newspaper. She pushed it out of the way hurriedly, revealing a three-by-three collection of glass vials underneath.

Vials?

"Janie," Orion said immediately. "Bring one of those to the light."

Rosalind plucked one out, tipping the vial closer to the flickering candle. It was half-filled with a liquid, obnoxiously green. The top was sealed with a metallic casing, but the kind that would have easily ripped if Rosalind poked a finger through.

Or a syringe needle.

"You sound like you've seen this before," she observed.

"I have. In Haidi's purse."

"*Haidi's* purse—" Rosalind was forced to clamp down on her surprise when there was another shudder on the door. She shoved the vial into her sleeve, then grabbed the crate lid with the mail label affixed to it. This was going to be their evidence. As soon as she figured out what those vials were.

"Come on," she said to Orion. "The window."

"Wait." Orion had his head tilted, concentrating on the voices. A moment later, he blinked with surprise and remarked, "The people in the foyer—they're soldiers. Someone is giving orders. It sounds military."

Rosalind snatched her hairpin off the floor, then hauled the curtains aside and pushed the window open into the night outside.

"*Climb.*"

The door heaved against its hinges. Rosalind made her exit first, swinging her legs over the windowsill and landing smoothly in the alley. She checked her arm. The red scratch wasn't healing. It wouldn't until the poison was counteracted.

"Let's *go!*"

Summoned once more, Orion clambered through the window, his shoes hitting the alley ground just as the door to the office burst open. Narrowly, Rosalind hauled him out of view, the two of them breaking into a run before the soldiers inside could see them.

"Main road is that way," Orion said, casting a glance over his shoulder.

Rosalind shook her head. "They're too close behind, and the main road is too wide. They'll see us. Back roads might throw them off."

Orion didn't argue. So long as they could navigate the labyrinth of unmapped alleys and lane apartment walkways, they would reach Avenue Road and have a far better chance of losing their pursuers there. Rosalind could already hear yelling in the distance. After they passed an old woman watering her plants and took three sharp turns, the woman's loud, angered protests some few seconds later warned Orion and Rosalind that their pursuers had entered the back alleys too, probably kicking over her plants.

"Why are imperial soldiers hiding out at a residence in the International Settlement?" Orion hissed. He wasn't really posing it as a question; they knew. If you started a scheme to prepare for invasion, you needed your soldiers ready to swoop in.

"I would guess they probably have secret bases all over the city."

The sound of bullets rang into the alleys. Rosalind and Orion both flinched, their breathing heavy, visible in the brisk night air.

"This way." Orion tugged them to the left, then under a stone gate, then past two residential houses. The ground started to move up on an incline, the pavement turning to smoother stone. The path should have led to an exit, bleeding out onto a main road.

But they ran right into another curved alley and hit a dead end.

"Shit," Orion hissed. He tilted his head up, up, up, scanning the wall. Only one alley light around the corner illuminated their surroundings. "Is that too high to climb?"

"*Way* too high," Rosalind replied, her throat tight. She didn't know if her increasing dizziness was a result of their desperate sprint or the toxins rapidly entering her system. They would have to abandon the crate lid she was holding. Toss it aside somewhere and act clueless when the soldiers caught up. The soldiers hadn't *seen* them, after all. Perhaps Rosalind and Orion could play it off. Make it seem like they were such unlikely suspects for intruders who could break into an undercover military facility that the thought was laughable. They were only a couple out on a night stroll.

Rosalind looked around. Except there was nowhere to hide the evidence, not a single trash bag or an abandoned piece of furniture. Of all alleys to keep clean, it *had* to be this one.

Orion seemed to come to the same conclusion. "We need to hide that."

"*Where?*" Rosalind demanded, her ears roaring with noise as she shook the object of theft in her hands. Her arm, too, had started stinging where she'd been scratched.

"Maybe we can fold it?"

"It's wood, Orion. How do you fold wood?"

Orion made a noise that sounded like a whistling teakettle. "Can we break it into pieces?"

Rosalind gave him an incredulous look. "IT'S WOOD!"

They were going to get caught in no less than ten seconds. They were going to get caught and then hauled off for execution.

"Can we *throw* it?" he suggested next.

"Over the wall? Are you out of your *mind*—"

Suddenly, Rosalind looked at the crate piece again. It wasn't heavy enough to throw over the wall because it was too thin.

It was *thin*.

"Orion," she said.

Orion was so deep in his panic that he didn't register the eerie calm coming over her. The strike of an idea—one so absurd that she blamed it purely on her poisoned mind—lit a match and caught ablaze.

"What?" he nearly screeched.

She shoved the crate piece to his chest, then pressed up against him, putting her hands around his neck. Just as the soldiers entered the alley, she rose onto the tips of her toes and kissed him, hiding the damning evidence between their bodies.

She didn't know if it was the poison or adrenaline causing the buzz that ran from the back of her neck to the tips of her fingers. All she knew was that something was different from the last time they had done this, that it was electric when their lips met, like she had plugged herself directly into an outlet. Faintly, she heard the soldiers call out what sounded like an all-clear in Japanese, then their footsteps fading as they went to check the next alley, but something was holding her still, something stopped her from pulling away when Orion set his hands around her waist and pressed closer.

Rosalind drew back slowly, several delayed beats after the danger had passed. Her head was spinning.

The poison, she reassured herself. Not Orion. Definitely not Orion. Definitely not his dark eyes, wide and volatile while she was the subject of his astounded stare. The crate piece started to slip between them. Rosalind seized it before it could fall, her hands clumsy.

"Hey," she said breathlessly. "Do me a favor."

Orion blinked once. "Anything."

"Catch me."

And with the barest second for him to heed her instructions, Rosalind collapsed into his arms, falling unconscious.

35

A concerned neighbor was crossing the courtyard when Orion hurried through the building door, shifting Janie in his arms so that she wasn't jostled. Of all times to run into a neighbor he had never met before, the universe chose now?

"Don't worry!" he exclaimed, swerving out of the neighbor's path. "This is my wife. She just drank too much at a banquet."

He hurried away, beelining for Lao Lao's apartment. He knew that Janie's situation had to be serious, because if she were even slightly conscious, she would have scolded him for making it sound like she couldn't handle her alcohol.

"Lao Lao!" he called outside her door. "Are you home?"

There was no response. Gritting his teeth, Orion marched for the stairs instead—at the very least, he had the key to Janie's apartment. Though it was a small struggle that involved a slight adjustment, he was nudging through the doors before long, tossing keys and bag and crate piece onto the couch and maneuvering Janie carefully into the bedroom. He set her on her bed as gently as he could manage.

Janie looked too pale. It scared him.

"What's this ruckus?"

The familiar voice boomed from the apartment front door, croaky and tired. Orion hurried out, skidding into the living room to see Lao Lao standing outside in her nightgown.

"Lao Lao," he heaved. "I don't suppose you have poison antidotes?"

The moment Janie dropped into his arms, he had run a cursory inspection for wounds, frantically searching for what had taken her down. He found the red scratch after a minute of panic, then remembered what she had said before about her hairpins being poisoned. Damn Janie and her silent burden-bearing.

"Antidotes?" Lao Lao echoed, taken aback.

"She's breathing," Orion went on. He had started rambling. "It's shallow and it's not getting worse, so I didn't take her to the hospital. I don't want to risk blowing our cover, but I also don't want to risk her *dying*—"

"What was she hit with?"

Orion stopped. Took a ragged breath. "Her own hairpin."

"Ah. I should have something downstairs. Talk to her, bǎobèi. Make sure she keeps breathing." As calm as anything, Lao Lao turned on her slippers and started back down the stairs. Orion was left standing in the dark living room, wondering if the old woman had grasped the severity of the situation.

"Talk to her?" he called back. "She's unconscious!"

Lao Lao was already in her own apartment, rummaging about loudly. Orion had no other option except to hurry back into the bedroom and crouch by Janie's side, watchful of her breathing. It hadn't been hard to carry her around the city. He was barely winded. The only part of him in distress was his pulse, beating at a hundred miles per hour.

"Please don't scare me," Orion muttered. A thin gleam of sweat remained on her forehead. He had never seen Janie Mead like this before: eyes closed, withdrawn from the world. For as long as he had known her, she didn't seem like she was capable of shutting down. She seemed as if she might have been born with her eyes wide open, keen and observant.

It felt like he was witnessing something he wasn't supposed to see—but he didn't want to look away. The storybook thief who had managed a glimpse into the dark and foreboding caves, only to find glimmering treasure instead of terrors. This wasn't supposed to be his to claim.

He wanted it nevertheless.

Orion brushed Janie's face, moving her hair out of the way. There was a tightness in his chest, spreading from the cage of his ribs to the hollow of his throat. He thought it might have been the start of a headache, but when he looked up and down to test the tension behind his eyes, he felt perfectly fine. It wasn't his head; it was his flesh and insides, his raw heart, pounding and pounding.

"I've split every memory of my life into two categories, Janie Mead," he said aloud, as if she might hear him. His touch trailed from her cheek to her chin. "Before my family broke and after my family broke. The way I lived when my world felt whole and the way I live now to mend those fractures."

Orion sighed. Janie returned a shallow exhale. He reached for her hand, clasping her burning-hot fingers in his palms.

"You were my first hope that there might be something else." She was not a remnant from his life before who expected a foolhardy version of him. She was not a discardable tool of his life after who could be exploited for some task. "A third category of memory. A future separate from the past. I have spent years thinking that if I just do the right thing, then I can go back to how it used to be. But maybe I don't want that anymore."

Maybe he wanted her laughing at him over the sound of traffic. Maybe he wanted her threatening him with a straight razor in her hand. They could continue to perform national missions under a joint cover because they worked well together, not because he needed to play hero and prove something. Once this assignment was finished, he wasn't ready to lose her. He didn't want to lose her *now*.

"Why am I talking to you when you can't even hear me?" Orion muttered. "You are a daunting force, beloved. If you fade away because of some measly poison, I will not forgive you in the afterlife."

"*Not . . . measly.*"

Orion jolted, his spine going ramrod straight. He hadn't imagined her response. Her lips had moved.

"Beloved, are you awake?"

Janie huffed. It was strained with effort, like she needed to summon every bit of energy in her body to make the noise. Her eyes remained closed. "*Dizzy.*"

Lao Lao finally returned, her slippers clattering across the living room floor. She barged into the bedroom and started telling Janie off for poisoning herself as if she had done it intentionally. Orion was too afraid of the old woman to do anything other than step out of the way when she neared the bed and eased Janie's mouth open to pour something down her throat.

Janie emitted a single cough, almost choking on the liquid. Lao Lao took away the cup and dabbed a wet cloth over Janie's face, satisfied.

"She will be perfectly fine," the old woman said, shuffling away from the bed and handing Orion the wet cloth. "I'll check in again when morning comes. Now let her rest. She's not used to it. I'm going back to sleep too."

Without waiting for a response, Lao Lao exited the bedroom, letting herself out of the apartment. Orion wrung the cloth in his hands and approached Janie again, setting it onto her neck gingerly. Her breathing had already improved. There was more color in her cheeks.

"You're awake?" he asked hesitantly.

"Pas vraiment," Janie replied. She was mumbling in French, the side of her face buried in her pillows. She hadn't seemed to notice her switch in language.

Orion hovered. He suddenly didn't know what to do with his arms. He suddenly forgot how normal people stood.

"Okay," he decided eventually, his voice quiet. "I'll leave you be—"

Just as he backed away from the edge of the bed, her hand shot out, grasping his wrist weakly.

"Stay," she whispered.

Orion stared at her grasp. He wasn't sure if he had misheard her.

"Stay," she said again, clearer this time. "Please. I don't want to be alone."

"All right." Slowly he shuffled close, sitting hesitantly on the bed. "I can stay."

"Tell me," Janie managed slowly. "Tell me more."

"More?"

"Your family." She paused. "You."

He thought the tightness in his chest might ease now that Janie was recovering, but it was only worse. And he knew—he tugged at the piece of string hanging from his thrashing heart and traced it to its source.

"Well." He tried to tamp it down. Janie Mead was a girl with so many secrets. If he followed that string, he was following it to his own heartbreak. Even though he couldn't release his hold on it. Even though he refused to release his hold on it. "It all started on a hot August night when I was born . . ."

Rosalind had been poisoned once previously during her training— on purpose, no less, so that Dao Feng could instruct her on how to handle it. That prior experience was the only thing that kept her from going into a panic when she woke up with a start, struggling to remember that it was normal to be confused, that nothing was wrong if she couldn't immediately place her surroundings.

For someone who never slept, being forced into a shutdown was a bewildering experience.

Rosalind opened her bleary eyes wider, trying to take inventory. She was lying on her own left arm—that much was certain when she felt the pins and needles of her limb waking up. As for the other one . . .

It was draped over a torso. A warm body, its chest rising and falling with even rhythm.

Rosalind froze in place. For several very long seconds, she didn't dare move, afraid that it would stir Orion out of sleep and he would see them tangled up. But then she remembered her last groggy wisps of memory before Lao Lao's antidote had dragged her unconscious again and could have sworn that she had reached for him while they were both still awake.

Jesus. This was so embarrassing.

She lifted her head in a daze. Outside her window, she caught a glimpse of purple-hazed skies, which made no sense, because that would mean a whole day had passed—

"Orion," Rosalind gasped, giving him a rough shake. He jerked awake, his eyes flying open and turning as round as coins. "Orion, what *time* is it?"

"Hey, hey—"

Rosalind lunged to the side, intent on lurching to her feet even as her head spun. The moment she sat up, however, Orion's reaction was whip-quick, grabbing her shoulder and pushing her back onto her pillow.

She started to rise again immediately. "We need to go."

"*Janie.*" He swung an arm around to her other shoulder, scrambling to keep her down.

"What are you so calm for?" she exclaimed. "The whole day has passed—"

"Will you hold *on*?" Orion demanded firmly. Before she could fight him further, he outright clambered over her and pinned her wrists over her head. "Now look what you made me do."

Rosalind blinked. Her heart leaped to her throat.

"Well, don't be dramatic." She tried to pull her wrists down. His grip was iron. Where she should have scoffed, the memory of her face pressed to his chest was still warm in her mind, and she found herself swallowing nervously instead. "You could have said it nicely too."

"There's no fun in that. Are you going to behave if I let go of you?"

"*Behave?*" Rosalind echoed. You share the bed with a man once and he starts thinking he can tell you what to do. The power was getting to his head. "First of all, I'll smack my skull against yours if you don't release me in three seconds. Second of all, we have a cover to keep at our jobs, and it's *dusk* outside—"

"Janie. It's okay. I called in and said you were sick. People get sick." He grinned, visibly waiting three seconds before tapping his forehead to hers. "Don't smack me. *I'm* behaving now."

With a bounce, Orion let go of her, easing away and returning to his side of the bed. Rosalind sat up, eyeing him suspiciously. "Oh."

Now that they were both awake and Rosalind had calmed down, Orion's expression turned serious. "How are you feeling?"

"Like I got run over by a military tank." Her muscles hurt. Her organs hurt. She ought to stop making her poison so strong. If it was the next day, then Silas was arriving shortly to debrief. She needed to freshen up and shake herself back into commission. It probably would have been less miserable if she *had* gotten run over by a military tank.

"You gave me a fright." Orion slid off the sheets, running a hand through his hair. He ducked to look into her vanity, peering at his reflection while he spoke, but his eyes were unfocused while he tucked and untucked his wrinkled collar, as if he was only doing so as an excuse to turn away. "A very big fright, Janie. Please never do that again."

Rosalind's lips parted. She didn't know what to say in response to that. How could she promise to never be in harm's way again? They were national operatives. It was a part of the job description.

"At the very least . . ." She shook her sleeve, and the vial they had stolen fell out. When she placed it on the bedside table, her eyes also wandered out to the living room, where Orion had tossed the crate piece upon one of the couch cushions. "We're one step closer to the end."

"Yes." Orion didn't sound too pleased by the rationalization. He had a strange look on his face. "I suppose we are."

He did up his top button. Before Rosalind could stop him, he said, "I'm going to fetch Lao Lao to check on you once more. Give me a minute," and strode out of the room.

The apartment door opened and closed. Rosalind swung her legs off the bed, frowning.

"Why are you being so weird?" she asked the empty bedroom.

36

Despite the fact that she hadn't been told about their rendezvous with Silas tonight, Phoebe showed up at the apartment ten minutes prior.

Orion almost closed the door in her face.

"Dearest sister," he bemoaned. "Why can't you stay safely tucked away at home?"

Phoebe ignored his question. She looked around. "Where's săozi?"

"Janie is downstairs fetching some food from the landlady." He sighed as Phoebe came in, reluctantly letting the door shut after her. "Now I suppose she must fetch extra to feed your big mouth."

"My mouth is perfectly sized," Phoebe shot back. "I have a question I want your opinion on. Has Silas mentioned Priest to you before?"

What a strange question. One he did not have the brain space to be pondering at this moment in time, quite frankly. But because he was a good big brother, Orion begrudgingly walked to the couch and dropped down, sifting through his memory. Of course Silas had *mentioned* Priest before. He was working a complicated triple agent identity while still doing work for the Nationalists, running their auxiliary mission on the chemical killings. He had offered small updates to Orion here and there—contact secured, communication initiated, signals exchanged.

Orion looked at his sister warily. He knew how she operated.

He didn't know if he should be afraid of why she was asking or brace himself for secondhand embarrassment.

"Nothing in particular," he said.

"Well," Phoebe sniffed, perching on the couch's armrest. "Did you know Silas is convinced that Priest is a woman?"

Orion threw his feet up on the coffee table. "Oh, mèimei, don't tell me you're getting possessive."

Phoebe pushed his feet off the table. "He has loved me since we were children. *Me*. Not this Priest."

Despite Phoebe's usual flippancy, this attitude now hardly came as a surprise. She could pretend to be clueless as much as she liked when Silas followed her around. She would still glance at Silas every time she made a joke to make sure he laughed. She would still check his reaction before everyone else's if she said something intentionally terrible, hoping to catch the roll of his eyes and tease him about it.

"First," Orion said, holding up a finger, "my goodness, Phoebe, that is *unhealthy*. Second"—he held up another finger—"Priest could be an old grandma for all you know."

His sister was fuming. "It's not about who she actually is. It's about him choosing—"

"You have gotten far too used to having his undivided attention for a decade," Orion interrupted, adopting his elder-brother voice. "In fact, you have gotten far too used to shrugging him off, so now you simply have to live with the consequences."

Phoebe did not look like she wanted to live with the consequences. In fact, she looked like she wanted to hit him for saying so.

"Don't you lecture me."

"You *started* this conversation by asking for my opinion. You know what—" Orion brushed his hand over his face, forcing himself to remain calm. "Forget it. Come back to this conversation with me when you're ready for a wake-up call. Have you found anything through Liza about Janie?"

The sneer on Phoebe's face morphed to eagerness in a blink. Their relationship had always been like this, even in childhood. They would have a screaming match, throwing death threats at each other because Phoebe stepped on Orion's book while she was coming in, and the next minute Orion was asking if Phoebe would like to go get some milk together at the corner shop. Without parental supervision most of the year, they had been each other's greatest allies and greatest enemies. Close as anything because they were a two-person family, but then pitted as competitors whenever their mother came to visit for a sparse two weeks and Orion was forced to step back, instructed that Phoebe needed the time more, that she was younger, that she required the grounding force.

He had been young too. He had needed his mother too.

He really should have suspected that their family was dysfunctional earlier on. Somehow it had taken total collapse for him to make the realization.

"Not yet," Phoebe said, drawing his attention back to the present. "But I'm following a source I sighted in Liza's apartment."

Footsteps were coming up the stairs. Quickly, Orion mimed zipping his lips to his sister, the two of them preparing to switch topics.

When Janie came in, holding a glass tray in her hands, she halted at the doorway. Her face was still a little pale from the previous night's poisoning, but she was moving around fine, and Lao Lao had given her the all clear. Before Janie could voice her confusion at Phoebe's sudden presence in her living room, Phoebe was swooping toward her, hands outstretched to help with the food.

"Hello," Phoebe chirped. "Let me give you a hand with that."

Rosalind had walked into the middle of a conversation. She could feel it in the way the room had a heightened sense of awareness, in the way Orion's spine was perked straight and Phoebe had already prepared a smile the moment the door opened. She didn't know what exactly they were talking about just before she entered, but it didn't take a genius to guess it must have been her.

She set four pairs of chopsticks down on the coffee table. A moment later, there was a knock on the front door, bringing Silas in.

"I thought they would never let me leave," he said, stepping through. "I've been awake for so many days that you will have to excuse me if I start talking to the wall."

"I promise you that getting too much sleep isn't making anyone in this room more sane," Rosalind returned.

"Didn't they excuse you from the forensic investigation this morning?" Orion added, moving along the couch for Rosalind to sit.

Silas plopped down on the opposite seat. Phoebe remained perched on the armrest. "Yes, and then I was summoned into Jiangsu to meet a fellow agent who had my contact. He was confused about why he hadn't heard from Dao Feng in so long. He didn't even know Dao Feng wasn't in active status."

Rosalind winced, pushing the food closer to the middle of the table. She lifted her chopsticks. Her grip felt weak, no matter how hard she pressed her fingers. "I suppose communication does break down when your handler is taken out of commission."

There was a reason the covert branch was made unknown to most of the party, after all. The fewer people who knew about it, the fewer people there would be to demand some sort of input on their missions. The fewer people who knew about it, the fewer victims to torture if one person was captured and couldn't clamp down on the information they knew.

"Why did the other agent want to meet?" Orion asked, an immediate note of suspicion in his voice.

"It was for his mission," Silas answered. "I've always had an ear perked toward his progress in case something proves useful for us." He offered a plate to Phoebe, and she took it gingerly. "The agent is code-named Gold Bar, presently making contact with an underground weapons ring moving through Shanghai. Their base is out in Zhouzhuang, but somehow their people keep smuggling weapons of every kind into this city."

Zhouzhuang. Rosalind sat back. Wasn't that where the letter Jiemin had been writing was addressed to? Why did that little town seem to be popping up everywhere recently? She gestured for Phoebe to take a pair of chopsticks.

"Shanghai has a weapons shortage at present," Orion stated.

Silas nodded. "Which is exactly why it's related to us. Once Seagreen's terror cell is uprooted, there is a small chance we might end up combating the Imperial Japanese Army while making arrests. The Kuomintang need to be armed for the worst-case scenario. Our fastest market right now is this underground ring."

Orion made an inquisitive noise. When Rosalind glanced at him, he was frowning.

"Most other supply chains lead back to the foreigners," he said. "Could we not use those?"

"My friend . . . ," Silas replied. "Capitalism and higher prices say no."

"You're sounding like a Communist," Rosalind muttered, not unkindly.

Silas shrugged. "That was actually how this underground ring got on our radar at first. The mission was to shut them down because they were supplying the Communists with weaponry, only now we need them too."

"And they're willing?" It didn't sound right. "Which side of the war are they on?"

"Neither. They're anti-Japanese and anti-imperialist. They'll give both parties what they need by connecting suppliers outside the city with points inside Shanghai, though heaven knows how they have so many black-market connections. That sort of business usually takes years of guānxì building from inside the city too."

Rosalind leaned onto her elbow, almost nudging Orion's leg. He was deep enough in thought that he did not protest. How peculiar. How did a ring operating out of middle-of-nowhere Zhouzhuang have the connections to move through Shanghai's black market? Ever since the White Flowers dissolved and the Scarlet Gang got swallowed into politics, the black market was composed of old Scarlets and foreigners, ex–White Flowers and businessmen who would claim they had never heard of the city's former gangs so that the Kuomintang didn't shut them down.

"Anyhow," Silas continued, "Gold Bar divulged his progress connecting with the heads of this ring. They're willing to supply, so by the time we make arrests on Seagreen, our side should be armed for smooth operation."

"Who are they?" Rosalind asked, latching on to the minor part of Silas's information. "The people spearheading the smuggling."

"A married couple. That's about all we know." With a grimace, Silas chewed more slowly on his food. "Gold Bar tried entering their base of operations and almost got knifed in the face. Better to leave them alone unless we really need to shut them down. People in the countryside are frightening."

He patted his jacket suddenly, setting his plate down. "Speaking of frightening things . . ." Silas retrieved something from his pocket. At once, Rosalind and Orion shot to their feet, jostling Phoebe so badly that she almost spilled her plate.

"Where did you get that?" Orion demanded.

Silas put the glass vial onto the table, his eyes growing wide behind his glasses. The green liquid inside shimmered under the overhead light.

"I found it in the alley, with the dead bodies," he answered, taken aback. "I would have turned it in immediately if we had a handler, but . . ." He trailed off, looking at Phoebe. Phoebe only shrugged her shoulders, indicating that she didn't know why the two of them had reacted like that. "Do you know what it is?"

The room fell into silence. On one side: Silas and Phoebe staring in bewilderment. On the other side: Rosalind and Orion exchanging a single glance, coming to the same conclusion.

"That's the murder weapon," Rosalind said, as if she had known all along, as if the thought had not finally taken shape a mere second ago. "It's what gets injected into the victims. Seagreen has been sending it out."

"Which means," Orion added, "Haidi is our top suspect for being the killer."

After Silas and Phoebe departed, Rosalind spent a long time sitting on the couch, staring at the green vial in her hand. She had turned off the lights overhead, planning to enter the bedroom, but then the concoction had drawn her interest and she had moved to go examine it, turning the vial this way and that by the moonlight coming in through the window. She had a bizarre itch to use it on herself, if only to see what would happen, if only to test its potency. But that was suicidal, given that the concoction would ravage through her body in the same way that poison did. Though she refrained, she did not let go of the vial.

"You okay?"

Orion joined her on the couch, his sleeves still pushed up from doing the dishes in the kitchen. He shook his hands to dry them, flinging water droplets everywhere. Rosalind's eyes flickered over briefly to see what was landing on her, but they returned to the vial almost immediately.

"Just thinking," she said. "I held something similar to this once before."

"A lethal chemical mixture?" he asked, his brows drawing together.

"No." She heard Dimitri's voice as clearly as if he were right in the room with her: *To rule the world, we have to be willing to destroy it. Aren't you willing, Roza? For me?* "Do you remember that epidemic a few years ago? When madness struck the streets and people started clawing their own throats out?"

"How could I forget?" Orion shifted higher on the couch. "It was around the time of our return. I banned Phoebe from going outside."

Rosalind set the vial down on the coffee table. She had been about to speak without thinking, to say that she'd had a hand in the madness, that a lover of hers caused its second wave after inheriting the sickness from the foreigners. But the city knew that narrative well, knew of Juliette Cai shooting Paul Dexter to stop the first madness, knew of the two gangs working together once Dimitri Voronin took up the mantle. If she admitted to her role, then she was no longer Janie Mead; she was the tragic and terrible story of how Fortune came to be.

"It only reminds me of that," Rosalind said quietly. "Strange science moving through the city once again."

Before Orion could reply, there was a knock on the front door, and both of them jolted into high alert. They were not expecting anyone.

Orion rose to answer, pressing a finger to his lips. Rosalind held still. The door opened a small fraction.

"This the Mu residence?"

At the sight of the paperboy, Orion visibly relaxed, pushing the door wider. The boy was holding a fruit basket in his hands, struggling to keep upright when it was half as tall as he was and stuffed with many obnoxiously large durians.

"Yes," Rosalind answered from the couch. "Darling, help him out, would you?"

The boy breathed a sigh of relief, shaking out his arms as Orion took the basket. He saluted and hurried away, leaving Orion to sniff at the fruit, a look of utter confusion on his face when he kicked the door closed again.

"Who is sending us durians?" he asked. "Is this supposed to be an insult? Like how the Victorians communicated with flowers?"

Rosalind waved for him to set the basket on the table. "Or," she said, peering in and spotting the note, "there is actual communication in here."

She pulled out the square of paper, smooth and cream in color, bleeding with black ink when she unfolded it. After a quick scan, she turned it around for Orion to see too:

> *High Tide—*
> *This is your new handler. Report at 08:00 tomorrow*
> *to the Rui Food Market, along Avenue Edward VII.*
> *Look for the yellow hat.*

"Dao Feng's replacement," Orion said, with considerable surprise. He peered down at the rest of the basket in search of another note, perhaps about Dao Feng himself, but there was nothing else to be found.

"We will bring everything we have so far." Rosalind looked to the side. The crate piece remained nestled on the cushion. "It's about time we start wrapping up the mission."

"Yes," Orion echoed hollowly. "I suppose so."

His tone drew Rosalind's attention, but he was turning away before she could meet his gaze, hauling the basket up and lugging it into the kitchen. Rosalind stared after him, puzzled.

There was a loud thump in the kitchen—the basket being dropped onto the counter. Then Orion's voice calling:

"I have a question."

Rosalind frowned, calling back, "Go on."

Orion returned, leaning on the kitchen doorframe with his hands in his pockets. "How old are you?"

It took every ounce of control for Rosalind not to grow tense. Why was he asking?

"Nineteen," she said. "I thought you knew that."

"I did," Orion replied. "I only wondered if I misremembered."

He fell quiet again. There had to be some reason for this query. He must have stumbled onto something.

But would it be so bad if he knew? a little voice whispered.

"My birthday was in early September," Rosalind offered. It would help her believability—make her seem like an ordinary girl. "The eighth on the Western calendar." She paused. "Why? Do I look older?"

Orion offered a smile, studying her from afar. A while passed before he gave an answer.

"No." There was an edge of disbelief in his voice. As if he didn't know how. As if he couldn't wrap his head around it. "No, you don't."

"Careful." Rosalind touched the edge of her eyes, padding her fingertips around lightly. "You'll make me self-conscious about my wrinkles."

"You'd be beautiful with wrinkles too."

Something seized at Rosalind's lungs. But she was never going to get them. She was going to stay this way forever, then blow away with the wind when her body chose to give up, as it had once before.

"Ah, what a compliment." She put her hands to her chest, pretending to swoon. "You've hit right at the mark. Now I will forever be in your debt."

Orion shook his head good-naturedly.

"Do you want to know something?" he asked. He made a quick stride over to the windows, where the blinds were still pushed wide open. Rosalind rose to her feet too, walking over to see what he was looking at. It wasn't the street, nor any of the cars idly parked in the vicinity. Orion's gaze was tipped up at the sky.

Rosalind craned her head to get a better view, but she couldn't tell what held his attention. Not until he reached for her chin and tilted her head a little to the left. Blotted in the inky fabric of the sky, situated just at the right place to see from their window, there were three prominent stars that shone a little brighter than the rest.

"Shen," Rosalind said, identifying the constellation in Chinese. "It's one of the mansions of the White Tiger."

"Consult the European brain instead," Orion said. "What do they call it?"

Rosalind sifted through her schooling. It must have been obvious to Orion when it occurred to her, because his lips twitched.

"Orion," she said. "It's called Orion."

He nodded, eyes still locked on the constellation. When that perennially stubborn lock of hair fell into his eyes, Rosalind wanted to brush it away. She forced her hand to stay at her side.

"Before I was High Tide," Orion began, "I was Huntsman. They weren't very creative with their code name designations. I thought it was a little funny."

Tell him, she thought suddenly. *I was Fortune. I was not a spy. I was an assassin.*

She couldn't make herself form the words.

"If the Nationalists can't have anything else," she said, "at least they have a sense of humor."

"Comedians, all of them." Orion brushed his hair away before Rosalind could. "But they did do an intensive job of building my identity. A near-complete merge with who I actually was, so that no one took me seriously, so that my targets were none the wiser to the intelligence slipping out while they thought they were only being wooed."

Rosalind thought back to the Frenchwoman. "Yes, you do appear to be very good at that."

"All the best spies don't look like one," Orion returned, the glint wicked in his eye. Slowly, though, the wickedness faded as he turned away from the window, regarding her in earnest instead.

A moment of silence passed.

"You liked it, didn't you?" Rosalind asked. "Being a spy, I mean."

She didn't know where the question had come from. Possibly a place of surprise, that a job he had forced himself into performing for the sake of his family wasn't some undertaking of doom and gloom. Rosalind was not the same. Much as she knew being Fortune gave her a purpose she could find nowhere else, she also couldn't stand that part of herself. The immortal, unstoppable assassin that sent people trembling to their knees. She only wanted to be a girl who was deserving of the world.

"I suppose I did." Orion considered the matter. "I don't know if I want to go back to that cover anymore though."

"Why not?"

He nudged his elbow against hers. "Because I've grown a little attached to High Tide."

That was right: they were neither Huntsman nor Fortune now. They were High Tide. Rosalind's brooding faded. In its place appeared a flicker of amusement.

"Attached to High Tide?" she echoed, her voice teasing. "Have you grown attached to *me*, Hong Liwen?"

"Yes." His reply came easily. It didn't sound like he was teasing her in return. "I have."

Her eyes snapped up. She hadn't expected that. Nor had she noticed that they were now standing precariously close, the window draping moonlight on their shoulders, two silver silhouettes with every edge blurred.

"Oh?"

Orion shifted even closer. "Beloved . . ."

Nothing followed. He had said it just to address her. When had he started doing that? As if he meant the endearment instead of it being a joke or a cover for witnesses?

A surge of panic shot into her veins.

"Good night," Rosalind blurted, taking a sweeping step back and breaking the spell. Though there was little chance that either of them would be tired when they had woken mere hours before, Rosalind whirled on her heel and took the excuse to hurry away, closing her bedroom door behind her before she could catch a single glimpse of Orion's reaction.

She pressed up against the door. Her heart was going too fast. Her forehead was sweaty.

"Stop it," she hissed. "This isn't happening."

But she couldn't lie to herself. There it was: that dip in her stomach, like she was hovering right at the precipice of a cliff, seconds away from falling. There it was: that hum at her fingertips, like she was losing blood and it was frantically rushing out of her body.

Maybe it was the remnants of the poison. Rosalind marched in front of her vanity mirror, checking for the dilation of her eyes, sticking her tongue out for its color. She even tried to look into her ear canals, but they all showed the same result: everything was healthy. Nothing was left in her system. This time, her reaction had no poison to blame.

"Putain de merde." Rosalind rested her hands on the vanity. Struggled to catch her breath as if she had run a hundred miles to get here.

"You do not like him," she warned her reflection sternly. "You *don't*."

Liar, her reflection returned.

She ought to poison herself again.

37

Silas was already sitting at the food market when Rosalind and Orion arrived that next morning, a bowl of wontons steaming before him. He was distracted, staring off into the distance, but he snapped to attention as soon as Rosalind plopped down in front of him on the other side of the table. She put the crate piece beside their feet.

"Fancy seeing you here, pal," Orion greeted, closing a hand on Silas's shoulder before going to sit beside Rosalind.

She felt his presence like every inch of her left side was on supercharge. She did her best to ignore it.

"Where's our new handler?" Rosalind asked.

Silas looked around. Orion picked up his friend's spoon and stole one of his wontons.

"I came early. Haven't seen anyone yet. Maybe he's waiting to check if we were followed before he approaches." Silas frowned, flicking Orion away before he tried to steal a second wonton. "No yellow hats nearby thus far."

Rosalind rested her chin on her hand. Her eyes flickered to a figure three tables over. "There's Jiemin, though."

As if hearing his name, Jiemin turned around from his wooden seat, wiping his mouth with a napkin, and waved. Rosalind and Orion waved back, while Silas squinted, staring even when Jiemin resumed eating his food.

"Who is he?"

"A colleague at Seagreen," Orion answered. "We don't have him on our lists."

Silas was still staring.

"Do you recognize him from elsewhere?" Rosalind asked. Perhaps they shouldn't have been so hasty to decide that he was innocent.

"Well, no," Silas said. "I'm just curious why there is a yellow hat sticking out of his pocket."

Rosalind froze. As did Orion, the two of them swiveling fast to survey Jiemin again. He was rising now, tossing his discarded napkin onto his emptied plate, examining the back of his hands after he had wiped them clean. *Surely*, Rosalind thought, *he is leaving and is only walking our way to give a quick farewell.*

Instead, Jiemin dropped himself into the seat next to Silas and said, "Lovely to meet you in person, Shepherd." He nodded to Orion, then Rosalind. "High Tide."

The table fell silent. Orion dropped the spoon in his hand. It clattered onto the cement ground, loud even above the chatter that surrounded them at the food market. Several tables looked over to see what the commotion had been, but they returned to their own breakfasts after a glance.

"It's *you*?" Orion exclaimed. While he squawked, Rosalind bent down to pick up his fallen spoon, closing her dropped jaw before she was upright again. "Why would it be you?"

Jiemin shrugged. "Are you asking for technicalities or logistics? My father is someone important in the Kuomintang."

"As is mine!"

Rosalind reached over, patting Orion's arm before he was crowing so loudly that the people one table over could hear him. In her other hand, her fingers were so tight around the handle of the spoon that her knuckles were turning white.

"I know who your father is," Jiemin said evenly. "It is not the same concept, believe me."

"So you both make nepotism work for you." Rosalind tried not to grit her teeth. She put the spoon down. "It still doesn't answer how an eighteen-year-old got assigned as our handler."

Jiemin didn't look bothered by her disparaging tone. He pretended not to see the complete puzzlement on Silas's face.

"I was implanted a year earlier than the two of you, so they decided I had been working on this task long enough to lead it." Jiemin pulled the yellow hat out of his pocket and dropped it on the table. It was stitched with the logo of a restaurant in the International Settlement. "How do you think we confirmed that the terror killings were coming from Seagreen Press at all? I infiltrated Japanese social circles first and found the instructions sent to Deoka—instructions about setting up in a warehouse outside the city and starting distribution on an unknown chemical compound. The next task was confirming those chemical compounds were linked to the killings that had started in the city."

"Then how long have these killings been ongoing?" Rosalind asked. "And why bring *us* in if you've been on the task for over a year?"

Jiemin folded his hands and looked at Rosalind. He remained unspeaking for several long seconds—eyes steady, gaze held—and with that alone, Rosalind knew: he was aware of her true identity.

"The two of you have talents that I do not," Jiemin answered eventually, when the silence drew on too long. He nodded to Orion. "Particularly that I cannot catch what they say in Japanese. It was faster to recruit and send more agents in than have me learn the language rapidly and misunderstand something."

"You cannot possibly tell me that you did not have finished lists in the year you were there," Orion said. "At the very least, you had suspicions—"

"Yes, it's likely that I've already marked down everyone you have," Jiemin cut in. "But that was never the point. That was the first task, and we needed to ease you in so you could figure out the next part. The *why*. What good is making arrests if we still don't know why they are killing our people with *chemicals*? It'll merely start again so long as we cannot find the root."

Orion glanced away, spitting a frustrated curse. Through his explanation, Jiemin's tone had been level, almost bored. If anyone were to observe them from a distance, no one could have possibly guessed that this boy was supposed to be their handler—their *superior*—looking so casual and melancholic. He seemed more like one of the restaurant waiters, underpaid and slacking off by sitting at the table with his customers.

"Dao Feng should have told us this to begin with," Rosalind stated. She was trying very, very hard to keep her tone level too.

Jiemin set his elbows onto the table. "To tell the truth," he replied, "I'm not sure why he didn't. When they gave me this task file, I looked over his directives. He was supposed to have presented all of it: arresting the guilty parties at Seagreen Press, tracing the killer, and finding an explanation for the killing method."

Rosalind had known about this oddity all along. It had prodded at her, had bugged her while she thought through the objective of the mission. But she had shoved it aside because she assumed Dao Feng would have provided the tasks if they were truly important. Now she was to believe that their work up until this point had been redundant, that their true mission had been withheld. They had wasted weeks finding information that Jiemin had already pieced together over the course of a year. What had Dao Feng been playing at? What did he know that they did not?

And why was Jiemin not privy to it either if he was stepping in as this mission's handler?

"Perhaps Dao Feng thought it would be too overwhelming," Silas supplied. "That Janie and Liwen needed an adjustment period first."

"Perhaps," Rosalind echoed, though she didn't sound certain in the slightest. "Well—we will have the rest soon, I suppose. Zheng Haidi is the likeliest suspect for the killer. We only need to catch her."

Jiemin made a sound. "*Haidi?* The office secretary Haidi?"

Rosalind frowned. "Yes. Don't underestimate her just because she seems airheaded. She was carrying around the killing weapon. I bet you haven't gotten your hands on that yet, have you?"

"I have not," Jiemin confirmed plainly.

"Here." She reached under the table. On their way over, Orion had scrimmaged up a black plastic bag to put the crate piece in, along with the vial that Silas had retrieved and the vial Rosalind had taken from Burkill Road. Rosalind pushed the bag to Jiemin. "Two vials of the murder weapon, as well as concrete evidence of Deoka's distribution. Last we saw, the rest of the crates are at a residence at 286 Burkill Road. If we move quickly enough, we might be able to catch the underground imperial base before they move."

Jiemin took the bag wordlessly. "Are you issuing instructions now, Miss Mead?"

"Yes," Rosalind said firmly. "The function at Cathay Hotel—let's close the mission then."

Orion and Silas both swiveled toward her at once, looking aghast.

"Are you joking?" Silas demanded.

"Did you not hear our prodigious handler?" Orion added. To his credit, he let out only the slightest hint of mockery. "He took a year to get to this point. How are we to finish it by Friday if it has taken this long to get everything else?"

But Rosalind was resolute on the idea. She had thought about this carefully last night when she had nothing better to do than to pace her bedroom floor and try not to let her mind wander to other places.

"It's our best chance," she said. "Jiemin, do you remain insistent on not attending the function?"

Jiemin nodded. "There are other ambassadors for the imperial force who will be present, brought in from other branches across Shanghai. Too many people in this city recognize me from previous missions. Once I make an appearance, it will have to be as a Nationalist, not as a Seagreen employee."

"Fine." Rosalind cricked her neck. "Then Orion and I will be on the inside undercover. We can run confirmation that all guilty parties are present before the Nationalists rush in to make arrests. When will we get another chance where our every suspect is in one place? No one can hear of what is coming ahead of time to escape. Rush Burkill Road at the same time, and that's everything wrapped up in a neat bow: suspects and chemicals all together."

It was far from a neat bow, but no one around the table had the energy to argue with her.

"Very well," Jiemin said. "Then you have until Friday to figure out their ultimate aim in these killings." He got to his feet. "I will feed this up our channels. We follow Miss Mead's plan. The function at Cathay it is."

Without another word, their new handler waved his goodbye and turned to go.

"See you at work," Orion muttered to Jiemin's retreating back.

Alisa left her building from the second-floor hallway window, jumping off the ledge and landing among the back-alley trash bags.

"Gross," she muttered under her breath, picking herself back up. She wasn't sure if her fugitive status was serious enough to necessitate jumping out windows, especially knowing how lazy the Municipal Police were, but there was no such thing as being too cautious. The late-morning light prickled her eyes as she exited the alley. A muggy humidity had sunken into the air today.

It was a new day of investigation. Though really, there weren't many avenues left as far as her investigation went. If Rosalind wanted a better job done, she really should have asked her own sister. Celia was more senior, and Celia had an even more senior agent wrapped around her finger. But since Alisa had been given the task, she supposed she would tie up the last loose end.

Something supernatural, sighted by an old lady. Something to do with why the Communists would want to chase after a couple of Nationalists.

She arrived at Bao Shang Road. The narrow street was hazy with smoke despite the bright blue sky overhead. Alisa bounded up the stairs of the building with a faded 4 affixed to its front, ascending and turning and ascending and turning until her head was dizzy. The memo had said the sixth floor. She had been preparing to knock around until she landed on the right apartment, but when she finished climbing six flights of stairs, one of the doors was already ajar.

"Hello?" Alisa called. She nudged the door as if to test whether the openness was an illusion. With a loud creak, it opened even wider. "The Kuomintang sent me. We were here some time ago to take a statement? I have returned to—" Alisa stepped in; at once she was blinded by a flash of bright light. *"Christ!"*

"Ah, you have to hold your pose, shǎ gūniáng. It will come out blurry otherwise."

Alisa blinked rapidly, trying to clear the seared patches in her eyeballs. Slowly the scene before her materialized: a quaint apartment, an old woman in a wheelchair by the window. The woman was holding a box in her hands, which—with some more rapid blinking—Alisa eventually identified as a personal camera.

"How could I be so thoughtless as to drop my pose?" Alisa made a final hard blink to clear the last of the blots. She smiled, refusing to be deterred from making a pleasant introduction. "Please forgive me, but when my superiors sent me here, they did not offer me a name, only an address."

The old woman pushed her chair away from the window, angling her wheels toward the couch instead. She waved Alisa over. Hesitantly, Alisa shuffled along after the woman and took a seat, perching at the edge of the couch cushions.

"That's probably because they did not ask for my name the first time," the old woman replied. "I am Mrs. Guo. Are you Russian?"

"Yes," Alisa replied. "My name is—" She paused. It wouldn't be good to use *Liza* in case it blew her cover with Seagreen. Though she supposed if the Kuomintang caught the Communists impersonating them around the city to get intelligence, there would be bigger problems to worry about. "—Roza."

Sorry, Rosalind.

The old woman looked her up and down. "And the Kuomintang trust you? They came knocking on my door after hearing of my story from a neighbor, you know. I'm truly beginning to wonder how many people they have recruited in every corner."

"Oh, I'm only a lowly assistant," she lied. "But listen to my Chinese—it's so good that they had to hire me."

Mrs. Guo considered the matter. Alisa held her breath, wondering if a Russian taken into the ranks of the Kuomintang was simply too far-fetched to believe.

"You do have quite an excellent way of speaking," the old woman decided.

Alisa grinned. She took out a notepad, her pen poised over the paper. "I won't take up too much of your time today. I am only confirming a testimony that you gave a while ago."

"Take up all the time you need," Mrs. Guo said, leaning back in her chair. "My kids don't visit me, and I cannot go downstairs to play mahjong anymore."

Alisa looked around. "Do you eat okay? Do you want me to get you something?"

Mrs. Guo looked amused. "Ah, don't worry about me. The only thing I might suffer from is utter boredom."

"Hopefully I won't bore you with this." Alisa pretended to consult another page in her notepad, though it was entirely blank. "I need to confirm what you saw through your window. You said it was . . . supernatural? Some people are having trouble grasping it, you see, so details would be appreciated."

Mrs. Guo stared at her for a moment. Then: "Details? How many more details do they want other than a serial killer in the alley outside my window?"

Serial killer? Alisa's eyes widened before she could suppress her reaction. Fortunately, Mrs. Guo was wheeling away, stopping by the table in her adjoined kitchen and sifting through a pile of magazines lying atop the table surface, so she had not caught Alisa's shock. Did this have to do with Rosalind's mission after all?

"Anything that you can recall would be wonderful," Alisa said evenly.

"I was shocked too, of course," Mrs. Guo went on. "The papers are writing about these killings every day. Corpse found on this road. Corpse found on that road. Holes in their arms. Expressions pulled in terror. I keep warning my daughter not to go outside, and she still goes out every night to dance at a silly wŭtīng."

"How did you know it was the chemical killings and not a regular criminal?" Alisa asked, scratching her pen down on the paper. "People are assaulted around these parts all the time for petty reasons."

"I gather other petty criminals are not stabbing syringes into their victims."

Alisa pressed the pen in harder. "So, you *saw* the syringe."

"Better than that." Mrs. Guo finally found what she was looking for, holding out a strip of photographic film. "Here. I already gave your superiors the photograph that showed the horrible scene, but I suppose information gets lost easily. I have copies of everything else already, so if you need the original dĭpiàn . . ."

Alisa didn't hesitate before snatching the strip. She held the negative panels up to the light, trying to discern the blots and shapes. While it was easy to identify the one in the middle as the photograph in question—it looked like it had been taken from above and through a window, with two figures at the bottom—the negative's tiny size and reversed colors made it impossible to pick out any detail. She needed to print it again as a proper-sized photograph first.

"Have they not made an arrest yet?" Mrs. Guo asked now, pushing herself back into the living room.

"They're getting around to it." Alisa waved the strip. "Thank you for this. It's very helpful."

Bidding Mrs. Guo goodbye, Alisa left the apartment, closing the door after herself gently. Why were the Communists concerning themselves with this? What did they know at the higher level that she still did not? If these pictures provided evidence of the killer, then the Nationalists could use it to haul Seagreen Press in. Her superiors should have passed the information on. Did the war matter that much? Did the war matter more than saving lives?

Alisa emerged from the building, picking up an urgency in her step. She turned onto the next street, then hurried into the first Russian corner shop she saw.

She held the negative strip out, alongside a wad of cash, and approached the counter.

"Do you have a darkroom?"

Orion was ambushed during his lunch hour while standing in front of a stall paying for dumplings.

"You're not going to believe this."

Fortunately, he recognized the voice in an instant, and despite being snuck up on, he didn't spill his large bag of dumplings in fright. Thank goodness. That would have been rather humiliating.

"Do me a favor, mèimei," Orion said. He counted his coins patiently to make sure he had the right amount. "Grab the two dòuhuā."

Phoebe sniffed, taking the two cups of tofu pudding from the shop owner. "Can I have one?"

"Yes, you can have mine. Leave the other one alone or else my wife is going to yell at me."

They moved to a table by the street side, Phoebe's attention focused wholly on not spilling the cups. She didn't dither before digging right in, shaking out a spoon from the utensil boxes in the middle. Orion set the dumpling bag down heavily, rather concerned with his sister's enthusiasm for the snack. Was Ah Dou feeding her enough?

"So what am I not going to believe?" he prompted.

Phoebe set her spoon down, like she had remembered again why she was here. "Remember when I said I got a glimpse inside Liza Ivanova's apartment?" With a glance around to make sure no one was watching, Phoebe reached into her bag and pulled out a magazine, setting it in front of Orion. The front cover was a pastel pink, featuring a woman in a lawn chair looking up at the sky. That was all Orion could discern from it. The text itself was written in Russian.

"Did you take this from her?" he asked, concerned.

"No! How irresponsible do you think I am?" Phoebe blew a breath up, getting her bangs out of her eyes. "Liza had hers framed. I thought it was bizarre—so I went around to every magazine shop in Shanghai to find another copy. Described the front cover enough times, and eventually a woman in Zhabei knew what I was talking about. She dug this out from the back for me."

His sister took another spoonful of the food. "I actually have to run—I need to catch a shoe sale at Sincere. Flip to the tab I made in the back. You won't be able to read anything substantial, but they printed the names in English with pictures. I have no clue what to make of it. I trust you'll have a better idea."

With a clink of her spoon against the cup, Phoebe got to her feet. Then, because she was always determined to be an irritant, she peered into the dumpling bag and took one before she departed.

"Don't spend too much!" Orion called after her.

"Don't tell me what to do!" she called back.

Left alone at the table, Orion turned the magazine around and opened it to where Phoebe had marked. The front cover had made the issue seem like it centered on lifestyle, so he was surprised when the page he turned to looked like an obituary.

Roma Montagov. Born 15 July 1907.

"The heir of the White Flowers?" Orion muttered, squinting at the picture. Why was this magazine printing his obituary? He flipped to the next page.

Juliette Cai. Born 15 October 1907.

With those two names together, everything suddenly made sense. Orion flipped faster. These back pages were all gangster obituaries. The magazine must have published them in remembrance shortly after the revolution that dissolved the gangs.

Dimitri Voronin. Born 2 January 1906.

Tyler Cai. Born 25 March 1908.

Kathleen Lang. Born 8 September 1907.

Kathleen Lang? Orion's hand stilled, his brows knitting together. He knew of Kathleen Lang—most people in this city knew the names of the fallen Scarlet Gang elite. But this picture . . . was a younger Celia, Oliver's mission partner. Orion had met her multiple times out in the field. Each time Oliver tried to make nice, Celia was forced to drag him away before Orion could throw a punch at him.

This didn't make sense. Unless . . .

"Oh my God," he whispered. If Celia was once Kathleen Lang, then he knew who Janie was. The connection wouldn't have occurred to him on his own—why would it?—but when placed in front of him, the resemblance between Celia and Janie was undeniable. He turned the page to the final obituary.

Rosalind Lang. Born 8 September 1907.

And there was Janie, looking exactly the same.

He had always suspected that Janie Mead didn't exist. Only this was something else entirely. He had assumed she was some other girl in the city. Perhaps with a tricky past, perhaps raised somewhere other than America. But *Rosalind Lang*—

Orion closed the magazine with a stunned finality. A police officer nearby blew into his whistle, the noise sharp and piercing. It did nothing to disturb Orion. Even as the world shrieked and scurried around him, he remained sitting stock-still, reeling from the bombshell that had landed in front of him.

38

After hours, Seagreen Press grew gloomy from the inside out, like some manor over the hills instead of a stout office building in the French Concession.

Rosalind should have clocked out already, but she remained at her desk, scribbling away on invoice sheets. She hadn't spoken much to Orion all day, intent on giving off the guise of busyness for anyone watching her. She had waved him away when he approached her around five, telling him they couldn't leave yet because she was mighty busy. In truth, she had a plan up her sleeve. Once she had waited out the rest of their colleagues, Rosalind could make her move.

Jiemin left his desk at five-thirty. He gave her a suspicious glance, trying to ask with his eyes what she was up to, but Rosalind merely offered him a mock salute and returned to her work. Soon, not only had the hallway lights turned off, but the department itself went dim, making it much harder to see the print in front of her. No matter. Twenty minutes later, the last woman at her desk walked out, emptying the department. Rosalind didn't need to look like she was working hard anymore.

She reached for her bag.

Much to her surprise, when she walked over to Orion's cubicle, he didn't look up. She had expected him to be impatient and readying to leave, but he didn't even hear her approach until she put a hand on his shoulder. He started.

Rosalind frowned. "Are you okay?"

"Yes," Orion rushed to say. "Ready to go?"

She nodded. The building had fallen entirely quiet.

"I've been waiting for everyone to leave so I could fetch the shipment logs in the mail room," Rosalind said as they descended the stairwell. "Can you have a poke around Haidi's desk too? I don't think she would store anything incriminating there, but we may as well cover all our bases."

Orion didn't respond.

"Orion," she prompted.

He took the last three stairs at once. For a moment, he seemed confused, like he was waking from a dream and finding himself already in motion. Then he said, "Yes, I can do that," and walked stiffly to the front desk.

What's wrong with him?

Rosalind shook her confusion off and hurried into the mail room, the door opening smoothly under her hand. There was no reason to protect the miscellaneous packages stored in here overnight, so there was no lock on the door, which made Rosalind's job a lot easier. She crept along the shelves in darkness, only the glow from the streetlights outside illuminating her search.

She thought she had seen Tejas rummaging down this aisle. Where was it?

Rosalind's eyes snagged on a box sticking out from underneath one of the farthest shelves. Its flaps were still open. When she tugged the box out and peered inside, she found a black clipboard lying right at the top.

"Aha, success," she muttered, opening the clipboard to its most recent page. There were some new entries—and one from earlier that very day, logging an outgoing crate for Burkill Road.

Rosalind ran the numbers in her head. It might arrive at the address tomorrow. Which meant there might be another hit tomorrow.

She unclipped the whole log. Rolled it up and shoved it into her bag before rising on her tiptoes and hiding the empty clipboard above one of the cabinets.

Rosalind slipped out of the mail room. Orion was still searching the front desk when she padded over quietly.

"See anything?"

"Only a lot of candy wrappers," Orion reported. "I don't think—"

A flare of headlights swept across the first-floor windows, interrupting Orion mid-sentence. The screech of a car's brake followed immediately, then a door slamming closed. Someone was coming back to the office.

"Hide!" Rosalind hissed.

"Here." Orion grabbed her wrist and pulled them both behind the desk, ducking under the heavy structure. The outer side of the desk extended all the way to the floor—anyone passing by would not see Rosalind and Orion unless they came around and looked from Haidi's chair.

A single set of footsteps entered the building. Rosalind didn't dare breathe, her hand fisted into Orion's shirt. His arm was wrapped around her waist, holding her unmoving in their tight quarters. She didn't know if it was her own heart hammering against her rib cage or if it was Orion's panic she felt passing to her. The space under the desk was cramped enough that she was half-sprawled on top of him, though the two of them entwined was nothing new at this point.

If they were found here after hours, there was little excuse for why they were acting so suspect, why the lights were off as if the office were closed. They needed to stay very, very quiet.

The late-night visitor went up the stairwell slowly. Their heavy tread was patient. It had to be a higher-up—Deoka or someone of his stature—or else they wouldn't have had access to drive through the front gates after the guards went home.

"Should we go?" Rosalind whispered when the visitor disappeared onto one of the higher floors.

"What if there's someone in the car too?" Orion whispered back.

"We're going to have to lie our way out." Rosalind perked her ears, trying to gauge if there was movement in the gravel lot outside. "It's more dangerous to wait it out. Leaving now is passably suspicious. Leaving in an hour is utterly guilty."

"Suspicious is still suspicious."

"We don't have any other choice!"

Orion searched her gaze. They were having a whispered argument about the matter as if they were debating different sides, but they both knew it was imperative that they slip out without getting caught. They were so *close* to finishing this assignment.

"Okay," Orion said. "If there's someone waiting in the car, I have an excuse we can have prepared."

Rosalind looked to the darkness outside the desk. She thought she heard pacing from the floor above. She tried to loosen her grip on Orion's shirt, laying her hand flat on his chest instead. His heart was beating so viciously that she could feel the thrumming against her palm.

"What is it?" she asked, turning back to face him. A snap of something dangerous passed between their eyes. Perhaps at that moment Rosalind should have known exactly what Orion's grand plan was.

He leaned forward and kissed her.

It wasn't a chaste kiss for a watching audience. It was one of his hands locked tight on her waist and the other one pushed into her hair, loosening the pins and undoing her braid. It was her body pressing closer, a magnetic draw demanding her to move, to wrap her arms around his neck.

Her mouth parted with a gasp, and Orion took the invitation. His lips moved against hers like an enchantment, like the world was ending and this was his final grace. She couldn't form a single coherent thought amid the franticness, but she didn't care. In the burning fire there was damnation, and she wanted to throw herself right into it.

Orion pulled away abruptly, heaving for breath. Rosalind was so dazed that she could only stare at him, struggling just as much to make a full inhale that would fill her lungs. There was a smear of her lipstick across the top of his lip. Without thinking, she reached to wipe it off, but he caught her wrist, burning-hot fingers wrapped around her burning-hot skin.

"It's what we need," he breathed.

Right. Because this was a part of the plan. An act.

"Let's go," she managed.

They clambered out from beneath the desk, not fixing a single rumpled collar. Rosalind drew her bag close to herself, and Orion took her hand. When they hurried down the front steps, the car that was parked by the building flashed its headlights at them.

The two of them halted. The chauffeur opened his door, his expression set in a frown.

"What—"

"So sorry," Orion interrupted before the man could say anything. Even without seeing his expression, she could hear the grin in his voice. "We didn't realize it had gotten so late. Not disturbing any security, are we?"

The chauffeur's frown faded, replaced by annoyance in his brow. He waved a hand and started to clamber back into the car. "Please leave the premises when you are ready."

"We'll get out of your hair!" Rosalind called lightly.

They spun around. Hurried across the grounds. Rosalind didn't think either of them exhaled until they had passed through the front gates, out of sight from the building and far from the watching chauffeur.

"You okay?" Orion asked. His voice was soft.

Rosalind stopped him, making a proper effort at removing her lipstick from his mouth. He watched her swipe a finger across his upper lip. She didn't know if he noticed the slight tremor in her hand.

"Of course," she said. "We're excellent spies, after all."

The air was cool on their walk back to the apartment, which was good for the flush in Rosalind's cheeks. She kept stealing glances at Orion, he kept stealing glances at her, and the two of them kept looking at each other wordlessly before turning back to the road, opting to continue walking in silence.

When Rosalind pushed open the door into her building court-yard, she stopped short.

"Silas?"

Silas turned around. He was standing with Lao Lao outside her apartment, in the middle of conversation.

"Wait, what?" Silas blurted suddenly as Rosalind and Orion walked closer. "I thought you were upstairs already."

"Upstairs . . . in our apartment?" Orion asked. "Why would you think that?"

Silas looked to Lao Lao. The old woman was visibly perplexed too.

"Because Lao Lao said you were," he replied. "Lao Lao told Phoebe that her brother was inside waiting to talk to her alone. Called us over and everything."

The courtyard went deathly silent. Phoebe was inside, talking to her *brother*?

"Oliver," Orion spat, charging up the stairs.

"Oh God," Rosalind muttered. "Lao Lao, did you know?"

"I thought it was Liwen," she exclaimed. "He said he lost his keys, so I let him in. Then he wanted to call his sister over, so I made the summons."

Oliver Hong had taken advantage of how similar they looked and sounded. Rosalind lifted her qipao skirt and hurried up the stairs after Orion, taking two at a time.

"I'll be here!" Silas called. Lao Lao ushered him into her apartment, offering him food to keep him out of the family drama upstairs—and so he wasn't putting his triple agent cover at risk among actual Communists. When Rosalind skidded into her own apartment, she was right in time to see Orion charge at his older brother, going for his throat.

"Hey, hey!" Rosalind yelled.

Phoebe stood up, installing herself between them. On Oliver's side, a woman grabbed his arm in a blur of motion, speaking furiously into his ear.

Celia.

For a second, Rosalind was so relieved to see her sister that she only stood staring. Celia looked healthy. Her hair was tucked in a small bun at the nape of her neck, her skin a warm glow and her eyes bright. Then Orion was lunging forward again, trying to circle around Phoebe, and Rosalind forced herself to move, looping her arms around him and physically dragging him back.

"If you get hauled in for fratricide, I am *not* bailing you out," she hissed.

"Sometimes a little fratricide is okay," Orion returned.

Over by the couch, Oliver tilted his head. He really did look like a carbon copy of Orion, if only with more shadows under his eyes and a deeper sense of rage brimming in the frame of his shoulders. He also looked more like a persistently smug scoundrel, because where Orion shook off his air with a sense of flippancy, Oliver wore it proudly.

"You don't mean that," Oliver said. "I've missed Phoebe dearly. I only wanted to catch up with her."

Phoebe shot him a look, aggrieved to be dragged into this.

Rosalind stepped forward. She released her hold on Orion with a silent prayer that she wouldn't regret it.

"Sit down," she instructed Oliver. "You're in our household as a guest, so at least be polite about it." She nodded to Celia, pretending not to know her. "You too."

Celia sat without argument. Oliver, however, strode forward in challenge. "It was never my intention to be rude." He extended his hand. "I'm—"

"—not touching my wife," Orion finished for him, smacking his hand away. "Go sit down."

Celia met Rosalind's eyes, her brows shooting right up. *Wife?* she mouthed.

Rosalind shook her head. *Don't ask.*

"Fine, I'm sitting." Oliver moved away, dropping down next to Celia. Phoebe, watching him, sidled closer on the armrest, her eyes darting back and forth. "And you caught us—as lovely as it is to speak to Phoebe, we're here with a warning for you. Concerning your task."

"As if we would take *your* warning," Orion scoffed.

"No, it really is quite grave," Celia said. It was the first time she had spoken, and Orion's attention shot to her, his eyes narrowing the slightest fraction before moving to Rosalind. It took every ounce of effort not to fret. Could he see the resemblance?

"What is it?" Rosalind asked steadily.

"Do you have a map?"

The request was sudden, but Rosalind stood anyway, padding into the bedroom and searching her shelves. She was delighted to see her sister, but it was still very much out of the ordinary, and that could only spell trouble. Rosalind returned with an older map, showing the city and its outer periphery, colored and outlined where the French Concession and the International Settlement started and ended. When she set it on the coffee table, Phoebe leaned forward and helped her hold two of the corners down. Celia, a pen in hand, hovered over the map, drawing a circle on the uppermost left side.

"There's a warehouse out here moving around Seagreen Press's issues."

"Warehouse 34," Rosalind supplied immediately. "I've been following it too. That's where the vials are coming from."

Now Oliver was frowning too, easing away from the couch seat so he could get closer to the map. "The vials?"

"The chemical injections that have been killing people across Shanghai," Orion clarified. Even without turning around, Rosalind knew he had rolled his eyes at his brother. "You know, the terror scheme that the Japanese Empire orchestrated. Which the government can't focus on because we're also busy fighting a civil war—"

"Orion, qīn'ài de, please shut up," Rosalind interrupted.

Orion clamped his lips together. Phoebe gave his arm a reassuring pat.

Celia traced another line of her pen along the map. "For the life of me, I couldn't comprehend why the warehouse would take newspaper printings from the factories, then pack them right up again. Rather, I couldn't figure out what a foreign newspaper from Shanghai was doing so far up from the city to begin with."

"We had also gone rummaging through Warehouse 34 sometime before," Oliver added. "It looked like a mix between a lab and a storage facility. Crates littered everywhere. Beakers and test tubes on the tables. After some heated discussion on the car ride down, we came to one conclusion."

"Those newspapers are a guise to get the shipments through the postal system," Celia finished. "Seagreen Press only writes its issues so that it can funnel whatever Warehouse 34 is making into Shanghai."

With a sigh, Orion finally approached the coffee table too, slotting himself next to Rosalind and sitting on the floor.

"We already knew most of that," he said tiredly. "We were working on the other half of the supply line. It comes in from the warehouse, reaches Seagreen, and then Seagreen sends it to a house in the International Settlement, where someone else takes it and uses it to murder people. The Nationalists have the evidence already. We're set to make our arrests tomorrow."

The room fell quiet. Celia and Oliver exchanged a look.

"What?" Rosalind demanded.

"The warehouse," Celia said slowly, "is run by Nationalist soldiers."

"*What?*" Orion demanded. "That's ridiculous. This is a foreign imperialist scheme."

Oliver splayed his hands. "A foreign imperialist scheme working with Kuomintang defectors, it seems."

"You—"

"Stay down," Rosalind commanded before Orion could rise. She turned to Oliver. "You must know how unbelievable that sounds. A whole warehouse operation would not be run by just one hanjian. It would require a militia. How would something that large escape the Kuomintang's notice?"

But doubt was starting to creep into Rosalind's mind, turning her cold. She thought about everything she did not yet have an answer for. The file being taken. Dao Feng being attacked. Every bit of chaos on their own side. Had someone been working against them all along?

Rosalind stopped. "Actually, hang on." She turned to Celia. "Do you know why the Communists tried to kidnap us?"

Celia reared back. "I beg your pardon?"

"I made a copy of their file. There were three code names—Lion, Gray, and Archer—claimed as double agents from your party who are pretending to be Nationalists."

Rosalind was not watching her sister now. She was watching Oliver, waiting for the slightest slip to indicate that he knew something about this.

"Shortly afterward," she continued, "it was stolen from me, my handler was almost killed, and a car full of your agents came after us, trying to haul us in with rope. I sent Alisa to sniff around, but she has yet to report back."

A beat passed.

"Alisa?" Orion and Phoebe echoed at once. Rosalind froze. *Merde.*

"Liza," Rosalind corrected. "That was a slip of the tongue."

"No, you *said* Alisa." A thought pulled Orion's eyes wide. "Alisa *Montagova?*"

This was a disaster. She thought she had been careful in winding and unwinding the threads of her past, placing them where they needed to be, but instead they were coming alive like a python, intent on choking her with her own lies.

"They're very similar names," Rosalind maintained.

Orion folded his arms. He evidently did not believe her, but he chose to stop pressing the matter, looking at the map in front of them again.

"There is some connection among all of this," Orion said. "Or else Dao Feng wouldn't be in the hospital comatose right now."

"I'm really failing to see the connecting points," Oliver countered.

Orion's fists curled. "I didn't ask *you—*"

"I offered my opinion, nonetheless." Oliver got to his feet. "Celia, we need to go. We've dawdled long enough."

"Wait. You just got here," Phoebe insisted, letting go of the map. The paper rolled up, collapsing into its cylindrical shape and dropping off the table. Rosalind almost stepped on it when she lunged upright too.

"Sorry, xiǎomèi." Oliver tugged on a ringlet of Phoebe's hair as he beelined for the door. "Ask your èrgē not to threaten my life and I might visit more often. Celia, sweetheart?"

Celia nodded, indicating that she was coming. As Rosalind instinctively took a step after her sister, Celia closed a hand around Rosalind's elbow, leaning in to make a frantic whisper. She switched to Russian so Orion and Phoebe wouldn't understand.

"You have to be careful. There is something terrible at work here. I know the Nationalists put you on this task, but they're involved in some manner, even if I haven't figured out how yet." Celia pulled away. She looked at Rosalind as if she wanted to say more, but they were being watched, so Celia only squeezed her elbow, communicating her concern in that one gesture. "Take care."

With that, her sister hurried off, disappearing out the door with Oliver. Rosalind felt the night air sweep in with the open entranceway.

"Why do you keep sending him off?"

Phoebe's voice took Rosalind by surprise. Rosalind shifted away from the door, finding the girl to be hovering in the middle of the living room, her arms wrapped around herself.

"*I'm* not sending him off," Orion replied. He sounded exhausted. "The city is. I can't stop him from working for the other side of a war."

Phoebe drew her shoulders high, seeming to prepare for a whole spiel. But then, like a balloon deflating, she only exhaled and walked to the door.

"I'll have Silas take me home. Good night."

The door closed. It left Rosalind and Orion standing in their living room, the space suddenly feeling empty. Rosalind extended her hand to Orion in a gesture of amity, and Orion responded by taking her wrist, pulling her to him in an embrace instead.

"It's okay," she said immediately. She tucked her head beneath his chin, breathing in deep. She was tired of these battle lines too. Barriers drawn in every which direction, keeping her from her own sister. They had chosen their sides. She wished there didn't have to be sides to begin with, but that was the naive and careless part of her speaking.

She knew why sides formed. Change. Revolution. Disruption.

"I'm tired of this," Orion whispered.

Rosalind tightened her grasp on him. "It'll be over tomorrow."

She felt him shake his head. It was a shake to say, *No, it won't be.* The arrests could be made tomorrow, a terror cell and an imperialist plot could be unrooted tomorrow, but the war would not be over. The sides would remain.

Orion drew away. "Do you believe them? About the Nationalists?"

"I don't know." Rosalind tipped her head up, frowning. She knew Celia would never lie to her, regardless of the circumstances. The only matter was whether Celia had received the right information. These schemes were masterminded by people who swapped costumes whenever convenient—this much they already knew. "All we can do is be careful. It'll have to come to a head one way or another."

Orion nodded. She wondered if he might ask about Celia. If he might be curious why Celia had seemed familiar with her. But he did not. All that was unspoken between them would remain unspoken for another night. He only tugged her back and wrapped his arms around her again.

Oliver drove into the night with his foot pressing harder and harder on the accelerator.

"Slow down," Celia chided. He was worked up. His destructive tendencies came out in full force when he was deep in thought about something else.

"There's no one out here," Oliver replied, pushing them even faster.

"Great logic. When we hit a bump in the road and go flying, at least it's only us who dies."

Though he would never admit it, the rebuke in Celia's tone did prompt Oliver to slow down the slightest fraction. Celia drummed her fingers on her leg, watching the trees whiz by outside.

"Oliver," she said. "What do you know about Priest?"

"Priest?" he repeated in surprise. He took his eyes away from the road for a brief moment to meet her gaze. "Priest has nothing to do with this."

"Answer my question."

"I'm serious. Literally not a single connecting point—"

"But what do you *know*?" Celia asked again. "I've had enough! This lock on information isn't helping anyone! If we're caught, we're dead anyway, so you may as well tell me."

The car slowed further. Though it was certainly still going at a dangerous speed, Celia could feel Oliver easing and easing on the accelerator, taken aback by her outburst.

"It does help," Oliver said. "It helps me sleep better at night knowing the Kuomintang can't torture you for information that I gave you. That I didn't put you in more danger despite knowing better." His jaw tightened. He was trying not to look away from the road. "Fine. Audrey was right. I control Priest. Each trip I make into Shanghai is to make contact and move intelligence around. That's all I can say. That's all I *will* say."

Celia blew air through her nose furiously. "I'm getting out of the car."

"Don't be ridiculous."

She reached for the door handle. Oliver lunged an arm over and slammed the brakes at the same time, trying to lock her into her seat before she could throw the door open and hurt herself. "Don't! Don't, okay?"

The car screeched to an abrupt stop, falling quiet. Slowly, Oliver moved his arm away, seeing that Celia wasn't going to march off. She only watched him expectantly—waiting, waiting.

"Look, here's a compromise," Oliver said very carefully. He pulled the car to the side of the road, parking them properly even though there was no one else using these roads at this hour. "I think I know why our agents went after Rosalind and Orion."

Celia blinked. "What?" She hadn't expected the sudden pivot. "Then why didn't you tell them?"

"Because we're at war. It might misfire on our own agents. How can I report to our superiors that I've given our enemies a heads-up?"

"They're not our enemies," Celia hissed. "They're our *family*."

Oliver cast her a sidelong glance. "So are the people in the countryside," he said. "So is every forgotten worker and factory runner. I can't push for revolution and hold it back at the same time."

God. He was going to be loyal to the cause until the very end. She knew this. Of course she did. She both loved and hated him for it.

"Why," she gritted through her teeth, maneuvering her body so that she could face him, "are you *like* this?"

Oliver mimicked her motion. He leaned in. "Like what?"

Celia stayed very still. Her gaze dropped before she could help it, looking at Oliver's mouth, mere inches away. At once, every thought on her mind and every argument waiting on her tongue fled in a mass exodus. She considered nothing except his proximity, drawing nearer and nearer. She could swap her head with her heart. It would be so easy.

Then she whispered: "Don't."

Oliver stopped. He didn't pull away. He stayed where he was, the two of them separated by a breath.

"I'm sorry," he murmured.

"No—don't be *sorry*—" Celia broke off with a frustrated noise and made the first withdrawal, turning to face the dashboard instead. "We can't do this. Not with our duties."

"Our duties?" Oliver echoed. Something was different in the next blink of his dark eyes—it took Celia a prolonged moment to realize his stare had turned wholly unguarded. Where Oliver Hong was normally stoic, he had dropped the facade, letting her in on his confusion and disquietude. "Sweetheart, we work for the nation, but it doesn't *control* us."

Celia shook her head. Sooner or later they were going to get into trouble. Sooner or later they were going to get hauled in by the government, imprisoned, tortured. This was something every operative on their side knew. The war was long. They had signed up to fight it.

"You don't know what you're asking from me," she whispered. "I've seen what love does. It's powerful. It's selfish. It will draw us away from the battlefield, and we can't allow that."

It would build a path away. It would make death something terrible, and then who would want to be a soldier marching into war? Who would want to risk leaving the world if they held something beautiful in their hands?

Oliver was frowning intently, like he was sifting through a multitude of responses in his head first. Almost no light from the night outside entered the car save for the stars overhead, and still in the dark she could sight every wrinkle of his brow and every twitch of his lips.

"There's a small flaw in your logic."

Celia blinked, her hands clutching together in her lap. "What?"

Oliver sighed. It sounded like he was saying: *Sweetheart*. It sounded like he was saying: *How are you following along this slowly?*

"You can't ask me not to love you by keeping me at arm's length. I'll love you anyway."

Their car jolted to a start again, the engine resuming its loud hum. Celia stared forward, her mind an utter dead-signal screech. She might have completely forgotten how to breathe if Oliver hadn't pulled back onto the road and driven over a large rock, throwing her around in her seat and forcing instinct to take over and start inhaling-exhaling again.

"As we were saying," Oliver said evenly, as if he hadn't dropped the most unbelievable confession on her, "there are murmurings that the Kuomintang are closing in on a weapon. They don't have that many active covert missions ongoing, and fewer in Shanghai itself. Whatever it is, our agents want it first. I think this is one and the same with Rosalind and Orion's mission."

Celia tried to get back on task. It was near impossible, but she gave it her best shot, opting to meet Oliver's gaze through the rear-view mirror instead of head-on. His expression was a blank and even slate. The guardedness had been reinstated.

"What does that mean?" she asked. Her voice sounded too scratchy, so she cleared her throat. "They went after Rosalind to get a weapon from her? Or are they after *her* as a weapon?"

Her rapid healing. Her inability to sleep or age. Rosalind's alternate identity as Fortune was infamous in both parties, even if most people thought she was a myth.

Oliver shook his head. "Our agents know that no one has been able to understand her powers, so they wouldn't be stupid enough to try something this many years later. They're not after her for her talents as Fortune."

"Then what are they looking for?" Celia asked. What else could be a weapon? Short of guns and knives and poison, what else was there?

"I don't know," Oliver replied. "Genuinely. It's not our mission, only one we are intruding on, so very little intelligence is traveling down the line for fear of a leak."

There was something just out of grasp in Celia's comprehension of the situation. She could feel it, like a lifeboat floating in the distance.

"But you think our people went after Rosalind and Orion because they are the ones closing in on it? The only thing they're closing in on are the arrests of imperialists and hanjian." Celia stopped. "And Warehouse 34, I suppose."

Now something was starting to move into place. Some scattered parts of a whole picture, brushing closer to where they were supposed to be.

The dirt road up ahead split into a fork. Oliver took the right. In the midst of making the turn, he hesitated.

"What is it?" Celia prompted immediately.

He let the steering wheel straighten itself, waiting for the vehicle to proceed forward before speaking. "There was something about that warehouse. It reminded me of my mother's old science kits, the ones that she would lay on the table for us to play with if we complained about being bored. It felt like they were out there mixing concoctions for fun. What's so great about a chemical killing mixture? You can kill people by injecting air into their veins too."

Celia sat back. A thought occurred to her so quickly that she felt like she had been physically slapped. "What if the point isn't killing?"

"What?" Oliver made a left turn, taking them onto a narrower dirt road. They were exiting Shanghai's outer borders. "So it *is* for fun and games?"

"No," Celia said. The materials in Warehouse 34. The metal slab that had looked like an operating table, if not for the buckles down the side. And Rosalind: Rosalind being brought back to life when Lourens plunged that needle into her arm. "What if they're running experiments, and killing their subjects is just a side effect? What if these deaths through Shanghai isn't them *using* a chemical weapon—what if it's their attempt at perfecting one?"

39

"Take this information to Rosalind immediately," Celia had said when Alisa picked up the phone, having been summoned to her nearest liaison station. "I promised Oliver I wouldn't get involved, but I can give a warning at least. Her mission is not a terror cell. They're not killing people for an excuse to invade Shanghai. They're using people as guinea pigs and killing them to perfect a chemical weapon."

Across the city and outside of it, Friday arrived to the sound of war drums. Alisa hadn't gotten the call until late afternoon, and then she needed to return to the corner store to pick up her pictures. She figured she may as well get the pictures before finding Rosalind so she could present everything at once.

"Hello."

The girl behind the counter tapped an envelope, already waiting by the guide maps and mints. "For you."

Alisa picked up the envelope, ripping into it immediately. The contents inside weren't thick: only five photographs, printed from the five negative panels on the film strip. She thumbed along the first two. A bouquet of flowers propped against the wall. Mrs. Guo pointing the lens at her bathroom mirror with a silly expression, which made Alisa laugh.

She was moving the photos from one hand to the other, keeping them in separate piles of viewed and unviewed. When she got to the next photograph, however, she dropped all of them at once, scattering them across the corner store floor.

"Oh dear," the girl behind the counter said. She didn't bother coming to help pick them up. Alisa, too, stood unmoving, her jaw hanging agape. Suddenly afraid that the photo might blow away with the wind, she dropped to her knees and scooped it up, wiping at the surface as if she might be able to erase what it was showing her.

"It's *you?*"

Orion had received a phone call asking him to go to local Kuomintang headquarters again, so when the workday ended, Rosalind started making her way to Burkill Road alone.

"I'll meet you there if they finish our meeting sooner than expected," he had whispered in the break room. "If you see Haidi during the window of time that she might act, do *not* confront her."

"I know, I know. I'm only keeping watch," Rosalind had reassured him.

The function at Cathay was in three hours. There was no time to waste when it came to collecting their last pieces of information. Rosalind wasn't concerned about acting solo anyway. She couldn't get gravely injured—as long as *she* didn't get a needle stabbed into her arm, and even if she wasn't the best fighter, it was still hard to overpower her.

The sun started to set at a leisurely pace, turning the sky into an orange watercolor. One by one, the streetlamps on the roads hummed on.

When Rosalind walked, she put each step down with intention. She carried no bag, no purse, making it all the easier to maneuver. There was only poison, coated on the pins in her hair, hidden in the fold of her skirt, attached to the hollows of her shoes.

She waited for a tram to pass, each toll of its bell like a death count across the city, marking those who had fallen, remaining for-ever nameless.

It didn't take long to arrive at Burkill Road. It didn't take long to slink along the pavement, keeping close to the shop fronts and saloon chairs until she was approaching the residence, until she was winding around the back and making a full circle, scouting every exit in sight. There were a few low windows. One back door hidden behind a big pile of trash bags. She was willing to bet that the killer would be using that to enter and exit, so Rosalind has-tened to another building farther down the alley and hid herself beside one of its stoops, within view of the door.

She waited. She watched. The sun went down. The skies turned dark. And when one single bulb turned on at 286 Burkill Road, there was movement in the alley, a figure exiting from the back door with whip-quick movement.

Rosalind shot to her feet. She hadn't caught sight of Haidi's face—not for a lack of looking, but because whoever had just exited the door had their features covered, swathed with black fabric. From head to toe, it was all black, blending right into the night.

Rosalind was in pursuit immediately: not for combat, only to get a better *look*. The alleys were relatively empty, and she was already familiar with them after her escape with Orion. Though she stayed on the figure's tail, she knew she needed to keep at a dis-tance to ensure they wouldn't hear her in pursuit. A few times they seemed to surge forward, and on the third time Rosalind almost lagged too far behind, barely catching a flash of the figure turning right. With a brief glance at the alley up ahead, she took another route, knowing that it would converge with their path.

"Come on, come on," she muttered under her breath, pulling one of her hairpins out. Forget only keeping watch: she was too close now. She skidded into the new alley—the killer was already some paces away, turning the next corner. Though they were moving fast, they were not moving in a hurry. It was methodic. It was done in a manner that indicated they still had not noticed Rosalind following.

There was the sound of something crashing. A flowerpot? A laundry line? Rosalind drew around the corner with her heart in her mouth and her weapon raised. Before her stood the killer, holding down a man dressed in threadbare clothes.

"Haidi, stop," she bellowed, revealing her presence. "Move away."

But Haidi . . . if it was Haidi at all, didn't even register the command. A flood of doubt stilled Rosalind's hand. She was witnessing them make the kill. Didn't they care? Weren't they frightened in the least—wouldn't they try to combat her or run?

"Hey!"

The killer plunged a syringe into the man on the ground and pushed down.

In a furious motion, Rosalind finally rushed forward, colliding with the killer and pushing them off-balance. She tried to haul the man to his feet as soon as the killer was momentarily shoved aside, but he was already jerking and seizing, making it impossible to get a good grip.

"Don't worry," Rosalind gasped. "Don't worry. Hold on—"

A hand grasped her arm, throwing her back. The hairpin clattered out of her grip. She hit the wall hard, almost putting a dent into the plaster.

Her head spun. Suddenly she regretted every decision that had led her here alone.

The man on the ground stilled. The masked killer turned around, movements slow and deliberate. Rosalind wheezed to gather her breath again, reaching up to yank out another hairpin. Just as the killer was moving toward her, she attacked, kicking the syringe out of their hand and hooking her leg against their ankle when her leg came back down, relying on the force of her momentum. It worked—or at least it half worked, slamming the killer onto their back while Rosalind rolled to the ground, returning to a combative stance. When they recovered, however, they were much faster. Her attack had urged them to pull a knife from somewhere within their clothing, and then their arm was coming down fast. Rosalind blocked once, then another time, rolling to get out of the way. She braced on her knees, right at an angle where she could reach up—

—and snatch the fabric off their face.

Though that would have been the opportune moment to lunge away and avoid the next arc of their knife, Rosalind didn't move.

"Oh my God," she whispered, dropping her pin.

40

This is how it happens.

The summons is made across the city. Communication is easy when the streets are populous and tangled with electric wires: send a runner, make a phone call. The technique doesn't matter, only the trigger word. Oubliez. *Forget.*

Then the killer moves. Sometimes it is hard to get away. The blankness is conditioned to set in only when they are alone. It took an incredible amount of programming. Of experimenting. Only when they are alone will they make a change of clothes and head toward the same location. They have been instructed very clearly about the routes they should take to avoid detection. They are already skilled to begin with, so this work is easy to drill in. No free thought necessary—only muscle memory.

Instruction number one: take the vial and the syringe. It is new each time. Slightly altered, depending on the results of the last run.

Instruction number two: find the first person who is alone and give them the concoction. In previous months, there were certain streets that were better to hit, certain areas to enter first. It would minimize the likelihood of being sighted by a watchful eye in the window or a curious pedestrian on more well-kept streets. Now it does not matter. Now time is of the essence, and every part of the city is fair game.

The last batch was supposed to have been the final run. When the delivery was handed over, the instructions changed once again: use all six in the batch. Surely one ought to work. Drag the bodies together if it doesn't. Don't go too far from home; don't raise any suspicion.

It didn't work as they wanted. One more batch. One more run.

The killer finds the man and pushes the needle in.

"Haidi, stop! Move away."

Who? When the killer looks, there is a girl braced for combat in the alley, eyes blazing. There are instructions for this too. Carry a weapon. Take down anyone who sees, anyone who intervenes. Do a good job of it.

One swing, another.

None of this is real, after all. Only tasks to complete. Only instructions to follow.

It won't be long before a killing blow can be made. This girl isn't fully trained; this girl is careless with her swings and abrupt with her movements, pulling her hand forward for no reason and then pausing when she pulls at the fabric that had been hiding the killer's face.

But doesn't she look familiar? the killer thinks. *Don't I know her?*

There: take the opening.

I know her.

The knife, hurtling toward her with its sharp point forward.

Beloved. Darling beloved.

"Oh my God," the girl whispers. *"Orion?"*

And just before he snaps out of his trance, he stabs the knife into her stomach.

Rosalind felt the blade leave her stomach with a tearing sensation, spreading biting agony through her middle. Her hands came to brace around the wound, deep crimson blood seeping through the

lines of her fingers. The moment Orion pulled the blade out, something seemed to change in his manner. His eyes turned wide; his
lips parted with astonishment. When he looked down at his own
hands, he seemed terrified to find them covered in red.

"Janie?" he rasped, dropping the knife. It clattered to the concrete ground. "What—what am I—"

"Stay back," she warned. "*Jesus.*" It was always the gut that bled
so much for no reason. She kept her arm braced against the wall,
blanketed in cold sweat. One would think that being able to heal
from anything meant she had no problem taking injuries, but each
time was more traumatizing than the next, each one a risk that
reminded her what it felt like to be at death's door. She wasn't the
same girl who had died the first time. She didn't want to die anymore.

"I didn't—" Orion took a step forward.

"I mean it," Rosalind commanded. Her stomach was knitting
itself back together, but not fast enough. She wouldn't be able to
get away if he reached her. Blood was still running through her fingers, pouring from the wound. Her head was light, her skin shivery.
"Don't come any closer."

"You're *hurt.*"

"Stop—"

Orion suddenly collapsed where he stood, as if he had taken it
on himself to heed her exact instructions. A moment later, Rosalind
registered Alisa Montagova standing behind him holding a blow
dart in her hand, her eyes wide.

"I sincerely hope that was the right move," she said. "A small
sedative—don't worry. What happened?"

Rosalind gulped for air. The stab wound was starting to pull
itself together, sealing from the inside first. She was so unsettled
that she might throw up at any second, but she still managed to
keep her voice even when she responded to Alisa.

"I caught him red-handed. He's the killer."

Slowly Alisa walked up to Orion, giving him a little prod to make sure he was fully knocked out. "I actually knew that part already. Here." She passed Rosalind a photograph. If there was any doubt that this was a one-off misunderstanding, all chance of it flew out the window when Rosalind squinted at the image, holding it near the bulb flickering on the wall. It was Orion. It was Orion midmotion, a syringe in his hand and a woman lying on the damp alley ground.

Rosalind muttered a curse under her breath. Her stomach was almost done healing. Seconds later, when she poked her hand through the hole torn in the middle of her qipao, she found smooth skin, albeit sticky with blood.

"I don't understand."

"I do," Alisa said. "Celia called. She wants you to know that this whole thing was never about terror killings—they're experiments. The chemicals are not meant to be used for murder. They're creating a prototypical weapon. Each vial is a formula of some sort that has not been perfected, so they've been testing and testing until . . ."

A moan came from the alley. Rosalind tensed and pulled out another one of her hairpins with her bloody fingers, but it wasn't Orion who had stirred. It was the man he had injected.

"Is he *alive*?" Rosalind exclaimed, rushing to the man's side. "Can you hear me?"

"Where am I?" the man wheezed. "Who are you?"

Rosalind's head jerked up, seeking Alisa again. "Can you take him to the hospital?"

"I suppose," Alisa answered hesitantly, scurrying over. She helped Rosalind lift him, then took most of his weight when the man swayed, unable to stand entirely on his feet. "What are you going to do about—"

"I'll figure it out," Rosalind interrupted, knowing what Alisa was going to ask. "Don't tell anyone. Don't say anything. We're walking in completely unknown territory, and I need to figure out our footing first."

"You're playing *such* a dangerous game," Alisa muttered, but she did not argue. With as much support as she could offer to the injured man, they hobbled off to the main road.

Rosalind, left alone in the alley, spun on her heel for one of the building doors. She knocked loudly, then stood back and waited. A tall man with a rag in his pocket answered, wiping grease off his fingers.

"Are you all right?" he demanded, seeing the blood on her clothes.

"Oh, I'm great," Rosalind answered. "Can you lift something for me? I'll pay you handsomely."

Rosalind had gotten Orion home in his unconscious state with the stranger's help, blabbering the whole time about how her husband sleepwalked and it was a huge nuisance when she was in the middle of slaughtering chickens to cook. Once the man had left the apartment, probably puzzled over where the chickens were, Rosalind had tied Orion to a kitchen chair and put the chair in the middle of the bedroom, where there was nothing nearby that he could knock over and use to free himself if he woke up before Rosalind was back.

She had planned to dart out quickly. But then—because the universe was intent on being a nuisance—there was a knock on the door and Lao Lao's voice yelling that she had a phone call.

Dammit, she thought frantically. Silas. He would want a report on whether they had confirmed a sighting on Haidi.

"What's the situation, High Tide?" Silas said the moment she brought the receiver to her ear. "Are all ends wrapped up?"

Rosalind couldn't answer for a long moment. She stood there, her grip tightening on the telephone. Orion needed to be brought in for his crimes. He was the *killer*. It was even worse than being hanjian; it was the literal blood of innocent civilians on his hands.

"Janie?" Silas prompted. "Are you there?"

"I'm here," she said. "Yes. We saw Haidi. She's the killer."

Rosalind Lang had always been a rather good liar. Maybe she would never learn her lesson. Lie first; figure out the rest later. There was a terrible weight on her chest as she hurriedly told Silas the rest—the killings as experiments, the deaths as side effects—only growing heavier when she put the phone down and hurried out of Lao Lao's apartment to hail a rickshaw. Time was running out. The night was growing darker.

Now, clambering off the rickshaw, Rosalind held the syringe tightly in her hands—the one that Orion had dropped in the alleyway. There was still a small bit of green liquid inside, swishing as she walked. If her head hadn't been elsewhere, it should have occurred to her to run some tests as soon as she'd stolen that vial from Burkill Road. Then again, when Silas brought them that other vial from the alley behind Seagreen. Instead, they had handed both off to Jiemin. The Nationalists probably wouldn't do anything other than dump them in a drawer somewhere.

Why hadn't it occurred to her that perhaps knowing the precise contents of what exactly these chemicals *were* could have been important?

Rosalind pushed through the crowds in Chenghuangmiao, making her way closer to the Jiuqu Bridge and finding a familiar restaurant nearby. She had changed her ruined qipao and put on something red instead, for old times' sake. She used to walk by this area often. Here she had witnessed her share of terrible things, beautiful things, agonizing things. Here she had been given the news of her immortality.

Rosalind went into the restaurant, then descended the stairs to the old Scarlet labs hidden belowground. It looked the same from the last time she saw it: those high windows showing people's feet as they passed by outside, the floors sticky with spills, the corners piled with equipment.

There was one scientist present, who looked up as she entered the lab. Rosalind's shoulders tensed; she had been hoping that it wouldn't be anyone she recognized. But this was Hu Dai, the very scientist who had given her the diagnosis. She remembered his kind, elderly face screwed up in confusion, delivering his conclusion while looking as if he didn't believe it himself even with the evidence in front of him.

Your cells are entirely different. They revert back to a starter state the moment they are injured. They don't decay at all. They rebirth instead of dying.

"Hello." Rosalind passed the syringe. She wondered if Hu Dai would recognize her. It had been four years now. He must have seen hundreds of people in and out of this lab since then. "Please tell me what this is."

"What—"

"I beg of you," Rosalind said. "There's little time to explain. Please tell me if you've seen the substance inside before."

"I was only going to ask your name," the scientist returned nicely. There was no indication that he remembered who she was. He took the syringe and opened it, transferring the liquid into a beaker. "I am Hu Dai. You are?"

Rosalind wiped her palms on the skirt of her qipao, but it didn't help with absorbing her cold sweat. The silk only left her skin feeling lacerated.

"Not important," Rosalind said. Janie Mead didn't seem like a cover she could slip into anymore. It had always been ill-fitting, but now it felt like putting wet clothing back on after getting caught in the rain, and Rosalind would rather have revealed her true self than take it on again.

She watched as Hu Dai separated the beaker's contents into three petri dishes, then poured an array of different mixtures into them. Minutes passed as he worked, metal clinking against glass as he stirred the chemicals around.

"What are you seeing?" she asked, impatient.

A lengthy pause. Hu Dai frowned.

"Given how it is reacting, you've given me a mix of something," he finally said. "I can't tell you exactly *what* it is in such a short time, but I can take a guess at its effects: Aiding blood flow. Strength stimulants. Creatine overproduction."

But Alisa had said that this was a weapon. How could any of those results be weaponized? It only sounded like it would make its victims into aspiring athletes.

"It's being used with lethal intent," Rosalind said quietly. "Is there poison in there too?"

"Poison?" Hu Dai echoed, surprised. "I don't see any poison. Let me put it under a microscope." He picked up a petri dish. "It doesn't take poison to make something lethal. Any substance in large quantities can kill. Something good in large quantities will kill too."

Rosalind leaned on one of the worktables. Hu Dai put his eyes to the microscope. He fiddled with a lever. Moments later, he jerked away with a start.

"What happened?" Rosalind demanded.

"I have seen this once before." He put a droplet of something into the dish. It fizzled, then calmed. Hu Dai leaned into the microscope a second time. He nodded sagely, as if the outcome was expected.

When he looked up, meeting Rosalind's gaze, something had registered in his expression.

"Lang Shalin," he said. "I didn't think I'd see you back here again."

Rosalind's stomach dropped. Perhaps when the knife had carved into her gut, it had detached her organs from each other, and now they were jostling loosely in her torso.

"How did you recognize me suddenly?" she asked. "The thought hadn't even occurred to you when I walked in."

"Well—" Hu Dai pointed a thumb to the beaker, to the bright green mixture that was still leaving a tinge behind on the glass. "I think you just brought me what made you immortal."

Jiemin swirled the whiskey in his cup, distracted by the music wafting in from some corner of the hotel lobby. He ignored the socialites that walked by, the politicians that threw over a nod, even the children who only wanted to wave hello. By nature of this location—a mingling ground for the well-to-dos of Shanghai society—there would be plenty of annoyances trying to make a greeting while he sat at the bar, but there was nowhere else in the city that protected their doors this thoroughly and logged every visitor. It was safer than any place in Shanghai could be.

> *Final conclusion: the deaths are due to an experiment by the Japanese to create an enhancement substance— possibly to give their soldiers healing abilities alike to Fortune. The killings are unintended side effects, not an outright instigation of terror.*
>
> *High Tide confirms Zheng Haidi as the field agent responsible. Other guilty accomplices included in the sheet attached to this note. Arrests to happen tonight. Shut down the cell before the final enhancement substance is passed to soldiers. Okay to proceed?*
>
> *—Shepherd*

"Another glass?"

Jiemin glanced up slowly, then shook his head at the bartender. He had burned the note as soon as he had finished reading it, but Silas's words were still stark in his mind's eye, easily memorized and reread on command.

Evidence for Haidi? Jiemin had returned.

The reply note had arrived quickly.

Negative. Only a sighting. High Tide advises eyes pinned to each suspect on arrest list to ensure their presence tonight. Okay to proceed?

Jiemin had chewed it over. Had swished the cup of coffee in front of him while he was exchanging those messages, worrying the waitresses behind the café counter with how sad his frown looked. He was not a regular there, so they had no way of knowing this was simply his resting expression.

Eventually, he had written up his response and left the café to drop it off.

Proceed. I will ensure eyes are on suspects.

Despite giving the mission its go-ahead, something still felt off to Jiemin. How had they figured out that these were *experiments* without getting hard evidence that it was Haidi? Where had they retrieved this information?

Jiemin slid away from the hotel bar, walking the short distance through the lobby and toward the elevators. The bellhop, already eagerly hanging around, asked if he needed anything, but Jiemin did not stop and merely shook his head. A flood was coming for this country, crashing into city after city through fire and artillery, and these two civil factions refused to join hands and board an ark for survival. Perhaps they would make a pair of very strange beasts by walking together, but better that than to remain stranded, drowned fools.

Jiemin walked until he approached the telephone, hooked up to a cord in the wall and displayed on a small bronze table decorated with a white lace cloth. When the operator routed the line where he needed it to go, he wasted no time reporting in.

"I am monitoring the situation that you're concerned about," he opened with. "Something isn't right. Can you get me information from the other side?"

Alisa was sweating with exertion by the time she had the man checked into the hospital. She had directed the rickshaw to go into the French Concession, opting for a facility under foreign money rather than the understaffed and overrun hospitals in Chinese jurisdiction. Despite her efforts, the waiting room at Guangci Hospital was still relatively busy.

Once the nurse put the man onto a gurney, Alisa finally staggered back, dropping into a seat with a big exhale.

"Family emergency?"

Alisa cast a sidelong glance at the old woman next to her. She was knitting, waiting on the plastic chairs.

"Something like that," Alisa answered. Her frantic pulse was starting to level now. All that gripped her senses was the scent of antiseptic cleaner, overwhelmingly heavy in the air.

"They usually let family go in with the patients," the old woman said. "You don't have to wait out here."

Alisa watched the nurse and the gurney disappear down the corridor. "Yes, you're right. I do think I'll go keep an eye on everything."

She stepped past the woman's knitting, a prickle darting up her neck. There was no reason to follow the victim further, not when her job had only been to get him help. But some curious part of her wanted to see what the doctors said. She wanted to know why he had survived where the others didn't, and whether that meant something.

Were the chemical experiments finished?

Had they finally perfected what they wanted?

Alisa's shoes were completely silent when she proceeded down the corridor, searching for the nurse. They seemed to have disappeared into thin air, because when she got to the end of the corridor, there was no one there. For a few seconds, Alisa only whirled and whirled, thinking that she was simply not seeing something.

Nothing. Where had they gone?

She moved along the rooms, poking her head into the open doors and pressing her face close to the glass of the closed ones. Perhaps the nurse had been superbly fast while pushing the gurney. Perhaps they had made the transfer during the short time Alisa had spent in the waiting room.

But even after Alisa surveyed each of the rooms within the wing, she didn't see the man she had brought in. In his state, it wasn't as if he could have *walked off*.

Alisa hurried back to the waiting room and marched toward the reception desk. She ignored the line and went right to the front, slapping her hands flat on the desk surface.

"I think there is a patient missing," she said in French.

The receptionist's attention shot in Alisa's direction. Beside her, the telephone started to ring.

"Another one?" she blurted. "Mon Dieu—give me a second. Hello?"

With the phone occupying her attention, the receptionist didn't notice Alisa jerk away in surprise, her eyes widening. What did she mean by "another one"? Who *else* had gone missing?

Alisa didn't wait around for an explanation, knowing that it was unlikely the receptionist would say more. She plunged deeper into the hospital, running a scan of the floor plan and familiarizing herself with where the wings expanded. The little hairs on her arms were standing ramrod straight. She didn't think it was in her head:

there were eyes watching her—watching in every direction to see what she would do next. Whose eyes? Which faction? Japanese, waiting to observe the first survivor of the chemical experiments? Communist, hoping to swoop in? Or Nationalist, simply preparing to arrest her?

On the second floor, Alisa trailed along a white stair banister, searching frantically before she sighted a sliding window staffed with two nurses inside. She watched a patient walk up to the window, asking for an invoice slip. This had to be the hospital's administration office. She didn't hesitate before lurking around the corner and slipping through the office door, darting within the shelves before the two nurses at the other end of the room could notice her. Alisa shouldn't have worried. Once the patient departed, the two nurses were too distracted with conversation anyway, closing the window to continue chatting. Alisa started to rifle through the shelves, opening the outgoing patient files that had been left here for processing.

"Come on," Alisa muttered—to herself, to the papers she was scanning, to the hospital itself. "Answers. Give me answers."

"Reception says we have another one," one of the nurses was saying, meanwhile. "The patient was only checked in minutes prior, though, so we could erase it from our records and pretend he was never here."

Alisa froze, ducking lower into the shelves and turning her ear to the front.

"That doesn't fix the problem of the first one. He was too important—we're going to have Nationalists sniffing around soon."

"I don't pity whoever has to make the phone call. How do we lose a patient? It's as if he got up and walked out."

"He was comatose, filtering poison from his system. We would know if he got up and walked out."

Who? Alisa demanded silently. *Who are you talking about?*

"You never know. Nationalists, eh? I heard he might have been a part of their intelligence unit. Dao Feng, age thirty-eight."

"Oh shit," Alisa said aloud.

She took a step back and slipped out of the office.

41

Rosalind felt the shift in the room when Orion stirred back to consciousness. Her throat clenched, twisting with pain as if the air had turned serrated. Or maybe that was just a symptom of looking at Orion as he pried his eyes open, as he lifted his head slowly and blinked with heavy confusion.

"You're okay," was the first thing Orion gasped. "You're . . . you're okay?"

"No thanks to you," Rosalind returned. "You stabbed me."

"I didn't mean to!" The moment Orion tried to rise, he pulled hard against his ropes and dropped back down. He seemed surprised to find himself tied to the chair. "I don't even remember why I was in that alley. I don't . . . What was I *holding*?"

Rosalind's mouth opened, but Orion wasn't finished:

"*Did* I stab you? How are you healed?"

"*Yes*, you stabbed me," Rosalind spat. "Look at your hands, Orion!"

He looked. Made a small exhale, his energy deflating. His hands were bound right in his lap, giving him a full view of the dried blood smeared there, the remnants of his violence. "Tā mā de. I don't understand."

"Which part?"

"All of it. You. Me."

Rosalind walked a small length of the room. She had turned on one lamp by the bed and left the other lights off. What did she need so much illumination for anyway? It would only make it harder to look at Orion's pleading expression.

"You're the one who's been killing people across Shanghai, Orion. I don't suppose you'll try to deny that."

"I'm—"

He wanted to deny it. She could hear the strain, the frantic search for an explanation. But he couldn't, not when the evidence was bright red in his palm. Rosalind drew out the photograph Alisa had given her and held it in front of him.

"Deny it," she ordered. "Deny it, Orion."

For what felt like a short eternity, Orion only stared at the image. If it were possible to have pierced paper by gaze alone, he would have embedded a dozen holes into the photograph.

"I cannot," he said eventually. "Somehow, I cannot. But I—" His voice faded, weak and addled. "I don't know why. I don't have any memory of this photo. I don't have any memory of trying to hurt you. All I remember is walking toward headquarters. I was *thinking* about how I needed to hurry back. And then . . . then . . ."

Missing time. Losing control. Selective consciousness. It was the oldest explanation in the book. The one that removed him from blame—but only if it was *true*.

Rosalind took the photograph away, setting it down on her desk. There she already had another newspaper waiting, an issue from one of Shanghai's domestic presses. They had run a column two weeks ago, listing every death that had been attributed to the chemical killings, going as far as to draw a map beside the list to pinpoint where each body had been found.

"Zhang Hua Road on September 16," she read out. "What were you doing that night? Were you nearby?"

The interrogation was harsh enough that Orion only stared at her, unable to reply.

"What were you *doing?*" she demanded again.

"I don't know," Orion gasped. "I don't—"

"Lu Ka Peng Road on September 12." Rosalind traced her finger up the column, relentless. "Where were you that night? Zeng Tang Road on August 24. Where were you? And August 19. August 8. July 22. Jesus, Orion, do you know how long this list is?"

He did know. He was her mission partner; he knew every component of this mission as well as she did.

"I can't *remember*," Orion insisted. He squeezed his eyes shut, then forced them open again. "I'm trying, I *am*. But reaching for those memories is like reaching for fog. It's as if I am actively repelled from thinking about what is missing. All I ever remember is walking toward local headquarters. Then *nothing*. Nothing until late at night when I return."

Rosalind crossed her arms tightly, gripping at herself hard enough to hurt. This could be a grand act. Skilled performers were aplenty in this city, feigning weakness with weeping eyes and pleading stares while plotting the next plunge of their knife. She shouldn't trust him. Being tricked once was a tragedy, a strike from the merciless universe when it selected its random victims. Being tricked twice was stupidity, a fault of hers for not learning her lesson the first time.

Four years ago she could have turned Dimitri in at any point. Instead, she'd let him deceive her over and over again, until the city on fire made him finally leave, and then—only then—did she come to her senses.

She couldn't watch this city burn again.

"You must recognize," Rosalind said tightly, "how hard that is to believe."

"I don't know how else to make you believe me."

Orion was staring at his hands. He turned them over, and there was only more blood on the other side. Rosalind thought about offering him a wet towel, but another part of her wanted to witness this. She needed to see it, needed to watch every minute change in his expression, waiting for cruelty to slip out.

"You're trying to claim that you have no memory of every time you have wandered into Burkill Road, taken a vial, and killed a person on the streets," Rosalind said. Each of those words said aloud sounded more outrageous than the last. "That you had no clue of your own actions even though we were investigating *you*." Her voice rose in a crescendo. "How can I possibly believe you?"

Orion closed his fists. It did nothing to take the blood out of his sight, not when it was smeared up to his wrists.

"Because of this."

And then, in a motion so smooth that it almost looked effortless, Orion broke out of the rope, rising to his feet. Rosalind scrambled to get back, lunging for the pistol on the shelf. She didn't hesitate. She pulled the safety off and pointed the gun forward.

He hadn't loosened the rope. His restraints were sitting as broken frays on the floor, one piece snapped from the other. He had used brute force to tear right out of it.

Rosalind's breath escaped with a whoosh.

I can take a guess at its effects, the scientist had said. *Aiding blood flow. Strength stimulants. Creatine overproduction.*

"You're an experiment too."

Orion could be wounded—she had witnessed that for herself. He wasn't like her. But if they were using him as a killer, then he had to be something distinct too. He was strong. Fast. Hadn't she watched him fight before? Hadn't she seen how easily it came to him?

"An experiment?" Orion asked. He took a step toward her. He was still going along this route. Absolute cluelessness and ignorance.

Rosalind put both her hands on the gun. It occurred to her in an instant. She knew what Warehouse 34 was making: a perfect merge between what she and Orion could do separately. Put supernatural healing *and* supernatural strength in a person, and they were a walking weapon, entirely indestructible in battle.

So who gave Orion this ability?

He took another step forward. Rosalind's finger tightened on the trigger.

"Don't come any closer," she warned.

"Listen to me," Orion said. "I could have broken out of those ropes the moment I woke up." Despite her warning, he was still inching toward her. "I didn't. I have no interest in hurting you."

Rosalind let out a cold laugh. "But that's not the matter at hand, is it?" Voices from the past snuck up behind her, whispered furiously into her ears. "Just because you wouldn't hurt me doesn't mean you haven't hurt others. I mean nothing."

"I have no interest in hurting *anyone*. I myself can hardly comprehend this."

"Stop walking," Rosalind snapped. "I'll shoot. Don't think I won't."

"Rosalind. Please."

She almost dropped the gun.

"*What* did you just say?"

When Orion came within range, he did not yank the weapon away. He made the last step to close the distance between them, and then his chest was pressed up against the muzzle, the dark steel of the pistol blending in with the clothes he wore.

"I used your name," he said. "I know who you are."

Since when?

"And what about it?" Rosalind returned shakily. She couldn't get stuck on this. "It changes nothing when the matter is *you*—"

"I ask for your trust. Whatever I am guilty of, I will fix it. Whatever I have done, I will atone for it. But you have to trust me first. I need you on my side. We're supposed to be a team. I can't do this without you."

"You must think I am a fool," she said. Her words were hard, biting, unsympathetic. "I have no reason to trust you."

Orion closed his hand around the pistol. Rosalind geared herself to fight, her arms locking, but the attack did not come. Instead, Orion was gentle, making a push of her hand, moving her aim to the very center of his chest.

"Then shoot me."

Rosalind blinked. His fingers tightened over hers, urging her in encouragement.

"Take my life," he said, "and all that I have done will be answered for."

"Enough," Rosalind demanded. "At the very least, have the decency not to play games—"

"This is not a game to me," Orion cut in. "I would rather die by your hand than have you believe me a traitor. I would rather take a fast bullet than have us pitted on different sides of an agonizing battle."

A quick flash of light came in through the window then, indicating a car pulling up to the curb outside. Neither of them paid it any heed.

Rosalind's grip had turned unsteady. If Orion chose to disarm her now, he would be successful. He did not. He waited. He said, "So shoot me. Shoot me now if you do not believe me," and let her press the gun into his frantically beating heart.

"Why are you allowing this?" Rosalind asked. Even to her own ears, it sounded like begging, like, *please, enough.* "What trick are you leading up to?"

Orion breathed out. "There is no trick," he said. "I allow this because I love you."

Her mind came to a halt. Each cell in her body screamed for air. *We have done this once before,* they were saying. *We have heard this before.*

Promises once made, never kept. *Roza, we can run away. Roza, it will not matter what your family says. Roza, it is not betrayal if they never cared about you in the first place. No one cares about you as much as I do.*

But Dimitri Voronin had never cared. How was this any different? She already had a hard enough time telling nothing from something. All she had ever known was love wielded as a weapon, love wielded as a falsity to lower her guard.

"Do you think I won't shoot?" she snarled. "Who are you deluding here? We have never been real."

Orion shook his head. There was a devastating shuttering in his gaze, a darkening of his eyes when they looked upon her—almost, *almost*, fooling her . . .

"We were to me," he said quietly. "You accused me of being a philanderer, and suddenly I wanted to prove you wrong. You wanted daffodils at your wedding, and suddenly I wanted to be the one beside you at the altar watching you hold them. I wanted it to be real. I wanted it all to be real."

It was so tempting to believe him, to throw in her faith and taking a flying leap. Except she had believed once before, and look where that had gotten her. They always knew just the right things to say, and she was always played for a fool. She felt her finger twitch on the trigger. She could shoot. She knew she could.

"I backed you into a corner, Orion. I think you would make up any lie to escape."

"How good of an actor do you think I am?" Orion whispered in reply. "I've never told anyone before that I loved them. Not like that. Only you."

God. Rosalind *ought* to shoot. But there was so much swirling in her head, rooting her with doubt. Orion seemed to gather that his life was not in immediate danger, because he started to move slowly, setting his fingers on her arms, doing nothing more than holding her with the most delicate decorum. He was leaning in, even knowing that his life was in her hands, even knowing that she might choose to pull the trigger at any moment.

Time trickled between them like water caught against a windshield: stalling, interrupted, waiting for something to push it back into motion.

There were voices outside. A double beam of headlights flashing again.

"Janie! Orion! Are you ready to go?"

The function at Cathay Hotel. The arrests.

With a furious curse under her breath, Rosalind withdrew her pistol and took a step away from Orion.

"We will resume this at another time," she said. Maybe deep down she did believe him already. It would be foolish to allow him on the mission if she genuinely thought him a traitor. But her heart was a terrified, meager little thing, and it refused to take a decisive stand. "Don't think I'm letting you off the hook. Go get changed."

"These are for you," Phoebe said when Orion and Rosalind clambered into the back of Silas's car, extending her arm from the passenger seat.

"For the love of all things holy, Phoebe—why are you here?"

Orion reached forward. Phoebe passed him two thin wires, both looped in a circle.

"I'm your eyes outside the hotel," she answered, waving her own wire. "You'll be reporting to me using the newest technology that hasn't hit the market yet—Jiemin gave it to me."

"Jiemin gave it to *me*," Silas corrected. His eyes flicked up to the rearview mirror. "Orion, are you okay?"

"I'm fine," Orion answered quickly, too quickly. His face was visibly pale. Where Rosalind had the advantage of cosmetics that covered her shock and reddened her cheeks, there was nothing to hide Orion's distress. "How do we use this?"

"Put the end into your ear and twist the wire around your lobe. It should be thin enough not to draw any notice."

Rosalind did as she was told. "And you can hear us through this?"

Phoebe flinched, pulling her wire out of her ear. "Ouch, that was loud. Yes. Yes, I definitely can."

Still peering curiously into the rearview mirror, Silas pulled the car out of its idle parking. The vehicle jolted as it merged onto the road, running over a bump. Rosalind smoothed her hands along her skirt, trying not to breathe too heavily. She had changed into the deep green qipao she had bought for the occasion. Though she had loosened the collar and kept the topmost buttons undone until they reached their destination, her throat felt clamped, like the fabric was closing in tighter and tighter.

"Take a weapon," Orion instructed quietly from her side.

At the front seats, Silas and Phoebe were deep in debate about whether they were supposed to have made a right turn when the lights were red. Phoebe had her wire in her hand instead of her ear.

"To the hotel?"

"Yes." Orion drew something from his sleeve. Rosalind almost hit him when she saw what it was.

"The knife you stabbed me with? I'd rather not."

"Rosalind." She wished he would stop using her true name. It sounded too real on his tongue. Too intimate. "Take it. In case . . . in case I hurt you."

"And then what?" she replied. "I stab you in return?"

"Yes," Orion answered easily. "You stop me. If something comes over me. If I can't control myself."

He had made quick work of washing the blood off his hands when Silas was honking outside. While Rosalind pinned her hair up, she had been watching him. Watching the panic and horror, the scrubbing and frantic rinsing.

He's acting, she'd wanted to insist. It was more uncomplicated to assume that everyone was out to get her instead of them being victims too. It gave her reason to be cold to the world, and she had been cold for so long.

"You can stop yourself, I'm sure," Rosalind said evenly. She had left his pistol behind. There was nowhere to conceal it on her body. She would have to make do with her poisoned pins. "You did it earlier."

"I don't know how. It just happened." Orion turned toward his window. "Even so, you still got hurt."

Rosalind fell quiet. She looked out her own window, nothing to say. Their surroundings bled and blurred together, each flare of light merging with the next along their route. Casinos and cabarets were migrating their activity outside: tables and booths set up under the streetlamps, gamblers playing with their cards and striking match after match for an endless row of cigarettes. As the car slowed to give way for a line of rickshaws at the traffic lights, Rosalind leaned into the glass, wondering how well the card players could see the hand they had been dealt as they played in the night.

The light turned green. The table by the traffic broke into raucous laughter, the sound growing fainter and fainter as they drove away.

"There we are."

Silas pulled into a spot between two cars. The Huangpu River was shortly ahead with its docked ships and busy ramps. Without any unnecessary drivel, Rosalind got out of the car, turning her head away from the breeze.

"Keep an eye out for any cars that try to leave when the hour turns," she heard Orion tell Silas. Then his door closed too, and it was the two of them standing on the street, postures stiff and countenances awkward.

"Do I need to plead?"

Rosalind blinked. "What?"

Before she could stop him, Orion took matters into his own hands, dropping onto one knee so that he was level with her hip. The knife's sheath came with a band, one that he lifted to her leg and fastened so quickly that Rosalind scarcely got a protest out. It would be easily accessible through the slit of her qipao, but that meant it would be easily visible too, so Orion pushed it higher, snapping it in place at her thigh.

Orion's eyes flickered up, an unspoken *That wasn't so hard, was it?*

"There," he said. His hands were still clasped around the band, fitted like a second holster. "Does that not make you feel safe and sound?"

"Hardly," she said. She tapped the wire in her ear. "Phoebe, can you hear us?"

"Loud and clear." Her voice was not coming from inside the car. It sounded right into Rosalind's ear, and Orion's too, if his flinch was any indication.

Orion rose upright again, giving her his arm. "Off we go."

42

athay Hotel was a glimmering structure plopped right where Nanjing Road met the Bund, a double-building threat that stood tallest among the other uproar overlooking the Huangpu River, located right at the edge of the row. Its roof resembled a giantess's weapon: copper-sheathed and pointed right at the stars, making the hotel appear even taller than it already was.

Rosalind craned her head up. A gust of wind blew hard around them, heightened by their proximity to the water. With her hand at Orion's elbow, her fingers curled around the fabric of his suit jacket, seeking comfort in his proximity despite the tightrope they were both walking on. Familiar faces started to come into view, colleagues and higher-ups waving down from the hotel entrance.

"Phoebe, how are we doing on time?" Rosalind asked quietly.

"Reinforcements are set to arrive when the hour strikes ten," Phoebe reported into her ear. Her voice was sugary even with the static disruptions. "It is a quarter to ten right now."

Rosalind's grip tightened. A few buildings over, the clock tower on the Custom House stood silent and ominous. It tolled every hour—a grand, sonorous sound that blanketed the Bund—which meant it would be tolling when the Nationalists rushed in, a final warning squirreling into every listening ear within the vicinity. She hadn't decided what she was going to do when the arrests started happening. Give Orion up? Protect him?

Celia's voice rang in her head, again and again. *The warehouse is run by Nationalist soldiers.*

One task at a time, Rosalind decided.

She tugged Orion forward.

They entered Cathay Hotel through the East Entrance Hall. The glamour reverberated from the building's exterior, but it was even more potent upon stepping through the doors: lush carpeting under their feet that tried to swallow them whole; tall, arched ceilings that bowed with soaring elevation; a heavy chandelier dangling between two marble staircases, one on the left and one on the right to ascend into the main banquet room. There were sofas lining the golden walls, occupied by laughing women and drunk men, all of whom did not look familiar to Rosalind. She could only assume other patrons were out and about as well. The Sassoon House, which the Cathay Hotel was situated within, always had something going on.

"This way, darling," Orion prompted. He nudged her toward the left as soon as they finished climbing the stairs, but he hardly sounded certain either. The atrium glowed tall and luxurious around and above; though Rosalind had attended events and dinners at the Cathay Hotel before, it seemed like some other world tonight with this many people present and mingling.

When they walked into the main banquet lounge, it was clear that they had found the beating heart of the function. Waiters hovered by either side of the two doors, balancing champagne on their silver trays, bowing each time someone lifted off a flute. Rosalind took one, then gave a cautionary sniff. It didn't give any indication of being poisoned, but who could say?

"There's Ambassador Deoka," Rosalind said quietly. She leaned her chin onto Orion's shoulder under the guise of affection—it afforded him a better view of the stage when he turned around and put his arms around her.

She wouldn't lean into the touch. She wouldn't relax under it. She wouldn't.

Deoka stood beside a floor vase, one that was almost as tall as he was and blooming with an array of flowers that extended in every direction. He was speaking with a group of men in suits, making introductions and shaking hands.

"Twelve others in the room," Orion reported to Phoebe.

"Another car has arrived outside," Phoebe returned through the line. "Your list has a total of sixteen."

Rosalind surveyed the attendees around them. "It is thirteen in the room," she corrected. "You missed Hasumi Misuzu in the corner."

The Kuomintang would have the profiles of every person on the list that Orion and Rosalind had handed in. So long as they were present tonight, it would not be hard for the soldiers to match their faces to their pictures and make the necessary arrests.

"I can sweep through the remainder of this level if you want to do the smaller floors above," Orion said. There were more attendees scattered past the other entranceway into the lounge, to the side of the stage where a jazz band was starting its set. The musicians counted down, and then the opening notes from a saxophone swirled through the room, drawing couples to dance on the cleared floor.

"Stay right here." Rosalind unwound her arm. "I'll do both sweeps."

"Is everything all right?" Phoebe asked through the wire.

"Perfectly fine," Rosalind replied easily. "We just need eyes on Deoka at all times. Right, Orion?"

He nodded stiffly. If he stayed surrounded by people, chances were that he wouldn't do anything outrageous—whether consciously or unconsciously. Giving him a tense look, Rosalind turned to exit the banquet lounge. She followed the gilded hallways out, passing the mirrored decoration pieces. Once or twice she thought she heard whispering behind her, but when she turned around, there was no one there, only sound carrying strangely from the high ceilings.

There was an elevator to the side of the building, but Rosalind took the old-fashioned stairs, using the handrails to heave herself up the steep climb. The rooms she poked her head into were largely empty: whole suites that were themed around a particular country, filled with objects made to resemble elsewhere. They were open tonight for attendees to wander in and out of, but it seemed the majority of the party remained downstairs. Rosalind sighted none of the faces she was looking for. As she was turning out of the Indian Suite, she bumped into someone, apologizing before she registered their face.

"Alis—" Rosalind cut herself off before she could finish the exclamation, tearing her wire out. She clamped her hand over the ends, hoping that would muffle her voice from Phoebe.

"What are you doing here?"

"Keeping an eye on your task, what else?" Alisa retorted. She was dressed in the uniform of a waitress, a tray balanced on her hand. "What's going on? Why is Orion here?"

Rosalind grimaced, waving for Alisa to follow her along the hallway so they could check the rest of the rooms.

"He claims"—she peered into the French Suite, sighting only one businessman who was probably a hotel guest—"that he has no memory of what he has done."

"Oh. I suppose that makes sense."

"What?" Rosalind was so surprised that she released her wire for a short moment before holding down the ends again. They continued walking. "How did you accept that so easily?"

"Because he doesn't have motive," Alisa replied, opening the last door along the hallway before Rosalind could. "Orion Hong has no power if the Japanese come in. He won't rise in rank; nor does he have men underneath him that he can turn into a battalion if he's cooperating as hanjian. Unless he's hiding some other life desire that you don't know about?"

"He could be making the conscious decision to work for someone," Rosalind countered. They both looked inside the last room. Empty.

"Then why investigate himself?"

"To mislead us."

"Then why not mislead you from the very beginning? Why not pin the accusations on another company? Why not move your investigation away from the chemicals?"

Just as Rosalind was going to object against Alisa for thinking too well of him, someone bellowed, "Mrs. Mu!" from behind. Alisa ducked her head immediately, pretending to be following after Rosalind, making herself invisible to Yōko as she bounded over to Rosalind's side.

"There's supposed to be a speech at ten," Yōko said. "You are heading down now?"

"Yes," Rosalind replied. "After you."

They descended the stairs at the end of the hallway, Alisa following a few paces behind. Yōko's step halted when they returned around the main atrium, pausing to check her lipstick on the smooth gold surface of the wall.

Rosalind was going to excuse herself, finding no need to stick around Yōko for long given that she was not on their lists, when the girl said, "You know, I had a feeling you didn't like me. But I think that of a lot of people. I know the entire world cannot possibly hate me, right?"

Rosalind jolted with surprise. The dagger at her thigh suddenly felt heavy. Like it had doubled in weight, dragging down on its sheath and preparing to detach from her leg and clutter to the floor.

"Where did you get an idea like that?" she asked.

Yōko shrugged, her bottom lip sticking out. The movement

made her look young, far too young to be working for a place like Seagreen.

The girl didn't know the difference between personal hatred and the burning resentment that Rosalind had for the empire that had sent Yōko here. Even if she wasn't to blame, she would feel its heat all the same.

"I like you perfectly fine," Rosalind said simply.

Yōko beamed, switching out of her dark mood in a blink. When they returned to the lounge, she waved her goodbye and went off to join Tarō in the corner. From behind, Alisa walked closer again and said, "You were far nicer than I would have been."

"Why blind someone who is in the dark?" Rosalind said quietly. It reminded her of herself: the naïveté, the worry that was wholly internal. She thought it was her against the world once too. That being disliked meant it was something she had done rather than the circumstances splitting people into their positions on the city's stage.

"On the chance that they might take to the light instead," Alisa retorted. She paused, glancing down to see Rosalind still pinching her wire. "There's one more thing: your handler is missing."

Rosalind whirled around fast. *"Missing?"*

"He's not in his hospital room. Whether he was taken or left of his own free will remains to be determined. The man we saved in the alley is also gone. Vanished into thin air."

Dao Feng was missing. The Nationalists were shortly arriving at the hotel. Rosalind could barely hear her own thoughts past the blood rushing frantically in her ears. She shook her head, trying to clear the din.

"I'll touch base on this after the arrests. Give me a moment." Rosalind put the wire back into her ear.

"—that's everyone in the building. Janie, for heaven's sake, can you hear me yet?"

"I hear you," Rosalind said. She spotted Orion standing by the table where she had left him. "What did I miss?"

"The point of having fancy technology is to use it! Why did you take me out? Ugh, whatever. Sixteen of sixteen are present. Keep your head down until reinforcements arrive."

"Understood."

Rosalind nodded to Alisa in farewell, then returned to Orion's side. He pulled a pocket watch from his jacket as she approached, showing her the time. Five minutes until ten. From the stage, the jazz band switched sets, putting a woman in front of the microphone. The speakers screeched with feedback for a quick second, then cleared as the woman started to croon an American song. They used to sing it at the Scarlet burlesque club. Rosalind had almost built a routine to the jazzy tune before deciding the song was too long, more fitting for swaying and slower movements.

She watched the guests dancing near the stage. Watched them twirl under their partners' arms and rest their heads down, eyes closed in peace.

"Dance with me?" Orion extended his hand.

Rosalind hesitated. "That's not a good—"

"Dance, Janie!" Phoebe's voice piped into her ear. "Don't act suspicious."

"I'm not acting suspicious," Rosalind hissed, but she took Orion's hand, nonetheless. Their fingers met with a shock.

The music fell quiet for a moment. Orion drew her close, arms around her waist. Rosalind held herself stiffly, keeping her face turned away.

"If you keep doing that," he breathed, "people are going to take notice."

"I'm not doing anything," Rosalind said tightly.

"Exactly."

She shot him a dirty look. He raised his arm and made her do a twirl.

"Answer this very seriously," Rosalind said when she was facing him again, her hands landing on his chest. "Say I believe you. Say everything you told me is true. Who forced you into this? Who is giving you instructions and wiping your memory?"

"What is she talking about?" she heard Phoebe mutter over the wire. The hour was fast approaching. There was no time to fret about Phoebe knowing the situation.

"I must admit that I haven't really been racking my brain yet," Orion answered. "First I had to reel over acknowledging the matter and then try to walk through every empty blank I have. . . ."

"Don't stall, Orion." Rosalind touched his cheek. She had meant for it to be threatening, to urge him to think, but she surprised herself when her hand was gentle, cupping against his face with the tenderness of a lover in agony. "Who could it be?"

He breathed out unhappily. "It has to be someone on our own side. Otherwise, I don't see any opportunity. Otherwise, I don't understand why the summoning call comes from headquarters."

Rosalind glanced up at the stage. The microphone screeched once with feedback as the singer adjusted the stand, finishing her song and stepping aside for one of the foreign investors at Seagreen. He waved for the musicians to quiet down on their instruments, a bright grin on his face when he greeted the banquet lounge.

"Who do we trust now?" Rosalind whispered.

"Janie Mead, *what* are you talking about?" her earpiece said.

The investor was summoning Deoka up to the stage when a bell rang through the room. Deoka was raising his glass to a round of applause when the clock tower atop the Custom House boomed across the Bund, at last signaling the turning of the hour.

The Nationalists did not delay a single second. Rosalind heard the rumble of footsteps first. Then a shout of alarm—someone pushed over in the atrium outside—before the squeak of shoes echoed down the corridors and soldiers were rushing in, fanning into the lounge and lining the walls, rifles pointed to every person in the room.

"Attention, all." It was Jiemin, leading the operation. He had changed into uniform, the army-green color stark against his pale skin, well tailored to his every movement as he raised a megaphone to his mouth. "No one is to leave this room until we have cleared it of suspects under arrest for inciting terror through the city."

The room shrank back in fear. Most of them had nothing to be concerned about. Those who already knew themselves guilty tried to make for the exits, but there were soldiers waiting, pushing them back in as soon as they tried. Ambassador Deoka stood very still. He looked like an animal caught in bright lights, trying not to move and hoping that it meant he would not be spotted.

Another soldier, standing beside Jiemin, was scanning the room, a clipboard in his hands instead of a weapon. When his eyes stopped on Rosalind and Orion, he gave them both a nod, indicating that he had recognized them as the agents of this mission. He started to move through the room, flipping a page on his clipboard, comparing attendees against printed photographs of each person that they were after. When he got to Haidi, he signaled for two of the soldiers to shake out her bag.

Three green vials rolled out. Rosalind watched the scene with her breath held.

"Those aren't dangerous," Haidi shrieked. "They're for me. I'll die without them!"

Rosalind frowned. Orion's hand tightened in hers. She'd *die*?

"Oh, I know." Jiemin picked up one of the vials. From across the room, Rosalind's concern was building steadily. What did he mean, he knew? "Ah Ming, grab the additional accused, would you?"

At his command, one of the soldiers strode for a far table, then hauled a waitress by her upper arm. She cried out indignantly, her hat falling and landing on the floor with a soft thud. *Alisa.* Why were they grabbing Alisa?

"Alisa Montagova," Jiemin said. Now that a hush had settled over the banquet lounge, his voice carried a harsh echo. "You're under arrest as an enemy of the state, in protection of the nation's welfare."

Whispers thrummed from corner to corner, the other witnesses barely able to keep up with the sequence of events. "Montagov" was muttered from mouth to mouth; the city had not heard that name in some time.

Rosalind pushed forward, goose bumps prickling at her arms. "Jiemin," she said. "What are you doing? She has nothing to do with the mission."

"I'm aware," Jiemin replied. He had always had a calm and slow disposition, but now it presented in a frightening manner, each instruction coming out of his mouth utterly void of emotion. "But it is useful to conduct business at once, is it not? You've got perfect timing too."

Rosalind blinked. "What?"

Jiemin signaled two soldiers beside him to proceed forward. He waved one toward her, then one toward Orion.

"Hong Liwen and Lang Shalin," he said. "The two of you are under arrest for murder, conspiracy, and national treason. Who did you think you were fooling?"

43

"Hong Liwen and Lang Shalin," the wire fed over. "The two of you are under arrest for murder, conspiracy, and national treason."

Then there was nothing.

"Hello?" Phoebe demanded. She thudded the wire, but that didn't do anything except hurt her own ear. "Orion? Janie? Can you hear me?"

"What happened?" Silas demanded.

Phoebe ripped her wire out, releasing a feral scream. She had observed that something was strange in the air between Orion and Janie, of course. After giving her brother that magazine, she only assumed it was because he'd found out his wife's true identity. What other sort of *murder* were they getting up to in their spare time? And why hadn't she *known*?

"Phoebe!" Silas reached over, taking the wire before she could tear it to pieces. "What *happened*?"

"They've gone dark." Phoebe's voice trembled in utter disbelief. "Jiemin just arrested them for murder and conspiracy."

Silas stared at her. "Did you mishear?"

"How do you mishear *murder and conspiracy*?"

The roads ahead were all blocked by military vehicles, caging in the perimeter of Cathay Hotel and ensuring that not a single occupant of the building could slip out unnoticed. Soldiers lined the

– 457 –

street, standing like sentry guards under the moon-tinged clouds. Silas's car happened to be parked just outside the frontline.

"Janie Mead isn't her real name." Phoebe pressed as close to the windshield as she could, scanning the scene. She stared unblinking until her eyes started to blur, until the night melded together as one big kaleidoscopic blot. "Her real name is Rosalind Lang."

Silas put the wire into his own ear. He tapped a few times, as if it would only take some more prodding before the sound started working again. There was no use. The soldiers must have confiscated the two corresponding wires.

"That's impossible." Silas was trying to sound matter-of-fact, but he was reeling too, trying to catch up on a race when a whole section of the trail had been cut out from underneath their feet. "The Scarlet Gang's Rosalind Lang? She would be an adult. Or rather, she is said to be *dead*."

Phoebe closed her burning eyes, knocking her knuckles to her forehead. *Think, think,* she told herself.

"How much of her brief to you was complete falsity?" she asked soberly. "The killings across Shanghai as a chemical experiment. Haidi being the one responsible for the deaths."

Silas hesitated. "There must be a mistake—"

"There's no mistake!" Phoebe exclaimed. "Both of them have been taken in as part of the scheme! They are no longer agents— they're suspects!"

Silas fell silent. He took his glasses off, rubbing the bridge of his nose.

"Impossible," he muttered again. "Janie gave us the conclusion herself. What reason is there to lie?"

The last few minutes of what she had heard through the wire played back in Phoebe's mind. What was it that Janie—that *Rosalind*— had been saying to Orion? Phoebe thought she had been mistaken, the sound coming weakly while it picked up Rosalind's whispers.

Say I believe you. Say everything you told me is true. Who forced you into this? Who is giving you instructions and wiping your memory?

"She's protecting him," Phoebe said aloud.

"Janie is protecting Orion?"

Phoebe remembered a cold winter day several years ago. The grounds outside husked and dry, the house inside heated by the roaring fireplace. She had been tucked into the couch, flipping through her books, when Orion came downstairs, looking dazed. It was some time after his first month working for the Kuomintang, when he was momentarily housebound because of his headaches. He had taken a fall, or so he had explained, after he hobbled into the house with an ice pack to his head.

But there was so much angry bruising around his neck too. And each time Phoebe asked him to recount how the fall happened, lurking around him to prod at the purple by his veins, he pinched his expression in concentration and gave the same details, saying he slipped onto his temple.

"I'll be back in a few days," he had said on the last step of the stairs. "There's some work to tend to."

"Can I come?" Phoebe asked immediately. "I want to come."

"You're not needed for this, Feiyi." Orion didn't give his usual wave. When he left, she sighted another bruise on his neck, and all she could think was: *How are you so insistent that you took a fall? You look like you were beaten up. Repeatedly.*

In the car, Phoebe put her thumb to her mouth, biting down hard on her nail. What was the question that Rosalind had asked him inside? *Who is wiping your memory?*

"Orion is the one being charged for murder," Phoebe concluded surely. She leaned back into her seat, placing her hands in her lap and her feet flat on the floor. "Let's go. We have to find where they're being taken. We have to break them out."

44

Rosalind paced the cell, stomping on the stone flooring as if she might be able to put her foot clean through. She could hear grumbling from the other cells too, where the rest of Seagreen's guilty employees had been placed.

Ambassador Deoka was in the cell across, looking curiously at Rosalind through the bars.

"I always knew there was something a little off about you."

"Shut up," Rosalind snapped immediately.

"When I sent Miss Zheng to investigate that picture from 1926, I had suspected that you were lying only about your age. Who could have thought it was a whole other identity? Lang Shalin, former Scarlet, reduced to a mere office worker. Aren't you angry at your government for that?"

Rosalind thudded the bars with her fist. It rang loudly, clanging with vibrations that shook the whole cell. Quickly, Orion tugged at her elbow, moving her back. Whether for better or for worse, the soldiers had decided to put her and Orion in the same cell, figuring there would be no trouble between them.

"Don't rise to the bait," Orion whispered.

"How can I not?" Rosalind returned. She struggled against his hold, facing Deoka again. "Did you think you were being sly, sending a tail after us on that tram? Stealing that file back?"

Deoka only looked at her evenly. If he had been given a

typewriter in his cell, he would probably have used this spare time to do some work. "I have no clue what you're talking about. Again, you may wish to look at your own government. Some spy you are."

Before Rosalind could scream through the bars, Orion lifted her off her feet, forcibly transplanting her to the corner of the cell. Rosalind let herself be moved, too annoyed to fight. There was a bed pallet that waited there, and she plunked herself down, her spine stiff and alert.

Deoka was right, in a way. There were so many lies at every corner that Rosalind had no faith in her own government.

"Dao Feng is missing."

She dropped the statement without any prelude. Orion needed several long seconds to register her words and several more seconds to ensure he had heard correctly. Slowly, he lowered himself onto the pallet too, observing her reaction as he sat next to her. He seemed prepared to bolt up at any moment if she sounded any protest. She did not, so he remained.

"Missing . . . from his hospital bed?"

"If he ever needed a hospital bed to begin with."

Orion drew his knees up, propping his arms upon them. "Are you saying . . . ?"

"I don't know what I'm saying," Rosalind kicked her heel. "I am trying my greatest to look at it from above. I am trying to imagine what I would say if this were something happening to someone else and I had no stake of my own in it."

Her eyes were downcast, staring at her hands in her lap. When Orion set his knees straight, shifting to get comfortable, he mimicked her position exactly, the two of them on the pallet, legs drawn out in front of them. Slowly, Rosalind nudged her hand an inch over, then another. The side of her left hand touched the side of Orion's right. When he hooked his pinkie finger around hers, she returned the gesture, keeping their hands together.

"Dao Feng is your handler," she said quietly. "There are no restrictions when it comes to giving you missions away from prying eyes and erasing your memory afterward. His hit was unlike any of the others. He was the one who trained me on poisons. He would know more than anyone in the city about how to hurt himself for the show and survive it unscathed."

"But we never would have suspected him of anything," Orion said. "Why hurt himself to begin with?"

That was the big question. Rosalind had no hypothesis. Orion, too, was simmering in thought, his brows knitted together. In the midst of it, he gave their joined fingers a tug, turning Rosalind's hand over and slipping his palm in properly.

"I must ask," Orion began hesitantly. "Does this mean you believe me?"

At the far side of the holding cells, there was someone yelling noisily, demanding something of the guards. The Nationalists had placed only two uniformed men on guard inside—their numbers were needed elsewhere, searching Burkill Road and getting to Warehouse 34 to put a stop to whatever was being made.

"Stranger things have happened," Rosalind replied. "I can heal a knife wound in seconds. Someone is brainwashing you. It's the world we live in."

Orion sighed. His hand tightened on hers. "Of course you would sound so pragmatic about it down to the eleventh hour. Lady Fortune, how did you come to be?"

"Just Fortune," Rosalind corrected. She leaned her head onto the wall, its cold press of stone cooling her body. "Do you know what year I was born?"

"Yes, 1907," Orion answered in a flash. Slightly embarrassed a second later, he added, "I saw it in your obituary."

Rosalind blew a breath up at her loose hair. She had so many obituaries across the city. Would whispers start to move after Jiemin made his declaration tonight? Would Shanghai once again know that she lived among its crowds?

"And yet I remain nineteen years old," she said. "It is not my own refusal to grow up: my body is halted, my mind locked in along with it. I did so many terrible things, Orion. I trusted the wrong person. The city blew up, my family fractured, and death came to take me in retribution." She dared a glimpse at him. He was listening raptly. "But my sister saved me. She knew someone who could help while I was feverish and ill, and he plunged something into my arm that brought me back to life. Now I cannot age. I can heal at monstrous speed."

Sometimes Rosalind thought she could still feel the invasive material that had rushed into her veins four years ago. A fiery sensation—running alongside her blood cells as her supplementary life force.

"It was like a burning, wasn't it?" Orion asked, as if he had read her thoughts. "Like it was ravaging a course to consume everything it touched, remaking your body in its path."

Rosalind blinked. She hadn't expected him to describe the feeling so aptly. "Yes. Exactly."

"Sometimes I dream about that sensation." Orion brushed his thumb against the soft pad of her wrist. "I think it was like that for me too."

But he couldn't remember. He could break through thick rope as easily as if it were string, he could probably punch a hole right through stone if he tried hard enough, but he could not say how he had come to be that way. At least Rosalind had been given her strange abilities in an effort to save her life. It seemed that Orion had been changed for someone else to use him.

Anger roiled in her stomach. Whoever had done this to him— whoever was creating these damned experiments—Rosalind would make them answer for it. For all the deaths, and then this one, terrible crime.

Orion's lips suddenly quirked into a smile. The sight was bizarre while Rosalind was thinking such dark thoughts.

"What?" she asked.

"Nothing," he answered. A moment passed. "So, you're a former showgirl, huh?"

Rosalind rolled her eyes. Of course. Trust him to start making jokes while they were locked in a cell.

"No, I will not be dancing for you."

His smile grew stronger. "You already have, remember?"

"That didn't count. I was in disguise."

"If you say so." He brushed his thumb over her wrist again. He seemed to like doing that. "I know a lot about showgirls."

"Oh, trust me," Rosalind said. "I *know*."

The vague noisiness at the far side of the cells finally faded. The quiet did not last three seconds before there was a startlingly loud clatter. At once, Rosalind scrambled to attention, jumping to her feet. Orion did the same, waiting to see what the sound was. They watched the soldier hovering near the door clutch his rifle warily, making a move to investigate. As soon as he had wandered out of their view, there was a shout and then a heavy thump.

Rosalind and Orion exchanged a glance.

"What was that?" Rosalind hissed.

"It was me. Don't worry."

The voice was familiar. Really, neither of them should have been surprised when it was Alisa who popped in front of their cell, prancing around like she owned the place.

"What?" Orion demanded. "How did you get out?"

"What kind of a question is that?" Alisa returned. She had a whole set of keys in her hands, sifting through them while she tried to find the right one to free Rosalind and Orion. From the other cell, Deoka was watching with a mix of horror and fascination. "I can get out of anywhere. I'm Alisa Nikolaevna Montagova."

Rosalind put her hands on her hips. Alisa stuck the key in and turned.

"All right," Alisa admitted. "I annoyed the soldier enough to lunge at me through the bars, and then I stole his keys. If it works, it works." She swung the cell door open. "Come on. Before the rest of Seagreen tries freeing themselves too."

Rosalind had been expecting a whole fight outside. Instead, there was only a handful of Nationalist soldiers standing guard in the station itself, and they were all dead.

"Was this your work?" she asked, astonished, turning over one of the men and finding a single bullet hole in his neck. The blood around him had not seeped far. Its puddle was restricted to a generous red smear.

"When would I have had the time?" Alisa demanded. "Of course not. My plan was for Orion to fight off everyone in the station."

Orion frowned, a silent protest at being used for strong-arming their way out. But there was not a soul to fight off. It looked like a battle had already passed through, and yet no one had barged into the holding cells. Why do any of this? *Who* had done this?

A door to the side slammed. The three of them reared around. Rosalind spotted her confiscated knife lying on the desk and scooped it up, immediately drawing it from its sheath.

But it wasn't Nationalist reinforcements entering the station: it was Phoebe.

She stopped short. "What . . . happened here?"

"What are *you* doing here?" Orion asked. He rushed over, then pulled her in for a hug. "You are single-handedly responsible for causing me stress hives."

Phoebe pulled a face, then wriggled out of his grasp. "I came to help you. Silas plugged into every network he could to get a report on what is unfolding with the mission. They raided Burkill Road, but no one is going to Warehouse 34. The motion got blocked somewhere along the chain of command."

It was looking more and more undeniable. That someone on the inside, someone with enough sway on the covert branch's affairs, was heavily in collaboration with the scheme.

"How were you going to help?" Orion exclaimed. "By marching into a station alone?"

"Silas was going to pull the lights!" Phoebe insisted. She gestured at Alisa. "We did it once before, didn't we?"

"That was a municipal station! This could have been so dangerous if—"

Orion looked around. He trailed off, still caught on the question of what exactly had happened here. It looked like the work of an assassin. But there were only so many assassins in this city, contrary to popular belief.

"Warehouse 34," Rosalind said aloud. "Orion, we have to go."

If those chemical experiments had finally reached success in the man who survived, then they were ready to be distributed. A concoction that turned someone as strong as Orion and as unkillable as Rosalind. It needed to be stopped. It couldn't be allowed to spread.

Orion nodded. "Hurry."

Outside, parked in a nook near the station, Silas was fiddling with the electric box, looking outrageously surprised to find them coming toward him.

"I haven't even pulled the—"

"I need you to take Phoebe away from here," Orion ordered.

"What!" Phoebe screeched. "I got you out!"

Alisa pulled a face but did not contribute to the argument. She didn't need to.

"Alisa Montagova got us out of there. Because she is an agent. Because we are all trained. You're putting yourself in danger, Phoebe."

"But . . ." Phoebe thinned her lips, searching—desperately searching—for an argument.

"Please," Orion begged. "You heard everything through the wire. You heard what I got hauled in for. My memory is being erased; I'm being controlled. If I cannot stop myself when it happens again, then I want you nowhere near me. I've already hurt someone I love. I'm not going to risk hurting you, too."

Rosalind felt the pang in her stomach like a physical sensation. Like her earlier wound was opening itself again, tearing from the inside out. Phoebe, meanwhile, took a shaky step back. She didn't look happy. But how was she supposed to argue with something like that?

Silas passed Orion the car keys. "I'm going to contact Jiemin again," he said. "Get a better explanation for what's going on with our forces and try to convince him to send people out to that warehouse. How did he even find out about you?"

"Hell if I know," Orion muttered, his expression tortured. "Up until this point, *I* wouldn't have known if it weren't for . . ."

He trailed off, looking at Rosalind. He wasn't trying to hide his anguish. He wanted her to know how sorry he was to have hurt her. That he knew he might hurt her again and wished she would sit out like Phoebe instead of risking it.

Rosalind opened the car door, sliding into the passenger seat. It wasn't realistic to keep her away. This was their mission. High Tide was their combined unit, unable to be separated. One without the other was unthinkable.

"Alisa," she called. "Are you coming too?"

Alisa slid into the back seat. "Of course. Silly question."

45

Orion followed the dark roads carefully, his eyes in constant movement to ensure they were not taking a wrong turn. He didn't have faith in himself anymore. Each decision came plagued with doubt, and then a sudden anxiety that the thought was not coming from his own mind.

He didn't realize his hands were shaking on the wheel until Rosalind touched his elbow, offering a steadying presence. The map books were open on her lap. It was easy to identify the bit of land where Warehouse 34 was supposed to be. Now it was only a matter of getting there.

"Take the turn ahead."

The night was eerily quiet outside the city borders. Orion's gaze caught on a house in the distance, then again when they passed, realizing it was not a house at all but an abandoned farm mill.

"We need to decide what our approach is going to be," Rosalind said when the trees around the roads started to grow denser. "If we find Dao Feng there . . ."

She trailed off. Could they treat him as a traitor? Could they forget everything about him and focus on taking him down, even if it meant taking his life?

"What *do* you expect to find there?" Alisa piped up from the back.

"Hard to say," Rosalind replied. "But someone stopped our forces for a reason. The weapon is finished. The last test subject survived. Whatever the cost, we cannot let it continue."

Orion tightened his grip on the steering wheel. He could feel his fear, putting ice in his breath and rushing into the car with his every exhale. What was about to befall the city? If they could incite this much damage with him alone, then what were the consequences of an army, a battalion, a whole military force?

Alisa poked forward suddenly, nudging her head between the two front seats.

"There's a military vehicle up ahead."

Orion slowed on the accelerator, holding his breath while they passed by. But the other vehicle was unoccupied. Unmarked.

"Someone is here," Rosalind guessed. "Or multiple someones."

Orion didn't want to keep driving forward. He wanted to turn the wheel and take them off-course, away from the warehouse. Unfortunately, that was not an option.

The warehouse appeared in view. Orion pulled the car to a stop before they could get too near, his heart thudding in his rib cage. The scene looked familiar to him in a hazy way, like getting déjà vu about something he was certain had never happened. The moment he tried to dig into his memory, intent on uncovering whether he had been here before, there was a physically painful sensation blocking his path.

There was another vehicle parked in front of the warehouse.

"Let me check first," Alisa said, already opening her door. "It could be my side."

"What?" Rosalind returned quickly, throwing her own door open to stop Alisa. "Why would it be?"

"My superiors had photographic evidence of the killings in action, remember? I'm willing to bet that they've known about this for a while—all of it, including what its ultimate aim was." Alisa paused. Her eyes went to Orion. "After their failed kidnapping attempt, they must have decided it would be more beneficial to wait until the experiments actually succeeded, then hurry to the source to steal the weapon."

Perhaps he was predisposed to be bitter toward the other side because of his brother's defection, but Orion felt a deep, dark resentment for those superiors. They had known, and they hadn't stopped him. They had known and had chosen to *monitor him* for their own gain instead of stopping him. *God.* Had *Oliver* known?

"What's wrong with them?" he muttered.

"It's warfare," Alisa said, albeit reluctantly. "Of course they want this weapon. Of course they would play dirty to secure it for the greater good."

It would change the course of the war. Orion flexed his hands in his lap. Beside him, Rosalind closed the map books with a thud. They could imagine it easily. Soldiers who could throw a man across the room, who wouldn't sleep nor age nor suffer from flesh wounds. Victory would be imminent.

"Stay here until I survey the surroundings," Alisa instructed. She closed her door. "Just in case. I'll yell if it turns out to be people we need to fight instead."

She walked off before either Orion or Rosalind could voice their agreement. It wasn't as if she had been asking for permission anyway. The car fell silent. Rosalind tossed the maps to the floor.

"It makes sense," she said quietly. "On all sides. Why they want this weapon so badly. Power is more important than anything else. You can't fight for your values without power first."

Orion leaned back in his seat, dragging his fingers through his hair. Everyone was so desperate for power—so why had they given it to him first? He didn't want it. These bastards should have taken it themselves. Done their *own* dirty work.

"I want nothing to do with any of this," he decided. "I want a cure."

"Maybe we can find one." Rosalind was staring ahead absently. "Maybe we don't have to be like this forever, wielded around as national tools. Maybe we can just be people."

Right as Orion was about to ask if she truly believed in such a sentiment, her eyes slid to him, and he didn't need to ask anymore. In that one motion, she switched from vacant to purposeful, calling forth a bone-deep resolve as easily as some people smiled. Orion had never met anyone quite like her.

"Tell me something," he said, though he had a feeling he knew already. "Why do you let yourself be a tool now? Why not walk away?"

Rosalind pursed her lips. His gaze followed the movement down. She didn't notice.

"Because I haven't done enough yet. I was given a power to be used. So I'll use it until there's no need for it anymore."

"Then you won't rest until the city is at peace and healed?" He turned in his seat properly, bringing his knee up so he could face her. "Shanghai will never heal, beloved. It is broken, as is every place in some way."

"I have every night unsleeping," Rosalind countered. "Spend long enough gluing together a shattered glass vase, and you will have a vase again."

Orion couldn't stop looking at her. Those determined eyes and the set of her brow. Artists would scramble to paint a face like that onto their war posters. Render her expression in vivid enough lines, and the sight alone could lead the world into battle.

"But Shanghai is not a glass vase," he said gently. "It is a city."

Rosalind sighed, searching the night outside. There had been no signal from Alisa. For the next minute, they settled into a tentative silence, not because there was nothing else to say but because too much had been said and there needed a moment of pause. Then:

"If you want the truth, I didn't used to be like this." Rosalind leaned onto the dashboard, hands tucked under her chin and elbows splayed to either side. Her voice quavered a little. "I didn't care enough, not for my family, not for the city, not for the world. Then I let someone I loved wreck it all, and it was the worst thing I'd ever done." She paused. When she tilted her head to the side, the blue-white moonlight lit up the high planes of her cheeks, making her look like she was glowing from within. "Isn't it strange how we say sorry in Chinese? In every other language it's some version of "pardon" or distress. But 'duì bù qǐ . . .' We're saying we don't match up. Sorry I didn't do what was expected. Sorry I let you down. Sorry you expected me to save you from harm, and I didn't—I didn't."

"*Rosalind*," Orion said. He had to admit—ever since he'd learned her real name, he'd been obsessed with the sound of it on his tongue. It suited her far better than Janie Mead did. "You don't mean to say that you're trying to save the whole city from harm. You'll spend your whole life trying, and you'll still fail. There is a reason why duì bù qǐ is duì bù qǐ. We're only human. We will never match up to what everything could be."

Rosalind gave him a little smile, almost looking confused. "With enough time—"

"No," he insisted. "You cannot save the world. You can try to save one thing if you must, but it is enough if that one thing is yourself."

Rosalind cast a glance out the windshield again. Still nothing from Alisa.

"You keep looking at your hands, do you know that?"

Oh? He hadn't expected the sudden turn in the conversation.

"In the apartment, in the holding cells, and on our way here," she continued. "Every few minutes, you look at them, and this panic crosses your face. That's how I knew to believe you. Another lover of mine never felt any shame when he hurt me. But all I feel coming from you is wave after wave of it."

Orion blinked. She had said "another lover of mine." Did that mean Orion was one too? He wanted that—he wanted it so deeply.

And yet he had wrought a sort of damage that he had not even fully comprehended. He didn't know *what* he had done. How could he know what to repent for?

"I'm . . . sorry," he said instinctively.

Rosalind sighed in defeat. He would have apologized again for inciting the frustration, but then she reached over, setting a hand on his cheek.

"Your life is mine as mine is yours." It was an echo of her statement from days earlier, but now it was ringing with an entirely different caliber. "If I promise to save myself, can you promise to forgive yourself? Can we make an exchange?"

I can't, he thought, only the words halted at his throat. She was looking at him with such earnestness that he could not bear to strike her down.

"I'll try," he answered instead. He would promise to wander the ends of the earth and find where the sky began if it meant she would keep her hand there, if it meant he could drown out the rest of his frantic fears by focusing on the sound of her voice. He had gone beyond getting attached to her. She was his guiding saint, the Polaris of his heart.

"Good," Rosalind said. Then she leaned in and kissed him once, like she was taking it for a vow, like she was delivering her own oath, and Orion could have gotten lost in it.

Despite the cars parked in the vicinity, the perimeter of Warehouse 34 was quiet, absent of activity. Alisa's boots crunched down on the drying leaves while she made a small circle of the grounds. Her own footfalls were the only human sounds she caught. When she came around to the front of the warehouse, she didn't call for Rosalind and Orion first—she nudged the door open slowly, waiting for a reaction.

But there was no movement. There was only darkness.

Alisa stepped into the warehouse, making an effort to be as quiet as possible. She didn't search for the lights; she navigated by the glow of the moon, letting her eyes adjust while the dark shapes started coming into clarity. There were the expected boxes and crates, the tables populated with equipment and liquid spills. Had they simply arrived at Warehouse 34 before anyone else? With most of Seagreen arrested, perhaps the scheme's communication lines had been broken.

Alisa paused, eyeing a door at the other side of the warehouse. She picked her way over, then nudged the handle.

But as soon as she opened the door an inch, it slammed closed from the inside. A screech swept through the warehouse, so loud that Alisa clapped her hands to her ears, whirling around. An alarm? What *was* that?

Something flickered in her periphery. When Alisa made a frantic search beside the shelves and cases, it occurred to her that there were some shapes that had blended into the flooring quite well.

"Oh dear," she said aloud.

The warehouse wasn't empty.

Soldiers lined the walls in tight formation, all *sleeping*. Alisa counted no less than twenty, some of them in the uniform of the Imperial Japanese Army, others with Kuomintang colors, somehow mixed together in collaboration.

One of them shifted. Another turned.

They were waking up.

Out of nowhere, the warehouse started to shriek with the continuous sound of an alarm. Rosalind tore her gaze from the map she had picked up again, scrambling to open her door. Alisa hadn't returned. Something had to have gone wrong.

"Be careful," Orion warned, moving just as fast. They circled around the car, eyes pinned to the warehouse. "We don't know what we might find."

Wind howled like a wolf's call around them, its gusts pulling ghostly fingers through Rosalind's hair. She plucked two hairpins out, letting her curls slip to her shoulders and fly out behind her. Orion took the lead, plunging into the warehouse first. Rosalind held her pins tightly—sharp ends forward—before following him.

Alisa was nowhere in sight. Instead, they came upon Japanese soldiers, standing guard in the middle of the warehouse, turning to face Rosalind and Orion as soon as they heard the sound of intrusion.

At the very least, they were weaponless.

Orion said something in Japanese. It didn't work. They charged forward.

"Rosalind, move!"

At once the two of them sprang in different directions, countering the soldiers' attempt at capturing them in place. Rosalind ducked to avoid the first blur of an arm shooting toward her but wasn't fast enough for the second. The moment the soldier gave her a shove to put her off-balance, she slammed down, her elbow making an unpleasant crunch against the concrete floor.

"They're not altered," Orion called over. "But . . ."

He trailed off, too distracted defending himself to continue, though Rosalind knew what he was going to say. These soldiers—their gazes were eerily blank, unblinking in the same way Orion had been when she encountered him in that alley. They *were* altered, if only in mind.

Here she was, thinking they were so fortunate that the soldiers weren't holding weapons. Instead, they were being *made* into weapons. Erased and rebuilt, rendered inhuman by some greater force's agenda. By sheer luck, the last batch of the experiment either had not come back to Warehouse 34 yet or had not been put into effect, else this would not be a fight at all—it would be immediate annihilation.

She watched Orion retrieve his pistol and shoot two of the soldiers. They hardly flinched before going down. Rosalind wheezed in a breath. So this was the battlefield now. This was what combat would soon look like: toy pieces being moved around, each life as expendable as incense paper.

Rosalind twirled the hairpin in her hand and stabbed its whole length into the calf of the nearest soldier. For a moment, he didn't react. For a moment, she thought that the scientists might have found a way around it, that these soldiers were enhanced to be immune to poison, too.

Then he collapsed.

Some few paces away, Orion had abandoned his pistol, out of bullets. Three soldiers surrounded him, and Rosalind didn't hesitate. She lurched forward. Stabbed one, ducked the attack of another. When Orion got a grip around the third, she shouted, "Hold him!"

Orion froze, his grip secured along the soldier's underarms. Rosalind pushed the poisoned pin into his stomach. The moment Orion released him, they repeated the same tactic on the other.

"We have time," Rosalind said breathlessly. "The successful batch hasn't been used here yet—"

"*Watch out!*"

One of the soldiers threw her down. Before she could recover, he kicked her stomach hard, and Rosalind recoiled, rendered immobile under the attack. Even if Rosalind couldn't bruise, it sure as hell *hurt*.

The soldier lifted his foot again. Just as he was about to make contact and probably flatten her lungs, he lurched back, a heavy *thunk* sounding in the warehouse.

Orion had thrown a crate at him. He swooped down and picked up another one, but instead of throwing it, he swung his arm and smacked it against the soldier's head, spitting: "Don't"—he swung again—"touch"—another hard thwack—"my"—the crate broke into two pieces—"wife."

The soldier dropped. Orion wiped a small sprinkle of blood off his face. Two more soldiers closed in.

This was a terrible battle. There was far too much going on at once, and they were greatly outnumbered. When another soldier neared before she could haul herself up, Rosalind was narrowly saved by a blur of motion dropping down from the ceiling slats. It took her a moment to realize it was Alisa: falling onto the soldier's shoulders and reaching forward to twist his neck with a sickening crunch.

In the same motion, she tumbled off, landing hard on her knees before righting herself.

"Ugh, I feel like my brother," she said, shaking out her hands. She looked at Rosalind, who finally got to her feet. "There will be more—they were waiting idle."

Right on cue, there was a burst of noise from the corner of the warehouse. Rosalind squinted into the dark, unnerved. She hadn't even noticed.

"We have to go," she said. "We're outnumbered."

"There's someone in that room over there," Alisa countered. "I think we walked into an active operation. Something is starting."

But this wasn't a fight they could manage. They could keep trying, or they could flee. And if the sacrifice of trying was their lives . . .

A gunshot rang into the warehouse. Rosalind whirled around, her eyes wide. She thought Orion's pistol had run out of bullets. Where was it coming from?

Another gunshot took out the second soldier Orion had been

fighting. Though it was hard to see anything without the overhead lights, Rosalind was close enough to catch the gaping hole in the dead soldier's chest.

The bullets were coming from *outside*, shooting through the open door of the warehouse. Again. And again. Each of them landed with deadly accuracy.

"Priest," Alisa stated in disbelief. "The Communists *are* here."

Rosalind was reeling in bewilderment. Why was Priest taking out the Japanese soldiers but leaving her and Orion unharmed? And where were the rest of the Communist agents if their sharp-shooter was outside?

Barely a second passed between each firing. The last bullet found its target, taking out the final soldier who posed a threat.

The warehouse swept into silence. They were surrounded by bodies. Orion rushed to the warehouse door hurriedly, looking out into the night, but if his expression was any indication, he could not see where the bullets had come from.

"Why would Priest help us?" he demanded.

A thought occurred to Rosalind. The Nationalist station, with all those soldiers killed so that they could escape without trouble. Had that been Priest too?

"We don't have time to figure it out." Rosalind caught sight of a door at the back of the warehouse, the one that Alisa had been talking about. As Rosalind marched toward it, Alisa called out a warning, yelling, "I told you, someone is—"

Rosalind threw the door open. She turned a questioning glance to Alisa.

"What the hell?" Alisa muttered, hurrying over.

The room was unoccupied, but there was another back exit that led into the night. If Alisa had heard someone in here before, that someone had fled. Only they had left behind a crate, half-turned over on the table in a rush.

Rosalind made a beeline for it, plucking out the newspapers shoved in with the vials. Within the rougher newsprint pages were sheets of white lined paper, careful handwriting penning formulas and equations. She hadn't rummaged too deeply through the crate they opened at Burkill Road, but she wondered if the same had been present there. Progress, passed on.

Rosalind picked up one of the vials. The glass was biting cold against her hand. Behind her, she heard Orion slowly enter the room, cautious as he approached.

Was this an old batch? Or was this the same version that had been sent out to Burkill Road—that had ended up working exactly how it was intended?

I want nothing to do with it. I want a cure.

"Alisa," Rosalind called. She gave her the vial when the girl sidled up to her side. "Can you take this to Celia?"

Alisa raised her eyebrows, though she accepted the vial. "Why does Celia need it?"

"She doesn't." Rosalind smoothed her shoulders back. Orion was watching her. "I'm destroying the rest. But assuming this is their final experiment run . . . we might need one fail-safe. To make a cure. She's the only person I trust to hold on to something like this."

"What—"

Alisa mocked a salute, cutting off whatever Orion was going to say. "Can do. I'll see you back in Shanghai."

She ran out of the room, leaving through the warehouse's entrance. Orion turned to Rosalind. Though he must have had something on his mind, Rosalind was not listening: she got to work emptying the papers out from the crate—news headlines and formulae alike—and started to tear them apart, ripping the papers in halves, then quarters, until they were illegible snowflakes of paper.

"Wait, Rosalind," he said suddenly. Before Rosalind could tear the paper into even smaller snowflakes, he reached for a piece, bringing it closer to his eyes. There was little light to read by. There was little light to see that Orion had turned pale, but Rosalind saw it, nonetheless.

"What is it?" she asked.

Without warning, the back door flew open.

Rosalind reached for the knife strapped to her leg, drawing it fast. She didn't know who she had expected. Some part of her had been mortally afraid that Dao Feng would walk in.

She didn't know whether to be confused or relieved that it was not him.

It was a woman.

"Rosalind," Orion said suddenly. "Put the knife down."

She frowned. "What?"

"Put it down, please," he said again, quieter this time, shock seeping into his voice. "That's . . . that's my mother."

46

"Your *mother?*" Rosalind demanded. She didn't lower the knife.

The woman who stepped through the door was dressed primly, a long pencil skirt sweeping past her knees and a pair of circular glasses on her nose. Her black hair was clasped in a low bun, a hesitant smile on her lips. Though, on closer inspection, her face was lined with age, she had a youthful look from afar, easily passable as the newest teaching assistant at the nearby university.

Rosalind didn't know what she had expected for Lady Hong, but it wasn't this. The newspapers had painted a picture of a shrinking former bookkeeper who had flinched at the first signs of trouble, opting to slip away and abandon her family. Either someone who lacked such a spine that she would have preferred quietude to the public eye or someone who held too much national pride to be associated with traitorous behavior. No matter which avenue they went down, it was always with an air of wild emotion.

This Lady Hong before them looked well kept. At ease.

The only discrepancy was the dirt on her nice shoes. Caked in mud, as if she had plunged into the forest, but . . .

"Liwen," his mother said. "I *thought* it was you. I recognized the car."

Rosalind's free hand snapped out, grabbing Orion's elbow as

he started toward his mother. He turned back suddenly, confused about why she was stopping him. In perfect contrast to his amazement, Rosalind was ice cold.

"This really isn't my ideal way of meeting my in-laws either," she said, "but what are you doing here, Lady Hong?"

Tension swept into the room. Lady Hong had clearly been set to flee, then had realized Orion was here and come back.

Beautiful as it was to imagine this a deserved mother-son reunion, Orion Hong was valuable—a living weapon. And *someone* had made him this way.

Lady Hong hesitated at the question. In that pause, Rosalind swiveled her eyes to the shredded paper in Orion's hands again, looking closer at the scribble. He had probably put it together a second earlier. It was his momentary elation that was pushing the conclusion aside, that was trying to force it down. But he had recognized the handwriting. He knew who was behind this scheme.

"Fine, we'll try an easier question," Rosalind said. "What was in it for you? Money? Power?"

"Rosalind," Orion whispered, but he didn't put his heart into the admonishment. He knew as well as she did what situation they were in.

Lady Hong threw her shoulders back. "I was an academic at Cambridge before I married. Did you know that?" She walked closer; Rosalind gave Orion a firm tug, pulling the two of them a step away. "Of course you didn't. The papers never mentioned it. Elite society didn't like it when I talked about it. The Nationalists were more than happy to ask for my expertise when they wanted to run some experiments, but the moment we approached some potential, the top gave the veto and *oh*—that was that. Forget what I *could* find."

Orion's breath was coming shallowly. Rosalind tried to take them backward once more, reaching for the crate of vials at the same time. Though she managed to secure a grip on the crate alongside the knife in her hand, she halted before she could take another step. Orion was resisting.

"Rosalind," he said. "Hold on."

"For what?" she demanded. "Your mother did this to you."

Lady Hong tugged at her sleeves. She looked disappointed, like this was an event that had gone awry rather than the very culmination of an investigation into a terror cell. Like she wasn't at the beating heart of it.

"Miss Lang, don't jump to conclusions," she said.

Rosalind pressed the crate closer to her chest. So his mother knew her identity. His mother had had an eye on them for who knew how long.

"I don't think it's a jump in the slightest," Rosalind replied. "I think the Nationalists brought you in to perform experiments when the civil war started. Make a soldier stronger, faster, more lethal. Make soldiers who would win on the battlefield." She remembered the look on Dao Feng's face when she screamed at him after that mission, when she raged about the innocent scholar's death early in her days as Fortune, claiming that she wouldn't work for their war. Concern flashing in his face, then his hand patting her shoulder and urging her to remain calm, urging her to remember that they were on the same side, that he knew she was her own person, that it was okay if she didn't want to kill like that.

You are not just our weapon, Lang Shalin. You are an agent.

"They cut you off, didn't they? Stopped your research. They thought it was immoral. You were turning real people into weapons."

Lady Hong's expression turned dark. "It was foolish," she said. "We were so close to a breakthrough."

At last the pieces clicked into place. One by one.

"The Nationalists pulled your funding," Rosalind went on. "But you weren't ready to give up. So you went to the Japanese and took *their* funding in exchange for giving them your research. You ran your next experiment on your own son. Did General Hong know? Or did you just let him take the blame for it when the remnants of your paper trail got him accused of being hanjian?"

Underneath her touch, Orion had frozen entirely. It had been a guess on Rosalind's part, but by Lady Hong's frosty silence, she knew she was somewhere along the right path. Nationalist soldiers and Japanese soldiers alike ran this warehouse, eyes blank.

"Or," Rosalind continued, "was this a collaboration? Have you been giving him instructions at every moment, having him make the calls to summon your son for your dirty work?"

Lady Hong remained unspeaking for a very long moment. Then: "I will not explain myself to a child."

Orion had finally heard enough. Enough to lay part of the full picture ahead of him. Enough to rob him of whatever hope had surged to life when his mother appeared at the door. "Not even your own child?"

On the table to the side, there was a tray, a pipette, and a Bunsen burner. The burner was connected to the gas lever below the ground already. Rosalind made a rough estimate of the distance.

"Your father and I drew out a very careful plan," Lady Hong said tightly. "Perhaps he is not happy with how slowly it has been moving, but we were clear with our ultimate aims. The Kuomintang cannot provide for us anymore. The Japanese Empire can. This is for you, too, Liwen. Us as a family."

"*How* is it for me?" Orion demanded. There was a sneer on his face, but it couldn't hide the sadness there too. "You both sat back and watched me kill people. Is your research that much more important? Is Father getting a larger army that much more important? You let me *investigate* myself."

Rosalind drew an inch to the left. When Lady Hong spoke again, she pretended not to hear Orion's questions, only his final accusation.

"We should never have gotten to this point. I told your father to shut your operation down. He claimed he didn't have the power to affect the covert branch. He has always disapproved of your involvement in the covert branch."

Orion's jaw tightened. He shook his head, though the gesture looked more defeated than anything else.

"I thought you were dead. You *abandoned* me—"

"I've always been nearby," Lady Hong cut in firmly. "I keep an eye on you and Phoebe. Heaven knows it's hard when you and your sister are so good at shaking tails off. Chasing them away for no good reason."

While no one was paying attention to her, Rosalind shuffled another inch to the left.

"In what world could I have guessed it was *you* sending blank-eyed men tailing after us?" Orion, meanwhile, demanded. "You left our lives. And now I learn I've been seeing you every few weeks to have my memory erased? What is *wrong* with you?"

"Listen to me," Lady Hong said. She sounded like she was delivering a lecture at the front of an auditorium. There was no remorse for what she was doing. No remorse for what she was promising to an enemy nation for the sake of being the first to make a scientific discovery. "You have a very early strain. I only gave it to you because it was less dangerous—before we added the research to allow healing. The human body doesn't like remaking itself. Every casualty we have had stemmed from that side."

Casualty. As if the guinea pigs she plucked off the streets were soldiers and not murder victims. As if she didn't focus on choosing people in Chinese territory, knowing there was little governance and that no one would care to investigate.

"But you have to keep taking it," Lady Hong went on. "Your headaches are a side effect. Without a new dose of that old strain every few weeks, they will get worse and worse before taking your life. It took us some time to figure that out. It took us some time to figure out that the only way to fix those side effects permanently"— she nodded her chin toward the crate in Rosalind's arm—"is to give you the final version. I told you. Everything I'm doing is for you, too."

Haidi's scream echoed in Rosalind's mind. Her desperation in the banquet lounge. *Those aren't dangerous. They're for me. I'll die without them!*

Another experiment. A later run.

"This is—" Orion broke off, unable to keep arguing. His sadness had turned bitter; his eyes, which had been large and shocked before, had narrowed with hostility. Rosalind wanted to reach out and reassure him, but she knew he would have to come to terms with it himself. His mother might claim to be doing this all for him, but if she hadn't experimented on him to begin with, his life wouldn't even *be* in danger.

"Let me guess," he said. "When I take the final version, I'll turn as mindless as those soldiers back there."

"Untrue—that is an entirely different strain," Lady Hong countered. Rosalind almost laughed aloud. She sounded so damn blasé, treating this as no matter at all. Orion clearly had *some* version of that mindlessness if they were ordering him around the city without him remembering a thing.

Rosalind must have made a noise, despite her best efforts. Lady Hong's gaze flickered over to her. To the crate.

"Miss Lang," she said, "for Liwen's sake, hand it over."

Rosalind took a step forward obediently.

"Rosalind!" Orion hissed in warning.

She turned back to look at him. *Your life is my life.*

And she could save it on her own.

Rosalind threw the crate onto the floor. At once, the glass vials smashed into pieces, little shards mixing with bright green liquid that trickled in all directions. Before Lady Hong could react,

Rosalind lunged for the Bunsen burner and shoved her foot against the gas pedal beneath the table. A piercing blue flame shot to life.

"I won't aid national traitors," she said coldly. She dropped the burner. In a burst, wooden crate and newspapers and green liquid alike erupted with flickers of fire, eating up everything in its vicinity.

The horror was stark on Lady Hong's face. It was too late to save anything. All she could do was watch it burn.

Her eyes flashed up to meet Rosalind's. "You don't know what you have done."

"I know exactly what I've done," Rosalind replied, and before she could think better, she readjusted the knife in her grip and made a swing.

She missed—narrowly.

Lady Hong surged backward, her lips thinning as the arc of the blade barely whispered past her nose. Now anger was encroaching into the pinch of her mouth, curdling away her previous calm.

"Lady Fortune, you play foul," she said contemptuously. "But so can I. *Oubliez.*"

Rosalind tried to stab again, though she couldn't help frowning at the switch into French. *Forget?* Forget what?

Suddenly, Orion's hand closed over her upper arm and threw her backward. The attack was so forceful that Rosalind slammed into the opposite wall, her shoulder making a loud sound. Her knife clattered to the floor. She was given a mere second to gulp air into her winded lungs. In the next, Orion was hauling her up again.

No.

"Orion," she gasped. There was nothing in his gaze. No recognition or humor, no sense of anything save for a blank, misted-over stare. "Orion, *don't*—" Rosalind swerved, avoiding his fist. "Snap out of it!"

He aimed low; she felt her shoulder click back into place and start to heal, giving her the strength to catch his wrist and push it up, slamming a foot behind his knee when his body turned to follow the movement. Though Orion stumbled, he dived forward deliberately, circling a foot around him as soon as he had balance again to throw Rosalind off stance.

She hit the floor. Swore viciously under her breath. She was going to lose this fight. It didn't matter how fast she could heal. Orion was too strong to be deterred.

His shadow loomed over her. Before she could roll away, he had her pinned, hands around her throat. Rosalind clenched her jaw hard to counter the pressure, pushing as hard as she could to pry away his fingers, but it was like fighting against steel.

"Orion," she wheezed.

His grip tightened.

"Orion, Orion"—the barest recognition stirred in his eyes—"it's me. It's *me*."

Orion's hands loosened a fraction. Though his expression was still blank, there was *something* there, something trying to fight toward the surface.

Rosalind did the only thing that she could. She reached her arm out, her fingers barely brushing the blade of the knife—reaching, reaching, and just as her vision turned entirely black, she secured a grip on the handle and plunged the blade into Orion's shoulder.

Orion flinched with a gasp, releasing his hold on her.

Without a moment to spare, Rosalind freed herself and clambered to her feet, heaving for breath as she put distance between them. She expected him to attack again immediately, but the knife in his shoulder had done something to affect his altered state. Small droplets of blood trickled in front of him, oozing from his shoulder to the floor.

"Orion?" she tried cautiously.

"*Go*," he snarled. Rosalind lurched back, startled out of her skin. From the other side of the room, Lady Hong had drawn her pistol, seeing that the fight had been put on pause. Rosalind barely paid his mother any mind, despite the threat she posed. Orion held all her attention.

He was letting the blood run. His hands were pushed hard into the floor, braced on the concrete. He looked like a conquered deity barely contained in its human vessel, head bowed and on his knees, palms down in supplication.

"Rosalind," he managed. "Go. Please." And he was. He was a deity, begging. "Rosalind, go! *Go!*"

"Hong Liwen, get up this moment," Lady Hong instructed, and pointed her pistol at Rosalind. Without a moment of hesitation, she pulled the trigger.

The bullet embedded deep. Rosalind hadn't even thought to move. Her hands flew up to clasp her stomach, in sheer disbelief that she had just been shot. She was at an utter loss for direction. Orion was shouting—"*Go! Please, go!*"—and Lady Hong was aiming again, and Rosalind couldn't even hear herself *think* because of her lightheadedness after almost being choked to death and now with half her guts about to tumble out.

She couldn't leave Orion here. The pain in her stomach was agonizing. The decision in front of her was even worse.

Lady Hong fired again. Another bullet pierced higher, into Rosalind's ribs, blooming with deep, deep red.

"*Go!* Rosalind, *go!*"

She needed to. She could heal a gunshot wound. But if Lady Hong aimed any higher, she could not heal her head blown clean off.

It hurt more to move away than it did to take the bullets. But Rosalind stumbled for the back door, pushing out into the night just as a third bullet tore after her, striking the doorframe instead and spraying wooden pellets everywhere.

Though Rosalind ran, she could not resist looking back. The shooting had stopped. Lady Hong was striding for Orion instead, tossing the pistol aside.

Get up, she wanted to cry. She wanted to scream, to brandish every weapon she had ever learned to use and take to battle. But when Orion was being wielded like this, she was no match for him at all—and it wasn't him she wanted to hurt.

Lady Hong had taken something out of her pocket. Orion was still kneeling, still shaking as he tried to keep himself from going after Rosalind.

A syringe came out. Orion refused to look up. This one wasn't green. It was filled with a red liquid.

Rosalind stopped running. "Orion, come on, come on—"

His mother drove the syringe into his neck. The plunger went down; Orion's head snapped up. In Rosalind's terror she might have shrieked aloud, but she barely noticed. If her greatest fear had come to fruition, then he had just been given whatever had wiped the minds of those other soldiers. Whatever Lady Hong instructed him to do next was lost to Rosalind as she turned fast on her heel and ran into the trees, gasping for air. She felt her body throbbing, blood pumping furiously around the bullets embedded inside her.

She couldn't stop. Even when she tripped on a rough part of the foliage, tumbling down to her knees, she gathered what remained of her strength and was up in a blink, barreling deeper into the forest.

On and on, she ran.

Because if Orion found her, he would kill her.

47

Alisa came to the stoop of the photography shop, looking around to confirm that the location was right: *240 Hei Long Road*. This was it.

She went around to the back door, banging noisily with both fists. She didn't care if the neighbors heard; there was nothing overly suspicious about a late-night visitor. "Celia! Celia, it's me!"

A lock turned on the other side. When the door opened, it wasn't Celia waiting but Oliver Hong.

"Hello," Oliver greeted, tilting his head curiously. There was a cat in his arms, purring as he scratched its small head. "Who are you?"

"Where's Celia?" Alisa demanded in return.

"Right here." At Celia's voice, Oliver shifted aside, making room for her at the doorway. Celia, already wearing a dressing gown, looked taken aback when she walked out. "Alisa, what are you doing so far outside the city?"

Alisa's fingers tightened on the vial in her pocket. She was moving to pull it out, but then she hesitated, eyes flickering to Oliver. Everything she knew about him flashed through her mind at once: all the casualties he had caused while in the field, all the people who were afraid of him for what he was capable of. If the grapevine wasn't lying, some even whispered that he was the handler for Priest.

"Rosalind asked me to give you something," Alisa said carefully. "But you—just you. She doesn't trust anyone else."

Celia blinked, then exchanged a glance with Oliver. The unspoken part of that statement was clear. Alisa would not be giving Celia anything if it meant Oliver would also get his hands on it.

"Alisa, it's okay," she said. "If you trust me, you can trust Oliver, too."

Slowly, Alisa released her hold on the vial, letting it settle safely back into her pocket. What a bizarre idea. Trust didn't come in package deals. Just because Oliver treated Celia well didn't mean that same kindness would be extended to everybody.

Alisa turned to Oliver. "Did you know?" she demanded. "That your brother had been made into a killer?"

The only indication that she had surprised Oliver was the cat's meow of complaint. His grip had tightened on the small animal. "I beg your pardon?"

"You must have known that something was off," Alisa continued evenly. "Even if you didn't know the outright reason, you must have considered that one must exist if our people were going after your own brother. You had the power to figure out why. Why didn't you? Why didn't you chase it until the end? Why didn't you nudge higher and higher until someone could tell you about Warehouse 34?"

Oliver took a moment to absorb her accusations. She had been speaking as if each one was a sucker punch, and now that she was finished, it was his turn to be on the offense.

"Alisa, was it?" Oliver confirmed. "*What* are you talking about?"

He didn't seem to want to take the offense.

"Orion Hong was brainwashed into making the kills across Shanghai!" Alisa said, her volume rising. For Rosalind's sake, she was suddenly furious. "And we *knew*. Some branch on our side has been sitting on photographic evidence for who knows how long, only so that we could steal the finished experiment. How could you let that happen? Why didn't you put it together?"

Alisa knew she had thrown her blame too far. She couldn't have expected Oliver Hong to have clairvoyance into the future. All the same, he was supposed to be a terrifying, powerful operative. What was the point of that if not to be used?

When Oliver and Celia said nothing in response, Alisa took a step back. Celia had pressed a hand to her mouth, taking in the information. Oliver's expression was carefully neutral.

"Why didn't you *care* enough to figure it out?" Alisa finished, landing on the question that she had really been wondering this whole time.

"I did," Oliver finally replied. "Just in the wrong goddamn direction."

Celia blinked. She lowered her hand. "What?"

"From that very first visit, I recognized my own *mother's* work in Warehouse 34," he said, each word strung close to the other, like he could only say this in one breath. They had reached the very end of the line: no secret had any meaning remaining. "It had to be a Nationalist operation in some manner—there was no doubt on that. But I didn't want to bring a fight to her, so I stayed out of it. I never even reported it. I was so intent on leaving her alone that I couldn't have imagined Orion was connected to this. That *she* was hurting Orion, her own *son*."

Alisa didn't know what to think.

She didn't need to. She was done here.

Alisa turned on her heel and ran. She heard Celia call after her, but she ignored it. She ignored everything except the world around her, the night howling and the trees rustling as she picked her way through the forest.

When Alisa reached into her pocket again, the glass vial had turned so cold that it stung her palm. It wouldn't do to lose it.

She slowed and took the vial out, letting her breathing return to normal.

The Nationalists wanted it. The Communists would kill for it. The Japanese would conquer them both with it. Her brother had sacrificed so much because he'd wanted to see the city changed, and Alisa was only ever going to work toward seeing that to fruition. And right now, no faction deserved her loyalty when they were making the very same scramble for power that would split the city apart once again.

Alisa looked up at the moon, regaining her directional bearings. Rosalind trusted her to protect this vial, and Alisa *would* protect it. The moment she fell off the grid, no one would be able to find her.

That was a promise.

48

The killer does not have a name. He has never had a name.

That is what his memory tells him. The dark road rushes ahead of him, and he stares out blankly, counting the streetlamps that fly by. Someone is driving the car—his mother. He knows that much, but he should not think of her as his mother anymore.

This is his controller: the one he must listen to and protect above all. Nothing else is more important. He should not allow urges of his own. He *will* not allow urges of his own. He only listens, only heeds commands.

The car brakes suddenly. In the distance, there are multiple dots of light, growing larger and larger. The headlights of other vehicles, fast approaching.

"Out." His controller drops a pistol in his lap. "Fend them off."

The killer gets out. When the other cars pull up, a host of soldiers pour onto the road, the blue and white of the Nationalist symbol stitched into their hats and their division numbers slapped above their olive-green chest pockets.

It is hard to identify faces in the dark. It is hard to identify faces at all, and every person before him now looks vaguely the same—features blurred and indistinct.

He charges forward. He lifts his pistol and starts to shoot, and it takes the soldiers some time before they scramble to combat him.

It does not matter what they do or who tugs his weapon away from him. He hauls the arm that comes near and breaks it; he pulls at the grip that encircles his neck and throws the combatant to the ground as easily as he would fling aside a crumpled piece of paper.

Nothing tires him out.

When the car drives up from behind him and pulls to a stop, his controller's expression is blank, peering at the damage that has been wrought.

"That's enough. Get in."

The rest of the soldiers have stopped trying to attack. They stand aside warily. They let him walk away. They watch him as he gets into the car and closes the door with a thud. This killer—this unthinking killer—wonders if he hears someone yelling, yelling a name. Perhaps he knows who it is; perhaps he knows whose name is being yelled into the night. But it all fizzles away before it reaches his ear, before he can really register what the words are saying.

The car drives away.

49

Rosalind hazed in and out of awareness, her head leaning against a tree.

She was healing terribly slowly, and the blood loss was affecting her. The bullets weren't being pushed out. They were made of some strange material and had lodged themselves too deep. It must have been intentional, given how well Lady Hong understood her healing. Her body didn't know what to do. When there was a flashing light in her periphery, she almost thought it was a hallucination until her ears also caught voices. Blearily, Rosalind looked up, searching through the shapes and blurriness before a familiar face dropped in front of her.

"Jiemin?" she asked.

"Are you hurt?" he demanded. More voices surrounded them now: Nationalist soldiers fanning through the trees to check the area. "I thought you could heal."

"Bullets. They're not healing well. Pull me up." Rosalind held out her hands, and Jiemin hauled her upright. Briefly, her vision turned black when she stood, and she almost fell again before Jiemin caught her.

"You were careless for this," Jiemin snapped. "I was closing in on General Hong as soon as he tried to block our motion to enter Warehouse 34. I put Hong Liwen in a cell specifically to keep him away from his father's control."

"It wasn't just his father." Rosalind blinked hard, urging her sight to return. "It was his mother, too. If we hadn't appeared, she would have taken the vials at the warehouse. But I destroyed them." A burst of anger flared in her chest. She shoved Jiemin suddenly, though her strength was weak. "Why didn't you *say* anything to me? Why surprise us like that?"

Jiemin tried to hurry her along, warily eyeing the blood still pulsing from her wounds.

"Because I reached into a source I'm not supposed to reach into," he answered gruffly. "A source that has ears on every part of the city, including the Communists. I couldn't answer for where I got the information from. I couldn't explain how I knew Orion was the killer before anybody else on our side did, so I needed to act fast and act first. But you had to go and do your own little thing."

Rosalind struggled to a stop. There was no use arguing about it now. What was done could not be undone. She needed to think. She needed a plan of action.

"Orion was taken."

"I know," Jiemin said. "We encountered him on our way here. He left half our people dead. He is under some sort of spell."

Rosalind took her arm out of Jiemin's grasp. She almost teetered over as soon as she was standing on her own, but she needed to face him, needed him to understand . . .

"We have to go after him," she breathed. "His mother is controlling him, but if we take Nationalist forces—"

"We cannot."

"We can! We only need—"

"You're not listening to me. It's over. That is not our mission."

Rosalind staggered back. "How can you say that?" she hissed. "How can we abandon him?"

"*Listen* to me."

Jiemin reached forward and shook her by the shoulders. The

movement worsened her pain, sent her every sensation into over-drive, but she welcomed it. She could feel everything, *everything*.

"Hong Liwen has had his memory erased. He is a liability and a threat. We must cut our losses where we can."

Rosalind jerked away. Her head spun. "You are *callous*," she spat. "I will go after him myself. I will—"

But before she could finish her sentence, she dropped to her knees against her will, sensation lost below her waist. In a daze, she held her hands out in front of her and found them so slick with blood that it looked as though she were wearing a pair of scarlet gloves.

"Lang Shalin!"

Though Jiemin dived forward, he was not fast enough to catch her before her head hit the grass. She felt the soft soil press into her temple, and at that moment, she was content to let it swallow her up.

Her eyes fluttered closed.

50

The world did not return slowly; it came back in a sudden jerk, like her brain had been kicked into commission with the flip of a switch. Rosalind tried to rise right away, afraid that she was in danger, but someone at her side pushed her back down.

There was no danger. This was a hospital.

She was lying in a hospital bed.

With that initial verdict made, Rosalind registered her surroundings one after the other. Smooth white walls. Midafternoon light. An intravenous line plugged into the inside of her elbow, and Celia sitting in a chair by her bed.

"Don't pull that out," her sister warned immediately.

Rosalind's fingers were already twisted around the line, giving it a yank. The needle slid out. The miniature wound closed up.

Celia sighed. "I tried. How are you feeling?"

"Perfectly fine." Rosalind shifted up on the bed. The pain had disappeared. They must have operated to remove the bullets, and as soon as those were gone, her body knew how to heal its wounds. There were bandages swathing her middle, poking out under her thin gown, but there would be no injuries underneath.

"So, what do you want to hear first?" Celia asked. "Everything you missed while you were under, or how I'm sitting here without being hauled in by your Nationalists?"

"The first one," Rosalind said, flopping her arms over the covers. "I already know the latter: you're sneaky."

Celia lifted a brow, leaning into the chair. She was dressed in a qipao with her hair pinned in elaborate braids, two loops of jewelry around her neck underneath her usual jade pendant. She had entered the hospital as a member of the elite, not as an agent of the Communist Party.

"I always miss you, but I don't miss your sense of humor."

"Who said I was trying to be funny? I'm serious."

Celia shook her head, an amused titter escaping her lips. For several long moments, she remained unspeaking, gathering her thoughts. Then: "I heard about Warehouse 34. The whole rundown. Apparently, we had agents near the scene, but when they saw what was going on, we didn't join the fray."

Rosalind still couldn't work out what exactly had happened. Priest was there too and had helped them—didn't that count as joining the fray?

"How did they know to go?" she asked.

"That . . . that is the other matter I need to tell you."

Celia drew her legs up, propped on the side of the bed so that she could rest her arms on her knees. She cast a glance over to the door of the hospital room, ensuring that no one was lurking within hearing vicinity.

"One of our double agents has publicly entered our ranks. He has relinquished his previous Kuomintang association."

Rosalind pushed herself upright. Celia didn't stop her this time.

"He was near discovery," her sister continued. "The Kuomintang had heard about a file containing the code names of three under-cover Communists within their ranks. Once different branches sent people out to get ahold of the information and it started moving, it would be a matter of time before he and two of his men were exposed for communicating with each other when they were allegedly not in acquaintance. He faked his own incapacitation early to ensure he could get away."

"No," Rosalind whispered. Though her thoughts swirled with sheer incomprehension, she knew who this had to be. She had stolen that very file on his instructions. It had never been information about Priest. It had been his own identity on the verge of exposure.

Celia nodded. "Trust me, if I had known when you were telling me about the file, I would have shared it then. But this was too high up to reach me until now. Dao Feng was Lion. Two agents in the Zhejiang covert branch were Gray and Archer. Once their inevitable exposure was confirmed, there was no way to continue undercover work. The same night that Dao Feng pretended to be attacked, he sent messages warning Gray and Archer to wrap up and leave before the Kuomintang could catch up to them."

Rosalind dropped her head into her hands. This was cruel. Those messages in warning—*she* sent them. She pushed them into the mailbox, happily believing everything Dao Feng told her without a second thought. Was she doomed toward this narrative for all eternity? Was everyone she loved a liar intent on betraying her?

She thought back to every moment with Dao Feng, every piece of advice he had given her, every lesson he had imparted. How much of Dao Feng's care toward her had been genuine? Every time she thought she had sealed up her old wounds, another grand actor took off their mask and came slashing at them again.

She breathed out slowly, dragging her hands along her cheeks. Her own handler had been a double agent. She had a sister on the opposite side. The Nationalists were never going to trust her again—hell, she wouldn't even trust herself. Beyond the throbbing betrayal tearing at her heart, she was almost angry. Dao Feng could have told her. He knew she wasn't particularly loyal to the Nationalists.

Why hadn't he brought her *with* him?

Rosalind pushed her emotions away. Now that she was awake, there were more important matters at hand.

"Celia," she said quietly. "Orion's mother took him. Plunged a syringe right into his neck and wiped him clean. . . ."

Celia looked regretful. "I know." She leaned to her right, reaching for something on the bedside table. Slowly, Celia slid the newspaper in front of her, angling it so that Rosalind could read the text.

LANG SHALIN ALIVE. HONG LIWEN HANJIAN.

The sub-headline continued in large font. Rosalind made a brief scan of the page, catching "taking disguises at Seagreen Press" and "Hong Buyao arrested for collaboration with the Japanese," but she couldn't read any more. She pushed the paper away. Then spat a curse.

"Oh, it gets worse," Celia said. There was another newspaper waiting on the bedside table. This one Celia didn't even maneuver delicately. She put it right onto Rosalind's lap.

IS LANG SHALIN THE INFAMOUS LADY FORTUNE?

Rosalind breathed out slowly. "Dear God."

"I had a similar reaction." Celia took the two newspapers away. "Don't waste time fretting that the Kuomintang won't trust you anymore because your handler had the wrong loyalties. They *cannot* use you as an agent anymore. Your identity has leaked to the whole of Shanghai. In truth, I wouldn't be surprised if someone within their ranks leaked it themselves just to get you pulled from commission."

Rosalind felt the scream build at her throat. And build and build and build.

"Orion is not hanjian," she whispered. Of all the details plastered on the front page of a newspaper, that was the one that annoyed her the most.

Celia said nothing. She let Rosalind broil in her anger.

"One more thing," her sister added when a moment had passed. "Alisa has disappeared."

What? Rosalind sat up taller. "Is she in danger?"

"I don't think so. She came to give me something but . . . then she ran off. I cannot comprehend why."

Neither could Rosalind. Given how Lady Hong had reacted to the crate that Rosalind destroyed, Alisa was now holding on to the only version of the successful chemical experiment. Perhaps the Imperial Japanese Army would begin efforts to re-create it, but it would take considerable time.

"She'll be okay," Rosalind said. She didn't know if she was reassuring Celia or herself. "She knows what she's doing."

A knock sounded on the door then, though no nurse came in. Celia hopped to her feet quickly and reached out to squeeze Rosalind's hand.

"I must go."

"Already?" Rosalind sounded like a petulant child. She didn't care. It was almost bizarre—though the two of them had come into the world at the same time, Rosalind had always thought of herself as the eldest one. Only now Celia looked so much older, like a true adult who had become certain of her place in the world. Whereas Rosalind . . . Rosalind didn't know if she would ever find that.

"I can find you later. That was my five-minute warning before your Nationalists arrive at your room to debrief you." Celia tried for a smile. "Don't stir trouble in the meantime, understand?"

"When did you become the older sister?" Rosalind grumbled.

Celia tightened her grip once more, then let go. "When I aged past you," she answered quietly. "Au revoir, Rosalind. Take care."

"Goodbye," Rosalind whispered after her sister, a pang in her heart as Celia turned back to wave through the glass panel in the door. She blinked her tears away, then clambered out of the bed. Though she was healed, she was exhausted, her legs heavy as she walked to the window.

Shanghai bustled on outside. The hospital was on a hill, which meant she could see the rooftops of the other lower wings. Beyond those rooftops was the front courtyard and then the rest of the street: laughing children bouncing their rubber balls, old men selling fried skewers, women passing out flyers for a cabaret show.

Rosalind pressed her fingers to her temple, trying to smooth out the tension there. A wooden toy rolled onto the road. When a small child ran after it, his mother hauled him back by the collar. Rosalind could not hear what the mother was saying from her distant hospital room, but the stern finger spoke volumes.

God. Rosalind loved the city she saw before her. Like some epiphany, the feeling invaded her at once, so potent that she might choke on it. She could push it down. She could turn away and pretend it was something else. Yet still the love existed, ever patient.

All her love seemed to emerge in an identical manner. It wasn't that it would be absent one day and then present the next. It would move in without her notice and get comfortable and conquer more and more space, and she wouldn't even know that there was a new occupant in her heart until she started wondering where all this furniture had come from and love flashed its dazzling grin at her to say hello.

There was a dull ache behind Rosalind's eyes when she turned away from the window, too overwhelmed to keep watching the scene outside. She needed a plan of action. She needed to fix this.

Because she had left him. She had told him that his life was hers, and then *she left him.*

Another knock sounded on the door. This time a nurse poked her head in.

"Lang Shalin?"

Rosalind would have to start getting used to this: her real name, in the open again. She nodded tiredly.

The nurse held out a slip of paper. "There was a telephone call for you while you were in surgery, so the caller left a message."

Rosalind reached for the paper, her brow furrowing. Who would be calling her while she was in surgery? Her superiors would be on their way to debrief her in person. They hardly needed to leave a message first.

"Thank you," Rosalind said. The paper crinkled under her hand, its edges brown, probably dampened with spilled tea and already dried in the time it took to reach her.

The nurse closed the door, leaving Rosalind to open the message and scan it over once, then twice.

Her grip tightened, putting wrinkles across the ink. It didn't matter: the words had burned themselves into her mind instantly. Outside her window, the city carried on, tucking players of every faction into its various corners, all of whom were stirring, stirring, stirring to life for combat. In front of her, Rosalind's sense of purpose unfurled like a newly paved path, drawing out her very next steps.

> *I can help you get him back.*
> *Find me in Zhouzhuang.*
> *—JM.*

"JM," Rosalind said into the empty room. "Who the *hell* are you?"

EPILOGUE

Phoebe Hong walked through the gates of the orphanage with her handbag swinging. The set of her shoulders was rigid and proud, keeping her posture vigilant. She had been countering sympathies and sidelong glances all week, and she couldn't bear a second more of it. That was what happened when your parents turned out to be national traitors and hauled your brother along, she supposed. She didn't know if people were looking at her because they pitied her or because they suspected that she would be next.

"Jiějiě!"

A toddler ran up to her, clutching a jar of jam in her hands. She gave Phoebe a toothless grin. "Can you open this for me?"

Phoebe crouched down with a responding smile, setting her handbag on the grass. She took the jam from Nunu and pretended to struggle with the lid.

"Oooh, this one is tough. Does Sister Su know you're rummaging around the jam cabinets?"

Nunu raised her chubby fists, doing a small dance on the lawn. "Nooo! Don't tell on me!"

Phoebe bit down on her laugh, twisting open the jam jar. "Okay, okay. Here's your jam."

With a cackle, Nunu took the jar and ran away, skirting around the lawn and seating herself on the playground. The morning sun was bright today despite the cold, and Phoebe had trouble fully opening her eyes in the direction of the orphanage, where the stained-glass windows reflected a dozen colors. Despite its quaint appearance, the orphanage was enormous, hosting multiple guest rooms at the back.

Phoebe retrieved her bag and walked into the building, closing the heavy wooden doors after herself. Inside, Sister Su was dusting the pews while keeping an eye on the children playing around a plastic table, and Phoebe waved at the nun, saying her hello.

"I didn't expect to see you here anytime soon," Sister Su said when Phoebe approached. "I heard about your brother."

Phoebe breathed in. When Silas told her what happened that night, having gathered information from the Kuomintang the next day, he had braced himself as if he expected her to fall apart. To his surprise, Phoebe had remained calm. Her brother had not become a mystery, nor was he in immediate danger. They knew exactly what was going on and they knew that her mother would not hurt him. The Kuomintang's spies could continue tracking his movements as Lady Hong hauled him along, moving from base to base with the Japanese mobilization efforts. The problem was meeting him in combat. The problem was engaging in a rescue without losing their own lives in the process—which seemed impossible at present.

"He will be okay," Phoebe said firmly. She believed it. He was strong. "Can I hang around?"

Sister Su pursed her lips, her eyes darting once to the back rooms. "I suppose so. There is nothing else to tend to right now?"

She knew what Sister Su was asking. "Not at the moment, no."

With a yielding nod from the nun, Phoebe proceeded through the orphanage, coming into the kitchen and putting her bag down. There was a back door here that opened into the yard, where a tire swung from a thick tree branch. She heard the leaves rustling outside as she looked through the cupboards, rising onto the tips of her toes to fetch a teapot. The clouds were rapidly thickening while she poked around the kitchen. By the time she found a tin of dried chrysanthemum flowers and scooped out two heapings for her tea, the sun was mostly covered, turning her surroundings dreary.

"Hmmm," Phoebe said, craning her head against the window as the water boiled on the stove. Perhaps it would clear up later.

The water finished boiling. She filled the teapot, then set it on the table with two teacups. Just as she heard a door opening down the hallway, Phoebe eased into one of the seats, pouring the tea and watching the yellowish liquid swirl.

When Dao Feng walked into the kitchen, he did not look surprised to see her. He only sat down and picked up the cup of tea that she had set out for him.

"Hello," Phoebe said.

"Fancy seeing you here," Dao Feng replied. He took a sip of his tea.

Phoebe examined her nails. "I had to ask my questions somehow. I trust that you've made a full recovery."

"Indeed, Miss Hong. Did you come to inquire after my health? How kind of you."

Evidently not. Without any further small talk, Phoebe asked, "Did you know that Orion was the one doing the killings when you sent him to investigate?"

"Of course not." Dao Feng's reply came quickly. "We wouldn't waste our time like that."

"When did you find out?"

"Midway in. By then it was too late to pull him from the mission without raising suspicion from the Nationalists. It was easier to use him. Wait patiently and see if we could take the asset from him at the end."

Phoebe's fingers tightened on her teacup. It was bizarre that this was supposed to be business, nothing personal, but wasn't everything in politics personal? What was the point of politics if not for the individual people it claimed to represent?

"It didn't work, so you didn't do a very good job," Phoebe said. "And you had to poison yourself too? You couldn't have simply gone into hiding? So dramatic."

"I was hiding in plain sight, Miss Hong." He took another deep drink of tea. "If I had actually disappeared, I would have been investigated. It would have given the two others no time to get their affairs in order and remove themselves too. No one thinks to investigate a man at death's door. No one looks in that direction."

Phoebe leaned back, her fingers tapping on the table. With every movement, she felt her earrings swing, the pearls brushing against her skin; all her impractical accessories jangled with constant sound, making interruptions to the otherwise quiet kitchen.

"My judgment remains. I saw you fall. *Dramatic.*"

Dao Feng straightened in his chair. He was casting his mind back to that night, puzzling out this new information. He must have caught a glimpse of her when she slipped forward to see what on earth he was putting into his arm; she had fled quickly when someone else started running into the alley, summoned by Dao Feng's feigned shout.

"That was you," Dao Feng stated, as if he had solved one of his own internal mysteries. "You took the file from Lang Shalin. You were still lurking around that night."

"I had to sneak a peek at what the file said. I heard some rumors. Needed to make sure all my affairs were in order. Unlike yours."

Now Dao Feng understood. He released his teacup, the drink finished, a glint of satisfaction entering his expression because he had finally connected the dots. If he had been bothered before about why she was sitting in this kitchen, why she was familiar with this orphanage as a base, he was no longer.

"Hong Feiyi, you are a lot smarter than you act, you know."

Phoebe smiled. It was unlike her other smiles, quiet and subdued rather than a bright grin that aimed to dazzle. "I get that a lot."

Dao Feng reached for a handshake. Phoebe extended her fingers, meeting his enthusiastic grasp. When he spoke next, his voice was filled with warmth.

"It is a pleasure to meet you properly, Priest."

AUTHOR'S NOTE

The difficulties of telling a story rooted in history is that the author always has the power of hindsight, but the characters might not have the full picture for years or decades to come. Where does the line get drawn between omitting information for accuracy and providing information for the modern-day reader? How much can we hand-wave for the sake of telling a story?

The opening scene to *Foul Lady Fortune* is known to the history textbooks as the Mukden Incident. On September 18, 1931, a small explosion was set off on the Japanese-controlled South Manchurian Railway. However, the damage was so weak that a train passed over the site shortly afterward and arrived in Shenyang—or Mukden— about ten minutes later without trouble. Still, the explosion had served its purpose. The Nationalists had been moving through China in a unification campaign (*Our Violent Ends* depicted their success overtaking Shanghai in 1927); the Japanese were threatened that they would lose Manchuria if the Chinese Nationalists took the land, especially when Manchuria was crucial for defending Japanese colonization over Korea. In their bid to maintain the area, officers of the Japanese army set up the explosion as a false Chinese attack. The next day, Japanese troops attacked the Chinese garrison at Beidaying under the guise of retaliation and successfully occupied Shenyang. In the next few months, they would use this movement to occupy all major cities in China's northeast.

The League of Nations would issue their Lytton Report in October 1932 to declare Japan as the aggressor who had wrongfully invaded Manchuria. By the time that stance was taken on the international stage, Japan had already secured control. Mutterings within China about the incident being a set-up wouldn't be confirmed until much later, when investigators determined Japanese army officers set the explosion without authorization from their government. In chapter six of *Foul Lady Fortune*, Rosalind guesses that the Chinese weren't responsible based on her own observations, which was my decision to give the reader historical information before the characters could be realistically certain. In every book I write, the most important thing I want a reader to know is that history is not a set of facts and dates, but a narrative that gets drawn up in between. Along the same vein, my historical-based fiction isn't supposed to be a complete rendering of the time or a direct portrayal of everything that was going on—because that wouldn't be possible and isn't what I'm intending to do in a novel. Extensive research is important to me when ensuring my story is accurate to the atmosphere and climate of 1930s Shanghai, but ultimately, the historical events of *Foul Lady Fortune* are used to examine imperialism, nationalism, and cultural generational trauma that has lasted to this day, not to provide an overall textbook account of the era. As with my previous duology, I highly recommend nonfiction resources as the next stop if you're interested in the events that take place in this book.

Shanghai in the 1930s was not only a tense time of looming Japanese invasion, but also a time of domestic civil war that would carry on into the next decade. There were real spies on each side, with the fictional covert branch in this book loosely based on the secret Special Affairs Department within the Juntong (军统), which was the Kuomintang's earliest intelligence bureau formed around 1932. Of course, all operations, assassinations, and events are a figment of my imagination, as is the existence of a superhuman chemical concoction being fought over by every faction. However, even when inserting speculative elements into historical settings, my intentions are always to press deep into the tensions and nuances that did indeed exist.

Peach Lily Palace was based on the real Peach Blossom Palace (桃花宮) which was built on Thibet Road in 1928, allegedly the newest and most glamorous Chinese dance hall among the numerous in operation, modeled off Western-style cabarets for Shanghai's intellectual and artistic circles. Most street names mentioned were real places, as were the major department stores Wing On and Sincere. Seagreen Press was a fictional invention of mine, but newspapers were hugely important during this era for propaganda—both Chinese and foreign—within the city, and for taking news overseas to the Western public, which I wanted to pay homage to in a time where the movement of political news was critical.

Until the sequel to *Foul Lady Fortune* arrives, I'll use this moment to recommend some literature that was actually written in 1930s Shanghai for anyone particularly intrigued by the vibes. The stories of Mu Shiying (穆時英) are some of my favorites, including "The Man Who Was Treated as a Plaything," "Shanghai Fox-trot," and "Craven A." And, yes, Orion's and Rosalind's aliases at Seagreen were based on his surname. I'm sneaky that way.

ACKNOWLEDGMENTS

To tell the truth, I can hardly believe that we've reached the acknowledgments section of this book after the journey it took to get here—both within these pages and outside of them. Writing a new series is hard, because it will inevitably be different from the first series that introduced my work to readers. Writing a new series that also happens to be a spin-off of said first series is even harder when it comes to balancing new, unfamiliar content with old, familiar elements. So thank you, reader, whether you decided you wanted to stay in this world or whether you decided you wanted to jump in here as an entry point. This book wouldn't exist without you.

I also wrote this book during the chaos that was graduating college and moving to New York, so I couldn't have emerged in one piece without the help of my publishing team. The biggest, biggest thank-yous: To my agent, Laura Crockett, who works absolute magic to make my days in publishing run as smoothly as possible. To Uwe Stender and Brent Taylor and everyone at TriadaUS. To my editor, Sarah McCabe, who utterly transformed this book from its earliest scrawny state to this final well-nourished product. To my publicist, Cassie Malmo. To Justin Chanda and everyone at Margaret K. McElderry Books, including Karen Wojtyla, Anne Zafian, Bridget Madsen, Elizabeth Blake-Linn, Michael McCartney, Lauren Hoffman, Caitlin Sweeny, Lisa Quach, Perla Gil, Remi Moon,

Ashley Mitchell, Saleena Nival, Emily Ritter, Amy Lavigne, Lisa Moraleda, Nicole Russo, Christina Pecorale and her sales team, and Michelle Leo and her education/library team. To the wonderful team over at Simon & Schuster Canada. To Molly Powell, Kate Keehan, Callie Robertson, and the rest of the amazing team at Hodder. To the fantastic team at Hachette Aotearoa New Zealand. And to the many other superstar teams translating and working on *Foul Lady Fortune* in different languages.

Of course, huge thank-yous must also go to my parents and my family and my friends. A particular shout-out to the D.A.C.U. and to my Kiwis—Ilene Lei, Jenny Jiang, Tracy Chen, Vivian Qiu—who make New York feel like home. I would be here all day if I named more names, so I'm reemphasizing my thank-you to everyone in the acknowledgments of my previous two books.

Ginormous thank-yous to booksellers, librarians, teachers, and all the many advocates who pass young adult books into the hands of their target audience. This book can only get to where it needs with the help of its champions, and I'm forever grateful for your hard work.

And finally, I know I started by thanking the readers, but an extra special thank-you to those who have always been so generous with their support. This includes every blogger, every fan account, every Instagram user who posts a picture of my book, every TikTok user who cries/screams/raves on camera about my book, and every general cheerleader. My stories are made more precious because of you.

Oh, wait, one more—my eternal thanks to Taylor Swift for providing the perfect soundtracks while I drafted this book and every book.